ALL THE DAYS PAST,
ALL THE DAYS TO COME

ALL THE DAYS PAST, ALL THE DAYS TO COME

MILDRED D. TAYLOR

THORNDIKE PRESS
A part of Gale, a Cengage Company

GALE
A Cengage Company

Copyright © 2020 by Mildred D. Taylor.
Thorndike Press, a part of Gale, a Cengage Company.

ALL RIGHTS RESERVED
Thorndike Press® Large Print Striving Reader Collection.
The text of this Large Print edition is unabridged.
Other aspects of the book may vary from the original edition.
Set in 16 pt. Plantin.

LIBRARY OF CONGRESS CIP DATA ON FILE.
CATALOGUING IN PUBLICATION FOR THIS BOOK
IS AVAILABLE FROM THE LIBRARY OF CONGRESS

ISBN-13: 978-1-4328-7780-4 (hardcover alk. paper)

Published in 2020 by arrangement with Viking Children's Books, an imprint of Penguin Young Readers Group, a division of Penguin Random House, LLC

Printed in Mexico
Print Number: 01   Print Year: 2020

ALL THE DAYS PAST,
ALL THE DAYS TO COME
is dedicated to
The man I have loved from the writing
of my first books,
SONG OF THE TREES and ROLL
OF THUNDER, HEAR MY CRY,
And without whose love and support
my books
Would Not Have Been

And
To my father, the storyteller, who led
the family north;
To my mother, who made a home for
all who came;
To my sister, the activist, who raised the
banner high;

And
To my great-grandparents who
survived slavery

and set the standard;
To my grandparents, who bridged the
generations between
slavery and the fight for Civil Rights in
the twentieth century;

And
To my uncles who served in World War II
and with the thousands of African
American soldiers who served
helped change the nation;

And
To my aunts, all the family who came
before, and whose
lives I have chronicled;

And
To all my family, my cousins —
brothers and sisters to me — and
all of the younger generations who
continue to forge ahead under guidance
of more than
a century of family teachings,
passed from one generation to another;

And
To My Daughter,
The Future

AUTHOR'S NOTE

I was born in Mississippi.

When I was three weeks old, my father was involved in a racial incident and he made the abrupt decision to leave Mississippi. He left that same day. When I was three months old, he sent for my mother, my sister, and me, and we all went north. Many of my family followed, but each year we all returned to Mississippi, for that was where our roots were, where my grandparents and other family still lived. In Mississippi, I heard the "n" word often spoken. I heard it spoken late one night when our family was traveling a rural road and my father was stopped by police and taken off to jail, leaving my mother, my sister, and me parked in our new car, frightened, staring out at the blackness of the night. I heard the "n"

7

word when I went with cousins to an ice cream parlor in Jackson, the capital of Mississippi, and we were told to go to the back of the building to be served. I heard the "n" word when my sister and I wanted to try on clothes in a department store. I heard the "n" word just in casual talk whenever white people were around.

But it was not only in Mississippi that I heard the "n" word. I heard it in Toledo where I grew up. I heard it when I was fourteen years old and the first African American girl was elected queen of a Toledo high school and an effigy was hung on the school grounds.

All across America I heard the "n" word: in Iowa when my family was refused lodging, in Wyoming when we were refused seating in a restaurant, but were allowed to buy food for takeout. I heard it as a young married when my husband and I were stopped by police in Los Angeles. I heard the "n" word throughout my childhood and as an adult. It is derogatory, it is demoralizing, it is foul, it is painful, and it is part of our American history.

In the United States from the days the

first Africans were brought to this country in chains, the "n" word was used. My great-grandparents who were born into slavery endured the "n" word. They hated the "n" word, but they endured it along with all else to which they were subjugated.

In 1976 when *ROLL OF THUNDER, HEAR MY CRY* was published, I said that I wanted to show Black heroes and heroines in my books, men and women who were missing from books I read as a child. I also said I wanted to write a truthful history of what life was like for Black people in America. That truth includes the "n" word. It inflicted great pain, but it is a truth that needs to be told. I do not promote the word, but not to include it in my writing is to whitewash history, and that I will not do.

When stories were told around our family fireplace or on our Mississippi front porch, my father and the other storytellers always included the "n" word when recounting the speech of a white person about whom they were speaking. Through their words I saw the characters vividly. I knew who they were. Now, just as the storytellers of old, I continue to relate the truth as I have done in all my writing. *ALL THE DAYS PAST, ALL THE DAYS TO COME* includes that same truth, the truth about America.

Mildred D. Taylor, 2019

PROLOGUE

(MARCH 1944)

Man and I were waiting for the bus.

I had been visiting with Great-Aunt Callie down near McComb, and my brother Clayton Chester, whom we all called Little Man, had come from where he was based at Fort Hood in Texas and met me there. I had gone down to McComb at Big Ma's request during a class break from Jackson College because Aunt Callie was feeling poorly and Big Ma was worried about her sister. By the time Man arrived, I had been with Aunt Callie, helping tend to her, for almost a week. Man only spent the night catching up on all the news, and the next morning the two of us left amidst tears as we all mourned at the thought that we might not see each other again. Miles were distant, Aunt Callie was bedridden, and now there was the war, which could

11

separate us forever. Clayton Chester — Man — was a soldier soon to be in that war. As unbelievable as it was to all of us, he was the first in our family going to the war. Time was short, and within days, he would be overseas fighting a war in Europe that few of us cared about.

It was late Saturday morning and the March sun was shining brightly when the bus arrived. It was a local bus coming out of Biloxi and going all the way north to Jackson. There would be numerous stops along the way. With one more round of hugs we said our final good-byes to members of Aunt Callie's family who had taken us in their wagon to meet the bus, then we got in line. The bus driver asked where we were headed. Wallace store, we told him and gave him our fares.

And he told us, "Go on to the back."

That was something we did not need to be told. We knew where we were supposed to go. We did not like it, but we knew. I led the way down the aisle, past all the white folks seated. One woman glanced up at us, then turned her attention back to her child. She knew that we were headed toward the curtain that separated the front section of the bus from the back section, the curtain that separated whites from colored. Not all buses had curtains as a line of separation, only signs, but this one did. Once we passed through the aisle and behind the curtain, there was no longer any need for us to be seen. It would be almost as if we were not even there.

We reached the curtain. It was a tarp-like material that hung in two sections, one on either side of the aisle. The curtain was hung on a rod that, as more white people boarded, could be moved backward into the area currently set aside for colored passengers, allowing white passengers more seating on the white side of the curtain. Colored passengers were forced to move farther back. For that reason, most colored folks traveling went right to the long seat at the very tail end of the bus to avoid having to move again. I did not want to sit on that rear seat and neither did Man. Already the seat was almost full, and for us to sit back there would have made for an uncomfortable ride. All but one of the other seats were unoccupied. An elderly gentleman sat in the first row behind the curtain. Man and I chose to be more prudent and sat several rows behind the curtain on the other side of the aisle. I took the window seat; Man was on the aisle.

"I think we'll be okay here," I said.

Man only grunted his agreement, but I understood. His eyes were on the curtain. I too looked at the curtain and felt the humiliation of it. I hated that curtain. Then I looked at my brother. I knew Little Man was fuming. He had sat at the back of the bus behind a curtain all the way from Fort Hood. There he sat, forced into a segregated army to fight a white man's war against more white folks and the Japanese too in some far-off place on the other side of the world. There he sat, the most scholarly of all my brothers and me, forced to leave school and being shipped off to the Second World War as soon as possible. There he sat in a soldier's uniform behind a black curtain so that white folks would not have to be reminded of his existence.

"Too bad Stacey couldn't come get us," I said, attempting to distract his thoughts.

14

Our oldest brother, Stacey, lived in Jackson, along with his wife, Dee. Little Man had lived with them until he was drafted into the Army. Our other brother, Christopher-John, lived with them too, and so did I. Both Stacey and Christopher-John worked at the box factory, and even though it was a Saturday, they would be putting in a full day at the factory before leaving Jackson and heading down the rural roads to our land and family home. They knew the time the bus was expected at the Wallace store and planned to pick us up there. I glanced at Man, expecting him to say something. He did not, so I went on. "Would've made this trip a lot easier."

Little Man checked his watch.

"It's a long ride," I said.

"I just want to get home, Cassie. Could be the last time."

I looked at him, but did not say anything more. I did not want to admit that I was thinking the same thing.

More people got on the bus. A family of five came through the curtain and sat in front of us. They nodded at us in greeting and we returned the nod. The bus began to move. I pulled out one of my schoolbooks. Man had a book too. As we rolled past dormant cotton fields north of McComb, the bus stopped several more times, but no one else came through the curtain. Then, halfway through the trip, the bus stopped again. The bus driver came down the aisle and stood on the colored side of the curtain. "Move on back!" he ordered. "All y'all up front here, move on back!"

The family occupying the rows in front of Man and me got up and moved to seats several rows behind us. Little Man and I both stared at the driver without moving.

"Y'all hear me?" questioned the driver. "I said move on back! Folks're gettin' on the bus." He looked at the old gentleman seated in the first row behind the curtain. "Startin' with you, uncle," he said. "I said get up!"

The old gentleman raised his head. "Suh?"

"You deaf? You need to step quick, boy!" This time the bus driver did not use the politer form of "uncle," which most white folks thought a respectful reference to a colored man of years. "I got a bus to move!"

The old man seemed confused. Man immediately stood and went over to him. "Sir, may I help you?" he asked.

The man turned to look at Clayton Chester and, seemingly recognizing another person of color, smiled wide and toothless. "You a soldier, boy?"

"Yes, sir," Clayton Chester quietly answered.

"You here in this new war?"

"Yes, sir."

"What you doin' fightin' in this here new war, son?" the old man asked.

"Not my idea," said Man.

"Boy, you move him on back!" ordered the driver. "Then you and this gal here with ya move on back too! Got a lotta folks gettin' on."

Little Man's body seemed to freeze as he turned toward the driver. I held my breath, hoping Little Man would not do what was probably on his mind to do. But then he helped the old man up, and I got up as well. Clayton Chester, supporting the old man, walked with him to the back row, so he would not have to move again. Now there was no space for another passenger on that rear seat. As Little Man left the old gentleman in the care of the other rear seat passengers, the old man called after him. "You be careful now, son!"

Clayton Chester turned and nodded, then he and I moved our things farther back to another seat as the bus driver took the curtain rod and moved it, slipping our former seats into the front section of the bus.

Both Man and I stared at the curtain. "I'm not moving again," said Man.

I glanced over at him. "Then I guess we'll have to get off this bus."

Little Man looked at me, met my eyes, and I shrugged and went back to reading. More than an hour passed as we traveled the poor dirt roads through the lush pine countryside of southern Mississippi. The bus stopped twice more and we could hear more passengers boarding, but no one came through the curtain.

That was just as well. Too many colored folks on the bus could pose a problem for all of us if more white folks boarded and needed our seats. If they did and there was no more seating available, we would have to stand. Also, it was not unheard of for colored passengers to be ordered off a bus altogether and told to wait for the next bus when seats were needed for white passengers. Man and I well remembered when Big Ma, our grandmother, was on a bus headed to see Aunt Callie and she and all the other colored folks were ordered off because their seats were needed. Soon after putting Big Ma and the other colored passengers off the bus, the bus had plunged into the waters of the Creek Rosa Lee and many of the passengers on the bus had been killed. Big Ma and all the family had pondered on that, but we knew that retribution did not come every day. Today it was just good that the curtain was not moved back again.

Our good fortune did not last.

We were getting close to home. We came to a crossroads called Parson's Corner where the bus made another stop, and the bus driver stood before us once more. Looking straight at Little

Man and me, he announced, "All right, you two, y'all gotta move on back."

"We already moved once," I said.

"And y'all gonna move again and many times as I say, need be."

Without looking up from his book, Clayton Chester said, "We're not moving back."

There was a startled pause from the bus driver. "You sassin' me, boy?" he finally sputtered. "Nigger, I'll put y'all off this bus!"

I could see white passengers past the curtain turning to stare. I got up before things got out of hand. I knew we could not win this thing. "You won't have to do that," I said. "We already decided to get off."

Man too got up, looked directly into the bus driver's eyes, then turned and got our bags from the overhead rack.

"Y'all bought tickets to the Wallace store," said the driver. "Y'all ain't gettin' yo' money back!"

We let him have the last say. Man waited for me to step into the aisle. Without another word I led the way past the driver and through the curtain. Man, carrying our bags, followed, past the turned heads of all the white people seated on either side of the aisle. As we stepped off the bus, whites waiting to board, unaware of what the holdup was, stepped aside to let us pass. They would board the bus and take our seats. Now Little Man and I had no recourse but to walk the miles to home. A small store was at the crossroads and probably had a telephone inside, but we couldn't call home. It was 1944 Mississippi and there were no telephones in our community, no way to call ahead and ask Papa or Stacey or Christopher-John to come get us.

We got started.

The bus soon passed us and as it did, we stepped back into the forest to avoid the billowing dust. Once the dust cleared, we stepped back onto the road. Even with the sun shining down on us, the day was cold and soon the sun would begin to set. As we walked along the red road we said little. Little Man had slung his duffel bag over his shoulder and had wanted to carry my bag as well, but I told him I

21

would carry it. I had always figured to be as tough as my brothers. I shifted the bag from one hand to the other until finally Little Man said, "Cassie, just let me have the bag. We can move a lot faster. You want it back later, you can have it."

As much as I hated to admit it, I knew Man was right. Although we were of the same height, though not of the same weight, my little brother was now stronger than I, had been for several years, and with all the Army training he had an endurance much beyond my own. Still, I kept the bag. At nineteen, going on twenty in the summer, I refused to admit I couldn't carry my own weight.

The sun had already set when a wagon came rolling slowly up the road behind us. Lanterns hung from its sides to light the way. There was a full moon and we could still see the road as we continued walking until the wagon neared, then we stopped and stood aside, waiting for it to pass. We were both apprehensive, for we could not see who was driving. As the wagon approached we saw that a black man sat alone on the wagon seat. We did not know him, but that was all right.

There was always a kinship when seeing another black face, especially on a Mississippi road at night. The driver stopped. "Y'all lookin' mighty weary," he said. "Where y'all young folks headed?"

"Over toward Great Faith," I said.

"Well, I'm going a ways past there, far as that store, then I'll be headed on north. Y'all welcome t' ride far's I go." He gave us a studied look. "What happen y'all t' be walkin' this road after dark anyways?"

"Nothing much," answered Man. "Just lost our ride, that's all."

"Uh-huh," said the farmer, doubt in his voice, but he chose not to question us further about it. "Well, y'all get on up here, y'all want this ride."

We thanked the farmer, then both Little Man and I climbed onto the back of the wagon. It felt good to be off our feet. We rested our backs against the wagon side boards and listened to the farmer's talk, but said very little ourselves. Finally, the farmer grew quiet, and we rolled on through the darkness. After some while we passed Great Faith Church and School silhouetted in the night against the black forest and shortly after passing them reached the next crossroads and the Wallace store, dark and closed for the night. Clayton Chester and I again thanked the farmer as we got down from his wagon. He went on north, headed toward Strawberry. Man and I headed west. We had only a few miles before we would be home.

As we walked up the long dirt driveway, the dogs started barking, then quieted as they recognized us and came over wagging their tails. The driveway ran along the side yard of the house, past the well all the way to the barn. Stacey's car was parked at the top of the drive. As we approached the house, the side door opened to Mama and Papa's room. Papa was standing in the doorway. " 'Bout time y'all got here," he said.

Mama quickly joined him, and Big Ma was right behind her. "What happened to you?" Mama asked. "Why weren't you on the bus?"

And Big Ma exclaimed, "Lord A-Mighty! We sho been worried 'bout y'all! Get on in here!"

Little Man and I stepped inside and put down our bags, then hugged Mama, Papa, and Big Ma. Stacey and Christopher-John came over and we hugged them too. "We were waiting for you up at the store when the bus came in," Stacey said. He looked at Man. "We thought maybe you didn't get in from Fort Hood and Cassie was waiting for you before heading home."

"Yeah," said Christopher-John, "we were thinking of running down to Mc-Comb first thing tomorrow if you didn't make it in." He slapped Little Man's arm fondly. "You looking good! Course, looks like the Army took a few pounds off you."

"They'll take a few pounds off you too when they call you up," Little Man wryly returned with a slow smile.

Stalwart Christopher-John punched at his own stomach. "Well, maybe I can use that!" Then he laughed.

"Y'all all right?" asked Big Ma.

"We're fine, just dead tired," I said.

Big Ma put her arm around me, hugging me to her again. "How'd y'all leave yo' Aunt Callie?"

"She's about the same," I replied, "but her spirits are good. She sent love. Everybody did."

"Come on, sit down," Papa ordered, and we all headed past Mama and Papa's bed to the wooden chairs, their seats covered in deer hide, that sat in a semicircle in front of the fireplace. Light from the fire lit the chairs, and two kerosene lamps — one on Mama's desk at the windows overlooking the drive, the other on the nightstand beside the bed — lit the remainder of the room. There was no electricity. Stacey's wife, Dee, sat in the rocker closest to the hearth. Stacey had married Dee in March of 1942. Their first child, Marie, called Rie by us all, had been born in December that same year. They were now expecting their second child. Both Man and I went over to greet Dee. She was in the seventh month of her pregnancy and did not get up. I kissed Dee and asked about Rie.

"Already in bed," said Dee. Then she turned to Man, now bending to kiss her. "How're you doing, Clayton?" she asked. Unlike the rest of us, Dee always called Man by his given name. Like Mama, she had been a teacher at Great Faith and had tolerated no nicknames in her classroom. I sat down with a heavy sigh beside Dee, kicked off my shoes, and rubbed my feet.

"Both of you look beat," Stacey said.

"Guess we should. Man and I walked all the way from the Wallace store and then some before that."

"What do you mean you walked some before that?" inquired Stacey. I didn't answer.

"Rob," Dee said, tightening the shawl around her shoulders and rubbing her arms, "honey, could you put some more wood on the fire? I'm feeling a bit chilly and I expect Cassie and Clayton are too."

Stacey gave me a questioning look before going over to the bin at the far side of the stone fireplace. He took several logs and piled them high on the flames, then turned to Dee. "That better?" he asked.

Dee smiled up at him. "Much better, Robert, thank you." Just as Dee had chosen to address Little Man by his given name, she had also chosen to address

Stacey by his first name. She said she preferred to be the only person who called him that. Stacey smiled back and added still more logs to the fire.

When all of us but Stacey were seated, Papa turned to Little Man and me. "All right now," he said, "tell us what happened. Why weren't y'all on that bus?"

Man stared at the fire and didn't say anything, so I said, "We got off the bus. Got off at Parson's Corner."

"Parson's Corner?" Mama questioned in alarm. "Why? What were you doing getting off the bus there?"

Both Little Man and I were silent.

Papa frowned. "They put y'all off?"

I glanced at Man and answered Papa. "No, sir. We decided that on our own. Bus driver told us to move."

Mama looked from me to Man. "That's it?" She knew, we all knew full well what the policy was. "Clayton Chester, that's it? The bus driver asked you to move?"

Little Man's gaze left the fire and he looked at Mama. His voice was matter-of-fact when he spoke. "We decided we weren't going to move again."

28

For several moments no one said anything and there was only the sound of the fire popping. It was Papa who broke the silence. "That driver know who you are?"

"No, sir," I assured him. "Got no idea." Stacey moved from the fire and sat down. "So, how'd you get home? You couldn't've walked all the way from Parson's Corner."

"Would've if we'd had to," I said. "We were on our way to doing it when a man came along in a wagon and gave us a ride far as the Wallace store —"

"Colored man?" asked Papa.

I sighed. "Now, Papa, you know Man and I wouldn't have gotten on otherwise."

Again the room was silent; then Big Ma stood and went over to Little Man. He looked up at her and she put her hand on his head and rubbed his hair, now butchered into an Army cut. "Umph, umph, umph," she mumbled. "All that beautiful hair, gone." Aunt Callie pretty much had had the same sentiment, and so had I. Little Man's hair had always been wavy and long, often hanging in his face and to his shoulders. Big Ma said he had gotten his hair from Grandpa Paul-Edward's white father and his half-Indian mother, as well as her own mother's people. She sighed heavily and let her hand drop. "Well, I know one thing. Y'all must be mighty hungry. Y'all sit and rest. I got supper waitin'. Jus' needs warmin'." She moved briskly toward the kitchen. In her seventies, Big Ma was able-bodied, still strong, and moved almost as quickly as she always had.

Dee got up. "I'll help," she said.

"Girl, you sit down. I can manage."

"I've been sitting all day and I want to help."

Big Ma's eyes narrowed as she looked at Dee, then she shrugged. "Have it your way then. I recall, I felt the same way when I was carryin'."

As Big Ma and Dee left for the kitchen, Papa, looking first at me, then at Man, said, "There any trouble 'bout y'all getting off that bus?"

Little Man gave no answer. So again, I answered. "Not really."

Papa's eyes stayed on Man. "Clayton?"

Man looked at Papa. "No, sir, no trouble. We just told the driver we weren't moving back again. We'd already moved once and we weren't moving again and he told us we'd move when he said we needed to move. So we decided to move all right. We moved right off the bus."

"You back talk him?"

Little Man shook his head. "We just got off."

"Well, if that's the case," said Mama, "there shouldn't be any trouble about it."

Little Man turned to Mama. He spoke softly. "Maybe that's what you think, Mama, but tell you the truth, I wanted to kill that man."

"Clayton!"

"I'd've done that, I guess there'd been trouble all right." Then what I knew had been coming all day finally happened; Little Man's temper exploded. "Here I am forced to go fight their war and they make me and Cassie sit at the back of their bus behind their curtain so they don't have to see us! Like we weren't even there, and still that's not good enough for them! So they make us move,

31

not once, but twice, so the good white folks could have our seats and still that wouldn't have been good enough for them if they'd needed more seats! They'd have moved us right off that bus if they needed our seats and we all know that!" His voice grew louder. "Yet they want me to go fight their damn war! Took me out of school so I can go fight their white man's war and there's nothing I can do about it! Nothing any of us can do about it!" He jumped up suddenly, and his wooden chair clanged backward to the floor.

At that, Papa, Stacey, and Christopher-John sprang up. Christopher-John grabbed at Little Man's arm. "Ah, Man, come on!"

Little Man jerked away.

"Son, calm down," Papa said as Big Ma came rushing in.

"What's goin' on in here?" Big Ma demanded to know. "Heard all this shoutin' and ruckus!"

Little Man turned toward Big Ma, looked at her in silence, then hurried out the side door.

"Clayton!" Mama called after him.

"I'll talk to him," Stacey said, touching Mama's arm in reassurance, and followed Man out. We all watched Stacey as he left. If anyone could calm Little Man, it was Stacey.

When Clayton Chester was born, I was too young to remember the events of those days. Stacey, however, who then was going on six, did remember and over the years the story was told many times: how Mama had almost died from the birth and Little Man had too. His was a breech birth. It had not been an easy pregnancy for Mama. She had been sick throughout and when the time for Little Man's arrival finally came, he was premature. Big Ma was a midwife and had delivered Stacey, Christopher-John, and me, but she did not deliver Little Man because he came more than a month before expected. Big Ma was not at home. She had gone down to McComb a few days after Christmas to visit with Aunt Callie, and Little Man was born the day after the new year in 1927. Another midwife in the community attended the delivery.

Stacey said he remembered Mama's screams that night and when the screaming stopped, there were no sounds of crying from the new baby. He said he had listened at the closed door and when he had heard the traditional slap on a newborn's bottom to bring the baby to life, there was still no crying, no life. There had been another slap and yet another, and finally at last he heard crying. When Stacey, Christopher-John, and I were allowed in the room to see our new brother, Stacey observed that the baby did not cry much; then he rubbed Clayton Chester's tiny fingers and declared, "He's a little man!" All in the room agreed, and the name stuck.

From that moment, Stacey took Little Man under his big brother wings. That was partly because Clayton Chester was so tiny and remained in questionable health for weeks after his birth, and also because Papa had gone back to work on the railroad. As Little Man grew stronger, Mama returned to teaching at Great Faith and taking on other community activities. Big Ma, too, was busy cooking, taking care of the house as well as the fields, and Stacey, who was not that old himself, was a big help to them in seeing after Christopher-John, Little Man, and me — especially Little Man, who for a while seemed to be threatened continuously with some physical ailment or impending catastrophe. He went through a bout of pneumonia before he could walk and again almost died. Later, he fell from a wagon and his broken leg took a long time in healing. Another time a bull got loose; Papa had smashed a dexterous two-fisted punch into the face of the bull and stopped its charge toward Little Man. Through it all, though, Little Man lived up to the name Stacey had given him. He was tough in spirit, set in determination, and certainly had a mind of his own.

By the time he was six, it was difficult to get Little Man to do what he was determined not to do. Unlike other six-year-olds, he did not cry when he was hurt, although once he had cried when he was humiliated at the hands of whites, his brand-new school clothes covered with mud-soaked water. But he certainly did not cry when he got a whipping. That was troubling to both Mama and Papa, who did not hesitate to whip the boys and me when we did something wrong. They explained the whippings by telling us that they had to be hard on us, to make us understand right from wrong and what was expected of us in this life. They also said that the whippings were to keep us alive, for we needed to know and follow rules, and that no black person in Mississippi could survive without following those rules.

The years of slavery and Jim Crow had proven that.

While we were growing up, Stacey, being older and also having a determined mind-set of his own, did not cry when being punished, but Christopher-John and I certainly did. That let Mama or Papa know we were truly sorrowful, and also that we had been punished enough. Sometimes, as soon as the leather strap hit our legs, the two of us began to scream, just to get the whipping over with, and Mama or Papa would let us go. Knowing that Stacey had no intention of crying, after a few licks of the strap they let him go too. But they seemed not to know what to do about Little Man, who refused to cry and show his remorse.

"Boy, why don't you just cry and get it over with!" I once advised him. "They'd stop whipping on you if you'd just cry."

Little Man had given me a long look, then said, "It's not that I don't want to cry, Cassie. I just can't. Something won't let me. Stacey doesn't cry. I don't either."

So, that's the way it was with Little Man too. Little Man followed Stacey everywhere and tried to do whatever Stacey did. Many things Papa would have taught Clayton Chester had he been home, Stacey taught, and Little Man was eager to learn about everything. His mind absorbed all put before him. Everyone acknowledged that Clayton Chester had a brilliant mind. He had even skipped a grade. Everyone also acknowledged that whatever Stacey asked of him, Little Man did. Stacey was Little Man's hero.

With the Japanese attack on Pearl Harbor on December 7, 1941, and the United States' declaration of war a day later, we all worried that Stacey would be called up to fight. But when Stacey was drafted, he was deferred because of his health. At fourteen, Stacey had run away to the cane fields of Louisiana to try to earn money for the family. During that time, he had come down with some sort of fever that had sickened him for weeks and had weakened his heart. It was early in the war when he was called up, and a number of colored men were deferred for any number of reasons, including flat feet. It was said that the government was concerned about Negro soldiers and interracial mixing in Europe, but whatever the reason for the deferment, when we learned that Stacey was not being inducted into the Army, we fell to our knees in gratitude and thanked God.

We all prayed that the war would be over before Christopher-John was drafted. But by the end of 1943, we knew that was wishful thinking and that Christopher-John would most likely be called up. The war had escalated as Axis forces continued to maintain their grip over Europe and in the Pacific. The Army was no longer being as selective about its draftees. They needed every man they could get. We steeled ourselves for

Christopher-John's eighteenth birthday. Christopher-John turned eighteen in late 1943 and graduated high school. As required, he was registered for the draft within thirty days of his birthday. He had not yet been called. We figured we had another year before we had to start worrying about Little Man. That turned out not to be the case. Little Man was drafted before Christopher-John.

There had been a mistake on the birth certificate.

At the time Clayton Chester received his draft notice, he was a first-year student at Jackson College, one of the state's colleges for Negroes. He was enrolled in the college rather than high school because of the grade he had skipped and his test scores being so high. All of us in the family had always known that Little Man was smart, but his college testing proved it. Maybe too much so. He was sixteen when he graduated from high school and enrolled at the college, but without our knowing it, his government birth certificate identified him as seventeen. It was that birth certificate that caused all the trouble. Clayton Chester, though born in 1927, was listed on the birth certificate as being born in 1926.

Most Negro babies born in Mississippi were delivered in the homes of their parents by midwives. There were no hospitals, no nurses, no doctors standing by for deliveries. Babies were born, their names recorded in the family Bible and information about their births filled out by midwives who sent it to the county seat for filing. Everybody I knew had been delivered and their births recorded that way. The birth certificates, all handwritten, stayed in the government offices. Very few people ever saw their birth certificates unless something came up and they needed them; then they went to the county to get a copy. But few people had need of a certificate and certainly Man did not, until the notice came from the Army. Then he needed it. Problem was, the information on the birth certificate was wrong. Clayton Chester Logan was listed as one year older than he was.

He was only seventeen.

There were other seventeen-year-olds in the Army. They had volunteered. Seventeen-year-old boys could volunteer with their parents' permission, but Little Man had no desire to serve voluntarily in the Army, and none of the rest of the family wanted that either. Throughout our lives we had existed under the dominance of white people, had been required to be subservient to them, with no equal rights, and we had no desire to go fight more white people overseas for the white people oppressing us here. There would never be volunteering on our part.

Mama and Papa went to the draft board to try to straighten out the matter of the birth certificate. But there was no time to straighten it out. Once the draft notice was received there was little time for appeal. January 1926 birth certificates had been pulled and despite the fact that Clayton Chester had not even registered as eligible for the draft, the Army chose to believe the date on the birth certificate. The Army wanted Little Man and that was that. According to one of his professors, Clayton Chester's high test scores and his college enrollment made him prime to be a leader within the Negro ranks of the Army. He could even rise to the rank of sergeant; he could not, however, rise higher. Officer positions over Negro troops were for whites only. Still, the Army was looking for young men like Clayton Chester. So, in the end, there was nothing any of us could do about it.

Little Man had to go into the Army.

For Stacey, it was a particularly heavy burden of guilt that he did not have to go to the war. If Stacey could have gone in Little Man's place, he would have done so. He felt the same about Christopher-John, for we all knew that soon Christopher-John would be called up too.

Stacey and Little Man did not come back before I went to bed. I had eaten some of Big Ma's good cooking and then, hardly able to keep my eyes open, I fell asleep. The next morning at breakfast I asked Man, "You feeling any better?"

He shrugged. "What do you think? Least I'm home for now, and that's what matters." Then he smiled wide and turned his attention to Big Ma. "Big Ma, would you please pass me some of that fine ham we cured last fall, some of that hot sausage we made too? It's going to be a good long while before I taste the likes of them again!"

Little Man did not have to report back to Fort Hood. He was on what was called a "delay en route" leave and was headed to Camp Benning in Georgia, from which he would be deployed overseas. The day before he was to leave, the boys and I went to the Negro photography studio on Farish Street in Jackson to have our picture taken. I was long-legged, honey-toned in skin color, and the vibrant green suit that I wore, with its fitted bodice and A-line skirt cut off right below my knees, complemented me well. My hair was naturally long and thick, crinkly in texture, but for the photographs, I had straightened it. Mama had always objected to my straightening my hair, but Dee had shown me how. With my hair cascading several inches below my shoulders, my green suit and matching dark green high heels cut out at the toe and heel, I was looking good. The boys were looking good too. They were all handsome, my brothers. Stacey and Christopher-John had Papa's height, but the same coloring as Mama and me.

Clayton Chester had pecan-colored skin like Papa, but not his height. His wavy hair reflected our Choctaw heritage and so did the coloring of his skin. Little Man was not in uniform. All of my brothers were dressed in their finest Sunday suits.

It was a memorable day.

We stood arm in arm and had several photographs taken. In one we were joking and laughing. In another, we were somber, reflecting on what was to come. The photographs were bittersweet moments frozen in time, for after today, we did not know if we would ever be together again. A week later, Christopher-John received his draft notice and without delay, he too was inducted into the Army.

Basic training for Negro soldiers was reported to be anywhere from three to ten weeks. Mostly, they were trained to be in service details that kept the soldiers, mainly white soldiers fighting at the front, stocked with supplies. Negro soldiers did the grunt work. But whatever the duties of Negro soldiers, they would still be in harm's way. Christopher-John was shipped overseas in late April. Little

Man was already there. With both of them gone, we tried to adjust to life without them, tried to adjust to the daily fear of what they faced over in Europe and North Africa. Each day we read all the war news printed in the newspaper, and each evening we gathered around the radio to hear the latest word about the war. When I woke each morning my first thoughts were of my brothers. Some mornings when I woke I knew something was wrong, but I had to ask myself what. Then I would remember, and feel that tightening knot of fear in my gut. The boys were not here; they were off fighting in that war, only God and the Army knew exactly where. They could be dead for all I knew.

From the time Little Man and Christopher-John went overseas, I wrote them every week. Mama and Dee did the same. Papa and Stacey sent their love but left all the writing to us, though they were just as eager for a reply to come. Even when letters did not come, the next week Mama, Dee, and I wrote again. When letters finally did arrive, much of what Christopher-John and Man had written had been redacted with heavy black ink. Army officials deleted all information they did not want us to have. We had no exact idea where Christopher-John and Little Man were. Even the mailing address gave us no clue. Their letters did not show the country from which they were sent, but instead an Army mailing address in the States. The first time I received letters from the boys, I was incensed that so much of what they wanted us to know had been censored out. Later, though, I was just happy and relieved to know that at least on the day the letters were written, Christopher-John and Little Man were still alive.

The house on Everett Street where we lived in Jackson had never seemed more empty. The house belonged to our Uncle Hammer. Uncle Hammer had several rental houses in the city, though he himself did not live in Jackson. For years he had lived in Chicago, but now was living in California. The Everett Street house was the best of his properties and he had turned it over to Stacey and Dee when they married. Soon after, I moved in with them and later, so did Christopher-John and Little Man. At that time Christopher-John and Man were students at Lanier High School and I was at Jackson College. All of us had gone to high school in Jackson, since by the time we were in high school Great Faith School only went to tenth grade. Before the boys and I moved into the house on Everett, Christopher-John, Man, and I had lived with other family members in Jackson, and before his marriage Stacey had been living and working in Memphis as a truck driver. The house, though small, was perfect for Stacey and Dee, and for the rest of us too. It was only a few blocks from the college and the box factory where Stacey worked, and not that far from Lanier. We enjoyed being in the house together. There was always activity in the house, other young people stopping by, boisterous moments and laughter and youthful fun. All that ended when Christopher-John and Little Man went off to war.

Although thoughts of Christopher-John and Little Man dominated our days, our family, like everybody else who had boys in the war, carried on with our lives. I continued my studies at the college, where I was working toward a degree in education and was scheduled to graduate in the spring of 1945. Stacey continued driving a truck for the box factory and both he and Dee, and all the family, were looking forward to the birth of the new baby. With the delivery date near, Big Ma came to Jackson to be with Dee, and she helped to deliver this new great-grandchild, just as she had delivered Stacey, Christopher-John, and me. The baby was born in May at the Everett Street house. Stacey and Dee called her 'lois. Three weeks after 'lois's birth, Stacey shocked us all.

He announced he was going north.

For months Stacey had talked about going north, but Dee was always against it and so were Mama and Big Ma. Papa had told Stacey to wait until after the war, when Christopher-John and Man would be coming back. Stacey had conceded to them, even though we all knew the opportunity to go north was now. We had heard about all the good-paying factory jobs that were available in the North because of the war. Yet Stacey had kept in mind that Mama, Papa, and Big Ma were now alone on the land and he wanted to keep near to them, at least until Christopher-John and Clayton Chester returned. Now, all of a sudden, he had decided to go.

The morning Stacey made his announcement, he had gone to work at the box factory as usual, but came home unexpectedly soon after. Rie, now a year and a half, was down with Mama and Papa and Big Ma for a few days while Dee recovered from the birth and tended to the new baby. I had no morning classes, so I was at the house. Dee was seated in the living room rocking chair holding 'lois when Stacey came in. Her older brother, Ola, who also worked at the box factory, was with him. Dee looked up in surprise when they entered. "Rob, what're you doing back so soon?" she asked, then looked at her brother. "And, Ola, what are you doing here?" Stacey passed Dee without answering and headed for their bedroom, right off the living room. "Robert? Something wrong?"

At the bedroom door, Stacey turned and quietly answered her. "I'm leaving, Dee."

"What?"

"I'm finished with Mississippi. I'm going north. Today." There was no outburst of anger, no animosity in his voice, just a statement of fact. He opened the door, left it open, and went to the closet.

"What?" Dee repeated, as if not comprehending what he had said.

I stared at my brother. I was as unprepared for his announcement as Dee. I went over to the doorway. "Are you serious?" I asked.

Stacey glanced at me. "What do you think?" He parted the closet curtains and pulled out a suitcase.

Dee looked to her brother for explanation. Ola shrugged. "He means it."

With 'lois still in her arms, Dee got up from the rocker and stood beside me. When she spoke, her words were almost a whisper. "Robert, have you lost your mind?"

Stacey pulled open a dresser drawer and began to empty out his clothes.

"Yeah, I guess I have. I'm crazy not to have left this place long time ago."

"But . . . what happened?" asked a bewildered Dee. "I don't understand."

Stacey opened another drawer. "What's to understand?" He nodded toward Ola. "You'd better thank Ola that he was with me today because I'm sick to death of these white people down here. I'm going to kill one of them if they don't kill me first."

"Robert, you don't know what you're saying!"

Ola moved toward his sister. "Dee, Stacey and this white guy got into an argument on the loading dock. Cracker grabbed at him, hit him. Stacey here was ready to hit him back. Took me and couple other fellas working on the dock to hold him, keep him from making that mistake. Boy'd be in jail, or dead, he'd've hit that white boy."

Dee listened to her brother, never taking her eyes off Stacey, who was opening another drawer. As he began to empty it, she said emphatically, "You're not going anywhere, Robert."

Stacey just looked at her and tossed

socks from the drawer into the suitcase. At that, Dee placed 'lois in my arms and hurried over to the bed where the suitcase lay, grabbed the clothes from it and slammed them back into the drawer, then turned to face Stacey. "You're not going anywhere," she repeated. "You're not leaving me."

Stacey said nothing, just moved past her to retrieve his clothes from the drawer. Dee blocked him. "I got a new-born baby in this house, Robert Stacey Logan. We got Rie. You're not going to leave your babies and me. My father left and didn't come back, and you're not going to do the same. You hear me? I won't have it! I won't let you leave!" Stacey sighed and went back to the closet and pulled pants from a hanger. Dee snatched them away. "I said you're not leaving!"

Stacey now stopped and looked at Dee clutching the pants in her arms and quietly said, "I am going, Dee. Even if I don't take one thing with me, I'm going. There are plenty of factory jobs up in Detroit. When I get one and get settled, I'll send for you and the girls, but today I'm leaving here."

Dee, stunned, just stood there, holding the pants to her chest, her back against the dresser, guarding it to keep Stacey from taking anything more. Stacey, eyes on her, stood silent a moment, then, giving up the packing, moved past her and toward me.

"You sure about this?" I asked.

He gently cupped the baby's head with his hand. "I'm sure." His eyes met mine. "I want to see the folks and Rie. I'm going down, let them know I'm leaving."

"Stacey, it'll crush them, all of you gone."

"No, it won't. They're strong and they know how long I've been talking about going." He glanced back at Dee, then looked at me again. "Cassie, talk to Dee."

"You talk to her," I said.

"I will. When I get back. But, Cassie, know this. Come this night, I'm out of here." He kissed 'lois and left. True to his word, Stacey left Mississippi that night.

Now all my brothers were gone.

■ ■ ■ ■

One week later Stacey called and said he had a job. Although headed for Detroit, Stacey had stopped over in Toledo to see a family we knew from the Great Faith community, the L.D. McClaires. The McClaires had moved north at the start of the war, and Mr. L.D. now worked at Willys Overland in Toledo, where jeeps were being manufactured for the Army. Mr. L.D. told Stacey jobs were still plentiful at the factory. Stacey applied for a job and was hired as a welder that same day, exactly a month after 'lois was born. In late August, Stacey sent for Dee and the girls. I went with Dee on a segregated train to help with the babies. I helped Dee get settled in the one room she and Stacey and the girls would share at the McClaire house, then returned to Jackson. Ola and his wife, Sarah, and baby boy had already moved into the house on Everett and I continued to stay there with them. In the spring when I graduated, I too headed north.

PART I

Part I

Toledo, the Glass City
(1945–1946)

Dorr Street.

It was the main street of our community, it was a street in transition, and we lived in the heart of it. At one corner of our block, on the same side of the street as our house, was a small grocery store owned by a Jewish family. At the other end of the block was a much larger grocery store known as Roman's, owned by Polish immigrants. At that end of the block there was also a café, a pool hall, and a drugstore. On the other side of the street on the corner was a bar and next to it an apartment hotel. A quiet residential street divided that side of the block. That was Wheeler Street. One block down Wheeler was the elementary school. On one corner of Wheeler and Dorr was a fish market, and on the other corner, a beauty shop, and a little farther down

57

was a shoe repair shop. On the next block going west were clothing stores, a shoe store, a cleaners, and a barbershop. On the block to the east were a gas station, a furniture store, a cafeteria, and, best of all, the neighborhood movie theater. At the end of that block and right around the corner two blocks down was the church we attended. Initially, there was a trolley line on the street, but it had been replaced by buses to take a body to downtown Toledo. There did not seem to be all that much need to go downtown; just about everything anyone needed was right there on Dorr Street. It was a busy street, a main corridor in the city, and there was always something to do, with people walking up and down the street all through the day and early evening.

There were hardly any trees on the block. Sandwiched among all the businesses was a stretch of residential houses, including a large house known as the Colored Working Girls Home, where single young women working in the city boarded under a strict Christian discipline and were watched over by several elderly matrons. It was one house removed from our house, which was in the exact middle of the block, directly across from Wheeler Street.

541 Dorr Street.

Ours was a house of note, mainly because of its location and maybe also because it was freshly painted white and stayed that way. Maybe it was of note too because the sidewalk was shoveled in winter or because the grass was cut and neat in summer and petunias were planted in a front flower garden. Dee loved petunias and Stacey had created beds for her as soon as they moved in, both in the front and backyards. Maybe people took note just because we lived there, a rising young family in the community.

It was obvious as heads turned to look at the house that many people were impressed by it, and we took pride in that. The house was large, a duplex. On one side of it was a rundown ramshackle house with unpainted wooden siding blackened with age and a huge barn in the backyard filled with rats. On the other side was a neat house, a side-by-side duplex, but smaller than ours. When we moved in, families in both those houses were white.

That did not last long.

Despite having been in Toledo less than a year, Stacey and Dee had managed to buy the Dorr Street house in the spring of 1945. They had managed this by both of them working. Once Dee arrived in Toledo, she had left Rie and 'lois with Mrs. McClaire and gotten a job at a tool factory, and she and Stacey had saved their money for a down payment on the house. Stacey and Dee had good heads for business and they figured to pay the mortgage by renting the upper portion of the house. Their decision was a smart one. In May 1945, the war ended on the European front. In September 1945, the war ended in the Pacific. With Christopher-John and Man soon coming back from the war, Stacey and Dee figured they would need a house.

By the time I arrived in Toledo, Stacey and Dee already had the house. They and the girls and I stayed on the first floor, where there were two bedrooms, a bathroom, kitchen, dining room, living room, sun parlor, and what we termed the front or "Sunday" room, where we sat on Sundays with all the folks who came to visit. Dee furnished the room with her best furniture and sheer white curtains that draped across the only window, a large picture window that looked onto Dorr. The house was the finest in which we had lived and had more space than any of us had ever experienced. Even though I shared a bedroom with the babies, I felt the enormous size of the house and shared Stacey and Dee's pride in owning it.

We learned that the house had not always been a duplex, but once had been a one-family house. The room that was now Stacey and Dee's bedroom was evidence of that. Once most likely another common room for the residing family, the bedroom was adjacent to the dining room and had two sets of stairs. One set of stairs, closed off by a door, led to the basement. Inside the bedroom closet, another set of wide stairs with a heavy carved banister led to the second floor. At the top of the stairs to the right of the hallway was a large bathroom, then the hall turned and along the rest of it were four rooms, presumably once all bedrooms, one of which had been converted into a kitchen. A door near the end of the hall opened into the upstairs sun parlor, a room with windows lining the exterior walls and stairs going to the downstairs sun parlor and the front door. In addition to the front door, there were doors opening from the downstairs sun parlor into the living room and the Sunday room. Both the lower and upper sun parlors as well as the downstairs bathroom had been added to the house years before.

The remodeling and the additions were a boon for Stacey and Dee. Three separate families lived in the three upstairs bedrooms and all paid a monthly rent. They were all young couples, two with children younger than three. They all shared the bath, the kitchen, and the sun parlor, and they all were happy to be there, for this was their start in the North. All the families, like ours, had migrated up from the South looking for better jobs, for less discrimination, for all the opportunities of the North. Stacey and Dee were fair with all of them, friends with all of them, and when any of the families upstairs decided they needed more space and could afford to move, there was always another family waiting in line to take their place, for with the house came assurances of who Stacey and Dee Logan were, who we were as a family, and how tenants were treated. Those upstairs rooms were in great demand and were never vacant.

With all the rooms upstairs occupied I asked Stacey about rooms for Christopher-John and Man. Stacey told me not to worry about them. They would stay downstairs with us when they finally came home. When that would be, we didn't know. We didn't know either if they would be coming to Toledo or going back to Mississippi. Following the end of the war on both fronts, we had expected their return any day, but the months of 1945 had passed into the spring of 1946 and still both Christopher-John and Man were in service over in Europe. I was exasperated with the waiting. "How much longer do you think it'll be?" I asked Dee as she stood at the kitchen table rolling dough for a sweet potato cobbler. "Before they come home, I mean." I was at the ironing board ironing a dress for the night.

Dee looked at me and shook her head. "Have no idea. Clayton and Christopher-John don't either."

"Well, I hope it's soon. I want them home."

Dee smiled at my impatience. "We all want them home, Cassie. Have patience."

"You know that's something I'm short on."

Dee laughed. "You're telling me? You never were one for patience, Cassie." She glanced over. "You about finished with that dress? I want you to make the cornbread before we go. No telling what time we'll get back."

"I'll be finished in a few minutes," I replied.

"All right." Dee, always organized, checked the wall clock. "I just have to get this cobbler in the stove and finish up the collard greens. The beets are ready and the okra'll be done in a minute. Pork chops won't take that much longer. Soon as the cobbler's done, you can put the cornbread in."

I nodded, enjoying the smell of frying okra and smothered pork chops and onions slowly baking. It was Friday morning and we were preparing dinner early because we were going to see the doctor in the afternoon. Dee was taking the girls in for a checkup and I was going to have a physical exam for a job for which I had applied. It was a position as a counselor at a girls' summer camp sponsored by Stacey's union. If I got it, it would be something different, and a challenge too. I would be out of the city for the summer and back in the countryside. More important than that, it would mean a full-time paycheck for two months. Since I had arrived in Toledo I had not earned much money. Although I had a little part-time job at Roman's, which was fine while I attended the University of Toledo, taking courses I needed in order to teach in Ohio, the pay was minimal.

Dee finished rolling the dough and began cutting it into large squares. "So, what time is Moe coming?"

"About the same as usual. He'll go home from work, change, then get on the road." The iron was now cold. I took it over to the stove, took a second iron from the gas fire, and set the cold iron on the grill. I placed the hot iron upright on the ironing board to let it cool a minute and readjusted my dress on the board. "He'll be here in plenty of time for us to go to the movies."

"I still wish Moe would just move down to Toledo," Dee said. "I hate that he has to make that trip from Detroit every weekend."

"He doesn't have to make it," I said, testing the iron on a rag to see if the hot metal scorched it.

Dee laughed. "Oh, yes, he does! Moe would be lost if he couldn't come down to see you!"

I waved off her comment. "It's not just me he's coming to see. It's everybody, the whole family."

"Cassie . . . you know how Moe feels."

I shrugged. "You know I love Moe. He's my friend."

"But that's all, isn't it?"

"I'm not in love with him, if that's what you mean."

"But he's in love with you, Cassie, and you know it."

"Yes, I know it, and I've told Moe I don't feel that way about him, and that's okay with him —"

"Maybe for now. But that can't go on forever, his feeling the way he does and you not returning those same feelings."

"Dee, I think you're wrong. I like being around Moe. I like talking to him. It's good to have a man to talk to other than just Stacey."

Dee smiled. "That, and because you can wind Moe around your little finger. He always agrees with you, whether he really does or not."

I took up the iron, cool enough now to finish my dress. "Well, that's good, isn't it? Having a man who agrees with you?"

Dee eyed me in all seriousness. "Not all the time. That's sure not what I would ever want in a man." She began to layer the cobbler. Setting slices of uncooked sweet potatoes in a deep pan, she layered them with the thinly rolled squares along with pats of butter and a mix of sugar, nutmeg, and cinnamon. "If Robert had been that kind of man, we never would have gotten together. I need a strong man, and, Cassie, I know you do too."

I just looked at Dee and continued ironing my dress.

I knew Dee was right about Moe and me. But then Dee was pretty much right about everything, and she always knew what she wanted. Even as far back as when she had first come into our lives she had known what she wanted, and what she wanted as soon as she saw him was Stacey, and as soon as Stacey saw Dee, he wanted her too. That was back in early '42, when Stacey came home from Memphis, where he was working as a trucker driving big rigs and living with Aunt Callie's son Percy and his family. When Stacey arrived he already knew a lot about Dee. Mama, Christopher-John, Man, and I had written and told Stacey that Dee was beautiful, petite, and cocoa-skinned, a striking young woman.

Dee Davis had come into our community in the fall of '41 to teach at Great Faith School. She was a recent graduate of the Negro Teachers Training School down near Brookhaven, and like other young Negro teachers in the state, she looked for teaching positions in Negro schools throughout Mississippi. As part of her contract with Great Faith School, Dee was given housing and board in the home of members of Great Faith Church. Initially she boarded with the Caldwater family, but in January of '42, when the Caldwaters needed the room they had given her, Mama, having been a teacher at Great Faith School, and Papa, who was a deacon at Great Faith Church, invited Dee to stay with our family. At that time, I was a student at Lanier High School and Stacey was in Memphis, but Christopher-John and Little Man were still at home. Since I went home about every weekend, I got to know Dee soon after her arrival and I agreed with Christopher-John and Man that she was right for Stacey. The three of us repeatedly told Dee we wanted her to meet our oldest brother. We had all fallen in love with Dee, and we had a feeling Stacey would too.

We were right.

When Stacey arrived the two immediately hit it off. Within two months of their meeting they were married. In the summer Stacey moved back to Jackson, found work driving a truck at the box factory, and they moved into the house on Everett. In the fall, when school began again, Dee continued her teaching at Great Faith School and stayed during the week with Mama, Papa, and Big Ma. By this time Stacey and Dee were expecting their first child. Marie was born, and with her arrival came a new generation. Rie was a beautiful baby and, as Big Ma liked to say, she was the best thing since peanut and butter. Rie was the first Logan grandchild and everybody fawned over her. Actually, with so much attention, she carried the risk of being spoiled, but I knew that would never happen. Both Dee and Stacey were too sensible for that, and their own upbringing pretty much guaranteed that Rie would be brought up the same.

Although Dee had fought Stacey about coming north, once in Toledo she had adapted to the move and did all she could to make their lives a good one. She too had wanted a house. Unable to qualify as a teacher in Ohio because she had not graduated from an accredited college, Dee had worked the evening shift at the tool plant making machinery parts for the war. With the end of the war, her job was terminated, but by then, she and Stacey had bought the house and, like Stacey, she envisioned that once they had a house, the family would follow.

I figured she would be right about that too.

I had known Dee less than five years and she was several years older than I, but she was now a sister to me, the sister I never had. I listened to her and trusted her opinion. She finished alternating the layers of sweet potatoes and dough and topped off the cobbler with the final uncut thick layer of dough. As she headed for the stove, I finished my dress.

I hated going to the doctor's office. The few times I had gone, once for myself, the other times with Dee and the babies, the waiting room was full, with babies crying and restless children running about in play or pure frustration at the wait. The room was filled with working-class families, both colored and white. Sometimes there weren't enough seats and those left standing leaned against the walls or stood outside until they were called. In the winter, the room was overheated, hot and stuffy, and the air smelled thick. In the summer, the heat was different, a stifling hot muggy heat that permeated the small building and seemed only to be made worse by the open screen door that allowed in the racket of the passing traffic. Appointments, if one had an appointment, were mainly in the evening when people had time after work to go see a doctor. Afternoons, though, were first come, first served. But whether one had an appointment or not, whether it was evening or not, the wait was long. It always was.

So far, on this day, we had been waiting for more than an hour and I was tired of waiting. "This is ridiculous," I said.

Dee just looked at me and smiled. Finally our names were called by the white receptionist. All the medical personnel were white. We got up with the girls and followed the white nurse, uniformed in white, down a long hallway. Dee was shown into one room. I went into another. The nurse told me to take off my dress and shoes and handed me a gown. As she left the room, she said after I was undressed, I should sit on the examination table. I did as I was told, then waited for the doctor. I wasn't sure which doctor I was seeing, for several worked in the office and they saw patients according to the order in which they had arrived. The doctor came in. I had not met with him before. He was a middle-aged man, beginning to gray. He nodded and spoke. "Cassie, is it?"

"Miss Logan," I corrected. I was almost twenty-two now and expected to be treated as an adult, even by white folks in this northern town.

He just looked at me and sat down at the corner table. Opening the file, he perused it for a few seconds before looking at me again. "So, what's the problem today?"

"I don't have a problem," I said. "I just need a physical exam for a job I'm applying for."

"What kind of job?"

"Counselor at a girls' camp."

"Which camp?"

"One run by the union at Willys Overland."

"You work there?"

"No. My brother does. I have the medical form you'll need to fill out." I opened my purse, pulled out a long envelope, and handed it to him.

As the doctor looked over the form, he said, "I didn't know they were hiring Negroes for these positions."

I stiffened, but said nothing.

But then he went on. "As I understand it, girls that go to that camp are white."

This time I spoke up. "As I understand it, the camps are open to the children of anyone who belongs to the union. My brother belongs to the union and if his children were old enough, the camps would include them too."

The doctor just looked at me, then put down the form and came toward me. "Well, let's get started."

I glanced back at the door. "Where's the nurse?"

"We don't need the nurse for this."

The one other time I had come to see a doctor, a nurse had been in the room, but I didn't point this out as the doctor came over and wrapped the blood pressure cuff around my arm. He held my arm against his body as he took my blood pressure. "Don't move," he instructed. He noted the pressure then took off the cuff.

"How is it?" I said.

"Fine."

"I mean, what was the reading?"

"I told you it was fine."

"Well, that's not telling me what it was."

"One twenty over eighty," he said, sounding a bit exasperated. "Mean something to you?"

"Yes," I said, and looked straight at him. He was talking down to me and I didn't like it. "It's perfect, right where it's supposed to be." I had read about blood pressure in a class I had taken. I didn't tell him that. He chose to be superior, and it gave me satisfaction that in this particular thing, I knew the same as he.

His sandy eyes stared at me, but he said

nothing. He went on with the exam. He checked my eyes, my ears, my neck, then placed a cold stethoscope inside my gown and listened to my heartbeat. He did the same with my back and asked me to cough twice. After that, he struck my knees with a small rubber hammer and commented that my reflexes were fine. I didn't say anything. Throughout the exam, he had said little to me. But now he said, "All right, lie down on your back, scoot toward the end of the table, and put your feet in the stirrups. I assume the nurse told you to take off your underwear."

"What?"

He opened a drawer and pulled out rubber gloves. "I need to give you a pelvic exam."

"A pelvic exam?"

"You'll need to lie flat and do as I say. You need to put your feet in the stirrups and spread your legs so that I can check you."

I glanced at the iron shoes on either side of me on the examination table, then looked again at the doctor. I had never had a pelvic exam. "Why do I need a pelvic exam? There's nothing about a pelvic exam on that medical form."

The doctor turned to me. "The form calls for a full examination and a full exam for a female means a pelvic examination."

"Well, I don't see why. I've never had to have one before."

"It's simple enough," the doctor said as he pulled on the gloves. "They want to determine if you have any kind of medical problem in your uterus or if you're pregnant."

"Well, I'm certainly not pregnant!"

"Let's get on with the exam, shall we?"

I looked again at the stirrups and fully realized the position I would be in to get my feet into them. I met the doctor's eyes once more. "Can we get the nurse in here?"

"I told you there's no need for a nurse. Now, if you want this form filled out, get into position. I'm sure you know the position."

I was silent a moment, considering what he meant by that, then I said quietly, "I told you I've never had a pelvic exam."

"Come now. A pelvic exam has nothing to do with knowing the position. All you colored girls know it, married or not."

I got down from the table. I had never spread my legs for any man, and I certainly was not about to do so for the first time with a white man, doctor or not, not without a nurse present.

"What are you doing?" the doctor asked, looking startled.

"I don't think I'll take the exam," I said.

"But you need it for the form."

"I also need a nurse in here."

He became indignant. "Why? I'm a doctor!"

"I said I want a nurse in here for the exam, so why can't a nurse come in?"

"Because I said so."

I had heard those words from white folks all my life. Even more than this man's implications concerning my character, I hated those words from white people. They cut me to the core. "You need to understand something," I said.

"I'm not putting my feet into stirrups for you without a nurse being in here, so I guess this exam is over."

He turned red. "You think I want something from you? You don't have anything I haven't seen before."

"I'd like to get dressed now."

"Well, I won't be signing off on this form."

"Fine," I said.

He glared at me, took his file, and left the room. He left the unsigned form on the table. I got dressed, folded the form, and put it back in my purse. I returned to the waiting room, paid the office clerk for the visit, and waited for Dee. "How'd it go?" Dee asked when she came out with the girls.

"Not as expected," I said, hurrying from the office. I did not want to stay any longer in this place. "I won't be getting the job."

"What? How do you know?"

"I'll tell you about it in the car. Let's go."

■ ■ ■ ■

Dee told me I could go to another doctor to fill out my form, but I figured them all to be the same. They all were white. By the time Moe arrived, I was in a foul mood. My friend Brenda from down the street and her boyfriend, Henry, were going to the movies with us and Dee had invited them to join us for dinner. I stayed quiet all through dinner. When Stacey asked about the visit to the doctor's office and if I had gotten the form filled out, I said I would talk about it with him later. The whole thing was too embarrassing to talk about in front of everybody. Stacey just studied me without comment as Dee quickly changed the subject. When dinner was over, Moe, Henry, Brenda, and I headed downtown to the theater. We went in Moe's car. Whenever Moe and I went out, if not with the family, it was usually with Brenda and Henry, for even though I was a grown woman, the tradition of double dating remained, and that was expected until I married. That was simply the way things were with many of the families from back home.

Moe, a mocha-chocolate young man, tall and skinny, parked his car a block from the theater, and with Brenda and Henry a few feet behind us and out of hearing, he asked quietly, "What's wrong, Cassie? You've hardly had a word to say all evening."

"Didn't have anything I wanted to say."

"That's not like you."

"It is today," I said, and we walked the rest of the way in silence.

There was a line as we approached the ticket window located in a bubble-like structure in front of the theater. It was a long line and all who stood there were white. In Mississippi there was a separate entry for "colored," but in Toledo white and colored stood in the same line to buy a ticket. "So, are you going to tell me what's the matter or not?" Moe persisted as we waited.

"Just had a run-in about something."

"What kind of something?"

"Don't want to talk about it."

"Okay." Moe let the matter drop. That

was the way it was with Moe. He seldom pressed me about anything. Because of that, I usually told him just about everything, when I figured I was ready. Moe was aware of this and his easygoing nature allowed him to be patient with me. Moe bought the tickets and we entered the theater. At the concession counter, Brenda pulled me aside and told me she needed to go to the ladies' room. I didn't have to use the restroom, but I went with Brenda. The ladies' room was in the lower lobby. Brenda and I descended a winding staircase covered in plush, red, velvet-like carpeting to the lower lobby, which was smaller than the lobby upstairs but had the same thick carpet and was furnished with large, comfortable sofas where people were lounging while awaiting the start of the movie. All those people lounging were white.

We crossed the lobby to the door marked "Ladies" and entered first into a small room with a sofa and chairs. A mirror covered one of the walls. A counter and chairs were in front of it. Women and teenage girls, all white, occupied the chairs as they combed blond or sandy-colored hair, primped their faces, and reddened their lips. Then we entered the next room, lined with toilet stalls. We were stopped by a Negro woman in a maid's uniform. "There's a stall at the end next to the wall you girls can use," she said, "but you'll have to wait. Somebody's in there."

A door opened to a stall near us and a white woman came out. "There's one open," I said. "Go on, Brenda."

Brenda hesitated and the attendant said, "One at the end'll be open in a minute."

"Go on," I said again to Brenda. "Thought you had to go so bad."

Brenda looked at me, then went into the stall. The attendant stared nervously on. "You girls gonna get me in trouble," she muttered. "Colored girls usually use the one at the end."

I turned to her. "What?"

"Never mind," she mumbled as another white woman stepped from a stall. The woman washed her hands and the attendant, smiling, handed her a towel. The woman thanked the attendant, tipped her a quarter, and went out. Several other women, all white, came in. Not in line, I stepped aside. One of the women entered the empty stall. Then the door to Brenda's stall opened and Brenda came out. The second woman in line said to the woman in front of her, "There's a stall open."

And the other woman said, "I'm not about to use that toilet after *she's* been in there."

Brenda heard, but said nothing and went over to the sink. The attendant heard as well and she too said nothing. As another stall door opened and a white woman exited, the white woman who had made the remark started toward the stall. I stepped in front of her and looked back. "You too good to use a toilet after a colored person, you won't be able to use this toilet either." Then I entered the stall and closed the door in her face.

When Brenda and I returned upstairs Moe and Henry were waiting for us at the stairs leading to the balcony. "You two certainly took long enough," laughed

Henry. "We thought you fell in."

"We had better go on up," said Moe. "They're beginning the previews."

I stared at the winding staircase as several couples made their way up the stairs. Clusters of people were already gathered on the landing. All were well-groomed, well-dressed, and all were colored. The balcony was where colored folks always sat, and it was understood that it was where we were supposed to sit. I figured not to sit there today. I was sick of the bigotry. I turned from the stairs to Moe. "Moe, could I have my ticket, please?"

"Well . . . sure, Cassie," Moe complied, without questioning me.

"Thanks," I said, and moved away.

"Cassie, where you going?" asked Brenda.

"I think I'll sit downstairs this evening."

"What!" exclaimed Henry.

And Moe shook his head. "Cassie . . ."

"I'm not sitting in the balcony, Moe. Not today."

"Girl, you must be nuts!" surmised

Henry. "What's got into you?"

Brenda grabbed my arm. "Cassie, don't get us into trouble!"

My eyes locked on hers. "You don't have to come if you don't want to. Go on upstairs." I looked at Moe. "You too, Moe. I'll sit down here by myself." I didn't wait for Moe to respond. I left the three of them standing there and headed for one of the two downstairs entries into the theater.

I got in line behind a white couple. As the young uniformed usher took their tickets with a friendly smile and said, "Hope you enjoy the show," I stepped forward. With his head turned toward the couple who had just passed, the usher, still smiling, turned toward me and his smile vanished. "Uh . . . you're in the wrong line."

"I don't see any other line," I said. "Here's my ticket."

The usher reddened. "Like I said . . . uh, you're in the wrong line. You're supposed to be in the balcony." He nodded toward the stairs. "You just head up those stairs. Someone'll take your ticket up there."

"No, I don't think so. I'm sitting downstairs today. Here's my ticket."

"And here's mine." I turned. Moe took my ticket and held both toward the usher.

"But you can't —" objected the usher.

"We'll need our stubs back," Moe said.

The usher was baffled. He looked around for help, but the lobby had cleared and there seemed no one available. Most of the moviegoers were now inside.

"Could you hurry up?" I asked the usher. "The movie is about to start."

Seemingly not knowing what to do, the usher took the tickets, tore them in half, and handed the stubs to Moe. "I'll have to get the manager, you know," he said as we walked past him.

"Go ahead," I said. "We'll be down front." With that, I stepped into the darkened theater with Moe beside me and walked the plush red carpet toward the huge screen looming before us.

It was a long walk down the aisle and the audience began to take notice. A murmur rose against the backdrop of cartoons on the screen. I tried to ignore them. There were three sections of seating divided by two aisles, with the center section being triple the size of the two sections that ran along the walls. Four rows from the stage were empty seats right at the entry to the row. I took the second seat from the aisle and Moe sat in the aisle seat. I had finally made it to the main floor, the forbidden section of the theater. The irony was, though, as I sat watching the screen, I realized that the view of the massive screen was actually better from the balcony. But I kept telling myself it was the principle of the thing. Several seats separated us from the other moviegoers in the row, who nudged each other and turned to stare at us.

All eyes in the theater, it seemed, were on us.

I sipped the drink Moe had bought me. Moe looked at me and smiled. "Popcorn?" he said, offering me the box. I smiled back and took a handful. Then we both set our gaze on the screen. The main feature was about to begin. A few minutes into it, murmuring rose from the back of the theater and, turning, Moe and I saw a circle of light on the aisle floor. Then two men, one carrying a flashlight, were standing at our row. One was the young ticket taker. The other was a much older man who announced softly, "I am the manager. The two of you will have to leave."

Moe and I looked at the screen.

The manager continued. "Now, I don't want any trouble in here, but if you don't leave voluntarily, I'll have to call the police."

Moe didn't say anything, but I knew what he was thinking. He couldn't afford to deal with the police. He could have gotten up and left, but I knew he wouldn't. I had started this thing and he was leaving it up to me. I acknowledged Moe with a look and said to the manager, "Why do we have to leave? We paid our money just like everybody else sitting here."

The manager seemed startled by my question. "Why? You know as well as I do the answer to that. You want to see this movie, you'll have to move upstairs."

Moe and I just sat there, staring straight ahead.

The manager's voice rose. "Are you going to leave?"

Without turning to him, I repeated, "We paid to see this movie. We should be able to sit where we want."

"Then you give me no choice," said the manager. "I'll have to call the police." The manager left with the usher behind him. Murmuring rose throughout the theater.

Moe took my hand. "Cassie . . ."

"You'd better leave," I said.

"I need to speak to Henry," said Moe. "I'll be right back." Without giving me a chance to say anything else, Moe got up. I held the box of popcorn and my drink and gazed at the screen. The murmuring subsided and all grew quiet again, except for the action on the screen.

Moe did not come right back. He was gone so long I began to worry that maybe the police had already been called before the manager spoke to us and maybe they were arresting Moe. I hadn't been afraid before. Now I was. This had been a stupid thing for me to do. I knew it. I already knew too what would happen if we sat here and so did Moe, yet he had come with me anyway. I figured I needed to go see about him, but before I made up my mind to do just that he came back and sat down beside me. The moviegoers took notice with renewed mutterings.

"What took you so long?" I whispered.

"Wanted to ask Henry to call his father. He already had."

"Attorney Tate's coming?"

"If there's going to be trouble, maybe he can get us out of it."

"They didn't try to stop you from coming back in?"

"No," Moe said. "They didn't lay a hand on me. They've called the police."

"Then you'd better go."

"No." He looked at me and again took my hand. "Not without you."

As I looked at Moe I knew I needed to swallow my pride and not put Moe through this. He had too much to lose. I knew we had to leave, but still I sat there. I sat there too long. Light flooded the theater and the movie was stopped. The crowd reacted with a noisy swell, including a sudden rise of voices from the balcony. Heads turned as four men walked down the aisle toward Moe and me. The manager was one of the men, accompanied by two policemen. The fourth man was Stacey. The manager and the policemen stood back and it was Stacey who approached us. He stopped at our row, looked at me, and quietly said, "All right, Cassie, let's go."

I looked at Stacey, took a moment, then got up. So did Moe. "You call him?" I asked softly of Moe.

"Figured he was the only one who could talk sense to you."

Moe stepped into the aisle and I followed, and together we left with Stacey. The manager and the police walked behind us. As we passed down the aisle, someone said, not in a shout, but loud enough to be heard, "Damn niggers! Think they can do anything they want!" I turned, but Stacey, not stopping and not turning, took me by the elbow and led me out. We stepped into the lobby and the lights dimmed behind us and the movie resumed. All was calm now. The moviegoers could see their film in peace.

■ ■ ■ ■

Attorney Charles Tate stood at the far end of the lobby talking to two white police officers. Brenda and Henry stood apart from them, watching the group as Henry's father did most of the talking. Other than the two groups, the lobby was deserted except for three people behind the concession counter, who looked on curiously as they awaited the next wave of moviegoers. The manager headed straight for Attorney Tate and the other policemen. The policemen who had escorted us into the lobby, after warning Moe and me not to leave, went with him. Stacey followed, joining Lawyer Tate and the police. Brenda and Henry joined Moe and me.

The police talked only a few minutes to Lawyer Tate and Stacey, then, with only a glance at Moe and me, left the building. Through the glass doors of the theater we could see them standing outside, but they did not get into their cars. Attorney Tate and Stacey came over to us. "Enjoy the movie?" asked Attorney Tate with all seriousness. Then he smiled and waved us toward the doors. "Come on," he said, "we need to talk."

The manager watched us leave.

Outside, Attorney Tate herded us down the street. I looked back. The police had not moved. "What about them?" I asked.

"My car's around the corner," said Lawyer Tate. "Just keep walking." I glanced back once more as we rounded the corner. The police were still standing there. When we reached Attorney Tate's car, he said, "Miss Logan, I understand you're the instigator of all this." He set his lawyer eyes on me and waited for me to respond.

"Well . . . I suppose I am."

"Now, for my own understanding, I would like to know why you thought sitting down on the main floor of that theater was so important? Couldn't you see the screen just as well from the balcony?"

"Probably better," I admitted.

"Then what was so important about the main floor?"

I glanced at Stacey and Moe, then looked again at Lawyer Tate. I was finally getting a chance to explain myself. "It's the principle of the thing, Mr. Tate. All my life, living in Mississippi, it was understood everything was separate. Up here, this was supposed to be like the promised land."

The lawyer smiled. "And it's not?"

"It's a false promise, Mr. Tate. The signs aren't there, but the rules are there just the same. I wanted to sit downstairs, just because I wanted to have the choice to do so."

Lawyer Tate fixed his eyes on me. "And was it worth it?"

"Well, I didn't get to see the movie."

"None of us did," grumbled Henry.

"You do understand," said Attorney Tate, "if Henry hadn't called me and if I did not have an ongoing working relationship with these white people, you two would most likely have been arrested. You do understand that, don't you?"

"Yes, sir, I understand."

"I've worked with two of those particular officers before. As policemen go, they're okay. They listen to reason, and they allowed your brother to go in to get

95

you. They didn't want a racial incident any more than we did. But you do something like this again, it might not turn out so well. Take seriously what I am saying to you, Cassie. You go up against the system again, you could wind up in jail. Is that clear to you?"

"It's clear, Mr. Tate, but segregation is segregation, that's the plain fact of the matter, and the fact that there are no signs still doesn't make it right. It's the same, with or without the signs."

Lawyer Tate's legal eyes studied me for a moment, then he said, "Hold on to that thinking, Cassie . . . and remember . . . our time will come. Our time will come." He then turned abruptly to his son. "Okay, Henry, date's over. You and Brenda come with me. We'll drop Brenda off. Moe," he said, turning back, "you come by my office when you get a chance. Robert, talk to your sister. I'll see you and your lovely wife at church . . . and, Cassie," he continued, glancing over at me, "maybe when Moe comes to see me, you need to come with him. Robert, you come too. I think we all need to talk. And one more thing, Miss Cassie Logan, you stay out of trouble." With all orders given, he and Henry and Brenda got into his Lincoln and drove away.

We watched as they left, then Stacey said, "Moe, you get your car and we'll see you at the house. Cassie, you ride with me. Car's parked up the street. I want to talk to you."

I sighed, looked at Moe, and went with Stacey. I knew I was in for it.

"So, what were you thinking?" Stacey demanded to know as we drove toward home. "Or did you think?"

I looked out the window, not wanting to talk about it. "It's been a hard day, Stacey."

"It could've been a lot harder. You could be sitting in jail right now."

"I know."

"And all for a movie you didn't even get to see."

I turned to him. "What do you want me to say? Maybe I just didn't think about all that. It was the principle of the thing!"

"Cassie, you know as well as I do that

principle will land your behind in jail, and no, you did not think. You certainly didn't think about Moe."

I was silent as Stacey glanced over at me.

"Forget yourself and your principle for a moment. What if Moe had been arrested? What good would principle have served then?"

"Moe didn't have to go in with me," I protested sullenly. "I didn't ask him."

"Oh, come on now, Cassie," Stacey said, exasperated with me. He knew me like a book. "You know better than that! Moe would never have let you go in that theater alone, and he would never leave you, you know that too. You made up your mind about this thing and you just didn't care about the consequences."

I took his chastising, but then defended lamely, "Like I said, it was the principle of the thing."

Stacey scoffed that off. "The principle. If Lawyer Tate hadn't shown up to talk to those white people, Moe could have been arrested. You need to think, Cassie, before you go taking a stand about principle. How many times Papa and Mama tell us that?" Stacey again looked at me. "Your principle could have landed Moe back in Mississippi. Your principle could have gotten Moe killed."

I met Stacey's eyes in the dark and knew there were no further words to say. He was right, and that's all there was to that. He was right about everything. We drove the rest of the way home in silence. Like the night, the streets were beginning to quiet, and in silence I thought about the city of Toledo without its signs, but segregated anyway. I thought about Toledo with all its opportunities, but segregated anyway. At least down home in Mississippi and throughout the South, folks were direct and honest about what was expected. Everybody knew exactly where a body stood. There was no pretense to equality. The signs were everywhere. *Whites Only. Colored Not Allowed.* We had a place and they had a place. Everybody had a place, and everybody knew where and what that place was. *Whites Only. Colored Not Allowed.* But here in Toledo, there were no signs. There

did not have to be. It was simply understood.

Whites Only. Colored Not Allowed.

LAYOFFS
(1946–1947)

Moe Turner was Stacey's best friend, and they had been through a lot together. At the age of fourteen, the two of them had run off to the Louisiana cane fields looking for work. They had gone not out of rebellion, but because both the Turners and our family, like just about every family around, were struggling with their crops, with their debt. Our family in particular, one of the few black families in the community who owned land, was faced with losing that land. With no money coming in, Stacey and Moe had taken it upon themselves to get some money by going off on their own. They were gone for months and both Moe's widowed father and all our family had searched for them, worried about them, and prayed for them. In the end, we had

101

found them, sick and frail in a Louisiana jail.

Both had come home that time, but that was not the case when, a few years later, Moe took a crowbar and slammed it into three white boys, three white boys in Mississippi. He bloodied them, injuring them severely, then he had fled the county and Mississippi and gone up to Memphis with the help of Stacey and a white boy named Jeremy Simms. The year Moe fled was 1941, just before the bombing of Pearl Harbor and the country's entry into World War II. I remember thinking that at least Moe didn't have to worry about having to be a soldier. The government and the state of Mississippi didn't know where to find him.

"Moe," said Attorney Tate, crossing his long legs as he pushed slightly away from his desk, which was between us, "I asked you to come meet with me because I have a story to tell you, a story that might be of interest to you. It's about Mississippi."

Moe looked quizzically at the attorney, then quickly at Stacey and me, and again at Attorney Tate. "Interest to me?"

Attorney Tate nodded. "And I asked Robert and Cassie to come with you because I think they have a part in it."

Both Stacey and I kept our eyes straight ahead, focused on Attorney Tate, but my heart began to race, for I feared where this might be going.

"As you know, I have contact with the police department and also with a number of attorneys in this area, including the district attorney's office. Well, recently one of these people contacted me as a representative of the Negro community and asked me if I knew a young man by the name of Moe Turner who might live here. . . ."

His voice trailed off for a moment as his eyes studied us. I kept my eyes directly on him. I felt movement from Moe, who sat next to me on the office couch. Lawyer Tate's eyes took note. "Of course, I told this person truthfully that I was not aware of any gentleman by that name, but I did ask why he was inquiring. I was told that it had come to his attention that a man named Moe Turner from Mississippi might be in the area and that this young man was wanted by the law in Mississippi." Again Lawyer Tate paused. Again he set his gaze on each of us. Then he added, "Wanted for a brutal assault on three white men."

Moe sighed, and I looked at him. In Moe's face I saw the same look of fear as five years ago, when he realized what he had done and what he was about to face. Attorney Tate kept his eyes on Moe, but Moe's eyes were downcast and he didn't speak.

Stacey glanced over at Moe and at me, then said, "So, what does this have to do with us?"

"Well, maybe not a thing," replied Lawyer Tate. "But I felt I had to mention it to you, because your name came up, Robert."

"My name?" questioned Stacey.

"Oh, goodness," I murmured, no longer able to pretend disinterest in what Attorney Tate was saying.

My emotional disclaimer was not lost on the lawyer, who glanced my way but said nothing. He went on. "Seems there is a white boy from Mississippi working at Willys Overland. Seems he recognized you, Robert, and he said that he was there in a town called Strawberry on the day of the attack. He recalled that on that day you and your sister were there in town also, and that he knew your family and the Turner family were close. He told folks back in Strawberry about you. Said that perhaps you would know where Moe Turner would be. Authorities there contacted the Toledo police and said there is an arrest warrant in Mississippi for this Moe Turner for aggravated assault. Ironic thing is that your name came up on the same day Miss Cassie here decided to integrate the downstairs seating area at the movie theater." He smiled bemusedly my way. "Course now, the police didn't take any names about that theater incident and that was at my request. I didn't want any of this coming back on you or your family, Robert . . . or you, Moe."

Stacey was silent a moment, eyes on Lawyer Tate, then, without looking at Moe or me, he said, "Well, I tell you, Lawyer Tate —"

At that, the attorney held up his hand, stopping him from speaking. "I don't need explanations. I don't need to know anything. In fact, I do not want to know anything. All I wanted you to know is that there is a white person from Mississippi who knows you and Cassie and that if he presses this thing, somebody from law enforcement might come to question you. I assume no one has contacted you about this." Stacey shook his head in silence. "Well, maybe no one will come at all. You and Cassie weren't implicated in that attack on those Mississippi boys. Like I told the detective who asked me about all this, I don't know the name Moe Turner. Actually, the only Moe I know is a young man by the name of Moe McKlellan. . . ." He looked straight at Moe. "But, of course, I didn't tell them that."

Moe shifted uneasily. Since his arrival in the North, Moe had been using the name Moe McKlellan and had gotten his job under that name. He also had identification under that name.

"This man who said he recognized me, you know who he is?" asked Stacey.

Attorney Tate touched a file on his desk, thumped it, and put on his glasses before opening it. He checked a paper

106

inside. "Harold Rockmiler," he said. He took off his glasses and looked up. "You know him?"

Stacey shook his head and looked at me. I shrugged. I hadn't heard of him either.

"Well, as I said," continued Lawyer Tate, "I just wanted all of you to know there was an inquiry. Also, if you ever need legal advice, my door is always open." He pushed back from his desk and stood. With that, Stacey, Moe, and I knew the meeting was ended, and we stood too. We thanked Attorney Tate, but as we started to leave, he stopped me. "Cassie, I'd like to speak to you for a minute."

I turned back as Stacey and Moe went into the outer office. "Yes, sir?" I said.

Lawyer Tate came over to me. "I've been thinking about your stand the other night at the movie theater. Maybe it wasn't a wise thing you did, but I admired it."

I glanced at Stacey, standing now by the secretary's desk. "Well, my brother sure didn't."

Lawyer Tate smiled at that, then said,

"I know you're working on a degree in education from the university here and Henry tells me you're almost finished with your courses. How soon will that be?"

"I have a couple more courses to take in the fall. Once I've passed them, I'll be qualified to teach in Ohio, probably by next January. But why are you asking?"

"Well, I've just been wondering if you're planning on actually teaching once you do qualify."

I was surprised that Lawyer Tate had been wondering about me at all. "Well, to be truthful with you, I don't know if I'll teach or not. My mother's a teacher and she loves it, but I don't feel the same as she does about teaching and I figure I ought to love whatever I do if that's what I'm going to be doing the rest of my life."

Attorney Tate nodded. "I agree with you, Cassie, that you ought to love whatever you do and have a real commitment to it. So, think about this, Cassie." His eyes met mine. "Law."

"Law?"

"That's right, law. Just think about it.

You want to take a stand about injustices, this could be a way. Like I said the other night, our day is coming for change, and you could well be a part of it. Just think about it."

I was silent a moment, struck by the thought. "I will," I said, and moved to go.

"And, Cassie, one word of advice. If you do choose law, never give yourself away concerning your circumstances, or those of a client, when it is not in your best interest to do so."

"What do you mean?"

"During our conversation earlier, Cassie, you confirmed something to me that I already suspected, something a good lawyer would always recognize."

I thought a moment, then realized what he meant. My emotional murmur had given him insight into my thinking. "Oh," I said.

He smiled. "You ever want to talk further about this, I'm here."

"Thank you," I said. "I'll remember that."

Attorney Tate hadn't asked, so we hadn't told him what had happened that day back in Strawberry when Moe had thrashed those three white boys with a crowbar. If we had told the attorney, I knew he would have understood. He too was from the South — South Carolina — and even if he had not come out of the South he would have understood anyway. Anybody of color would have understood.

It was the taunting, the humiliation that led Moe to strike out at Statler Aames and his brothers. And it was the fear. The Aames brothers along with their cousin, Jeremy Simms, had already chased down a colored boy along the Creek Rosa Lee, and the boy had been injured. On that December day in Strawberry I knew I was thinking about what had happened along the Rosa Lee, and I knew Moe was too. Clarence Hopkins was as well.

Clarence was also a good friend of ours, same age as Stacey and Moe. He recently had joined the Army, and he was with us, in uniform, that day. Statler

Aames and his brothers saw Clarence and even though Clarence was in uniform, or perhaps because he was, they began to taunt him, to humiliate him with racial jokes. They had forced Clarence to take off his soldier's cap so that they could rub his head for so-called good luck. Clarence had bowed his head, scrunched his soldier's cap in his hands in silence, and they had rubbed his head with raucous laughter and invited other white men watching to do the same.

Stacey was not with us, but Moe and I had witnessed all that was happening to Clarence and had felt the shame of it. Only the appearance of Mr. Wade Jamison stopped the Aames brothers from further humiliating Clarence. Mr. Wade Jamison was a white man, a lawyer, a powerful figure in the county, and could be a formidable foe. Mr. Wade Jamison had befriended us on more than one occasion. He was the one white man we called our friend. But Mr. Jamison was not present a little while later when Statler and the other Aames boys tried to do the same thing to Moe as they had done to Clarence.

Moe chose not to bow his head.

When they approached, Moe was in the process of using a tire iron to remove a flat tire from Stacey's car. The Aames brothers seemed to take no note of the crowbar or that Moe might use it. They took no note that Moe might not submit to their taunting as Clarence had done. They took no note that Moe might strike back. They attempted to touch Moe's head and Moe had lashed out with the tire iron. He struck Statler first, knocking him to the ground, then the other two brothers, Leon and Troy, as they came at him. Moe had seriously injured Troy, whom he had smashed in the head, and Troy had been bedridden ever since. He lashed out at all of them for what they were attempting to do to him, for what they had done to Clarence, for what they had done along the Rosa Lee. He had lashed out for all of us; then he had run for his life.

Moe escaped the county in the tarp-covered bed of a truck driven by Jeremy Simms. Jeremy drove him as far as Jackson. From Jackson, Stacey had taken Moe out of Mississippi up to the train station in Memphis. I was with them, along with our friend Little Willie Wiggins. On that day we all feared we might never see Moe again as he fled far away from us, but we knew he had to go. There was no way he could stay in Mississippi and live. Moe, of course, was feeling all this too, and it was even more frightening for him. He was leaving everyone he knew, everyone he loved. He was leaving his widowed father and all his family. He was leaving with the laws of Mississippi against him. He was leaving and knew he could never return. He was leaving me, and that is why he kissed me. He was leaving me, and that is why he said he loved me.

That was the first time Moe had ever kissed me, the first time I had ever realized he thought of me as more than a friend, more than just Stacey's little sister. It was the first time and the last. In the years since, he had not attempted to kiss me again, and that was just as well for I had felt nothing when Moe kissed me. Moe was my friend, my close and special friend, but that was all and that was all I wanted him to be.

"Moe, I think you know it's best if you don't come down here for a while," said Stacey when we were in the car and heading back to the house. "You best stay in Detroit."

Moe was silent.

Stacey glanced over. "We'll come see you there."

"I don't want to put y'all in trouble."

"I think we'll be all right. White folks always known about our families, how close we are. I'm sure a lot of them know I'm up here, and Cassie too. The law in Mississippi's not interested in us —"

"Just me," said Moe.

Stacey nodded. "I think so. That's why I say you shouldn't come for a while."

Moe sighed and looked out the window. I was sitting between Stacey and Moe. I looked first at my brother, his eyes straight ahead, then at Moe. I knew how much Moe's weekend trips to Toledo meant to him. When he came on Fridays, he stayed until Sunday evening. He slept on the sofa bed in the living room. He ate all that good food Dee cooked, and for him it was almost like being back home. We were his family now. He went to church with us, played baseball down at the vacant corner lot near the school, listened to the radio in the evenings, enjoyed everything we enjoyed together. It was an escape from the loneliness of his own life living in a rooming house up in Detroit. It was an escape from being Moe McKlellan. With us, he could again be Moe Turner.

When Moe had first arrived in Detroit, he had gone to our people living there, extended family who had come up to Detroit from Canton, Mississippi, and who had never lived down around Great Faith. Moe told them nothing about what had caused him to come so suddenly, just that he was looking for work to help out his family, but he knew he could not stay long with them. There were many in the family and he was just one more body to take care of in their small space, so as soon as he got some work, Moe moved out and took a room in a boarding house. He took the room under the name of Moe McKlellan, just as he had taken his job under that name. When Stacey and Dee bought the house on Dorr Street, they asked Moe about coming to stay with us, but Moe had said no. He already had a good job working at the Ford factory and, besides that, he didn't want to bring any trouble to them in case Mississippi tracked him down. Despite all that, I knew what Moe was feeling now, and I knew also he did not want to stop coming to Toledo. Once we were at the house and Stacey had gone back to the kitchen to greet Dee, Moe sat next to me on the living room sofa and said, "I don't know if I can stay away. I know I oughta, but the truth is . . . I want to see you, Cassie."

"Ah, Moe . . ."

"I know. I know how you want things to be. You want us being friends —"

"That's important —"

"Sure, it is . . . but you know I want more, Cassie."

"Well, I'm not going there, Moe. We've been friends too long for us to go there."

Moe smiled. "You never know," he said.

"Well, I do. You best stay in Detroit and keep yourself safe. And don't worry. I'll be coming to see you along with Stacey.

116

You'll always be my friend."

Moe smiled again. "Yeah . . . that's what I'm afraid of."

That next week Attorney Tate called. The detective who had approached him about Moe wanted to talk to us. Stacey and I met the detective at Lawyer Tate's office. He questioned us briefly about the incident in Strawberry and asked us about Moe. We told him we didn't know where Moe was.

During the war years there had been no new cars. All the car factories had turned full attention to manufacturing for the war. In 1946, for the first time in five years, new cars began to roll off the assembly lines in Detroit, and Stacey was among the first to buy one. His purchase was even published in the newspaper. It was a 1946 Mercury, burgundy in color, with white-walled tires. It was a beauty. As soon as he had driven the Mercury from the showroom floor and brought it back to Dorr Street, people began to gather and marvel at the new car. Everyone, it seemed, wanted a ride in the Mercury, even if it was just around the block and — after a first ride with Dee, the girls, and me — Stacey obliged. He even let some of his most trusted friends drive it.

Stacey loved cars, always had. Part of his love for cars had come from Uncle Hammer, who always drove fine cars, even a Packard. Uncle Hammer had even driven the Packard down into Mississippi. But it was Stacey who had bought our family's first car in Mississippi, a Ford that had belonged to Mrs. Wade Jamison, and like his new Mercury it too had been burgundy. Stacey had driven that car north and had kept it throughout the war years. Now, with the enticement of the new models, he had traded in the Ford for the Mercury. He had a good income at the factory, the union was strong, and even though there was some concern that there could be layoffs, Stacey bought the car.

Later, he began to regret that decision.

Finally, Christopher-John and Clayton Chester came home.

Despite the fact that Man had gone first into the Army, it was Christopher-

John who came home first. He arrived in August and went directly to Mississippi. Stacey, Dee, the girls, and I went down to greet him, but he didn't come back with us. He stayed on awhile helping on the land, and came to Toledo in November. Man didn't arrive in the States until December. He too went directly to Mississippi. He was there for Christmas, but after the new year he too came to Toledo. Both Christopher-John and Man had decided they could no longer live in Mississippi. Actually, they had already made up their minds while still in service. Neither saw a future in Mississippi. Having endured the bloody battles of Europe, having been tested daily, they no longer had the stomach to live under the harsh rules of segregation.

With so many soldiers returning, the rumors of layoffs at Willys Overland were now rampant. Soldiers who had once worked at the factory wanted their old jobs back, the jobs that had been promised to them. In addition to so many returning soldiers, the Army would no longer need the production of jeeps as it had during the war. The plant returned to its prewar production schedule with no more of the overtime that had provided high wages to all its workers. There was no longer hiring. Christopher-John was fortunate to get a job with a car dealership, though it was part-time. Trained as a mechanic by the Army, Christopher-John had a skill that did not require work in a factory. Clayton Chester was not as fortunate. Unable to get work at any of the plants in the area, he decided to go back to school under the G.I. Bill, which would pay his tuition as well as allow him a living allowance. It was too late for him to enroll at the University of Toledo for the semester, so he enrolled in special classes offered to veterans at the local vocational high school. His plan was to enroll at the university in the fall. In the meantime, he was taking the vocational classes and any odd jobs he could get — painting, plastering, light electrical work, minor plumbing. Man was good at anything he set his mind to, and even if he did not know how to do a particular thing, it was of no worry to him. He simply went to the library, got a book on the subject, and when it came time to do the job he could do it.

With Christopher-John and Clayton Chester now in the house, Dee found places for them to sleep, one on the living room sofa bed, the other on the Sunday room sofa. At first, it seemed a bit crowded having five grown people staying downstairs, but soon it didn't matter. We had lived in smaller spaces together growing up at home and on Everett Street in Jackson. What mattered was that the boys had returned safely from the war and we were all together again. Now, here in Toledo, even with the threat of the layoffs, we could look forward to a future.

During the Christmas holidays, before Man came to Toledo, Moe had stayed with us while the Ford plant was shut down for the week. It had been months since the meeting with Attorney Tate and Stacey's warning that Moe should not come to Toledo. Despite that warning, Moe said he just wanted to be with folks from home. "You know, Cassie," he said, "how much I miss my daddy, all my family. These past months not being able to come down here every week, see all of you, I've been missing them even more. When Stacey brought me that last letter from my daddy, Daddy said baby brother Morris was about to finish up eighth grade at Great Faith School come spring and then he'll be going up to Jackson or over to Vicksburg to finish school. He said he'd rather send Morris up here to me so he could go to school in Detroit."

"Really?" I was surprised. "Thought he'd want to keep Morris there. He's always doted on Morris."

"Well, we all have since Mama died giving birth to him. We all took a hand in raising Morris. Always smart as a whip. Course you know I ain't seen him since he was seven. He'll be turning thirteen before year's end." Moe seemed reflective on the coming year. "Got the feeling my daddy is looking out for both of us, for Morris and for me. His youngest son and his oldest son. He wants Morris to have a good education. Education, that's important to Daddy, but I figure the real reason he wants Morris up here is for me to have family with me, and who better than Morris?" Moe smiled. "Daddy says I half raised him. Might as well finish the job."

"So, what are you going to tell your daddy?"

"Figure to do what he wants and send for Morris, have somebody bring him up to Detroit before school starts next year."

"They lay you off, are you still going to send for Morris?"

Moe nodded. "My daddy hasn't asked one thing of me in all these years I been gone from home, but he's asking this of me now and I'm not about to say no to him. Whatever happens, I'll make it somehow. Besides, it'll be good to have one of my family here. I won't feel so alone."

I understood.

The layoffs began after the first of the new year in 1947. Those workers who had filled the factory's high demand for labor during the war years were now being let go.

Stacey was one of those workers.

No one knew if hiring would begin

again or if there would be a callback. Uncertainty hung over the house on Dorr Street and over the city. All the renters had jobs at the plant and all of them, like Stacey, were laid off. Christopher-John had his part-time job and Man, his temporary jobs. I still had my job working a few hours each week at Roman's, but that only brought in enough to help with the groceries as well as my own personal expenses. None of us earned enough to pay the mortgage, and it was the mortgage on the house that worried us all. The renters paid what they could and some could pay nothing at all, but Stacey and Dee were not about to put them out. Like us, they were all hard-working people and were doing what they could to find work to support their families. Still, we all knew that there had to be money coming in soon from somewhere. Stacey and Dee fell back on their savings, but if the layoff continued and there was no full-time work, that money would soon run out.

"I have a good mind to go to California if things don't pick up here," Stacey said as we sat around the kitchen table late one evening. A sleepy Rie sat on his lap. "I figure maybe Uncle Hammer can find something for me."

"So, what do we do then?" interjected Dee. She repositioned 'lois, already sleeping, in her arms before demanding an answer from Stacey with a pointed look. "Move all the way out there like we moved all the way up here?"

Stacey smiled at her. "You want to move back down south to live? All you've got to do is say so," he teased.

"I wasn't saying that," Dee demurred.

Stacey laughed. We all did, for we knew how Dee now felt about going back south. "I'm telling you the truth," Stacey said. "I could not get the woman to come with me north and now she's the one who doesn't want to go back. For two years I begged Dee for us to move north and she fought me tooth and nail about the thing —"

"Well, I finally came, didn't I?" retorted Dee.

"Yeah, you came all right! You came after I had to get the hell out of that state, and on the day I left, as I recall — now, you tell me different if you recall something else — but on the day I left, as I packed my suitcase, you were busy unpacking it and you told me in no uncertain terms that I was not going anywhere. You told me I was not about to leave you and our babies and our folks to go off to some northern city we didn't know a thing about. Now, am I wrong?"

Dee allowed a contrite smile. "Well . . . that was different."

Again, all around the table laughed. Then I asked Stacey, "Have you written Uncle Hammer about coming out there?"

"No, figured maybe to ask you to write him for me since Dee already told me she won't do it."

Dee gave him a look. "You need to write your own letter if you want to go out there so bad."

"Well, you write so much better than I do." He smiled at that, but we all knew Stacey never wrote letters. He had never felt comfortable about his writing. Having gone to work full-time after tenth grade, he was the only one of us who had not graduated high school. "I guess if you or Cassie won't write the letter for me,

I'll just call Uncle Hammer." Dee gave Stacey a stern look that said they couldn't afford a telephone call all the way to California. Stacey ignored the look. "Uncle Hammer said there could be more opportunities out there for colored folks than here."

"But what kind of work could you get?" questioned Christopher-John. "We all know Uncle Hammer's not hardly doing factory work."

"Never has," inserted Little Man.

"Well, we all know that's a fact," Stacey agreed. "He's always been independent, his own man, but he's always had his hand in something. He told me he bought some houses out in Oakland like he did in Jackson, but I don't know what all else he's doing. I just know he's in business for himself and he knows lots of people."

"It could be worth the try," said Man, "what with things like they are here and in Detroit. You go out there, Stacey, most likely I'll go with you."

Stacey nodded. "Love to have you join me. That's a long drive."

"Maybe I'll go," I said. "I'd like to see

California. What about you, Christopher-John?"

"Well, y'all going, guess I'll be going too, least for a while."

"Well, before you all start packing your bags," interjected Dee, "I suggest you give more thought to finding work around here because I for one do not plan to move to any California. I like it fine right here."

"Yeah, I know," said Stacey, and he laughed again. "That last part, just what you said when we were down in Mississippi."

He might have laughed, but Stacey took Dee's words to heart. He scoured the city looking for work and finally found a job bussing tables during the day and sweeping and mopping the floor at night at a downtown restaurant. The pay was minimal, but it was honest work, and it was better than nothing. Dee wanted to go back to work as she had done during the war. She even suggested taking work as a domestic, cleaning white people's houses, but Stacey wouldn't hear of it. None of our people had worked as a domestic since slavery and neither had Dee's. "You want to housekeep," said Stacey within my hearing, "you just keep cleaning this one. I won't have you cleaning white people's houses."

And Dee said, "Plenty of good honest colored folks clean white folks' houses and take care of their babies. I'm not too proud to do it, if it means money coming in."

Stacey was adamant. "You've never done it and I won't have you doing it!"

"Well, look what you're doing! Cleaning tables and mopping floors!"

"Maybe I have to do it," said Stacey, "but you won't. You just stay here and take care of this house and our own babies."

I don't know how much more discussion about the matter they had in private, but in the end Dee stayed at home, taking care of Rie and 'lois and the house. That in itself was a huge job. It was Dee who washed and ironed most of the clothes and cooked the meals and cleaned the house and kept everything in order. At dinnertime each day she had a hot meal on the table for all of us. Although

Dee herself did not bring in any money, there was no way the rest of us could have managed without her. Financially, things remained tight, but somehow we came up with enough for Stacey and Dee to pay the mortgage each month. Then things got harder for all of us.

In late March, Papa called. I answered the phone. "Go ahead," drawled the long-distance operator. "Your party's on the line."

"Cassie," said Papa, having heard my voice when I answered the phone, "I've got some bad news for you."

I felt my stomach twist. "Sir?"

"It's your mama. She's in the hospital. I'm calling from there now. Doctors say she's had a stroke." It seemed to me, at that moment, I stopped breathing. "We need for y'all to come home."

"Papa," I muttered, hearing myself sounding like a little girl of years ago, "is it that bad? How could this happen?"

"It's that bad. Now, sugar, put Stacey on the phone. I need to talk to him."

Stacey talked to Papa, and when he hung up, he talked to all of us. "Mama

130

was just sitting at her desk working on her speech she's supposed to give to the Colored Women's League in June and she just slumped over."

"Oh, Lord," Christopher-John groaned, sounding like I had only moments before. "Oh, Lord."

Stacey cleared his throat. "We've got to go home. First thing, come morning."

Practical Little Man looked at Stacey. "On what? We don't have the money."

We all looked at each other and knew he was right. We didn't have the money to go south, to make this unexpected trip. We didn't have the money to go see about Mama.

It was late Friday night when we got the call. The mortgage note had been paid on that same day. So had the electricity bill and the coal bill and the water bill — the telephone bill too. It was the end of the month. We were all paid weekly, so now that the monthly bills were paid, we all had breathed easier, a sigh of relief for one more month. Dee had done the grocery shopping too that day. With all the bills paid and food stocked for the week, there was little money left in our pockets, but we had figured that was okay. We had just enough to see us through the week until next payday.

"So, what do we do?" I asked as we sat at the kitchen table drinking the hot coffee Dee had just perked. It was after midnight.

Stacey looked around the table. "Altogether, how much money do we have?"

We all counted our money and laid it on the table. Each of us had only enough for bus fare and a few personal items. Dee put in the remaining household money she had kept that was needed for the week. "Doesn't even amount to twenty dollars," said Man, thumping the pitiful pile of money. "Not nearly enough to get us home. Gas at about fifteen, eighteen cents a gallon, we'll need eighty to a hundred dollars to get us down there and back and take care of us while we're there. Few dollars for emergency too."

We were all silent, studying on the figure.

I broke the silence. "So, how do we get it?"

"Too bad it's Saturday morning already," said Dee. Stacey looked at her and she went on. "If it weren't Saturday, we could go to the safe deposit box at the bank and cash in the bonds."

Stacey's eyes stayed on her. "You'd want to do that?" The bonds, war bonds, were their savings, their total savings. All their other savings had been depleted by the layoffs. They had bought the bonds during the war. Each week money had been deducted from both their salaries and that money had gone toward the war bonds and the nation's war drive. The bonds were not destined to mature for many years, and if they were cashed in now, there would be a severe penalty, but still they could have gotten something on them. But that option wasn't available to them. Banks were not open on Saturday. Banks closed late on Friday and would be closed until Monday morning. Stacey repeated, "You'd do that?"

Dee's eyes met his. "Yes."

Elbows on the table, Christopher-John leaned forward. "Anybody we could borrow money from so you don't have to cash in the bonds?"

"Anybody close enough we could ask

for money is counting pennies just like we are," said Stacey, then smiled. "Fact, some folks are trying to borrow money from me."

"What about borrowing money from the church?" suggested Little Man.

"Church hasn't paid the pastor in more than a month," Dee informed us.

We all pondered this in silence. Then I took a deep breath and ventured, "What if we tried borrowing money from somebody not close to us?"

Stacey turned to me. "What do you mean, Cassie?"

I knew Stacey was not going to like what I was about to say. None of them would. "I mean . . . what about asking the Kondowskis for a loan?"

Little Man exploded. "Beg a loan of a white man? No way, Cassie!"

I gave him a hard look. "You'd go to the bank for a loan, and who do you think owns the bank? White folks."

"But that's not personal," reasoned Man. "The Kondowskis are people we have to see all the time."

"We do a lot of business down at

Roman's. Everybody in this house does, and the Kondowskis know that. They're decent people. Not one of them has ever been out of line with me, always treated me fair. They're at the store every weekday morning and Saturdays by six o'clock. We could get the money and be out of here first thing."

Christopher-John frowned. "You think they'd really loan it to us?"

"Can't find out unless we ask."

Christopher-John turned to Stacey for a decision. "What do you think, Stacey?"

Stacey looked around the table at each of us. "I'm like Man. I don't like it. But thing is, it might be the only way we can get the money before Monday."

"But, Stacey," objected Little Man, "the thought of going begging —"

Stacey stopped him with a wave of his hand. "Won't be begging. Dee and I'll put up the bonds. Dee can go to the bank on Monday and cash them in."

"Or I could put my salary up as collateral," I volunteered.

Stacey shook his head. "You might not be able to work there for a while if Mama needs you. Best thing we can do is use the bonds as collateral." He looked at Dee. "You sure, Dee?" Dee nodded without a word.

"If you use the bonds," I said, "we'll pay our part back to you." Christopher-John and Man nodded agreement. We would ask the Kondowskis for a loan of one hundred dollars.

Clayton Chester, still reluctant, said, "And what if they don't loan us the money?"

"Then we'll just have to wait until Monday and pray Mama's all right," Stacey said.

Dee got up. "In the meantime, I'll start cooking. Good thing I bought those two chickens for Sunday dinner. I'll start cutting them up and get them fried so you'll have food for the trip. All of you best go get some sleep."

I took my coffee cup over to the sink. "I'll help you. The boys can sleep."

"You need your rest too," said Dee.

"With three other drivers, I figure I can sleep in the car without ever having to take the wheel."

Dee seemed relieved at the help. "All right," she said, then put on her teacher's face as she calculated all that needed to be done. "First, we need to do the chicken, cook some hard-boiled eggs, make some ham sandwiches and maybe some sausage sandwiches. I bought two loaves of light bread today, so we can make quite a few. I'll make a pound cake so you can have something sweet. Bought some apples and bananas. You can take those too. We'll need to make a jug of Kool-Aid and some coffee —"

"We'll get it done, Dee," I said.

"Need us to help?" offered Christopher-John. Little Man echoed his willingness to help as well.

"No!" Dee adamantly exclaimed, and I backed her up, almost simultaneously, then we both laughed, breaking the tension of the night. "Too many folks in my kitchen! Last thing I need is a bunch of men in here trying to cook my food. I thank you all very much, but we'll do better without you. Go get some sleep."

Stacey went over to Dee. "Call me at five. That'll give me time to wash up and get packed before Cassie and I go down to Roman's." He glanced at me for approval of the time and I nodded. Then he folded Dee into his arms. "Thank you, baby," he said. They held each other close, then Stacey pulled away and, saying nothing more, went off to their bedroom.

They called themselves the Roman brothers, but in truth their given names were Stanislaus and Leo Kondowski. They had come to this country from Poland in the early 1920s along with their father, mother, and other family members. The two brothers and the family had worked hard and soon set up a little grocery store on Dorr Street. The two sons called the store Roman's in honor of their father, Roman Kondowski. Originally, the family had lived in the neighborhood, right next to their store, but as colored people began to move into the neighborhood, they, like other white people on the block, moved out. But they kept the store where it was and it grew, expanding to a larger building. The store was a focal point in the neighborhood, and its customers, both colored and white, came from many blocks around to buy goods from their store. Unlike other businesses on the block, the store was set back from the street, and even had a parking lot in front of it. They did good business.

Always aware of customer demands and the variety of foods wanted by its varied customers, they stocked everything from Polish bratwurst and sauerkraut to chit'lings, tripe, hog heads, pig feet, cow and pork brains, and the like demanded by colored folks coming up from the South. They also kept a pulse on the changing neighborhood, and in a city where the movie theater on the next block was still basically segregated just like the upscale theaters downtown, the Roman brothers had taken it upon themselves to integrate their grocery staff. When they hired me as a cashier, such a position in white-owned stores always had been held by white workers. There had been a few grumblings by a handful of white customers when I first began the job, but the Roman brothers had stood firm. Those customers who didn't like it could choose to go elsewhere, they said, and I had kept the job.

"So, a hundred dollars, that's it?" asked Leo Kondowski when Stacey and I presented our situation to the brothers. "That's enough to get you home to your mama, all the way down to Mississippi? You sure it's enough?"

"It'll get us there and back," Stacey said. "And, like we said, we'll pay you back on Monday. My wife will bring you the money. We have bonds."

"War bonds?" questioned Stanislaus, then looked at his brother and both shook their heads. Both Kondowskis were gray-haired and looked to be in their fifties, but Stanislaus was the elder. "No, no, you lose too much money you cash them in now," Stanislaus said. "You keep the bonds. You pay us over time."

"Well, we thank you for that offer, Mr. Kondowski," Stacey said, "but we'd rather pay you back soon as we can with the bonds. We'll sign a note to that."

Leo Kondowski waved away the suggestion. "No need for a note. You're good people and your word's good enough."

"We appreciate your trust, but we want to do this the business way," Stacey insisted. "We'll sign a note —"

"All right then, if you insist. We'll make you a loan, but like we said, not against the bonds." Stanislaus glanced at Leo, who concurred. "We'll call it an unsecured loan."

Stacey started to object, but Leo cut him off. "Not totally unsecured," he said. "It's secured by the kind of people you are. We admire your family, all of you. You and your wife buying that big house, making a home for your sister and for your brothers. Miss Cassie here going to school and your brothers fighting in the war, your whole family pulling together, just like we did to get this store, that's a fine thing. You're hardworking, all of you, and we'd be pleased to help you out so you can go see about your mama. Anybody raise such a family must be a fine lady."

"She is," I said. Stacey was silent.

Leo looked at his brother, then back to us. "So, shall we make out the note?"

Stacey looked at me, considering, and conceded. "We'll repay you as soon as we can and we'll pay interest, same as the bank. "

Stanislaus smiled. "If that makes you

feel better. Leo, get a pen."

I told the Kondowskis that most likely I would be staying awhile in Mississippi to help Mama after she was out of the hospital. They said my job would be waiting for me whenever I returned. They also said they would be praying for our safe journey and for Mama. As Stacey and I left the store, I glanced back at the Kondowskis. They were still standing in the doorway. They waved good-bye.

An hour later, Stacey, Dee, Christopher-John, Clayton Chester, and I formed a circle, held hands, and had family prayer. By eight o'clock, the car was fully packed and we were on the road, on a trip that would take us from the relative freedom of the North into the land of the Deep South.

GOING SOUTH

(1947)

I had taken the trip back to Mississippi twice before, once on the train and once with Stacey and Dee driving the two-lane Dixie Highway through southern Ohio and across the bridge that spanned the Ohio River, the Mason-Dixon Line that marked the end of our northern freedom. Once we crossed that bridge, everything changed. Once we crossed that bridge, we were in Kentucky. We were in the South, and there was no more pretense to equality.

Signs were everywhere.

White. Colored.

The signs were over water fountains. The signs were on restroom doors. The signs were in motel windows. They were in restaurant windows. They were everywhere.

Whites Only. Colored Not Allowed.

We didn't have to see the signs. We knew they were there. Even if there were no signs on display, they were imprinted in all our thinking. They were signs that had been there all our lives. When Dee and I had prepared all the food for the trip, it had been as if we were packing for a picnic. But of course that wasn't the case. We had packed all this food because once we crossed out of Ohio into the South we could not stop in restaurants along the way, even if we had had the money or the time. We couldn't stop at any of the motels or hotels either. We ate our cold food, knowing it was as good as or better than any served in the restaurants. We kept the signs in our heads, ate our food, and were thankful for it.

Now, rolling through the border state of Kentucky, we took great care to attract as little attention as possible as we drove through the small towns that stretched along the highway. We stopped only in the big cities for gas. We stopped in Lexington, and farther south we planned to stop in Nashville or Memphis and prayed that everything would be fine with the car. We did not want contact with white people any more than necessary. We kept to the speed limit. We obeyed every traffic sign. Once in hard-line Tennessee, we grew even more cautious. We all watched for the police, who could be hidden at any intersection, at any bushy turn of the highway, or in response to the call of any white person who had seen us with our northern plates riding through.

And then we entered Mississippi.

We were now in the Deep South and there was no state more menacing, more terrifying to black people than Mississippi. In each town we were wary of white men gathered on porches, standing in groups on the street, wary of their stares at four Negroes riding in a brand-new Mercury with northern plates. We were wary if they stared too long, if they pointed toward us, if they appeared ready to approach us. We held our breath and moved cautiously, slowly, on, obeying fifteen-mile-an-hour town speed limits, stopping at every red light, breaking no rules, and all the time as we drove, as we worried about being too noticeable, we worried about Mama. It didn't seem real that she was sick, that she had had a stroke, that she was in a hospital, that she possibly could die. We didn't want to think about it and none of us talked about it, but all of us knew we had to get through these small towns and down the road again toward home. Only once out of a town did we breathe normally again. Close to home, we drove through the town of Strawberry, its streets deserted in the predawn hours. We were glad of that; we did not want to be seen. We were in Mississippi, our birthplace, but it was now like being in a foreign land.

Morning was dawning as we drove up the driveway. Papa's truck was parked in front of the barn. As expected, Papa and Big Ma were up. They said Mama was holding her own. They had spent all day Saturday at the hospital in Jackson, but already this morning, the chores were done and Big Ma had breakfast waiting for us. As tired as we were, we enjoyed the smoked ham, the grits and biscuits and eggs, as well as molasses, everything washed down with the cows' morning milk. While we ate, Papa and Big Ma told us just what happened the night Mama had the stroke. It had only happened Friday evening and now it was Sunday morning, but time seemed to be passing so fast that Friday seemed long ago. As soon as we finished eating, Papa got up from the table. "You all get some sleep," he said. "I'm going to wash up and go on into Jackson. Y'all come later. Hospital got strict hours. Can't see your mama 'til visiting time anyway."

"When you go, Papa," Stacey said, "we're all going with you." He didn't ask Christopher-John, Man, and me how we felt about that; he already knew. We all wanted to be with Papa, and we all wanted to see Mama, no matter how tired we were.

Papa shrugged. "Up to you."

Jackson was the capital of Mississippi. It was the heart of the state. Like every facility in Jackson, like every facility in Mississippi run by the government, run by white folks, the hospital was segregated. All medical personnel were white. We entered through a separate entrance,

147

sat in a separate waiting room, and when we were finally allowed to see Mama, we entered a separate area for colored patients. Only two visitors at a time were allowed to see a patient. Papa went up first alone. When he returned, he told us, "I talked to your mama and I think she understood what I said. She didn't open her eyes, but when I told her all of you are here, I could see her eyelids try to move. She hasn't said a word, but I know she heard me."

Stacey and I went up next. Mama was hospitalized in a big room, a ward, with several other patients. When we entered the ward, we were directed to the far end of the room, next to the windows, and I was glad Mama was near the light, near where she could feel the sunshine.

Mama was asleep. She looked peaceful, but so pale, so frail. Both Stacey and I called to her, but she did not respond. We leaned past the tubes connected to her, kissed her cheek, squeezed her hand, then sat side by side, waiting for her to waken. During the time we sat there, Stacey reached out for my hand and then we softly prayed to give Mama strength, to bring her back to herself, to the Mama we knew, and to give all of us strength to help her.

We sat there for more than half an hour, but then, knowing how worried Christopher-John and Clayton Chester were waiting downstairs, we left so that they could come up. We went back and forth that way for as long as the hospital allowed us to stay. Right before we left the hospital, Mama opened her eyes. She didn't say anything, but she opened her eyes and she smiled.

That was enough.

There was no staying at the hospital beyond the Sunday visiting hours, so we headed home in the late afternoon. Besides, there were chores to be done and we didn't want Big Ma tending to the animals alone. But when we got home we found Little Willie Wiggins already there and the chores done. Little Willie had seen to them. " 'Ey, you scounds!" he hollered, coming from the barn as we drove up. He put the feeding bucket he was carrying on the ground and hurried toward us. Stacey was out of the car first, and the two old friends greeted each other with a warm hug. Christopher-John, Man, and I followed with hugs of our own.

"Things must be mighty good for y'all up north!" praised Little Willie in his good-natured way. "See you done got yourself a new car, Stacey. She's a beauty!" Little Willie stepped back a moment, admiring the Mercury, then turned serious. "How's Miz Logan?"

"Holding her own," Stacey said.

Then Papa smiled, as if letting Little Willie in on a secret. "Eyes opened today . . . and she smiled."

"You don't say! Ain't that something!" exclaimed Little Willie.

Inside, Big Ma had supper waiting. After hearing our good news about Mama's progress, Big Ma let out a "Praise the Lord!" then told us about all the folks who had stopped by asking about Mama. "Pastor was here. Stayed more'n two hours with me. We had us a houseful and a houseful of prayer. That's what's goin' to see us through. Prayer. Prayer and faith in the Lord." Then Big Ma turned to Little Willie. "Now, you joinin' us for supper, Willie." She said that more as a command than an invitation.

"Yes, ma'am, sure am," agreed Little Willie. "I done told Dora when I left home not to be holdin' supper on me. Figured to be here, and all of us had a lotta catching up to do."

Big Ma nodded with approval. "Good you told her that. Dora's a fine, understanding girl."

"She had to be to marry Little Willie here," teased Stacey.

"Can't argue with you there!" laughed Little Willie. Dora, Little Willie, the boys, and I had all grown up together, and Little Willie had married Dora as soon as he was drafted into service.

"Well, y'all wash on up now," ordered Big Ma, turning back to her kitchen. "Supper's ready for the table."

"I'll help you, Big Ma," I volunteered.

"Just wash on up, girl," Big Ma said. "You can help me with these here dishes after. Right now, though, don't need no help puttin' this food on the table. Go on with the boys now." I did as I was told.

151

No matter how old I got, or how old Big Ma got, there could be no arguing with my grandmother.

By the time the boys and I had washed with well water stored in buckets hanging from hooks on the back porch and gone back inside, kerosene lamps were lit and set on the table. The dining area was small in comparison to the Dorr Street house. The table filled most of the space. On one side of the room were two pantry cabinets. There the dishes and any desserts were kept. Next to the pantries, a door led into the boys' room. At each end of the dining room was an opening, one with the door leading into Mama and Papa's room, the center of the house that served as our family gathering place, while the other opening had no door and led into the tiny kitchen dominated by the wood-burning stove.

On the other side of the table, windows lined the wall. Beyond the windows were the back porch and the backyard, where the chickens and rooster, the peacocks and guinea hens roamed freely during the day, and beyond the yard, the garden, and beyond the garden, the orchard filled with fruit trees planted by Big Ma and Grandpa Paul-Edward long ago. The smokehouse and the outhouse were out there too. At each end of the table was a chair. Papa sat at one end, Big Ma at the other with ready access to her kitchen. Chairs also lined the table along the pantry side, allowing just enough walking space for a body to pass between the cabinets and the table. On the window side of the table there was a backless bench. That was where the boys and I sat for meals growing up. The room was small but the table had always been full, laden with Big Ma's good cooking. Once we were all seated, we held hands and praised God for His blessings, for keeping Mama in His care, for bringing us all safely home.

Then we ate.

Big Ma had cooked spareribs brought from the smokehouse and served with black-eyed peas, cornbread, and candied sweet potatoes, along with cha-cha, a mix of pickled tomatoes, peppers, and onions preserved last summer. For dessert, there was peach cobbler made with peaches canned in the fall. It was good home cooking like only Big Ma could prepare, and despite the reason for our coming home it felt good to be here.

"So, how long y'all plannin' on stayin'?" asked Little Willie after gulping down his clabbered milk. "Be here for next Sunday services? Reverend Stalnaker's preaching."

"Don't know yet," Stacey said. "Got to get back soon as we can. Course, everything depends on how Mama's doing. Doctor told us she's not out of the woods yet. In any case, expect to be here least until the end of the week."

"I'll be here longer than that," I said. "Mama'll need me when she comes home."

Little Willie acknowledged that would be the case and reached for another helping of the candied sweet potatoes. "So, how are things up north? Time I followed y'all up there?"

Stacey smiled at the thought. "Wouldn't hardly recommend it right now. Lots of layoffs with all the soldiers returning. Production for Army supplies has pretty much stopped and it's hard to get work. Fact is, I'm laid off."

"You don't say!"

"All of us working part-time jobs to put food on the table, make ends meet."

Little Willie was thoughtful. "Well, one thing 'bout being here is long as I got ground under my feet for farmin' and growing the food for me and my family, leastways I know we won't go hungry."

"That's a fact," Stacey agreed.

"And what 'bout that scound' Moe?" asked Little Willie. "He laid off too?"

"He's all right," Stacey replied. "Got laid off but he was lucky enough to get another small job that keeps him going."

"Good to hear that. No trouble from the law here?"

"Well, did hear there's a white fella from down here working at the factory where I worked and he's been talking about my connection to Moe, but that's about it. Police questioned Cassie and me, but we told them we hadn't seen Moe."

Big Ma frowned. "Hope that don't get y'all into trouble."

"Don't think it will, Big Ma," I said.

"We talked to them for just a few minutes months ago and they haven't been around since."

"Well, I don't like it," said Papa. "Y'all be careful up there."

"Yeah, be real careful," Little Willie warned, echoing Papa's words. "That law's got a long arm. Boy better watch hisself." Little Willie grew thoughtful. "Sometimes, it don't hardly seem real that trip we took up to Memphis with that boy to get him outta here. Took him up there to that train, come back, and here we was in a war! Lord have mercy! Ain't never gonna forget that weekend!"

"Don't think any of us will," confirmed Stacey.

"Wasn't long after that, Uncle Sam done called us all up. 'Member, Stacey, we got our notice the same time, went to the medical exam together. You sure was lucky, Stacey, getting that fever when you gone to those cane fields. Wish I had gone with you and Moe, gotten it too, 'cause I sure wasn't ready to go to that war."

"Who was?" questioned Christopher-John.

"Sho 'nough gave us plenty of worry 'bout all you boys," said Big Ma.

"Well, gave my family worry too," admitted Little Willie, "and I tell y'all, it was a scary thing. Got trained at Fort Hood, Texas, same as most other boys from round here unless they got sent to Camp Shelby. 'Cept for that trip up to Memphis, that was the only time I'd been out of Mississippi. Later on, after we done been deployed, heard Christopher-John and Man got called up." Little Willie laughed. "Lord have mercy! Jus' to think we was over there in Europe fightin' white folks!"

"Should have been fighting them over here," Clayton Chester sullenly interjected.

"That's the truth," agreed Little Willie with a sober face; then he brightened. "Couldn't believe when I seen both y'all over in France after Patton's Army come through. Just couldn't believe, so far away from home, and we all meet up. Y'all sure was a sight for these here sore eyes!"

"Felt the same," admitted Christopher-John.

"You know who else I seen over there?"

asked Little Willie. He gave none of us a chance to answer as he blurted out, "That white boy, Jeremy Simms!"

Stacey turned to Little Willie. "You did?"

"Sure did. Just heard a few days ago, though, he got kilt over there."

We all stopped eating. None of us had heard this news. I looked across at Stacey. Jeremy Simms had befriended him, had befriended all the boys and me while we were growing up. It was an odd thing. Jeremy was a white boy whose family were tenant farmers, whose family had less than we did. His father was Charlie Simms and his cousins were Statler, Leon, and Troy Aames, all of whom, because they were white, thought themselves superior to every black person. All that family did, except Jeremy. From the time he was a child until he was a young man, Jeremy had reached out to us. We had never understood why. Right before the war, he had risked all and had taken Moe, hidden in the back of his father's truck, all the way to Jackson. Jeremy had lost his family because of it.

Stacey's eyes were downcast. He said

nothing.

Big Ma shook her head sadly. "I'm sho sorry to hear that. I recall, that boy mostly tried to do right by us."

"Well, war," said Papa, "it don't make a difference 'bout a man's color when it comes to a bullet."

"Took my boys," said Big Ma softly, then was quiet. We all were. Both Papa's oldest brothers, Uncle Mitchell and Uncle Kevin, had been killed in the First World War.

"Well, least it's over now," said Little Willie, breaking the silence. "Now all we've got to do is keep ourselves alive down here without upsetting these white folks."

"Maybe we need to upset them," I said.

All eyes turned to me and Clayton Chester said, "It's about time we did." No one at the table disputed that. "They made us fight in that war and the war's won, now they expect us to go back to the way things were before the war. Well, I for one can't do that."

"We shouldn't have to," added Christopher-John. "It's high time things changed."

"Well, that'll be a long time comin'," predicted Big Ma, " 'cause I don't believe things ever gonna change down here. All these long years I been on this earth, things been the same. If change ever come, I won't live to see it. Maybe none of us will."

We all looked at Big Ma, afraid she was right.

After the dishes were done, I sat alone on the front porch swing. It was a chilly evening but I welcomed the chill against my face as I pulled my coat around me and looked out upon the land. It was almost dark, but I could see the roll of the long sloping lawn to the road below and across the road to the forest of long-needle pines. To the west of the lawn was the driveway and to the west of that, pasture land. To the east of the lawn was the land where the cotton had grown, land fallow now in the days before spring. Beyond the field the land rose to the hillside boasting the grand oak that marked our boundary with the Granger plantation, which dominated most of the

160

area north toward Strawberry. The once-owner of the land, Harlan Granger, was now dead, but the Granger family still prevailed and many in our Great Faith community still sharecropped on Granger land. I looked out at the field where a fire had once raged between the boundaries of our land and the Granger plantation, a fire that had destroyed our cotton crop, but had saved the life of a black boy, Stacey's friend T.J. Avery. I kept staring out across the land until all grew dark around me, then as kerosene lamps were lit in the front rooms, I went back into the house.

The boys and I stayed on throughout the week, visiting Mama every day, and each day she seemed better. She spoke a little and we were greatly encouraged. By Thursday, Mama was much improved and the doctor was talking about letting her come home early in the next week. He said it had been a relatively mild stroke and that Mama being young still, her body was otherwise strong and she should fully recover with no lasting side effects. There was some paralysis in her right arm extending from her shoulder into her hand, but with exercises and time, she would have the full use of her arm and hand again. She was to get plenty of rest and not take on anything strenuous for some time. With that good news, the boys planned to head back north as soon as Mama was home. Before leaving, Stacey wanted to go see Dee's family. He had promised Dee. I decided to go with him.

Early on Friday morning the two of us headed farther south toward Brookhaven. It was more than a two-hour drive. As we neared the Davis place, passing over rough backcountry roads, people were working in the fields. It was now April. It was planting time. When the people in the fields saw the big northern car, they stopped what they were doing to gaze at us, saw we were colored too, then gave big, friendly smiles and waved. Stacey honked the horn and we waved back. This was one of the good things about being home. All colored folks were a part of this life; none of us were strangers. We all lived under the same rules, no matter what our individual circumstances, and we all had to abide by them. Those rules and our color bound us together.

Like us, the Davises owned land. They were a significant family. It was even said that Dee's grandfather had served in the short-lived Mississippi legislature during Reconstruction. We passed several small houses and more people working the fields; they all were Davises. Dee's grandparents had had fourteen children and many of those children and their families continued to live on the land. The Davises stared, then waved as the others had, and we continued on our way to the main house. The Davis house was ranch in style, long and one-story with unpainted plank-board siding and a sizeable porch that connected the three sections of the house. At one end of the house lived Dee's mother, stepfather, and her fifteen-year-old brother, Zell. At the other end were Dee's uncle and his wife and their eight children, and in the middle section was Dee's grandmother, Big Ma Davis. Dee's grandfather, like Grandpa Paul-Edward, had passed long ago. All of the Davises not in the fields poured from the house to greet us. They all had questions about Dee and the babies and about Mama, when we told them why we had come south.

It was a warm day and after a huge meal served by Dee's mother, we sat on the porch, and soon many of the folks we had passed as we drove to the house came walking up the red road. Many of them were barefoot. Mostly, the children were shy of us, but all welcomed us with open arms and big hugs. As the afternoon wore on, long-legged, barefooted teenage Davis boys and Zell came from the fields. They sat on the porch railing and on the steps and stared in awe at Stacey's shiny new Mercury and talked with wonder about the North and their dreams of going there. They asked questions about what Toledo was like, questions about jobs and opportunities. Stacey told them about the layoffs and that life could be hard there too. Zell and the cousins listened intently to all Stacey said, but still clung to their visions of the North. They all talked about going north one day, and when Big Ma Davis asked Stacey if her grandsons could stay with him and Dee if they came, Stacey looked around the porch and into the yard at all the Davises gathered, eyes on him, and he said, "Well, long as Dee and I can keep our house and we have room, all our family's welcomed into it."

It was late afternoon as Stacey and I drove through Strawberry, headed for Jackson. We planned to visit Mama, then spend the night with Ola and his family at the Everett Street house. Traffic was heavy. As always, we drove slowly, obeying all the signs, all the lights. A red light stopped us right across from the courthouse and a voice called out to us. On the other side of the street was Mr. Wade Jamison. "Stacey Logan! Cassie!" he called. With a briefcase in one hand, he waved us over with the other. "Come to my office!"

Stacey touched the brim of his hat in greeting and nodded as the light changed and Mr. Jamison walked on to his office down the street. Stacey found a parking space and we joined Mr. Jamison, waiting for us at his office door. He held out his hand to each of us. "Good to see you! Good to see you!" he said, shaking our hands. "Come on in." He ushered us to some leather chairs near his desk and sat in one himself. Mr. Jamison was a gray-haired man in his late sixties. We had known him all our lives. He smiled. "Haven't seen you since you went north."

"Yes, sir, it's been a while," Stacey acknowledged.

"So, when did you come home?"

"Early Sunday," Stacey replied.

"Well, how's everyone at your place? Haven't been out that way in some time."

"Not so well." Stacey glanced at me. "That's why Cassie and I are home. Christopher-John and Clayton Chester are here too. Mama had a stroke last week. She's in the hospital in Jackson. We're on our way to see her now."

Mr. Jamison leaned forward. "How is she?" he asked softly. He looked from Stacey to me.

"She's doing better," I said. "Doctor said she'll be fine, full recovery."

Mr. Jamison sat back. "I'm glad to hear that. She's a fine lady, your mother." He nodded in affirmation to that and took up his pipe. As always, his words were genuine and so was his concern. From the time Stacey and I were children we had known of Mr. Wade Jamison and his sincerity. Back when I was nine years old, Mama had organized the colored people of our community to stop shopping at the local Wallace store owned and run by whites. Mama had been fired from Great Faith School because of the boycott. She had organized the boycott because the Wallaces had set fire to Mr. Sam Berry, a black man. The Wallaces had never been arrested, had never even been charged for the burning, and Mama was determined that we as colored people would not support men who had done such a thing. She proposed that we buy all our goods from the stores in Vicksburg instead. That is when Mr. Wade Jamison stepped in. He came to see us and said, if Mama would permit it, he would back the people boycotting the Wallace store. Papa, since he was a boy, had known Mr. Wade Jamison, and Big Ma had known Mr. Wade Jamison since he was a boy. Wade Jamison was the only white person in Mississippi we all trusted.

For several minutes we sat talking to

Mr. Jamison, answering his questions about the family and our lives in Toledo. He seemed to be enjoying our company. He asked me about my plans. I had once told him I was interested in studying law, to become a lawyer like him. "You pursuing that, Cassie?" he asked.

"Not yet," I said. "I've got a degree in education, so I suppose I'll teach."

"Well, you ever do decide to pursue law and I'm still around, you let me know."

I promised him that I would.

Mr. Jamison looked at his watch. "Well, I don't want to keep you from seeing your mother. Those hospital hours are pretty strict." We all stood. "Give her my best, and also to your father and your grandmother." We thanked him. He shook our hands once more and we left.

The next morning we went with Ola to Farish Street. Farish was the main commercial street of the black community. It was a brick-laid street lined with stores, restaurants, cafés, nightclubs, a movie theater, and Negro offices representing a variety of Negro businesses, including the photography studio where the boys and I

168

had had our photograph taken during the war. There were white-owned businesses on the street as well, but black businesses dominated at least one block of it. Running north to south, Farish bisected downtown Capitol Street, Jackson's premier business street. All along Capitol were the white-owned department stores and banks and office buildings. Capitol Street also boasted a splendid view of the sprawling Old Capitol Building built before the Civil War. Located on State Street, but facing Capitol Street, which dead-ended into State, the Old Capitol Building was the landmark building of Jackson.

We stayed in Jackson until the first visiting hours at the hospital. Christopher-John and Man came with Papa to visit Mama, but went back with Stacey and me. Papa said he had business to take care of in Jackson and would see us at home. While Papa was in Jackson, the boys planned to continue some of the work that needed to be done on the land, mainly clearing the forest of some of its dead trees and chopping them for firewood. They also planned to plow the field for cotton and plant the seed before they left for Toledo. We knew Papa needed the help. He no longer worked on the railroad and now Mama, Big Ma, and Papa totally depended on what they raised on the land. Although the cotton grown would be minimal, it would bring in extra money in the fall. Other money they earned would come from the firewood they sold along with the cured meats from the hogs and cows. Big Ma still sold canned preserved goods, vegetables from the garden, and fruit from the orchard in the market up in Strawberry. That money would be much needed, not only for the hospital bills but for other expenses, including the day workers they paid to tend the fields. There was much work to be done before the boys left, and we all figured to get a good start on it.

Before going home, we decided to go see Moe's family. Whenever any of us were back home, we always went to see them. On the way over to the Turner farm, we had the misfortune to run into Statler and Leon Aames, along with their uncle, Charlie Simms. The three of them were in a steel-blue pickup truck coming toward us on the narrow dirt road out of Strawberry. Stacey pulled over to let them pass. Statler, at the wheel of the truck, had already slowed down. We knew he was eyeing the shiny new Mercury with the Ohio plates. When he saw who we were, he stopped alongside us. One look at him and we knew he was still festering over Moe's attack. Statler rolled down his window. "Well, look who done made it back home!"

Stacey did not roll down his window. He glanced over at the truck, then looked away.

" 'Ey, boy! I'm talking to you!"

Stacey kept looking straight ahead. "We ought to get out of this car and show them who's a boy," said Man from the back seat. "We could whip them easy, Stacey!"

"Yeah, and get ourselves killed afterward."

"You not talking, boy?" yelled Statler. "Well, I want you to know we think that nigger Moe Turner is up north. Heard from Harold Rockmiler work up at that Toledo plant, you most likely know where that Moe is. Well, you tell him for us, he might be hiding up there now, but one day we'll get him. Our brother Troy still laid up, ain't never been the same! One day we'll get him! One day he's gonna pay for what he done to my brothers and me!"

Another car came along the road behind the Aames truck. It sat there a moment, then the driver honked to move Statler along. The driver in the car was white and, dressed in a suit, looked to be a businessman.

Statler glanced back at the car, then again at us. "You tell that damn nigger what I said! One day we'll get him! We'll get him sure!" Then he gunned the engine, and the truck took off in a swirl of dust.

The Turners were sharecroppers on the Montier plantation. Their family had been on the plantation since before the turn of the century. Their house was small, but Mr. Turner had raised his seven children in it as well as his deceased sister's four children. His daughters were now married and lived with their husbands, also on Montier land, and several of the boys were married as well, but the remaining children were still with him, including Maynard and Levis, who had just returned from the war. Levis was my age, and Maynard was a classmate of Christopher-John's.

"Good to see y'all," said Maynard, slapping Christopher-John on the back in warm greeting as soon as we stepped from the car. "Figured y'all be down here."

"Heard 'bout Miz Logan," put in Levis. "How she doing?"

We told him Mama seemed better each day.

"Good, good, glad to hear that. Come on in the house, see Daddy. He ain't been feeling too well." Levis led the way up the creaky porch steps and into the dark front room that served as both a living room and a bedroom. Although it was a warm day, there was a fire going in the fireplace. Moe's father sat in a rocking chair next to it. The boys and I went over to him and greeted him with hugs.

" 'Scuse me for not gettin' up," Mr. Turner said, "but my legs kinda weak today. I stand up, they might jus' give

way from under me. Sit down, sit down."
He too asked about Mama. "Well, you
know we all been prayin' for her."

"We know those prayers been heard,"
said Stacey.

Mr. Turner nodded knowingly. "The
Lord sho is good." We all agreed. "Well,
how's that boy of mine doin'?"

"Doing just fine last time we saw him,"
answered Stacey. "Didn't see him before
we left though, had to leave so sudden."

Mr. Turner nodded in understanding,
then glanced around the room. "Where
that Morris?"

"Last I seen of him," said Levis, "he
was out there slopping the hogs."

"Well, go get him," ordered Mr. Turner. "Tell him Stacey and them here."

Levis went to do his father's bidding
while Maynard sat down in a straight-
back wooden chair with rawhide covering and began questioning Christopher-
John and Man about the war and where
they had fought.

"Well, I was all through Europe and
even over in North Africa for a while,"
said Clayton. "Fought in the 123rd

Engineering Platoon. Became a sergeant over there."

"You name it, I was in it," contributed Christopher-John. "France, Normandy, the Rhineland."

"Wonder I didn't meet up with y'all," said Maynard. "Saw Little Willie though."

Christopher-John laughed. "Seems like Little Willie met up with just about everybody over there!"

While Christopher-John, Clayton Chester, and Maynard talked about their days in the war, Stacey and I answered Mr. Turner's many questions about his eldest son. "I sho do miss that boy," said Mr. Turner as the screen door opened and Levis came in with Morris behind him. Morris was a tall boy, chocolate in coloring, like Moe, and wiry. He was also outspoken, not at all shy for his thirteen years. " 'Ey, Daddy!" he called. "You all right?"

"Same as when you gone out from here," returned Mr. Turner. His voice sounded harsh, but there was a smile on his face. "Now, you come on over here and say hello to everybody."

Morris came right over and shook

hands with Stacey, Christopher-John, and Man. When he got to me I stood and said, "Boy, you too big to hug now?" Morris laughed. Morris was like a little brother to Stacey, Christopher-John, Man, and me and we treated him as such. As a little boy he was often with Moe and often at our house. He seemed to be as much a part of our family as he was of his own. We often called him Little Brother Morris.

"Not hardly, Cassie," said Morris, still grinning as he bent and gave me a big hug. He then pulled up a chair, along with Levis, and we all sat talking about Moe, the North, and what it was like for Moe to be there.

After a while, Mr. Turner said, "You know I want this boy Morris to go up north to school, be with Moe." He looked at Stacey. "Moe tell y'all that?"

"Yes, sir, he did." Stacey turned to Morris. "What you think about going north?"

Morris shrugged, smiled, and looked over at his father. "Fine with me, long as it's fine with Daddy."

"He'll be going then," declared Mr.

Turner. "Come the end of summer, my youngest and my oldest gonna be up there in Detroit together. That'll suit me fine." Mr. Turner then nodded, seemingly happy at the thought.

On Sunday all of us went to Great Faith Church, where so many people were asking about Mama and praying for her. Mama was a substantial member of the community, always active, and well loved as a teacher. After church all of us, including Big Ma, went to Jackson to visit Mama. Mama was scheduled to come home on Tuesday and the boys planned to leave Wednesday night for Toledo. After working through much of the day on Monday, both Christopher-John and Man washed up and got ready to go over to the McFaddon place. "You wouldn't by any chance be planning to do some courting while you're over there?" Papa teased as Christopher-John took the keys to the Mercury. Christopher-John smiled somewhat sheepishly. The McFaddons boasted a family of ten daughters, two of whom, Becka and Rachel, still lived at home. Becka was the older of the two sisters and she and Christopher-John had been seeing each other since before the war. As far as Rachel and Clayton Chester, they were only friends, nothing more. Still, they enjoyed being together and the two sisters and their mother had invited them to supper.

While Christopher-John and Clayton Chester were gone, Papa and Stacey continued chopping logs brought from the forest earlier in the day, stacking the split firewood in huge piles along the pasture fence. At suppertime, Big Ma sent me to fetch them. "Big Ma says she's about ready to set food on the table," I said as I came from the back porch and hopped the huge stones set as a walkway to the drive. "So she said finish and wash up."

"Won't finish this for a while yet, baby girl," Papa said. "Want to get as much chopped as I can while I got the help."

Sweat was beading on Papa's forehead. He looked worn. "Papa, you work too hard," I said.

Papa kept on chopping and said in his genial way, "You figure you grown enough to tell me that?"

"Well, it's the truth."

"Not working any harder than all those years when I worked on the railroad."

"But that was a long time ago."

Papa laughed outright. "So, you telling me, your ole papa, he getting too old for this kind of working?"

"Well . . . no, sir . . . but you know what I mean. Stacey, you tell him."

Stacey looked at me, then stopped chopping and looked at Papa. "You could slow down some, Papa. I'll chop the wood, and while you and Cassie go into Jackson tomorrow to get Mama, Christopher-John, Man, and I can finish all this up."

Papa chuckled. "Just how old do you think I am? I know you must think I'm awful old, but I'm not yet fifty."

"Not saying you old, Papa," Stacey clarified, "but you could take a break while we're here."

"Well, that's all fine and good for now," Papa said without missing a swing of his ax, "but what happens come another month or two and we need more firewood? You boys coming all the way from

Ohio and chop wood for me?"

Stacey frowned. "Maybe not next month, but we'll be back in August for revival."

"And what I'm s'pose to do 'til then?"

Stacey took a moment and thought on that. "Maybe Christopher-John, Man, and I can stay on another couple of days and chop enough wood to last you until we get back."

Now Papa stopped his chopping and looked at Stacey. "And what happens to your family while you're down here doing my work? What about Dee and the babies? They're expecting you back before the end of the week, needing you back. And what about the money you all trying to make just to hold on until things get better? Where's that money going to come from if you stay down here chopping firewood for me? No, son. You gotta get back, and so do Christopher-John and Man."

Papa returned to his chopping; Stacey didn't. "I could talk to Little Willie, get him and some of the other fellas to help out here."

"And what we gonna pay them with,

son?" asked Papa, back in the rhythm of his swing. "Those boys got their own work to do. Can't ask them to come here for nothing."

"We'll find a way to pay them. Can send some money when we get steady work again."

Papa struck his ax hard into a log and let it stay. "No. I said no. Now, both of y'all listen to me." He took a kerchief from his pants pocket and wiped his face. He said nothing for a moment as he refolded the kerchief and put it back into his pocket while Stacey and I waited respectfully for his next words. "I appreciate y'all, more'n you know. I'm proud of both of you, all of you, and I know I can always count on you. I know too you just thinking of me and your mama and your grandma when you talk about help for me and maybe stayin' on. But truth is, I'm not an old man yet, even if y'all think so. I got plenty of strength left in me. I can do the work.

"Now, there gonna be doctor bills to pay, hospital bills to pay, a crop to plant to help pay for all that. If I need more help, I'll let you know. I thank you for all you done while you've been here, but for now, though, all I need is Cassie staying on to help your mama. You boys, though, I want you to go back to Toledo and take care of your own lives, and, Cassie girl," he said, turning to look at me, "I want you to do the same once your mama gets better. We raised y'all to have lives of your own and we want you to have them without worrying 'bout us. We'll do fine."

"Papa," Stacey ventured quietly, "I know this is something you maybe don't want to talk about for a while, but you and Mama ever think about joining us up north?"

I shot Stacey an incredulous look. Papa did too. There was an audible gasp from him. "And leave this land?"

"Well, Papa, you know things up there are a lot better in a lot of ways —"

"That may be, but my life is here. Your mama's life is here. As for your grandma, you know what she and my daddy went through to get this land. Our lives are in this land. Our lives are this land."

"Papa, I'm not talking about giving up the land —"

"Leaving it would be just the same as

giving it up."

"But, Papa —"

"Now, listen to me, Stacey. You too, Cassie. I know y'all got more opportunity up there as young folks than you'd have here. More opportunities for Rie and 'lois and I'm glad for you. Stacey, you made the right decision to go north, and Cassie, Christopher-John, and Clayton, I'm hoping it's the right decision for them too. Now, I'm not gonna say it didn't take your mama and me a while to get used to the idea that all our children gone north and aren't coming to live back here, but we understand why y'all had to go. I'm still hoping one of you'll come back here one day to take care of this land when your mama and me are gone. But for now, your lives are up north and ours are here, and that's the way it's going to stay."

Stacey glanced at me, then turned back to Papa. "No changing your mind about that?" he asked.

"No changing my mind," Papa answered quietly as he picked up his ax and began to chop again. "And that's all I've got to say about it."

■ ■ ■

We all rejoiced when Mama came home. Papa and I had gone in the Mercury to get her while the boys continued working. It was late afternoon when we returned to the house, and Mama went straight to bed. The ride from Jackson had tired her out, but she was happy. She laughed a lot and talked a lot, and at suppertime, instead of our sitting at the table, we took a plate of food to Mama, who was excited to get Big Ma's cooking again, and holding our plates we sat around the bed and enjoyed our meal together. On Wednesday, the boys and Papa continued plowing and planting the cotton field while Big Ma and I got busy cooking food for the boys to take with them on their trip back north.

"Now, don't you let that chicken burn," warned Big Ma as I did the final turn of the wings sizzling in the iron skillet on the wood-burning stove.

"Big Ma, I know how to cook chicken," I said, giving her a look. "After all, you taught me."

"Well . . ." she said begrudgingly, "just

make sho it don't burn."

"Know how to kill one too," I bragged. "Wring its neck, dunk it in scalding hot water, pluck out its feathers, gut it, cut it up, make it ready for frying, seasoning, and battering, and all. Guess who taught me that too?"

"Now you jus' gettin' smart," Big Ma admonished with a big smile.

"Just saying I can do all this because of you, Big Ma. You taught me how to cook. You know, Mama never taught me much about cooking."

"That's 'cause your mama had better things to do. So you tell me now, who you gonna cook for? Here you are going on twenty-three years old. All the girls your age round here been married four, five, or more years, got two, three, four children, and far's I can tell, you ain't even got a beau. Time you got married! You need a good man in your life."

I turned from the stove and looked at Big Ma. "I haven't met the right man yet, Big Ma."

"What about that Moe Turner?"

"Friends, Big Ma, friends. That's all we are."

"Well, ain't nothin' wrong with marrying a friend. Love can come out of that. Child, there's all kinds of love, love that'll surprise you, love that'll sneak up on you when you ain't watchin'. Now, your grandpa and me, when we first met, I figured he was a nice man, but it was his best friend, Mitchell, that plumb swept my head. Oh, that man, he was big and strong and good-looking, wasn't afraid of nothing, and folks was always wantin' t' be round him and I was one of them. My heart was always racing when I was with that man, and I felt so proud when I married him. When he got kilt, it was your grandpa took care of me. Mitchell done asked him to. I was carrying Mitchell's and my child, your Uncle Mitchell, when Mitchell died, and I was far 'way from my people's home. Only person I had round me in my life was your Grandpa Paul-Edward.

"Paul-Edward, he was a quiet man, smart, smart man, stayed mostly to hisself and that was mainly 'cause he looked white 'mongst black folks, but he knowed how to get things done. Got this land, and, in time, he got me too. He wasn't nothing like my Mitchell, but I loved him. I loved him so. He was good to me. He become my life."

Big Ma nodded at memories and finished wrapping the biscuits in silence. I didn't disturb her from her memories; after several minutes, she said, "Cassie?"

"Yes, ma'am?"

"God got a way of bringin' the right man into your life to give you the happiness and the joy and everything else He wants us to have in this life. Man who love you, Cassie, make love to you and give you babies, ain't nothin' like it. Time come that man to enter your life, don't you turn your back on him. Not even if that man's Moe Turner."

I met Big Ma's eyes, and let it be.

The boys left before midnight on Wednesday. They wanted to get through as much of Mississippi as they could while it was still dark, before people were out and moving about and taking note of them. We received word from Dee's brother Ola that they had made it back safely. He drove down from Jackson to let us know. Mama, Papa, Big Ma, and I were all thankful to hear the news, but Mama, no longer having to worry about the safety of her sons, became restless about her confinement. Although she was able to be up a few hours during the day, the doctor had ordered her to get plenty of bed rest for several weeks, which she begrudgingly did.

I had been shown by the nurses how to administer the exercises for Mama's arm, but after a couple of weeks of bed rest and exercises Mama still could not fully use her right hand for writing, and she very much wanted to write. Mama loved writing. She was frustrated and grew increasingly more irritable. "Turn off that radio," she ordered from her bed. She was sitting with a book on her lap, and several books lay next to her. "That noise bothers me. Sometimes I wish Stacey had never brought that thing into this house."

We all understood that much of Mama's frustration came from the fact that until she was fully recovered, she could not work. Since Mama had lost her job as a teacher at Great Faith, she had taught students needing extra help in their studies. After the boys left home, she had used their room as a classroom, and sometimes the room had been filled with students on a Saturday morning or after school. She also went throughout the community working with young people who weren't able to go to school, children who were disabled in some way or whose parents couldn't spare them from the family workload in their homes. She taught adults too, anyone wanting to learn. Sometimes people paid Mama; most people didn't. They had no money to pay her. But Mama didn't mind that. She just wanted to teach.

I sucked in my breath and went over and turned off the radio. "Mama, when Stacey bought this radio he just wanted us to be in the twentieth century and know what was going on in the world."

"I never thought I'd say this, but I think I know enough."

"As I recall, Mama, you and Papa and Big Ma used to sit here every evening and listen to the war news. You were happy to have the radio then."

"And you know why that was. Your

brothers were over there fighting in that war. But there were times I didn't want to hear any of it. I was walking around scared most of the time. Now there's news coming in from all over, United States and all around the world, and it hardly ever is any good news. I don't need to hear it. Just the sound of it wears on my nerves."

I went back to oiling the furniture. "That's because you've been so sick, Mama. I figure having a stroke kind of makes things wear on your nerves."

"And you know about strokes and nerves?"

"No, ma'am, I just figure it makes sense."

"Oh, well, I thought maybe you were heading into the medical field now. It's obvious you don't want to teach."

"Obvious?"

"You were graduated with the courses you needed to teach, yet you're working in a grocery store. Our first college graduate in this family and you're working at a grocery store."

"Mama," I said in exasperation, "I'll

have a teaching job in the fall. I'll put this college degree to use soon enough, not that I want to teach." Mama looked disappointed. I tried to explain. "You love teaching, Mama. You've got a passion for it, something I don't have. Only reason I got the teaching degree was because everybody said that was the best thing and I'd always have a job if I were a teacher. I couldn't figure anything else. Maybe I'll teach a couple of years, but it's not really what I want." I could feel Mama's disapproval. I finished oiling the furniture, and with the mopping already done, picked up the mop bucket and headed for the dining room door. "Anything else you want me to do for you, Mama?"

"Yes," Mama said. "I want you to go empty that bucket, rinse out that mop, then come back in here and write a speech for me."

"Ma'am?"

"The speech I was working on when I had the stroke, it still needs to be done."

"Mama, I don't know anything about writing any speeches!"

"Then I'll teach you. That speech to

the Women's League is next month. I plan to give it, but I can't write it. You can. I'll give you my ideas, you put them on paper."

"Now, Mama, writing a speech wasn't what I meant when I asked if you needed me to do anything."

"Course it wasn't. But that's what I want from you, Cassie, and that's what I need. So come sit down at my desk and use your brain. That's one of your many blessings, Cassie, your brain. I want my speech."

During the next weeks Mama taught me the basics of good speech writing, and she was a hard taskmaster. She did not want a good speech, she wanted a superb speech, and she wanted it done her way. I got a little tired of all her demands and attention to details, all the changes she wanted made, but finally I managed to finish the speech. Mama read it and told me it was good, but it could be better. She instructed me as to the strong points and weak points of the speech and then told me to rewrite it. I did. She awkwardly edited it with her left hand, using a brutal pen, and told me to make more changes. When we both were exhausted with the speech and with each other, the speech was what Mama wanted. Not only was it good, it was better than good. Mama said that she would be proud to give it, and, for me, that made all the weeks of writing worthwhile. By the time the speech was finished, it was nearing the time for me to head back to Ohio. Mama was much better and able to be up and doing more things for herself. The only physical sign that she had had a stroke was in her hand, but we were all confident that soon she would have full use of it.

"I'm really looking forward to making this speech," Mama told me.

"I wish I could stay for it, but I need to get back to work."

"I understand." Mama smiled. "And come September, that teaching job's waiting."

A few days before I was to leave, Papa and I walked the land. It was reminiscent of the many times we had walked the fields and the meadows and the forest.

We walked up the hillside where Grandpa Paul-Edward's gravesite lay. Papa and I sat some while on the bench in our enclosed family cemetery and said a prayer of gratitude for those who had meant so much but were now gone. We looked out over the land from the hillside, then walked down to the pond nestled among the high pines of the forest. We sat on a log fallen so many years ago and talked of many things. Papa wanted to know my dreams, my plans for the future. Like Mama, he was concerned about me. "Your mama told me you're not too eager to teach," he said. "You don't teach, what you plan on doing?"

I sighed. "Tell you the truth, Papa, I don't rightly know. There was a time when I was twelve or so I wanted to be like Mr. Jamison —"

"A lawyer?"

"Yes, sir. Thought about being a lawyer like him. Seems there were so many things he could do because he knew the law."

Papa nodded in agreement. "But don't forget, things he was able to do wasn't just because of the law."

"I know that, Papa, and I'm not forgetting he could do things I couldn't begin to do because he's white. But I'm also not forgetting that his knowing the law, even the law that's set against us, helped us out sometimes."

"You decide that's what you want, you know getting to be a lawyer won't be easy. Now, you know I want you to follow whatever you want to do, but for a colored person it'll be a hard road."

"What road isn't hard for us?"

Papa acknowledged that fact. "Well, you pray on it, Cassie girl. You got the whole world ahead of you and I'm not doubting you can do anything you set your mind to do. You come from folks who done just that. You want to be a lawyer, then that's what you'll be." Papa put his arm around me. "But lawyer or not, there's another side of life and I want you to know about that too. So, you tell me, Cassie girl, who's courting my baby girl now?"

"Nobody in particular."

Papa frowned. "That a fact?" He pulled back to study me. "Just how old are you now?"

"Oh, Papa!" I laughed. "You know how old I am!"

"Time you started thinking about getting married, don't you think?"

"Nobody to marry," I said.

"Well, you tell me then, what's the matter with them boys up north? Can't they see a gold mine living in their midst? Young man marries my daughter will marry himself a prize."

"I don't know about all that."

"Well, I do," said Papa, getting up from the log. "Just make sure when that special young man finds you that he appreciates you, that he loves you, that he honors you, and that you trust him. That's important. You hear what I'm saying to you? Make sure you can trust him," Papa repeated.

"I will," I promised.

Three days later I said good-bye to Mama and Big Ma, and Papa took me to Jackson, where I boarded a segregated train and headed back to Toledo. The boys had sent money for my train fare. As the train sped north, I had plenty of time to think about what Mama and

Papa and Big Ma had said. I needed to decide on a course for myself. I needed to figure out what I was going to do with my life. One thing I did not need to think on was that I wanted someone special to share my life, to love me. But no matter what anyone said, I knew that someone was not Moe Turner.

California,
Here We Come!

(1947)

"I've made up my mind," said Stacey. "I'm going to California."

That was all it took. Dee had already accepted his decision, and Christopher-John, Clayton Chester, and I had just been waiting for him to say it. It was now July. The layoffs had continued into the spring and summer and other work was slow. I had the teaching job for the fall, but I was not looking forward to it. We had paid off our loan to the Kondowski brothers, so now, with all the bills paid, we pooled the money from our various part-time jobs. We figured we had enough to make the trip and leave money for Dee to take care of the girls and the house for at least three weeks. We hoped to have jobs in California by then. Once the decision was made, we left one week later. That week gave us time to take care of all business at hand, and that included my giving notice to the Kondowskis. They said they were sorry to see me leave, and I believe they were.

Moe wanted to go with us, but in the end he decided against it. "I've got that little janitoring job, and it pays my way," he said. "Out there in California, I might not even find that. It's too much of a gamble, especially with Morris coming."

Stacey tried to persuade him. "There's more distance between California and Mississippi than Ohio and Mississippi. Could be it'll be safer for you out there."

"And, besides," I said, "Morris might like California."

"Well, they haven't found me after all this time, I figure I'll be safe enough. Are you planning on staying there, Cassie?"

"Maybe. Depends on Stacey."

Moe smiled. "Well, then, maybe I'll come then, me and Morris too."

Before we left, news came from home that Troy Aames had died. We worried even more for Moe.

■ ■ ■ ■

We still couldn't convince Moe to go with
us, so we left without him. Clayton Chester had researched the routes, and the
four of us had studied the maps. We
would be traveling through Indiana, Il-
linois, Iowa, Nebraska, Wyoming, Utah,
and Nevada to Oakland, California. We
were all looking forward to it. We figured
at least four days to cross the country
and that included a stopover in Muncie,
Indiana, and Chicago to see family there.
Saying good-bye to Dee and the girls and
Moe was hard, but we were excited about
the adventure, and with food and water
and a cooler of lemonade, we headed out.
Before noon we were in Muncie, visiting
with Aunt Callie's son Percy and his family. They too had migrated north during
the war. We ate lunch with them, then in
the late afternoon headed on to Chicago,
where we spent the night with more family who had migrated north from down
home. The next morning before daybreak
we were on the road again, laden with
even more food provided by our Chicago
family. We figured to cross Iowa and be

in Nebraska before nightfall.

Things didn't work out the way we planned.

Midway through Iowa we ran into car trouble. Stacey, Christopher-John, and Man all looked under the hood of the new Mercury and agreed what was wrong. The alternator was busted and needed to be replaced. Problem was that although we carried a spare tire and fluids needed for the car, we would have to go to a mechanic to replace the alternator. We stood by the side of the road thumbing for help. A truck finally stopped and Stacey got a ride into the next town, a small town. When he returned in a tow truck, he said, "Looks like we'll have to spend the night, wait 'til morning before the car's fixed. Tow driver works for the only gas station in town, and the mechanic shop's already closed for the day."

"So, what do we do 'til then?" I asked as the tow driver hitched the tow to the Mercury. "Where do we stay?"

"Been thinking on that. Maybe we can find a motel. We planned enough for an emergency."

"Not for a motel," said Christopher-John. He looked at Man, who had done all the budgeting for the trip. "What do you think?"

"We can manage it," said Man, "depending on the price of a room."

"Just one room?" asked Christopher-John. "What about Cassie?"

"All I want to do is stretch out," I said, "and I can do that on the floor."

"I don't think you have to do that, Cassie," Stacey said. "You can have the bed; rest of us can sleep on the floor. We've sure done it before or slept on the ground." Both Man and Christopher-John nodded at that. "When the man gets finished hooking up the car, I'll ask him about a place."

Stacey rode in the truck cab with the tow driver. The rest of us stayed in the hooked-up Mercury. Once we were at the gas station the driver unhitched the car. Christopher-John, Man, and I started to get out, but Stacey motioned us to stay inside. As Stacey paid for the tow, the white driver said, "Now, they'll take a look at your car in the morning, but far's a room, you probably won't find one here. We've only got one motor court, but you probably won't get a room there."

"All full?" asked Stacey.

The driver glanced over at Christopher-John, Man, and me in the car. "It's right across the street there," he said, looking back at Stacey. "You can go on over and check for yourselves. They don't have rooms, you can spend the night here in your car." He folded the bills Stacey had given him and slipped them into his pocket. "See you in the morning. We open at six." With that, the driver got back into his tow truck and left.

Stacey leaned inside the car. "Well, what you want to do? Shall we try it?"

We all looked at each other, and I said, "Well, it is Iowa, not Mississippi."

"Yeah," Little Man pessimistically agreed, "but we all know it's still the United States."

Christopher-John opened his door. "Let's walk on down."

At the motor court a sign flashed "ROOMS AVAILABLE." At the office door the manager said, "Sorry, all full up. No rooms available," then shut the door.

We spent the night in the Mercury.

We wasted practically a whole day in Iowa. We held on to our patience and our tempers. The mechanics did not have an alternator for the Mercury, but they ordered one from a shop in another town. We ate the food Dee and our Chicago family had packed and counted the minutes and the hours. Finally, late afternoon, the alternator was delivered and in place and we were on our way again. As soon as the speed limit allowed, we were out of Iowa and into Nebraska. We had no trouble in Nebraska. Maybe that was because we didn't stop except for one fill-up. From Nebraska we headed into Wyoming. We drove through the night. We all had been looking forward to Wyoming, for we were eager to see the West, the mighty frontier West, and the Great Rocky Mountains. Soon after we crossed into Wyoming, we stopped by the side of the road to sleep. We did not want to miss the first sight of the mountains, so we took a few hours and waited until the sun rose to continue. It was worth the wait.

All of us had seen movies about the wild, wild West with images of majestic white-capped mountain peaks, pure clear expansive land that stretched to the edge of the world, it seemed, deep green mountain valleys, cobalt blue-sky country, ponderosa pine country, God's country. We were all astounded, hardly believing we were actually here. We imagined buffaloes roaming this land and the native people of this land, the keepers of it. We had all been romanced by the heroes and outlaws of the West portrayed in movies: Annie Oakley, Wild Bill Hickock, Geronimo, Cochise, Wyatt Earp, Buffalo Bill, Sitting Bull, Billy the Kid, and Frank and Jesse James. We knew the stars of those great western movies, like Gary Cooper, John Wayne, Randolph Scott, Tyrone Power, Henry Fonda, all figures so mighty that no one could defeat them. We were now in the true West, and like those mighty figures, maybe we were feeling we could not be defeated either.

■ ■ ■ ■

After two days of eating cold food, we all wanted something hot, and when we saw the sign advertising mouthwatering-looking hotcakes, cheeseburgers and fries, and steaming hot coffee at a restaurant just off the highway, we decided to stop. Still infatuated by the West, we marveled at everything made of logs in the restaurant, everything from the hand-hewn railing that ran along the steps we climbed and along the porch that stretched the full front of the restaurant, to the log building itself. The entry was two enormous pine doors, and above them were mounted horns from a long-horn steer. Everything was totally western. We stepped inside and waited as we observed the "wait to be seated" sign. Beyond the entry, in the dining area, brightly colored woven Indian rugs hung on the walls, and a massive fireplace constructed of rock, larger and grander than any we had ever seen, was at the back wall. We marveled at it and felt part of another world.

"Know what I want?" said Christopher-

John. "Stack of flapjacks this high." He indicated at least a foot of pancakes with upstretched hands.

Stacey smiled. "That all?"

"Nope, not hardly. Want some scrambled eggs, some ham this thick." Again Christopher-John indicated measurement with his hands. "Sausages and strips of crisp fried bacon, huge glass of milk, orange juice, and coffee. Lots and lots of coffee."

"Think that'll keep you?" I teased.

"For a while. What about you?"

"Maybe close to the same, minus a few of the flapjacks. I want to see a menu."

Christopher-John laughed. "What about you, Stacey? And you, Man? Same?"

Stacey didn't answer as he looked around the lobby and then into the dining area. He seemed apprehensive. Clayton too was unsmiling and his look was stern. There were no other colored people in the restaurant.

I chose to ignore it. "Well?" I said, following up Christopher-John's question, but before Stacey or Man answered, a man stepped from the dining area and approached us. He did not look western friendly, like the sign outside had suggested.

"Something I can do for you people?" he asked.

We all knew that tone.

I glanced at Christopher-John and Clayton Chester, then at Stacey, waiting for him to speak for us. "We'd like to be seated," he said.

"What? At a table?" the man questioned.

"We'd like to get something to eat," Stacey continued. "I think we'll need a table for that."

The man sighed and looked back into the restaurant before looking again at Stacey. "That's not possible."

Stacey looked past the man into the room. "I see empty tables —"

"Not for you," the man abruptly interrupted. "This is my restaurant and I've got a right to choose the people I serve and where to serve them. Now if you want something to eat, we'll serve you, but not inside. There's a door you can go to in back and you can order from there. Food will be the same as served in here —"

Clayton Chester stepped forward, his movement threatening. "We just came back from fighting your war!"

Stacey cut him off with an outstretched hand. "Clayton," he quietly said, and we all understood. It was an order. Man looked at Stacey and advanced no farther, like a soldier recognizing an order from a superior-ranking officer. "All right," Stacey said to the restaurant owner, "as long as we can get some food." I wanted to say something, but out of respect to my brother, I kept my mouth shut.

"Fine," said the man. "I'll send word that you're coming around." He turned to go.

"Wait," Stacey said, stopping him. "You don't mind, could we just order here? Both my brothers, they're veterans. They just came back from fighting over in Europe. I figure it's a shame we have to go all the way to the back door just so two soldiers can get some food. Even in Germany they didn't have to do that.

They fought the same war as these fellows did." Stacey motioned toward the soldiers seated in the dining area.

The restaurateur looked again at Christopher-John and Clayton Chester. "All right, all right, since you're veterans, I'll take your order, but you'll have to wait outside until we bring it to you." He pulled a pad from his vest. "Now, what do you want?"

Man looked at Stacey and went outside without another word. Stacey watched him go, then said to Christopher-John and me, "You both go with him. I'll order for us." Christopher-John immediately did as Stacey ordered, but I stayed. "Cassie —"

"I want to order with you," I insisted. "Go ahead."

"I'll take care of it, Cassie," said Stacey. "Go on out."

"Are you going to order or not?" The restaurant man was growing impatient.

Stacey ordered. "We'll have eight cheeseburgers, four milkshakes — two strawberry, two chocolate. Four large orders of fries, four orders of onion rings, and —"

"Wait a minute, wait a minute!" the man said as he tried to keep up with the order. "Give me time to get this all down." He took a moment and said, "What else? You want some dessert?"

"You have apple pie, chocolate cake?" asked Stacey.

"Yeah, got both."

"Then we'll take both. Four apple pies, fours slices of chocolate cake."

"That it?"

"And oh, yes, coffee. Four large coffees with sugar and cream."

"All right, I'll figure this for you and get it ordered. You can pay me, then you can wait out at the bottom of the steps."

Stacey glanced toward the seated uniformed soldiers. "You make all your veterans and their families pay before they get their meals?"

The man glanced back too and relented. "All right, go on, wait outside. We'll bring your order to you."

Outside, Christopher-John and Little Man were not around. We figured they had gone back to the car, parked on the other side of the building. "You'd better go on and join them, Cassie," Stacey said as we went down the restaurant steps.

"No," I said. "I'll just wait here with you, but I want to know why you ordered all that food when we can't eat in there."

"Just go on, Cassie," was all Stacey said. I stayed with him.

The wait was some thirty minutes or more. Restaurant patrons came and went. Finally, the restaurant door opened and the restaurant owner emerged with a young man behind him carrying a large box. The owner motioned to us. "Come on up, you two. I got your food."

Stacey had been leaning against the post railing with his back to the restaurant. Now he straightened and turned toward the restaurant and looked at the man. "On second thought, we decided we don't want your food."

"What?"

"Said we don't want your food. Changed our minds. We can't eat your food inside at one of your tables, we decided we don't want to eat your food at all."

"You — you can't do that! Not after we fixed all this! We've got a bill here!"

"You said you've got a right to serve who you choose, and we figure we have a right to refuse your service. So, we are refusing your service. We don't want your food."

The restaurateur's face turned fiery. "This is what I get for trying to be nice to you damn niggers! You're going to pay for this order!"

Stacey said nothing. He took my arm and started away.

"You get back here!" yelled the man. "I'll have the police after you!"

Stacey now stopped and looked back. "Won't be the first time," he said. Then once again he turned, and we walked on with the manager yelling after us. Refusing food we had ordered might have seemed an insignificant way of fighting back, but at times, insignificant ways were all we had, all that allowed us a little dignity as human beings. We knew the way of things down home in the South, but this was Wyoming. We had thought maybe things would be different here, in the great American West. We were wrong.

It was clear.

Being colored was a way of life in America, and it was a full-time job.

None of us had ever driven through mountains like these before. Stacey was at the wheel. He was the most experienced. He had driven trucks throughout the South and knew better than any of us how to handle the road, but the curves of the mountain roads were challenging. Massive rock formed a sheer mountain wall towering far above on one side of the road while on the other, the land dropped off steeply into the far depths of a valley. I was afraid of this rugged land, yet had never seen land of such awesome beauty. As Stacey swerved around the mountain curves, hitting speed limits way too high, we all kept looking back, waiting for the siren of a police car. We were in Wyoming, the wild West, but we might as well have been in Mississippi. The romance of the West as portrayed throughout America was not for us. For us, America remained as always, the same. *Whites Only. Colored Not Allowed.*

I was learning about America.

"Well, it's about time you all got here," said Uncle Hammer when he opened the door to us. It was midmorning and we had driven through the night, but had seen the sun rise over California.

"We were getting worried," his wife, Loretta, said, standing beside him. "Come on in, come on." Aunt Loretta was a vibrant woman, voluptuously built, with bright red lipstick and long red fingernails and formfitting clothes. She was a divorced lady with two grown children whom we had never met. Uncle Hammer had married her ten years ago. He had brought her only once to Mississippi so we all could meet her. Soon after that, he had made his move to California, and though he had been back to Mississippi since, Aunt Loretta had not come with him. She was a Chicago woman and very much unlike the women back home in our community. She was a looker, as the men liked to say, and dressed loudly, as the women liked to say, but she seemed to fit Uncle Hammer. I liked her.

"So, what took you so long?" asked

Aunt Loretta as we seated ourselves on plush gray furniture.

"You know we told you on the phone," said Stacey, "trip would take us three or four days. Would have made that time if we hadn't gotten held up in Iowa."

"Car broke down," Christopher-John explained.

"Well, why didn't you call?" asked Aunt Loretta. "We're not in Mississippi, you know." The reference of course was to the fact that no one in our Mississippi community had a telephone. That in itself had been unnerving to Aunt Loretta when she visited. "We've got telephones here," she finished.

"I think they know that," Uncle Hammer said brusquely, and leaned back in his chair. "Now that you're here, what's your plan, Stacey?"

"Like I told you, Uncle Hammer, get a job if I can. If I can do that and it seems steady, I'll bring my family out."

Uncle Hammer took a cigarette from a silver box. Aunt Loretta came over and took one as well. I had been surprised the first time I had seen her smoke. No other woman in our family smoked. In fact, I had seen no other woman in our community smoke. Out of respect, Aunt Loretta had not smoked in the house or in the presence of Big Ma, Papa, or Mama, but she had lit up in front of the boys and me. She lit Uncle Hammer's cigarette with a lighter, then lit her own, and sat back down. Uncle Hammer watched her, then looked again at the boys and me. "And what about the rest of you? You all planning on jobs out here too?" He looked directly at Christopher-John.

"Well, I don't know yet, Uncle Hammer," Christopher-John answered. "I've got a part-time job at a dealership and the owner said maybe I could be full-time if I come back. Right now, I'm just on leave, but they're holding my job for me for a few weeks."

Uncle Hammer drew on his cigarette. "What about you, Little Man?"

I laughed. "He doesn't answer to 'Little Man' anymore, Uncle Hammer. Says that's the name for a child."

Clayton Chester spoke up for himself. "Man's okay, Uncle Hammer, you want to call me that. I still answer to family, no one else. I just don't like being called 'Little' Man anymore."

"Why should you?" stated Uncle Hammer. "Childhood names sometimes stick a little too long. Sometimes folks forget your given name, they call you by these nicknames so long. Folks used to call me 'Babe' 'til I put a stop to it. So, in answer to my question, you planning on staying here?"

"Haven't made up my mind yet. I've been accepted in the engineering program at the University of Toledo under the G.I. Bill, but if I stay here, I'll apply to a California college. Depends on Stacey."

"You got a girl?"

Christopher-John laughed. "Yes, sir, he's got a girl all right! Man's always got a girl!" Man shot him an annoyed look, but didn't say anything.

"And what about you?" Uncle Hammer asked of Christopher-John. "You thinking on marrying soon?"

Now it was Man's turn to laugh. "More than likely, he'll be married before the year's out." Christopher-John smiled and made no reply.

Uncle Hammer nodded at that. "The boys have all had their say, Cassie. Still waiting on you. What are your plans, or are you waiting on what Stacey does too?"

"Pretty much. Course, too, I just wanted to see the country."

"And what do you think about the country?"

"Learning about it."

"And just what did you learn?"

"You really want me to tell you?"

"I ask a thing, I expect an answer."

That was a fact. So I told him in detail about Iowa, about Wyoming. I told him about the food we had ordered and walked out on, leaving the threat of the police coming after us.

"Y'all did that?" exclaimed Aunt Loretta. "Oh, y'all bad!"

Uncle Hammer looked at her. "Could've done worse."

"Oh, baby, I know you have," she said, grinning widely at him. Uncle Hammer only grunted and looked away. "Well, on that note," said Aunt Loretta, "looks like that's my sign to go fix some food for y'all. This man's already grumpy from waiting for y'all, so I better get this food on the table."

I rose to help.

Aunt Loretta waved her hand at me. "Ah, girl, sit down! You're tired and fact is, I do better by myself. Just talk to your uncle. He's been talking 'bout hardly nothing else since he heard y'all was coming. I'll call you when the food's on the table." As she passed Uncle Hammer, she leaned down and kissed the top of his head. Uncle Hammer showed no reaction except to look after her as she passed. The boys and I smiled at that. As gruff as Uncle Hammer could be, it was obvious that Aunt Loretta was his match. We also knew that though Uncle Hammer could be gruff in manner, there was always love in his heart for his family, and there was nothing he wouldn't do for the people he loved.

After we had eaten, Uncle Hammer said, "Now that you got food in your stomach, there's a man I want you to meet, Stacey. He's a colored fella, owns a trucking company. Man named Strickland. I've talked to him about you. Told him you'd had experience driving big rigs. We can go see him now, 'less you feel you need some sleep first."

"Slept in the car. I'm not tired. Course, I would like to wash up first."

"We all would," I said.

"Well, then, I'll show y'all upstairs," Aunt Loretta volunteered, getting up from the table.

I got up too, picked up my empty plate, but then Aunt Loretta stopped me.

"Girl, you leave those dishes. And I mean that! I'll get to them later."

"But —"

"No 'but's! One thing you have to understand, Cassie, is that I'm lady of this house, and though your Uncle Hammer takes care of everything else, I take care of this house, and what I say about this house, that's what goes!" She laughed good-naturedly. "Right, Hammer?"

Uncle Hammer looked at me and lit another cigarette. "Leave the dishes, Cassie."

I put the plate down.

"Now, come on, follow me," said Aunt Loretta. "All of y'all now."

We did as ordered. We gathered our luggage and followed her upstairs. Aunt Loretta led the boys to a room the three of them would share. There were two twin beds and a sofa that unfolded into a bed. The boys were more than pleased. She then led me to a room of my own. I had never had a room of my own before. It was beautiful, like out of a movie. She showed us the bathroom, which was large and spacious and had not only a tub but a separate shower stall too. The floor was tiled in gray and coral ceramics, and so were the walls. It was elegant.

"Now, you all figure out your own schedules about this bathroom, but don't worry about your Uncle Hammer and me. We've got our own bathroom off our bedroom."

None of us had ever heard of such a thing, but we marveled at it. So, this was California. The boys, out of courtesy, let me have the bathroom first, and I chose to shower. It was exhilarating. I had never had a shower before. The house on Dorr

Street and the one on Everett, in Jackson, had no shower, and, of course, down home on the land, there wasn't even a bathroom, only a round washtub into which I had to squeeze myself for a bath with water drawn from the well and heated on the wood-burning stove. After the shower, I eyed the tub, looked around the sun-filled room, and promised myself a long, luxurious soak later. Aunt Loretta had already told me to take advantage of all the bottles of bubble bath and lotions lined along the tile shelf encasing the tub.

I figured to like California.

Once we all had a chance to clean up and unpacked the Mercury, we headed out, taking both the Mercury and Uncle Hammer's Cadillac. Aunt Loretta went with us. She said she wanted us to see the sights after we went to the trucking company. I rode in the Cadillac with Uncle Hammer and Aunt Loretta. At Stacey's insistence, our first stop was at a car wash. Stacey always demanded a clean car, just like Uncle Hammer, from whom he had gotten his love of cars, so Uncle Hammer understood. After the car wash, we went to the trucking company.

Stacey and Uncle Hammer went into the trucking office, but the rest of us stood by the cars. It was a warm day and the sun was shining. Aunt Loretta was quite a talker and we laughed and talked with her, enjoying her stories, until Stacey emerged and said, "Cassie, they want to see you inside."

"Me?" I asked. "Why do they want to see me?"

"Uncle Hammer told Mr. Strickland about you." Stacey glanced over at Christopher-John and Man. "Fact, he mentioned all of you were looking for work, but Mr. Strickland said he only needs one driver right now. Thing is, though, he said there might be an opening for Cassie in his brother's office in Los Angeles."

I stepped away from the cars, totally surprised. "Los Angeles?"

"That's what he said. Uncle Hammer knows Mr. Strickland's brother too. Actually, said he knew him before this brother here. Says he's a good friend. You interested?"

I went with Stacey. As we entered the office, Mr. Strickland came over to greet me. He was an older gentleman, older than Uncle Hammer. "Your brother has been telling me quite a bit about you, Miss Logan," he said affably as we all sat down in comfortable chairs next to Uncle Hammer. "Understand you're looking to find a job in California."

"That's right."

"Well, I don't have any openings myself that might suit you, but my brother might. He has several businesses down in Los Angeles with a partner of his. Primarily, he's in the insurance business, but he's also doing a bit in real estate too, and now he's expanding into a little local trucking serving the Negro community. He's got an assistant to help him with the insurance and another with the real estate, but he just told me the other day he'll be looking for someone to assist in taking care of the trucking paperwork. Of course, he could hire someone down there, that wouldn't be a problem. But I'm sure because of your uncle and his recommendation, he'd hire you with no hesitation, sight unseen. Stacey here tells me you know how to type and that you're a quick learner. Now, I know you're a college graduate, so I don't know if you would be interested in this kind of work."

"I could be interested, but I've never worked in an office."

"No need to worry about that. You don't even need shorthand. Typing is the only manual skill you need. The main thing is that you present yourself well and learn the office routine. You can do all that, I think you might be helpful in my brother's operation down there. If you're truly interested, I can contact my brother. He'll go with my recommendation of you and, of course, that of your uncle."

I glanced at Stacey and Uncle Hammer. All of this was so unexpected.

"I am interested," I said, "but what about the salary?"

Mr. Strickland laughed. "Got a lady here after my own heart. First things first! But to tell you the truth, Miss Logan, I don't know right off. I'll check with my brother. One other thing. Hammer tells me you've never been to Los Angeles and that you don't know anyone there."

"That's right."

"If you decide to take the job, I'm sure

226

my brother and his wife will welcome you to live with them. Now, my brother's wife is in a wheelchair and she needs some help getting around and taking care of the house. Would you be willing to take care of those duties in exchange for room and board with them?"

I didn't hesitate. "Of course."

"So, can I tell my brother I've found just the person to work with him down there?"

"Well, Mr. Strickland, the job — if the pay is all right — and the living situation both sound good to me. But my decision depends on my brothers and what they're doing, so I'll need to think about it."

"Far as your brother right here," Mr. Strickland said, nodding toward Stacey, "I don't think that's a problem. We'll need to test-drive him and I'll be doing that myself personally in a few days. Can't do it before then. I've got to run up to Sacramento tomorrow, but if he passes the test-drive, he's got a job. You keep that in mind."

"I will," I said.

■ ■ ■ ■

When we left the trucking company, Aunt Loretta rode with Stacey and me in the Mercury, and Clayton and Christopher-John rode with Uncle Hammer. As we followed Uncle Hammer, Aunt Loretta was our tour guide, pointing out every item of interest and making an observation on just about every place we passed. It was clear to us that even though Uncle Hammer led the tour, Aunt Loretta was in charge of it and had scheduled the itinerary beforehand with him. We doubted if Clayton and Christopher-John were getting as detailed a tour. We rode through Oakland's downtown, then crossed the Bay Bridge to San Francisco. Aunt Loretta said San Francisco was her town. She loved it and much preferred it to Oakland, but Oakland was where Uncle Hammer had wanted to settle. She gave us a quick tour of the city. Although we didn't stop, we drove through San Francisco's Chinatown and a place called the Embarcadero. She said we would come back another day to get a better look. We then drove onto the Golden Gate Bridge and Aunt Loretta told us about its construction and history. The bridge spanned waters of the Pacific Ocean, was more than a mile and half long, and connected San Francisco to cities to the north.

By now it was late evening and we were all hungry. We stopped at a restaurant on the wharf. The experience of dining at an oceanfront restaurant was a new one for my brothers and me. Unlike in Wyoming, we were welcomed here. Our family were the only people of color in the restaurant, but we were greeted with a smile and great service and none of the other diners paid any attention to us. Aunt Loretta recommended the lobster, and to my amazement, a tank was wheeled before us loaded with live lobsters. We made our pick. Uncle Hammer made it clear that we were to order whatever we wanted, that we were his and Aunt Loretta's guests for the meal, and that he wanted no argument about that. He recommended we add some prime rib to the order, and Aunt Loretta declared there was nothing like it. Prime rib and lobster! She was absolutely right. It was a royal meal.

At the end of the day, when we returned to the house, the boys and I were exhausted and looking forward to sleeping in beds for the first time since we had left Chicago. The day had been a good one and as we said good night to Uncle Hammer and Aunt Loretta and to each other, we were all agreed that we liked California. Maybe we could just make a home here.

The next day we slept in late, but after breakfast Uncle Hammer, without his wife, took us on a different kind of tour. He took us to the heart of the Negro neighborhood in Oakland. As in Toledo, colored people had bought where they could, had gathered there with their churches and businesses and identified themselves with other people of color. He took us to the three apartment houses he had acquired during his stay in California and introduced us to some of his tenants. There was one house in particular he wanted Stacey to see. He told Stacey if he decided to stay, he could have one of the apartments rent-free in exchange for managing the building. The apartments were spacious, each with two bedrooms and almost as big as the downstairs on Dorr Street.

After the tour of the apartment houses, we had a late lunch at a neighborhood café, then Uncle Hammer took us to land outside the city. The road to the place was unpaved and dusty and the property held no more than a shack of a building, similar to what we had known back home in Mississippi. It was occupied by a middle-aged couple who enthusiastically welcomed Uncle Hammer. They invited us inside and offered us steaming hot coffee and warm molasses bread. We learned that they had migrated to California from Louisiana during the 1920s and had made their living working as a maid and butler to a white family. As part of their compensation, they had been allowed to stay on this parcel of land owned by that family. When the family dismissed the couple and put the land up for sale several years ago, Uncle Hammer had bought it.

Uncle Hammer charged them no rent, just asked that they look after the place.

There was a pen filled with hogs, and several horses roamed freely in a pasture beyond the pen. Chickens and guineas had the run of the yard. There was an orchard of orange trees, lemon trees, pear and fig trees too. There was even a vegetable garden. Uncle Hammer had planted it and looked after it himself. He said he liked working in the garden, feeling the soil between his fingers. "I figured I couldn't stay in Mississippi, not like the way things are down there," he said, "so I carved out a little bit of home for myself right here. Fact is, I'd like to live here one day, but Loretta, she's a city person, so I bought that house in town for her. This place though, this here is where my heart is. This place, it reminds me of home."

The boys and I understood.

In the days following, before Stacey went on his test run with Mr. Strickland, we checked the Bay Area for other job possibilities. Uncle Hammer had made a list for us. There was another company, a white company that might be hiring, and both Stacey and Clayton Chester filled out applications. Several garages had openings for a mechanic and there was also a service department in a dealership that was interested in Christopher-John's qualifications. He would have no problem getting a job. I found that I could get a job as a sales clerk, but I could not get an office job in a white firm without shorthand. Also, most of those jobs, even here in California, remained lily-white. Still, we all had good job prospects. Man's decision about staying in California was totally dependent on what Stacey chose to do. Christopher-John, however, was torn. He had his part-time job waiting for him in Toledo and even though he wasn't admitting it yet, we knew his heart belonged to Becka and he wanted to marry her. As for me, I was waiting as well on Stacey's decision, but I wasn't certain if it would affect my own. If Stacey stayed and brought Dee and the girls out here, I would want to be here with them, not in Los Angeles. But if all my brothers left, I wasn't sure what I would do. I loved my family, wanted to be with them, but an opportunity had presented itself, and like Christopher-

John, I was torn as to what decision I should make.

We had been in California almost a week by the time Stacey went on the road with Mr. Strickland. On that same day, Dee called. Uncle Hammer was gone and Christopher-John and Man were with him. Aunt Loretta answered the phone. The call was station-to-station, not person-to-person, allowing Dee to speak to whomever answered. Aunt Loretta told Dee that Stacey was not at the house, then handed the phone to me. "It's Dee," she explained. "Has to be something wrong, her calling on day rates."

As I took the phone, I nodded in agreement and said to Dee, "Dee, what is it? What's the matter?"

Dee laughed and I was relieved. "Nothing's the matter, Cassie. Fact, everything's fine. They're calling everybody back!"

"What!"

"You heard me! Everybody's being called back to work! They go back to work next Monday!"

"You're kidding!"

"It's all over the radio. The union called too. It's official! You all better get started back right away."

I frowned. "You know Stacey's not here. He's on a test run with Mr. Strickland. He's the man owns the trucking company."

"I know. Loretta told me. When will he be back?"

"Not 'til this evening probably. You know, Dee, he could get that job here."

"Well . . ." Dee went quiet. "He's got a job here too . . . and the girls and I are here. You tell him to call me soon as he gets there. This call is costing. I've got to go."

When Stacey returned, I met him outside by the car and told him about Dee's call. Stacey smiled and shook his head in dismay. "That's something, isn't it? I'm getting called back to work?"

"That's what Dee said."

He walked around to the front passenger door of the Mercury, opened the glove compartment, and pulled out a soft clean cloth. Coming back to the front of the car, he began buffing a spot on the fender, then laughed. "The Lord sure does work in mysterious ways! Two jobs in one day!"

"So, you definitely got the job with Mr. Strickland?"

"Sure did!" He grinned and continued buffing the chrome.

"So, what're you going to do?"

"Truth is, Cassie, I don't know. I've got to think on it."

"I don't think Dee wants you to think on it," I said.

"I know what Dee wants. We've got a house already in Toledo with a decent rent that'll be coming again, what with folks going back to work at the plant and all the back-rent due. All that'll certainly help with the mortgage. We've put down roots there, made a life, know people, and there're good working conditions at the factory. Could have that job for life."

I pointed out that if he stayed here, he could not only work with Uncle Hammer but have a rent-free apartment, along with the trucking job.

"That's the thing. I'd like that, working with Uncle Hammer. Maybe with him I

236

could do something that'd be good for Dee and the girls. Maybe one day be my own boss."

"But?" I said, reading my brother's mind.

Stacey smiled at me. "But there're no guarantees. It's risky. If I were on my own, no wife and children to think about, maybe I'd chance it. But the way things are, Cassie, I just don't know if I can take that risk when it comes to Dee and my girls." He was quiet a moment, then stopped his buffing and looked at me. "And what about you?"

"What about me?"

"You going to take the risk and stay here? Give up that teaching job? That offer Mr. Strickland made about his brother and business in Los Angeles, what're you thinking?"

"Like you, I'm thinking on it." I turned to go, then looked back. "But you, you'd better make up your mind quick. Dee's waiting on your call."

Stacey didn't call Dee right away. He talked first to Christopher-John and Clayton Chester, then went to Uncle

Hammer's office at the back of the house and the two of them talked. Afterward, Stacey left. We sat down to dinner without him. Aunt Loretta asked about Stacey, and Uncle Hammer said, "He's a man grown. He can miss dinner if he wants."

Aunt Loretta gave him a look, but then dismissed his surliness. "Well, he's missing a good dinner." Dee called again, but this time person-to-person to Stacey so that she would not be charged for the call if Stacey wasn't here. We all knew Dee was anxious to hear from him.

Stacey did not return until late. It was already past midnight in Toledo. He asked Uncle Hammer if he could use his office phone to make the call. Uncle Hammer was in his leather chair reading the newspaper. "You know where it is," Uncle Hammer replied.

Several minutes later Stacey returned to the living room. "Well, we've decided. I'm going back. I'm leaving in the morning."

"You sure about going back?" I asked.

"I'm sure. Dee agrees. She wants to stay there."

"Well, we were sure hoping you would stay here with us," said Aunt Loretta.

Without looking from his paper, Uncle Hammer said, "He's made his decision. He has to do what he figures is best for his family."

"Wasn't an easy decision to make," Stacey admitted. "I told Dee how beautiful it is out here. I told her about the apartment house too. That's where I went to think things through before I talked to Dee. Dee's worried about if something down home happens, if her mama or grandma or anybody else got sick and they need her to come down, she couldn't hardly make the trip from California back home like she could from Toledo. Admit, that bothers me too. Much as I want to stay here — and I probably would if I wasn't married with a family — I figure it's best to go back to Toledo, at least for now."

Uncle Hammer put down his paper. "May not get another chance to leave," he said.

"I know that. But I prayed on it. Decision's made."

"Well, I hope you all aren't going back,"

lamented Aunt Loretta. "It's been so good having all you young folks here."

"It's been good being here too," said Man, "but since Stacey's going back, I'll be going too. I can start classes at the university in a few weeks."

Christopher-John looked at Man, then over at Aunt Loretta and Uncle Hammer. "Mainly I came out here to be with them, but like Stacey, I figure it's best I go back."

Aunt Loretta laughed. "I know! You got a girl to think about!"

Christopher-John grinned. "Well, I suppose she's got something to do with it."

Aunt Loretta's eyes turned to me. "So, that just leaves you, Cassie. What're you planning on doing? You've got that offer."

I was quiet a moment, then sighed. "Don't know yet."

"Well, like you told me a couple hours ago," said Stacey, "you better make your mind up quick. I want to be on the road come daybreak. Car's already tanked up, ready to go."

"Cassie, you know you're welcome to

stay here, job or no job," said Aunt Loretta. "Isn't she, Hammer?"

Uncle Hammer looked at me. "She knows that. Boys too." With that said, Uncle Hammer rose from his chair. "Come on back to my office, Stacey. We need to call Strickland, let him know your decision."

Christopher-John, Clayton Chester, and I stayed talking to Aunt Loretta, waiting for them to return. Finally, Christopher-John and Man said they were going up. They had packing to do. Aunt Loretta asked if I was going up too, but I told her I wanted to wait for Stacey and Uncle Hammer. She then made us a pot of hot cocoa, and after pouring a cup for each of us, she kicked off her shoes and tucked her long legs close to her body on the couch and encouraged me to do the same. We sat there talking until Uncle Hammer and Stacey returned.

Uncle Hammer said good night and Aunt Loretta said, "I'll be down early to get breakfast on the table and fix some food for y'all to take. Now, Cassie, you leave those dishes where they are. I'll get them in the morning." Then she and

Uncle Hammer headed upstairs.

Stacey started to follow them up, then turned back to me. "You made up your mind yet?"

"Not quite. I'll tell you in the morning."

"Well, time is short."

"I know that."

Stacey was silent, his eyes reading mine. He understood the difficulty of the decision I had to make. "All right then. See you in the morning."

With the family upstairs, I sat alone in the quiet room and pondered my future. I was still there when Stacey, Christopher-John, and Man came down, ready to leave.

I told them I was not going back to Toledo.

It was not easy saying good-bye to my brothers. "I guess you know what you're doing," said Stacey. "You're giving up a good teaching job come fall."

"Good teaching job maybe, but you know how I feel about that."

242

Christopher-John frowned. He was concerned about my being alone. "No family down there in L.A., Cassie. Won't you be lonely?"

"Probably so, but think on it," I said, playfully tugging on his arm. "Los Angeles! It'll be an adventure!"

"Adventure's not always what it's cracked up to be," warned Man. "Don't be too quick to jump into anything doesn't feel right."

I smiled. "Believe me. I won't do anything you wouldn't do."

Little Man smiled back. "Well, that's not saying a whole lot."

Stacey hugged me. "Just make sure you keep yourself safe, Cassie. Keep yourself safe."

As I stood in the driveway with Uncle Hammer and Aunt Loretta and watched the Mercury roll down the street, then turn the corner out of our view, I felt a new kind of loneliness sweep over me. My brothers were going, leaving me behind. I had been without them before, but this was new. Before they had been the ones going into the unknown. Each

of my brothers had gone off on his own.
I never had.

Now I was going into the unknown.

Cassie's Love Story
Chapter I
(1947–1948)

I was on my own.

For the first time in my life I was without Mama and Papa and Big Ma and my brothers. Uncle Hammer and Aunt Loretta had driven the nearly four hundred miles down the coast to take me to Los Angeles and had stayed several days with the Stricklands, enjoying vacation time with them while I got settled. Before they left I had already started working at Mr. Strickland's office on Central Avenue, where he and his partner, Rowland Tomlinson, ran their trucking, real estate, and insurance businesses. Like Farish Street in Jackson and Dorr Street in Toledo, Central Avenue, simply called "the Avenue" by many, was the main corridor of the Negro community. Businesses of all kinds, from auto repair shops to medical, dental, and law offices, clothing stores and grocery stores, record shops, restaurants and cafés, theaters, and nightclubs were on the street. Real estate and insurance businesses like Strickland-Tomlinson were also there.

Strickland-Tomlinson was a quiet office and pleasant enough. Everybody working at the agency was colored. That was the way Negro businesses were back in Toledo and certainly down in Mississippi. Black business owners employed other black people. Los Angeles was no different. I had never worked in an office setting before, but I soon learned my duties and I felt comfortable during those first few days while Mr. Strickland was in the office. But then a few weeks after Uncle Hammer and Aunt Loretta left, Mr. Strickland had a stroke, and things began to change.

Mr. Strickland's stroke was severe. He was partially paralyzed, could not speak, and it was expected that he would stay that way. Full recovery seemed doubtful. With Mrs. Strickland already in a wheelchair, the Stricklands' adult children decided to move their parents in with them. That left me without a place to stay, but then Rowland Tomlinson and his wife invited me to stay with them.

It seemed to be working out all right for me. Instead of taking care of an elderly Mrs. Strickland and helping with the housecleaning in exchange for room and board, I now was responsible for some light housecleaning on weekends and helping care for the Tomlinsons' four children before they were off to school as well as some weekends. The children were all under twelve, and I enjoyed being with them. I liked Mrs. Tomlinson too. She was fair with me and gave me every other weekend off from household and child-caring duties once the house was cleaned on Saturday mornings. Then I was free to do whatever I wanted. It was seemingly a good arrangement, but there was one problem. I was not comfortable with Rowland Tomlinson.

A much younger man than Mr. Strickland, Rowland Tomlinson seemed nice enough. He was always polite and smiling, but both at the office and at home I often found his eyes on me, following my movements a bit too much. It was never anything he said, but I just had an uneasy feeling about him. I tried to dismiss it. There was no one I could talk to about how I was feeling, so I kept my thoughts to myself.

All of Mr. Strickland and Mr. Tomlinson's businesses were located in one building, and there were two floor levels. On the first floor were desks for the individual insurance salesmen who walked throughout the neighborhood selling insurance and collecting payments, for two real estate agents, and for a receptionist. A set of stairs led to the second floor, which opened onto a balcony partially overlooking the lower floor. Two secretary desks were located in the balcony portion of the office. A hallway led from the outer office to the private offices of Mr. Strickland and Mr. Tomlinson. When I first came to work for Mr. Strickland, I was at a desk on the first floor working as a receptionist, answering the phone, greeting people as they came in, and handling paperwork for the newly formed trucking company. At first I was concerned that since Mr. Strickland had hired me and he was no longer in the office I might lose the job, but that turned out not to be the case. Although Mr. Strickland's trucking venture was put on hold, I was given other duties, and one week after Mr. Strickland's stroke, Mr. Tomlinson moved me upstairs to a secretary's desk. The woman who previously had sat at the desk was moved to a desk downstairs.

The other desk in the balcony office was occupied by a woman named Justine Curry. Just one look at her and I could understand why Mr. Tomlinson had dared not move her. She had been Mr. Strickland's secretary, had been with him more than ten years, and she looked formidable. Justine was square-built in size, in her mid-thirties. She was not friendly, actually rather gruff in manner, but Mr. Strickland had trusted her totally. She knew the insurance business inside and out. She never smiled, at least not while I was around. Sometimes I found her staring at me from her desk across the balcony, but she spoke not a word to me unless necessary.

I got the feeling she didn't like me.

When I said good morning to her, her only acknowledgment was a grunt. Basically, that was our entire communication for the day unless office work required our interaction. I chose not to let her attitude bother me. I had learned some time ago that how other people saw me was up to them. I had been taught by Mama and Papa and Big Ma to live up to a certain standard, and I tried my best to do that. The fact that I had done nothing to Justine, yet she chose to be abrupt with me, was irritating, but I let it be. I continued to say good morning and daily she continued to grunt acknowledgment until finally one day, while sitting at her desk, she said, "Don't it bother you?"

I glanced up from my work. "What?"

"That you sitting up here and Louise sitting downstairs. That's her desk." There was a slight accent to her voice, but I didn't know from where, and I wasn't interested enough to find out.

"It wasn't my idea," I said. "Mr. Tomlinson moved me up here."

"Yeah, that's just it," said Justine. "Mr. Tomlinson moved you up here. You ever wonder about that?" Before I could answer, she swiveled in her chair, turning her back to me, and returned to her work.

Her words were not lost on me. I did wonder about it and even more so when I was in the Tomlinson home and Rowland Tomlinson was there. The Tomlinsons had made space for me on the first floor, in Mr. Tomlinson's den, where there was a sofa bed. Mrs. Tomlinson told me that the room was mine and that I should make myself comfortable there despite the fact that Mr. Tomlinson had a desk and files in the room. She said he seldom used the room and whatever work he might bring home, he could do in another room. Mr. Tomlinson had affably agreed with his wife, but said I would have to forgive him if he barged in from time to time to retrieve some of his files. I had thought nothing of it at the time, but already on more than one occasion after I had retired for the night, he had knocked softly on the door and said he needed to get a file. The first time he knocked, I had not yet pulled out the bed and was not undressed. The second time he knocked I was already in bed and the lights were out.

"Yes?" I said when I heard the knock. "Who is it?"

Without giving an answer, Mr. Tomlinson opened the door and stuck his head in. "Oh, I'm sorry, Cassie," he said. "I didn't realize you were already in bed. Apologies, but I need to get a file from my desk. I know exactly where it is. Won't take but a minute." He started into the darkened room.

I was startled by his intrusion. "Could you wait a minute please?" I sat up, pulling the covers close to my chest and switching on the lamp next to the bed.

"Oh, you didn't have to turn on the light, Cassie," he said pleasantly. "Light from the hall is sufficient. I know exactly where the file is, and like I said, this won't take me but a minute." He came farther into the room, leaving the door open. "Don't mind me, Cassie. Go on back to sleep. I'll be out of here in a jiffy." He went directly to his desk and opened a lower drawer. I watched his every movement. I heard him flicking through files. His eyes were concentrated on the drawer, then he pulled out a folder and held it up with a victorious smile. "Got it!" he said, as if he had just scored a feat of some sort. He closed the drawer and headed for the door. "Sorry to have disturbed you, Cassie," he said as he put his hand on the doorknob. "Good night."

"Good night, Mr. Tomlinson," I said.

"By the way, that's a very pretty gown." He smiled, then closed the door.

I sat for a moment listening to his footsteps going down the hall, then jumped up and hurried over to the door. There was no lock on it. A heavy leather chair was nearby. I pushed it over and jammed the top of it under the doorknob. After that, I had done the same every night before I went to bed. Rowland Tomlinson hadn't come back for another file since that night, and I didn't mention his coming to the den to Mrs. Tomlinson. I didn't want to make something of what maybe could have been nothing, yet I watched myself around Rowland Tomlinson as I felt him watching me.

After that first brief conversation initiated by Justine we went back to our daily acknowledgments of one another, my good mornings and her grunts. I was cordial, but I wasn't going out of my way to make friends with her. It was now clear she didn't like me, and the truth was I didn't care much for her either. We mostly ignored each other until one day after Rowland Tomlinson had come from his office and stood next to me as he dictated a letter. When he left with the first draft of the letter, I glanced up and saw Justine watching me. I turned and went back to my typing. Seconds later I was startled by Justine, who had come over to my desk and was standing directly in front of it.

"You seeing anybody?" she abruptly asked.

I was totally not expecting such a question. "What?"

"You had a man, maybe Mr. Tomlinson wouldn't be so interested in you."

I was surprised that she had noticed Rowland Tomlinson's attention toward me, but I said, "What are you talking about?"

"You ought to meet my brother." She turned then and went back to her desk. I just sat there puzzled, wondering where all that had come from.

A few weeks later as the weekend

neared, Justine approached me again. I was standing at a table close to the hallway, pouring a cup of coffee to take to Mr. Tomlinson. "I know you staying with the Tomlinsons," she said, "and you working with that man too. Don't he get on your nerves?"

I was not about to confide my feelings to Justine and get into an office mess. Mr. Tomlinson had done nothing to me except make me feel uneasy and I certainly didn't want to say anything that could get back to him or Mrs. Tomlinson. "Justine, what are you talking about?" I said, putting the cup on a tray.

"Girl, you know what I'm talking about. I see him watching you. Like I said, you had a man and he knew you had a man, maybe he'd leave you alone."

"He's not bothering me, Justine."

"Yeah, well, you just wait. I've seen men with that look before. You young and you pretty." I was surprised by the compliment. That was the first nice thing Justine had said to me. She paused a moment. "You ought to meet my brother. He's got a woman right now, but she's not right for him."

"And you think I would be?"

"You're different." Justine studied me as if to see my reaction to what she said. "He's my baby brother, lot younger than me, more your age, just returned from the war not too long ago. Maybe somebody like you'd be good for him. I guarantee you'd like him."

This was the second time Justine had mentioned her brother to me. She might have wanted me to meet him, but I certainly wasn't interested in meeting her brother. If he was anything like Justine, I didn't want anything to do with him. In fact, I didn't want anything to do with anybody connected with Justine outside the office. "I'm not interested in meeting anyone right now, Justine," I said, adding sugar and cream to the tray. "I'm just trying to make a living."

Justine stepped away, then came back as I turned toward the hallway. "I got a sofa at my place you can stay on you ever want to get away for the weekend. I got two kids and my man, J.D., there, but I'll see they don't bother you."

I smiled at her invitation, thinking that was the last way I would want to spend a weekend, but I said, "Well, I thank you, Justine, but really —"

"Just let me know," she said, ending the conversation and walking away.

I tried to figure Justine out. She was gruff and unfriendly, yet she had extended this invitation to me. I wasn't about to accept it, but I thought on it, and as my free weekend approached, I thought on it more and more. Thursday night made up my mind for me when there was a soft knock on the door and Rowland Tomlinson called quietly, "Cassie, may I come in? I need to get a file." I said nothing. I was already in bed. The lights were out. I held my breath, listening as the doorknob turned. There was nothing more from him. I heard him walk away. I left the chair in place. The next day I rose early, tended to the chores I was to do on Saturday, and told Mrs. Tomlinson I would be away for the weekend.

After work on Friday I went with Justine to her apartment. Outside stairs led to the apartment on the second floor. The apartment was cramped and not in the best order. Clothes and papers were scattered around the living room. Dirty dishes were on the kitchen table and pots from previous cooking were on the stove. Justine made no excuses for the mess, except to say she had two children and a man. She implied that cleaning the apartment was their responsibility. There were two bedrooms in the apartment. Her children, a girl, twelve, and a boy, five, shared one of the rooms and she and her man slept in the other. Her man, J.D., was in the apartment when we arrived. He was a scrawny-looking man and had little to say. The children were not there. They were staying with a friend of Justine's for the weekend. Justine showed me to their room. The room had twin beds. Justine gave me some sheets, then announced that she and J.D were going out for the evening. She didn't invite me to go with them. Justine said there was food in the refrigerator I could cook. After she and J.D. left, I realized that maybe staying at Justine's was not the best idea, but I had committed to the weekend so I figured to make the best of it. I put the clean sheets on the bed, then went to the kitchen and got started on the dishes. I thought that was the least I could do to show my appreciation to Justine for her hospitality.

"My brother's here," Justine announced. "You, Cassie, you get the door."

I had already showered and dressed and was planning to spend the day reading in the bedroom, away from Justine and her boyfriend. I had only come into the living room on the way to the kitchen for a cup of coffee. I stopped and stared at Justine.

"Well, go 'head!" she ordered. "Don't keep him waiting out there all day!"

Her order rankled me, but it was her place and I was only a guest in it. Though not happy about it, I went to the door and opened it. I was not prepared for the man on the other side. He looked nothing like I expected; he looked nothing like Justine. "You must be my sister's houseguest," he said, smiling, and his smile was like sunshine.

I nodded, feeling suddenly light-headed.

"Well, I'm Flynn. I hope Justine told

you I was coming."

"Well, let him in, why don't cha, Cassie!" hollered Justine. "He won't bite!"

I unlocked the screen door and pushed it forward. The man with the golden smile stepped inside and, unexpectedly, he bent his head toward mine and whispered in my ear. "Don't let my sister get to you. She'll bite, but I won't let her bite you."

I looked into dark eyes and was silent. "What you gawking at, boy?" Justine demanded to know. "Like you ain't never seen a pretty girl before?"

Flynn kept his smile. "Don't embarrass us, Justine."

"What you mean? Ain't embarrassing nobody! I see the electricity! Well, what I tell you, Cassie? Ain't my baby brother fine?"

"You know what?" said Flynn, and to my surprise he took my hand. Also to my surprise, I let him. "Let's get out of here," he said. "My sister's impossible when she figures she's done something right." He pushed the screen door open and I followed him out without a word spoken.

"All right! Be that way!" Justine hollered after us. "But be sure you name your firstborn after me!"

Flynn closed the door on her and led me down the steps. He never let go of my hand. When we reached the street he leaned against a foreign-looking car, silver-gray, parked there and I said, "I think we're safe now."

"She speaks," he said, and fixed his eyes on me and again he smiled.

I felt the sensation of his look, then glanced down at our hands. "You can let go now," I said.

"You sure you want me to?" he asked. His voice was evocative. His eyes were piercing.

I pulled my hand from his, hoping he had not felt how my body was trembling, but I could tell from his smile that he had. I felt my face growing hot. Trying to recover, I turned from him, then leaned against the apartment fencing, putting the sidewalk between us. "We weren't introduced," I said. "I'm Cassie Logan."

"Yes," he acknowledged, his face solemn now. "And I'm Flynn de Baca, and

I must say you're even prettier than Justine said you were."

I glanced away, not sure how to respond to that, then turned back to him. "I'm surprised Justine told you that. I didn't even think she liked me."

He laughed. "Well, obviously she does. She's been after me for weeks to meet you."

"Really?" Now I laughed. "She's been after me to meet you too."

His laughter settled into a smile. "My sister, the matchmaker."

There was silence between us for a moment, then I said, "De Baca, you said? I was thinking of you as Curry, but, of course, that's Justine's married name."

"No," he said. "She's always been a Curry. I've always been De Baca." I just looked at him. He shrugged. "Different fathers" was all he said.

"Oh." I was feeling nervous. I changed the subject. "I don't know what Justine told you about me, but I'm staying with her just for the weekend. I actually am living with my boss and his family. I was feeling a bit like I was in the way, so Justine invited me to stay with her over the weekend."

"Yes, she told me."

"Well . . ." I cleared my throat. "I don't know what else she told you, but I'm not from Los Angeles. I'm originally from Mississippi." I rattled on about my move to Ohio and how I had come to California with my brothers, been offered a job, and decided to stay. When there was nothing more for me to say, I finally grew quiet. I had never been one lost for words, but I was now. I took a deep breath and just let the quiet settle in. This man's gaze was still upon me so I finally met his eyes and took him in fully for the first time. The man was gorgeous. He was tall and lanky and his skin had a reddish-golden tint. His dark hair was coarse like mine, clipped close to his head, his cheekbones were high, and his lips were tantalizing, once again ready for a smile. When the smile came, I knew at that moment this man was about to change my life.

He pulled away from the car and extended his hand to me. "Yes, my sister had pretty much told me all that. Now, if you'll allow me to hold your hand again, we'll walk."

"Why do you need my hand to walk?" I asked coyly.

He leaned toward my ear once more. "Because I'm as struck by you as you are by me."

I hesitated, then responded, "You're sure about that?"

"Aren't you?" he asked, his hand still extended.

Again I hesitated, then placed my hand in his. "Where are we going?"

"No place in particular, just walking. But don't worry, you're safe with me. You'll always be safe with me."

I knew it was a flirtatious remark, but without really understanding why, I actually did feel safe with him and, holding the hand of a man I had met only minutes before, I walked down the street with him and listened as he talked and my world began to change. All that I could think was that he was beautiful, the moment was beautiful, and I felt beautiful too.

It was magical.

■ ■ ■ ■

I wanted to know more about Flynn but he seemed reluctant to talk much about himself. "Justine is the talker in our family," he informed me.

"She didn't tell me much about you except that I needed to meet you. She said she could guarantee that I'd like you."

He flashed that smile. "And we both know that you do."

I laughed at his cockiness, but I felt there was no need to hold back. Something about him made me want to be honest with him. "Yes, as a matter of fact, I do."

"Well, we're off to a good start. By the way, Justine was right about another thing."

"What's that?"

"She said I'd like you too."

I smiled. "So what about you? Tell me about yourself."

"Me? Oh, I'm not very interesting. Just a soldier returning from the front in

Europe, trying to get on with my life." That was all he said about himself. He spoke of other things. He talked about the school we were approaching and proceeded to give an architectural history of it, and he did the same for several other buildings we passed. He seemed absorbed in all of them. When we reached a nearby church, he stopped. The church looked to be quite old. "Made of adobe," Flynn said. "Built by Indians under supervision of Franciscan monks back around 1800." He pointed to the belfry. "You see that bell up there? Took more than twenty men to raise it."

I was impressed by what he had told me. "How'd you get to know so much about all these buildings?"

His eyes still on the belfry, Flynn said, "I love buildings, Cassie. They're my passion." He looked at me. "I work construction. One day I plan to be an architect. A builder." Flynn then looked back to the church and continued giving more history about it, and as he spoke, he never let go of my hand. I listened intently to his every word. I was intrigued by him.

This man.

■ ■ ■ ■

When we returned to Justine's apartment building, Flynn saw me as far as her front door but said he would not be coming in. "Justine will have too many questions." Justine, however, opened the door before he could leave.

"Well, you two back, huh?" she said. "Where'd you go?"

Flynn ignored her. "I'll see you again," he said to me, and only now released my hand.

I wanted to ask when, but I didn't want to seem too eager, so I said instead, "I'd like that."

"Well, what I tell you, boy?" Justine asked. "Wasn't I right?"

Flynn smiled that fantastic smile and, without another word, kissed his sister on the cheek and left.

I received a letter from Moe. Moe wrote me at least once a week, and I always wrote him back, but not always before his next letter came. He told me he was back to work at Ford, but his best news

267

was that Morris was now with him. Levis had brought Morris in time for him to start school. Moe said it felt great to have family living with him in Detroit. Morris was doing well and though he was homesick, he was adjusting to Detroit. Moe also told me Morris looked forward to the frequent trips they took to Toledo, just as he did. Moe added that Dorr Street was not the same without me. He asked when I was coming back. I wrote and told him I didn't know. I told him about my job and about Los Angeles. I described the city to him. I told him I missed everybody from back home, and I did. One thing I didn't tell him was that I had met a man who filled all my waking hours with dreams and my nights with longing.

When Flynn said he would see me again, I thought he meant soon, within a few days, a week. But then the days and the weeks passed, and I did not see Flynn again. After several weeks, I attempted to put the fantasy about Flynn to rest. There was a young man at church name of John Means who was interested in me and had asked me out. I wasn't interested in John Means, but I finally said I would go to a movie and dinner with him. I mentioned the date to Justine when she asked about my weekend plans, and the very next day she asked me to dinner at her place for that same Saturday evening. "I'm sorry, Justine, I can't," I said. "I told you I already have plans."

Her face soured into a look of disappointment as she sat at her desk sorting papers. "This man you're going out with, he anything special to you?"

I just looked at Justine, smiled, and continued with my work. I figured it was not Justine's business whether the man I was seeing on Saturday night was special or not. Besides, I had no intention of getting any closer to Justine or her family. It was clear to me now that I had not affected Flynn as he had affected me.

"Well, that's too bad you not being able to come to dinner," Justine went on when I didn't answer her question. "I was going to invite my brother too." I didn't say anything to that. "You know, I wish you and my brother could get together. You'd be good for him. Maybe you'd find he could be good for you too."

I pushed my work aside and rose from my desk. "Well, we'll never know that, will we?"

"I told you before he's got a woman. Older woman. Almost old as me. I don't like her. She's not good for him, and besides that, she's crazy."

"He's in love with her?" I asked without emotion.

"No. He just don't know how to get rid of her. You're the kind of girl he needs, not this vampire woman!"

"Well . . . it's none of my business." I headed for the hallway.

"Too bad you think that way, 'cause it ought to be," said Justine.

I turned at the doorway. "Why?"

" 'Cause, he likes you. He didn't say anything more than that, but I can tell. He was struck something powerful by you, and, girl, I know you was struck something powerful by him too."

I just stared at Justine without acknowledging her comment and with papers in hand went down the hall to Mr.

Tomlinson's office.

Christopher-John called. He said he and Becka were going to be married the Sunday after Christmas at Great Faith following church services. That is how most couples married, right after the services, and the congregation attending the services just stayed on for the wedding. No invitations were sent out, just the announcement was made in church and everybody was invited. I wished I could be there. Christopher-John told me he wished that too, but Stacey and Man were going south with him. He planned to bring Becka back to Toledo and the two would be staying in one of the upstairs rooms. I was happy for him.

Mr. Tomlinson closed the office during the holidays and I went to Oakland by train to be with Uncle Hammer and Aunt Loretta. Aunt Loretta had family in the area and she invited them all over for Christmas dinner. It was a good time to be around family and it helped take my mind off Flynn. I returned to Los Angeles New Year's Day and went back to the Tomlinsons. The children were happy to see me, and so was Mrs. Tomlinson. Mr. Tomlinson was polite and smiling. I kept my guard up.

There was nothing specific I could put my finger on about the way Rowland Tomlinson was with me. I knew I was in so many ways naïve around men. I had always been protected, sheltered, by Papa, Mama, Big Ma, by my brothers. I kept telling myself that maybe I was reading more into Rowland Tomlinson's movements, his looks toward me, his choice of words to me than there actually was. I kept thinking I needed to give him the benefit of the doubt. But I also kept telling myself I was not stupid. Then there came a Friday afternoon in late January when Rowland Tomlinson asked me to work late. He said that there was a contract that had to be finished. He said he would need my help to do it. I asked Justine if she was staying to help with the paperwork. She said she was not. Rowland Tomlinson hadn't asked her to stay. Her eyes narrowed. "You staying here alone with him?" Her voice was full of apprehension.

"The contract's got to be done," I explained, choosing not to voice my concern.

"Uh-huh." She was silent a moment, then said, "You want me to stay? I can find something to do."

I thought for a moment about asking her to stay, but then decided against it. I figured I was probably being foolish about Rowland Tomlinson. So far, there had been nothing overt in his actions. "No, there's no need for you to do that. Besides, Deacon Barnett will be here. He always cleans up on Friday."

Justine nodded hesitantly. We both trusted Deacon Barnett, who was deacon at the church I attended and a close friend to Mr. Strickland, and who also worked as janitor at the office. "So, I guess I'll go on, huh?"

"All right," I said. "I'll see you on Monday."

Justine gathered her things. "S'pose if you work later, Mr. Tomlinson, he'll take you home too?"

"If it's not too late, I can still take the bus. I'd like to go to the library."

"On a Friday night?"

"Well, that's what I'll tell him." I didn't say anything further. I did not want to confide in Justine. I did not want her becoming my ally; yet, as she studied me, I felt that she was.

At the end of the day, after Justine and the rest of the office staff had gone, Deacon Barnett had not yet arrived. On Fridays, like clockwork, he arrived just before five o'clock, quitting time for the rest of us. But today, as I checked the wall clock at ten past the hour, he had not arrived. I chose not to worry about it as I tackled the pile of papers before me. They were handwritten papers that Mr. Tomlinson said needed to be typed so that he could file them on a trucking bid with city hall first thing Monday morning. The forms were familiar and I knew from my weeks working in the office that Mr. Tomlinson always submitted such forms typewritten.

I typed steadily for more than an hour, and during that time Rowland Tomlinson stayed in his office. As I made my way through the pile of papers, I kept checking the clock. Deacon Barnett still had not come. I concentrated on my work and tried to dismiss the time and Deacon Barnett's absence. But with half the typing finished, Mr. Tomlinson emerged from his office. "So, how is it going, Cassie?" he asked.

He came around the side of the desk to stand behind me. I didn't look up at him. I just kept on typing. "I should be finished soon," I said.

"How soon?" he asked.

Still not looking up, I replied. "Maybe another hour."

Rowland Tomlinson stood behind my chair and looked over my shoulder. I felt nervous with his standing there, but I continued typing. Then, after a minute or two, he reached over my right shoulder and placed one hand on the desk to the right of the typewriter, and then placed his other hand to the left of the typewriter, enclosing me between. My back was to him. I stopped typing. He leaned down close and whispered, "You think that'll give us enough time?"

I was naïve, but I wasn't stupid. I knew exactly what he meant. I jerked backward, attempting to rise, but Rowland Tomlinson blocked me with his arms.

"Oh, come now, Cassie. You didn't answer my question," he said softly, his breath against my ear. "I know you want this as much as I do."

I pushed back in the chair and tried to stand, but he laughed at my effort, keeping his hands firmly on the desk, his body obstructing my movement. Then suddenly his laughter stopped and he released me. He stepped back and I immediately sprang from the chair, looked into his face, and stepped away from him. He was no longer looking at me. I followed his gaze.

Flynn stood on the landing.

"How'd you get in here?" asked Rowland Tomlinson, clearly irritated. "We're closed, and that front door's locked!"

Flynn looked at me, then at Rowland Tomlinson, and there was no smile this time. He studied us both. "Man downstairs let me in from the back. Says he's here to clean."

"Deacon Barnett?" There was surprise in Rowland Tomlinson's voice. "He's not supposed to be working tonight."

"Well, he is," said Flynn.

Rowland Tomlinson looked dismayed. "Who are you? What are you doing here?"

Flynn, still standing at the landing, fixed his eyes on Rowland Tomlinson. "I've come for my lady." Then he looked at me. "Cassie, are you all right?"

"Of course she's all right!" Rowland Tomlinson declared, his tone indignant. "Why shouldn't she be?"

Flynn kept his eyes on Rowland Tomlinson and repeated, "Cassie, are you all right?"

I was startled, but I tried not to show it. "Yes," I said.

"Then are you ready to go?"

"Yes," I said again, and pushed past Rowland Tomlinson. "I'm finished here."

"But, Cassie, we've got work to do," objected Rowland Tomlinson.

"I'm finished," I said once more. I gathered my coat, my other few things, and left with Flynn, leaving Rowland Tomlinson standing speechless at my desk.

I waited until we were outside before I stopped Flynn and asked, *"What are you doing here?"*

"Like I told the man, I came to get you. Justine got worried. She asked me to come. She also called your Deacon Barnett to see if he was here. She found out your boss had told him not to come today. Justine told the deacon to get right over here and unlock the door. When she called me, I got a little worried too."

I stared at Flynn. "Why would you be worried? You don't even know me."

"True. Come on, let's go to the car."

"I was thinking I would take the bus," I said.

Flynn glanced back at the office building. "You sure you want to do that? Your Mr. Tomlinson could come out any minute and see you standing there. You plan on going back to his house?"

"He's not *my* Mr. Tomlinson, and no, I do not plan on going back there, least not tonight." Then I just stood there, thinking what I should do next. I looked up and down Central Avenue. Most of the businesses on the block and most of the stores had already closed for the day, but the theaters were open and the jazz and other nightclubs soon would be. A whole different crowd would be on the street.

Flynn seemed to read my mind. "Why don't you come with me and you can figure out what you want to do."

He held out his hand to me. I didn't take it, but I went with him. I had no other place to go. Once inside the car, I thanked him for coming for me. He smiled that fantastic smile and began to drive. As I tried to think of a place for Flynn to take me, I took note of Flynn's car, the beauty of the upholstery and the design of the steering panel. "What kind of car is this? I've never seen one like it before."

Flynn glanced over, looking surprised that those were my next words. "Mercedes."

"Never heard of it, and I thought I knew all the car models. All my brothers love cars, talk about them all the time."

"It's a German make. I saw a couple like it while I was over in Germany, wanted to get one. It's secondhand, about eight years old, had to fix it up, but it'll do for me."

He said nothing further and we rode in silence until I said, "Flynn, I don't know where to go. I can't spend the night at the Tomlinsons', but I'll need to let Mrs. Tomlinson know I won't be home."

"You want to go by there now to talk to her?"

I shook my head. "Mr. Tomlinson might come while I'm there. I don't want to see the man and I don't want to hurt Mrs. Tomlinson. She's been good to me. Besides, I don't know what I could tell her, that her husband was coming on to me?"

"That's the truth, isn't it?"

"Yes, but I can't tell her that. I need to call her though. She'll want to know why I won't be home, where I'm staying."

"Tell her you're staying with a friend."

"She'll want to know who that friend is."

"You can tell her you're staying with me."

"I don't think that would go over very well."

"Then tell her you're staying with Justine."

"I don't want to lie."

"You won't be. We'll call Justine. She'll make a place for you."

I didn't like the idea of staying with Justine and her boyfriend again, but I didn't have much choice. I had no family in Los Angeles, no place else to go, no real friends either, no one except maybe this man.

Flynn drove to a café on the other side of town. He said we would call from the café and also have dinner. When I objected to dinner, he said, "You've seen Justine's place. You think she'll have dinner waiting when you get there?"

I relented. I was hungry and I admitted to myself that I would rather be with Flynn for as long as possible than without him at Justine's apartment.

The restaurant was small, almost like a big kitchen, and everyone there seemed to be Mexican. As we entered, some of the diners turned curiously to look at us. I felt out of place; it was as if we were interrupting a family dinner. A middle-aged man with a mane of luxurious silver hair came rushing over with a wide grin on his face. He spoke in rapid Spanish and embraced Flynn. Flynn returned the embrace, greeting the man in fluent Spanish. He addressed the man as Papá Miguel. Then he introduced me.

The gentleman was Señor Peña, proprietor of the restaurant, and he greeted me warmly, taking my hand in both of his before calling out to someone in a back room. Within moments a woman and several children emerged, and they greeted Flynn with the same enthusiasm as the man had done, hugging him warmly and smiling sweetly at me. Two young men also emerged and hugged Flynn. They were the Peñas' eldest sons, Jorge and Eduardo. Then the woman, Señora Peña, speaking only Spanish, gestured toward her kitchen and even I understood she had to get back to it. The children lingered around Flynn until their father shooed them back to the kitchen. Then, after a few words from Flynn, he led us to a large desk set behind a colorful screen in the corner of the room. It was obvious to me it was his own personal desk, with papers stacked high. A telephone was on it.

"Here, you sit," Señor Peña said to me, rolling back the desk chair. "You can make your calls from here."

"Thank you," I said.

Señor Peña smiled widely. "When you finish, *hijo,* you come over to the table in the corner. I'll fix it up real nice for you and your lady. And I'll bring you a feast for two." He hurried off, and for a moment my gaze lingered after him as I relished how he referred to me.

"I'll call Justine first," Flynn said, picking up the phone. After a couple of minutes of explanation to Justine of what had happened at Tomlinson's office, he hung up. "She said she won't wait up for us, but you can sleep on the sofa for tonight. I have a key, so that's not a problem. We get there when we get there."

The next call was to Mrs. Tomlinson. It was obvious from her tone that her husband had not yet made it home. I told her I was spending the night at Justine's and apologized for not calling earlier. She was understanding, knowing, she said, that young folks needed time to do fun things on a Friday night. She told me to be careful and I told her I would see her tomorrow. As I hung up the phone, I wondered what I would say to her tomorrow. I knew I had to move out. There was no way I could stay under the same roof as Rowland Tomlinson.

Once we were seated at our table, Flynn asked me what I would tell her and I admitted that I didn't know. "Like I told you, she's been good to me. She treats me like a daughter. If I could've given her two weeks' or even a week's notice about moving out, it would make more sense . . . but just moving out all of a sudden . . . how do I explain quitting my job?"

"You could tell her the truth."

"I told you I can't do that."

"Well, maybe you can just tell her that you met a man, fell madly in love, and you're running off with him."

I laughed. "And who would that be?"

"I could be there when you told her. It would be obvious."

"And you know what would happen then? Mrs. Tomlinson would be on the phone the very next minute calling the operator to get my Uncle Hammer up in Oakland and he'd be down here the next day."

"Well, it was a thought, and still a possibility."

I knew he was teasing me with the proposal, and I smiled. "I don't think so. You don't know my uncle. Nobody gets on his wrong side."

"He sounds like a formidable man. Maybe we'd better come up with a new plan."

"Maybe we'd better," I said, laughing. "He is a formidable man."

Thoughts of any new plan were delayed by the serving of our meal and a flurry of exchanges in Spanish. There was a lilt to the words, smiles on faces all around, and the discomfort I had felt earlier was gone. I asked Flynn about his relationship with the Peñas. "I've known them since I was a child. They're kin to my father." He did not elaborate, and from the brevity of his answer, I knew not to question him. This was obviously something he did not want to talk about.

As we finished our meal, the Peña family joined us at the table. The restaurant now had begun to clear and we lingered over a drink called sangria. I began to feel somewhat light-headed and put the drink down. "What? You don't like the sangria?" asked Señor Peña.

"No, I do," I said. "It's delicious! It's just that . . ." I glanced at Flynn. "Is this wine?"

"Yes, of course, special to Mexico!" Señor Peña responded proudly.

"Oh, well, that's my problem then," I said, feeling just a bit foolish. "I've never had wine before."

"Not any kind?" questioned Flynn. His arm was now resting on the back of my chair, not touching me, but close, oh so close. His nearness made me flush.

"Country Baptist," I said, as if that explained it all, "and there are some things country Baptists just aren't supposed to do."

Flynn laughed and so did the Peñas.

"You want, Miss Cassie, I'll bring you something else," offered Señor Peña, moving to take my glass.

I stopped him, putting my hand protectively over it. "Oh, no . . . the sangria, it's fine. Maybe this is what I need tonight anyway. It's been a hard day."

By the time we left, the café was closed. Flynn had kept saying we should go, but the Peñas kept insisting that we stay, that it had been too long since they had seen Flynn. Finally Flynn stood, asked for the bill, and pulled out his wallet.

"What!" exclaimed Señor Peña. "You insult us! We're family!"

"You see, that's why I don't come more often," explained Flynn. "Here, let me pay for this."

Señor Peña pushed away Flynn's hand and the money it held. "Would you pay for a meal if you came to the house? For you, this is the same as taking a meal at our home. Put your money away, *hijo mio*, it's no good here."

Flynn smiled. "Guess I don't come back again, you treat me this way."

"Well, that's up to you," retorted Señor Peña, "but you know always you're family and our door is always open to you."

Flynn then spoke to Señor Peña in Spanish. The two hugged, and as Flynn and I started out, unexpectedly, Señor Peña gave me a fatherly embrace and said softly, "You come again, Miss Cassie Logan. I can see you are special to our boy. He's never brought anyone here with him before."

I couldn't help but feel that despite the awkwardness of the day with Rowland Tomlinson and the uncertainty of my future, all had been worth it, for what I was feeling now as we left the café: a closeness to the Peñas and a closeness to Flynn and whatever world he was from. Maybe in part it was the sangria that made me feel this way, but more likely, it was because of Flynn.

I did not want to leave Flynn, and I knew he knew that. "You want to go to Justine's now?" he asked as we drove from the café.

I shook my head. "But I suppose I have to. . . . It's late."

"Cassie, when you're with me, you don't have to do anything you don't want to do. The time doesn't matter."

I didn't question what he meant by that. I decided to let him guide me through whatever was to come. I trusted him. I didn't know why, but I did. I nodded and rested my head against the car door. The sangria had made me sleepy. I covered my mouth as I yawned, then asked, "What do you want to do?"

He reached over and placed his hand over mine resting on the seat. "It'll take us a while to get there. You're sleepy, so sleep."

I didn't ask him where we were going. I just nodded again. I trusted him to take me where he chose. With his hand over mine, I fell asleep. I did not wake until the car stopped.

"Cassie, we're here," he said.

I looked around groggily. "Where?"

He got out of the car. I stared at what was before me, a framed wire gate with barbed-wire fencing running from each side. A large "NO TRESPASSING" sign, visible in the darkness, was spread across the gate. My door opened, and Flynn held out his hand to me. I took it. "Where are we?" I asked.

"My dream" was all Flynn said.

He led me to the gate. A padlock was on it. He pulled a key from his key chain, unlocked the padlock, and pushed the gate open. "Come into my dream," Flynn said. I entered and followed him across a grassy field. There was a full moon, and the outline of trees and mountains were visible against the sky. He led me across the field and just when it seemed we were about to fall off a cliff, the land opened up and before us was a bowl of trees and mountains outlined beneath the moon.

"Oh, my Lord . . ." I was awed by what I saw.

"Just wait 'til daybreak," Flynn said. "Maybe you will have seen something like it, but I never have." I took in his dream with silence. "Wait here," he said. "I need to go back to the car for a minute." I acknowledged his leaving with a slight turn of my head, then stared out at the wonder of the night. The sky was clear, the stars were bright, and the moon shone down like the sun. "I brought some blankets," Flynn said when he returned. "Flashlight too, if we need it."

I eyed the blankets. "And what do you

expect us to be doing on a blanket?"

He shook his head at my wariness. "Nothing you don't want to do," he said, tossing one of the blankets to me and spreading the other at the base of a tree. "For now, we'll just sit."

The night was chilly and I wrapped the blanket around me. We sat some distance from each other; Flynn's back was against the tree. We gazed out across the valley to the mountain range beyond and we talked. We talked through the night. Mostly, Flynn left the talking up to me. He seemed fascinated by my stories. But again, he seemed not to want to talk much about himself. He did not want to talk about his childhood. He did not want to talk about the war. What he did want to talk about was this land and his dream.

"Man who owns this land says it can be mine in a few years. I've got a contract with him. Minute I saw it, I knew it was something I had to have. I'd love to build a house on it someday. I'd design it and build it myself. That's my dream."

He was holding me by now. I sat between his long legs, bent at the knees, as

I rested against his chest. His back was still against the tree, his arms encircling me, but his eyes were on the sky, on the land. When the sun rose, we were both silent, watching its splendor. It was I who broke the silence. "Now I understand," I said.

He looked down at me and turned my face toward him. "I'm glad," he said. "I wanted you to." Then, for the first time, Flynn kissed me.

"You know what you want to do now?" he asked me.

"No."

The sun was well above the mountains. I pulled myself from his arms and sat directly across from him. "I was thinking. It's nice of Justine to ask me to stay, but I don't think it's the best idea. I mean, I'd pretty much be in the way. It'd be crowded, especially with Justine's children there. I've got a little money saved. I could maybe go to a hotel for a few days while I look for another job. Maybe a colored hotel on Central."

"Well, there is the Dunbar on the Avenue. But there is that other option,"

Flynn said quietly. "Like I said before, you can come stay with me."

"Don't forget what I said about my uncle."

"So your uncle doesn't come after me, I can always find another place to stay for a while."

"Justine mentioned you were involved with somebody. From the way Justine talked, I don't know if staying at your place would be such a good idea."

"Justine sometimes talks a little too much." He was silent, then spoke cautiously. "The lady Justine spoke about has her own place. I have mine." That was all he said.

"Doesn't matter. You know I can't stay at your place anyway."

Then together we both said, "Country Baptist."

"There's an older lady I know. Name's Mrs. Hendersen. Maybe if you stay with her, help her, you could have a place to stay without charge for a while, and a room of your own. There are other women staying there too."

"But I'll still need to find some outside

work. I'll need to earn some money."

"Well, first things first. Let's go and see what she says." Flynn pulled me up. He picked up the blanket and together we folded it. With the blanket squarely folded between us, his arms clasped at the back of my spine and mine clasped at his, he kissed me again. The sun warmed my skin.

I had never felt more glorious. *This man.*

Flynn arranged everything. He stopped at a pay phone, called Mrs. Hendersen, and told her about me and my situation. She told him to bring me right over and not to stop for breakfast. Her girls, as she called them, were with her and they had not yet sat down for breakfast. We could join them. Flynn and I accepted the offer.

Mrs. Hendersen lived in a modest-looking house, well-kept, a few blocks off Central Avenue. As soon as the door opened, we could smell coffee brewing. The three women who stayed with Mrs. Hendersen were older women in their forties or fifties and all seemed pleasant. Mrs. Hendersen herself was in her mid-eighties with a quick wit and a solid mind. Although confined to a wheelchair, it was obvious she was still in charge of her faculties and of her house. Mrs. Hendersen said she was from Louisiana and had come to California during the First World War while her first husband was serving overseas. She made me welcome as she explained that I could stay in her home rent-free in exchange for some of the housework, some of the cooking, and helping her with her personal care when needed. It was fine with her if I got a job, just as long as I kept up with my duties at the house. Once I got a job, however, I would be expected to pay a minimal amount to help with food and the house bills. Mrs. Hendersen made it clear that she was not out to make a profit from the boarding money. "Before my husband passed on," she said, "he made sure this house was paid for, so my only worry is ongoing bills. Mainly, though, I open my house to ladies to give them Christian living and share what I can with them. Keeps me from being lonely and feeling old."

Mrs. Hendersen said I would have my

own room. "Young lady needs some space to herself." She went on, though, to say, "Just because you have your privacy, that doesn't mean you can just do anything here. We have moral, Christian rules in this house and no gentlemen callers are allowed in the bedrooms, even when they're as handsome and fine as this young man here." She looked at Flynn and laughed, and Flynn smiled. "They're welcome to come visit at most anytime during respectable hours. But come ten o'clock at night, we lock the doors and all gentlemen callers better be out of here. Now, that doesn't mean you have to be in this house by ten. I'm not your mother, so I'm not setting that rule. All the ladies who live here, I believe, have good moral character and, I hope, good judgment about what they do with themselves. You'll have your own key, so you can come and go as you please, but if you break one of my rules concerning my house, you're immediately out of here. Is that understood?"

"I understand," I said.

"Good. Then welcome to my home."

After breakfast one of the ladies gave

me a general tour of the house, then showed me to my room, located in the basement, as were the other women's bedrooms. My room was small, but neat and clean with a bed, dresser, chifforobe, nightstand, lamp, and a comfortable-looking chair. A picture of Jesus hung on the wall. It was a pleasant room and I figured I would like it here. The bathroom that all the boarders shared was at the end of the hall. Mrs. Hendersen, whose bedroom was on the first floor, had her own private bathroom and I would be responsible for its cleaning.

Mrs. Hendersen gave me a key and told me to move in whenever I wanted. "Well, I'd like to stay right now, if that's all right," I said. "I'll get my things later, but right now, I'm really sleepy. Like we told you, we were up all night."

"Then you sleep, child," said Mrs. Hendersen. "Today, tomorrow, you don't worry about doing anything around here. You rest, go out with this young man, enjoy your weekend. You bring your things and on Monday, I'll show you what you need to do to be part of our home here. I'll also be thinking on maybe where you can find a job. I know a lot of people around here, so I believe we'll be able to find you something."

And so that was it. There were no papers to sign. No application to fill out. No money to be paid. I was accepted on Flynn's word, and I accepted this new home on his word as well. Better than all that, I really liked Mrs. Hendersen.

I walked to the porch with Flynn. I did not want him to go, but I knew we had to part at some point and now seemed to be the right time. "Are you going over to Justine's?" I asked. "Let her know I won't be coming?"

"I'll stop by there."

"Will you thank her for me? For making a place for me . . . and for sending you? Tell her I'll call her."

"I'll tell her. Now, you get some sleep."

"You too." He turned to go, making no effort to kiss me again. "And, Flynn," I said, stopping him. He looked back. "Thank you. For all this. It seems like I'm always thanking you for something."

He flashed that smile, then was gone.

■ ■ ■ ■

Flynn had said nothing further about the move from the Tomlinson house, and since he hadn't, I figured I had to handle that on my own. That was just as well. I didn't want to become dependent on this man; he made it so easy to do. It wasn't until the afternoon and several hours of sleep that I called Mrs. Tomlinson to give her some advance warning of my plan. I didn't want to just show up at her front door and begin to pack. Now that I had a place to stay I could tell her the truth, or at least part of it. I could tell her about the space that Mrs. Hendersen had offered me and that I would be helping her, that I wanted to go back to school — which I did — and staying with Mrs. Hendersen and helping her would allow me to do that. I knew she would ask about my job at her husband's office. I didn't know if he had told her that I had quit and, if he had, what reason he gave. I knew one thing for sure. Whatever he told her, it would not be the truth. I was pondering on just what I would say to her questioning when Justine called.

"You need help moving?" she asked in her brusque way. "Flynn told me to call."

"Yes, thanks. I don't have much to pack, but I'll need a ride."

"So when you want to go over, today or tomorrow? I'll get J.D.'s car."

"Today, I guess. I just don't want to see Mr. Tomlinson."

"That fool! He knows you coming, he probably won't even be there. Just let me know when." She hung up without another word. I wasn't offended. That was just Justine.

I decided not to put the matter off and called Mrs. Tomlinson, hoping her husband did not answer. I was in luck. One of the children answered. When Mrs. Tomlinson came to the phone, I tried to sound cheerful as I told her about the great opportunity to stay with Mrs. Hendersen and possibly take classes at the university. I apologized for giving her no advance notice, but told her that Mrs. Hendersen expected me to start my duties at her house Monday morning. So far, all true.

"But, Cassie, I'm so disappointed,"

Mrs. Tomlinson said. "What about your job with Mr. Tomlinson?"

"Oh . . . didn't he tell you? I told him yesterday I was leaving, wouldn't be back."

"You did? He didn't mention it."

"Well, he had a lot of paperwork he was trying to take care of. Maybe he just got busy and forgot." I didn't like making excuses for the man, but so far, Mrs. Tomlinson seemed to be accepting what I said. I added quickly, "I was wondering if it's all right if I come pack up my things in a little while. It won't take long. Also, I can do the Saturday cleaning before I go."

"Oh, Cassie, don't worry about the cleaning. It's already taken care of, and there's no rush on your packing. I tell you what. Why don't you come spend the night, go to church with us tomorrow, have dinner with the family —"

"I'm sorry. I thank you, but I can't do that. I'm already at Mrs. Hendersen's and there's a lot I need to do to get settled here."

"All right, Cassie, but I sure do hate to

lose you. The children are going to take this hard. You come whenever you want. We'll be here."

I arranged a time for later that day, then called Justine. When Justine and I arrived at the Tomlinson house, Mr. Tomlinson was not there. "What I tell you?" Justine whispered to me. Mrs. Tomlinson said he had business at the office and wouldn't be back until late. Mr. Tomlinson's absence made it easier on all of us and gave me additional time to pack and visit with Mrs. Tomlinson and the children. Mrs. Tomlinson insisted that we have something to eat with them, and without the stress of Mr. Tomlinson around, we accepted her invitation. I enjoyed Mrs. Tomlinson and the children and was glad we had this time together.

"Now, you come and see us again soon," Mrs. Tomlinson said as we prepared to leave.

"I'll try," I said, knowing it was not likely I would set foot in this house again. It would be too awkward.

She took my hand. "And, Cassie, don't worry about any of this, I mean about your leaving so suddenly. I understand."

Her eyes met mine, and in that moment, I wondered if she knew why I was really leaving.

That evening I called Uncle Hammer. I was not looking forward to explaining things to him. I just told him things hadn't worked out at the office with Mr. Tomlinson and that I thought it best to find another place to live. I told him about Mrs. Hendersen and my new living situation. I also told him about maybe going back to school. Uncle Hammer listened in silence as I did all the talking. When I finished, with nothing further to say, he finally spoke. "This man Tomlinson, he do anything to you?"

"Sir?"

"Are you all right, Cassie?"

"Yes, sir."

"You need me to come down?"

"No, sir. I'm fine."

He was silent a moment. "Well, you're a grown woman now and I know you've got a good head on your shoulders, so I expect you made the right decision for yourself. You need me, there's something

303

you can't handle, you let me know. I'll come down."

"I know."

When I hung up, I sighed, relieved that Uncle Hammer hadn't questioned me further. I knew he had sensed something was wrong. I also knew I couldn't lie to him. I didn't want him to come, yet it gave me comfort to know he would. Even though we were separated by all those miles, just knowing Uncle Hammer was in the same state allowed me a sense of having family near. Still, as I went to sleep my first night at Mrs. Hendersen's, I felt a loneliness I hadn't felt before. I was alone in the city of Los Angeles. I was alone now, except for Flynn, but I didn't know if I should count him in my life yet.

It wasn't until early Sunday morning that I remembered that I was supposed to go to Sunday dinner and a movie with John Means. I did not have his number and I wasn't planning on going to church since it was the same church the Tomlinsons attended. I also did not want to call the Tomlinson house to leave a message for

John Means, but the arrangement was that he was to call for me there. Once again I had to seek out Justine as my go-between. Justine usually did not go to church, but spent her Saturday nights enjoying herself with J.D. at a club. My call woke her. When she answered the phone, her voice was groggy and she was in a bad mood. I got right to the point. I told her that I wanted her to call Mrs. Tomlinson to tell John Means when she saw him at church that I had moved and to give him my new number.

"What about my brother Flynn?" Justine asked harshly.

"What about him?"

"You going out with this Means man after you spent all night with my brother?"

"Yes," I said, figuring this was none of her business, but adding, "Did Flynn tell you what we did all night?"

"He don't talk much to me 'bout those kind of things."

"Well, I don't either," I countered. "Will you call Mrs. Tomlinson or not?"

"All right. Give me her number."

Soon after church services, John Means called and a few hours later arrived at Mrs. Hendersen's house for our date. Because I didn't know John Means that well, and because it was the custom from my upbringing, I had insisted another couple join us. Of course, I had totally dismissed this custom when it had come to Flynn, but then Flynn was in a category by himself. There was no comparison.

I introduced John Means to Mrs. Hendersen, who was in the living room when he arrived, and she sat there chatting with him for a few minutes before she said it was time for her to retire to her room and asked me to help her there. Once we were alone, Mrs. Hendersen said, "You know I don't hardly know you, Cassie, so excuse an old lady for butting in, but I can't understand why your first gentleman caller is this Mr. Means and not that fine young man Flynn. I've seen a lot in my long life, and one thing I was feeling was something strong between you and that boy."

I liked her thinking. "You really think it was strong? On his part too?"

"Maybe because you kept looking away, you didn't see how he was looking at you. So, why are you going out with this John Means person? He seems like a nice enough young man, but he can't come close to Flynn, and I believe you know that."

I did know that, but I said to Mrs. Hendersen, "John Means asked me out. Flynn didn't."

I rejoined John Means, but throughout the evening I kept thinking on what Mrs. Hendersen had said, and about the night I had spent with Flynn. Dinner was pleasant enough; we went to a Negro café in the neighborhood and the food was good. The other couple kept the conversation going. I had little to say. John Means was very attentive and asked me several times if I was having a good time. I smiled brightly and told him I was, but my mind was on Flynn. At the movie theater John Means again asked me if I was enjoying myself and placed his arm around my shoulders as we watched the movie. I did not pull away, but I did not move toward him either, and I was glad he did not try to hold my hand.

After the movie, as the crowd spilled onto the sidewalk, John Means put his arm around me again, almost possessively this time, as we stood with a group of people he knew. Moviegoers for the later show were arriving and I was mostly silent watching them, ready to get back to Mrs. Hendersen's but waiting politely as John Means and his friends talked. Just as they finished their conversation and started to part, I saw Flynn. He was not alone. He was with a woman of very light complexion, almost white, in fact. She was tall, well-dressed, sophisticated-looking. She was a striking woman. I was totally caught off guard. I stared at them, then tried to move away before Flynn saw me. I was not successful. Flynn suddenly looked my way and our eyes met. He did not flash that smile of his, but his eyes did not turn away.

It was I who turned. "Are we going?" I said to John Means, who apparently had noticed nothing. His arm still around me, John Means smiled down and walked me away from the crowd. I do not know if Flynn's gaze followed me.

■ ■ ■ ■

I couldn't sleep. I did not know why seeing Flynn with that woman of his had upset me so. This was only the third time I had seen him. I hardly knew the man. John Means and his friends and I had gone to the early evening show. We were back at Mrs. Hendersen's before nine and I had gone to bed right after. Before ten o'clock, Florence, one of the women at the house, knocked on my door. "Cassie, there was a call for you," she said. "Mrs. Hendersen took it. She said that it was from Flynn and he wants to see you. Said he would be coming later."

"What?" I asked. "Why? What time?"

"Didn't say. Mrs. Hendersen told him he could just knock on the door. If you wanted to see him, you'd answer it."

All of this was surprising to me, and for a moment I didn't say anything. "Well," said Florence, "are you going to see him?"

"Don't know. Is Mrs. Hendersen still awake?"

"Was a few minutes ago. Usually stays

up late 'til maybe midnight."

I thought a moment. "Do you think she'd mind if I wanted to talk to her now?"

"You know what she says. Her door is always open."

I put on my housecoat and went to see Mrs. Hendersen. She welcomed me in. She was already in bed, but sitting up reading a book. "So! The young man wants to see you!" she declared as I came in. "He sounded pretty eager to talk to you, but why so late?"

"I don't know. Is it all right if I do?"

"You don't break any of my rules. You wait in the parlor for him. He knocks on the door, you open the door and sit on the porch and talk to him. That's not breaking any rule." She looked at me curiously. "You want to talk to him?"

"I do," I confessed, "but I don't know if it's the best thing. I mean, to talk to him tonight. Maybe I should wait." I hesitated then asked, "What do you think?"

"Well, I don't know if you should wait or not. I don't know what's going on between you." When I didn't say any-thing, Mrs. Hendersen patted the bed and motioned me to sit beside her. I sat down and she said, "I've known this boy Flynn for some time now and he's got a beautiful way about him. He's always in good humor, but tonight he obviously was upset. I've never heard him upset before. It wasn't the words he said, mind you, but mainly the tone of them. Now, I don't know what's between you except that powerful feeling, and it's none of my business, but if you want to tell me what this is all about, I'm here to listen."

"I saw him with another woman tonight and Flynn saw me with John Means."

Mrs. Hendersen smiled and slowly nodded. "Ahhh . . . that explains it then."

"You're smiling, but it's not funny to me. I want to see Flynn, but then again I don't."

Mrs. Hendersen studied me. "Cassie, how strong are you?"

"What do you mean?"

"I mean, how strong are you in keeping your womanhood to yourself until the time is right for you to give it away?"

I just stared at her.

"Look, child, I've been married three times. I know the ways of men and I know how a woman usually is with a man she's had relations with. If I'm right, just looking at the two of you together, I don't think you've been with him in that way. In fact, I don't think you've had relations with a man before. If you'd had relations with that boy Flynn you'd be moving different around him."

I was silent at the suggestion.

"That's all right if you don't want to say. If you're a good Christian woman, that's good. But sometimes forces more powerful than our Christian teachings can change a young woman's mind about her future. That Flynn is a powerful force. You've got to know your own mind before you meet it." She reached for my hand and held it with both of hers. "Did Flynn tell you how we came to meet?"

I shook my head and she went on.

"Well," she laughed, "it's a bit of a story. It was back before the war and I still considered myself somewhat young." She laughed again. "That was before I was in that wheelchair there. I'd already lost my husband, one who gave me this house, so I was making do for myself. I hadn't yet started opening up my house to ladies in need, but I had this friend name of Thelma lived right across the street there. Widow lady too. Thelma and me decided we weren't too old yet to do anything we wanted to do, so one day after we'd gone to the grocery store in my car, we had a flat on the way back, and there we were, two seventy-something-year-old ladies trying to change a tire!"

Mrs. Hendersen laughed heartily. "We didn't know what we were doing! Neither one of us had changed a tire before. We knew enough to get out the jack, then we tried to figure out how to attach the thing on the car. Somehow we got it set, then we had to jack up the car. Well, we couldn't get it jacked and that's when we heard this voice behind us asking if we could use some help. We both looked around and there was this tall young man standing there, this bemused smile across his face. I don't know how long he'd been standing there watching us fiddle with that jack, but I said, 'What do you think!' "

This time I laughed with Mrs. Hendersen.

"Yeah, that's just how we met. Flynn jacked up the car, changed the tire in no time flat. Thelma and me, we offered to pay him for his trouble, but he refused to take any money from us." Mrs. Hendersen paused, looked away a moment, then back at me. "I lost my only child, my son, to cancer when he was about the age Flynn is now." She let go of my hand and added softly, "Flynn's been like a son to me. I truly do love that young man. He's a good man, Cassie. You wouldn't go wrong with him."

"Do you think I'll look too anxious if I see him tonight?"

"Depends on how you handle yourself."

I thought about all Mrs. Hendersen had said, and said nothing. Mrs. Hendersen was fine with the silence and said nothing either. Finally, I decided and stood. "I want to see him. I couldn't sleep anyway. There's no point in putting it off."

Mrs. Hendersen nodded. "Good," she

said, giving me an approving smile. "Good."

Still in my robe, I sat in the parlor. It was past eleven o'clock. I read for a while, glancing at the wall clock every few minutes. All I wanted was for Flynn to be at the door. Impatiently I waited, but finally as it neared midnight I slammed down the book, turned off the room lamp, and headed for the hallway. I was furious. There was a knock on the door. I ignored it. There was another knock, then Flynn called softly, "Cassie?"

I took a deep breath, went to the door, and opened it.

"I didn't know if you would see me," Flynn said.

"I didn't know if I would either," I replied. "I talked to Mrs. Hendersen about it."

"And what did she say?"

"She said I had to be strong in my own feelings."

"And are you?"

"I'm talking to you, aren't I? What did you want to see me about? You called

315

more than two hours ago. What took you so long to get over here?"

"I had to take the person I was with home."

"And it took 'til midnight to say good night to her?"

"Cassie, would you please come onto the porch? I want to talk to you about tonight."

I pushed open the screen door and stepped out. I pulled my robe tighter and crossed my arms. "What about tonight?"

"You saw me with someone and I didn't want you to put that person between us in your mind."

"Well, you saw me with someone too. Were you concerned about him being between us in your mind?"

Flynn dismissed the suggestion with a wave of his hand, and I wasn't sure how to take that. Maybe I wanted him to be jealous, at least just a bit. I certainly was jealous. "It's not about him. It's about how you might be seeing this woman and me. We both know what Justine said to you." He moved away and leaned against the porch post.

"This woman, does she have a name?"

Flynn didn't answer my question. "Cassie, just a few short hours ago we spent the night together on my mountain. I've never taken anyone to my land before, but I wanted you to see it, to experience it with me. As soon as I saw that land, I wanted it. I felt the same about you. As soon as I saw you, I wanted you too."

I was startled into silence.

"I just wanted you to know that." He turned to go.

"Is that it?" I said.

He turned back. "For now. I just want you to keep the door open to us, Cassie."

"Why shouldn't I close it? Flynn, we've only seen each other twice before. We spent the night on a mountaintop together, but there is no 'us.' "

"Isn't there? Like I said, Cassie, keep the door open. I've got some things to work out, but once I do, I'd like to see you again."

"And you couldn't wait until morning to tell me that?"

"No. I wanted you to know tonight. I

didn't want there to be any misunderstanding between us. How I felt the other night is how I feel now. I hope the same goes for you." He stared at me in silence, said good night, then turned once again and went down the steps to the Mercedes. I watched him drive away.

CASSIE'S LOVE STORY
CHAPTER II
(1948–1949)

He had been born in Puerto Vallarta. His mother was of African descent, his father a native Indian. Soon after his birth his mother and father separated, and his father was no longer in his life. His mother had, in part, been influenced and educated by British colonialists in neighboring British Honduras, and therefore she named her children after them. There had been two other children, both boys, one older than Justine, one a few years younger. Both were now dead. A few years after Flynn was born, his mother returned to her native British Honduras and took both Flynn and Justine with her. When Flynn was eight, his mother died and Justine, who was sixteen, basically raised him. There were only the two of them left. When he was ten, Justine went to the United States, leaving him behind with a family in Mexico, the Peñas. When he was fifteen, Justine sent for him. Soon after, the Peñas migrated to the United States as well. In 1943, at age twenty, he was inducted into the United States Army even though he was not yet a citizen, but a resident alien. He served on the European front and was at the invasion of Normandy. While with the Peñas in Mexico, he had apprenticed as a carpenter, and upon his return from the war, he started working construction. He had hopes of designing buildings of his own one day and of building his own house on the mountain land. That was what I knew about him. It wasn't all that much, but for me it was enough. I didn't need to know anything else.

I already was in love with him.

The days following my midnight meeting with Flynn, Flynn did not call. He did not call the following week either or come to see me, and I got on with my life. With the help of Mrs. Hendersen, I got a job selling tickets at the Lincoln Theater. She knew the manager. It was a decent-paying job and it was a fabulous

320

one. Sometimes, too, I served as an usherette. The Lincoln Theater, one of several theaters on Central Avenue, was a Negro theater showing the most recent movies as well as showcasing live performances by some of the biggest Negro stars, like Duke Ellington and Billie Holiday and Nat King Cole. It also presented talent shows. Moorish in architectural style, the building had fascinated Flynn and he had pointed it out to me during our first walk together. I loved working there. My hours were mostly during the day, but sometimes I was called to work evenings as well, and when I was, I kept wondering if Flynn would come walking into the theater. I couldn't get him off my mind. I had been with him only three times, but thoughts of him ruled my days and my nights. I could not forget the words he had said to me. I also could not forget the woman clinging to his life, and that he was not ready to let go of her.

In some ways, I felt myself no match for this woman. I was a country girl and saw myself as that, pretty enough, I knew, but certainly no match for a woman schooled in the ways of men. I knew nothing about men in that way. As confident as I was most times, I had never slept with a man and was often unsure about my own feelings. What I was sure about was that I had strong feelings for Flynn, but despite what Flynn had said to me, I wasn't sure about his feelings for me. I wanted to see him again. I wanted to be near him again, to touch him again. I wanted him to kiss me again, hold me again. I could not let go of this feeling I had for him. In mid-March, Flynn unexpectedly reached out to me once more. He called. "You get your life straightened out yet?" I asked.

"I'd like to talk to you about that later, if you'll see me," he said. "You mentioned you like fishing. I know a great spot."

I agreed to go fishing. It was before dawn on a Saturday morning when Flynn came for me. He took me to the pier. There we climbed into a rowboat and Flynn handed me a fishing rod, already baited. "Can you swim?" he asked.

"Not very well. Used to wade a little in the Rosa Lee." His look was questioning. "Creek near our place back home," I explained. "Used to fish there too."

Flynn rowed the boat, leaving the rod in my hands. As the morning sunlight began to settle on the water, he stopped rowing. "You thought about what I said that last night we talked?"

"Is your friend still in your life?"

"Her name's Faye," he volunteered. "She's still a friend. Does that make a difference?"

"Why should it? I figure a person can have more than one friend."

He was quiet a moment, then said, "She won't be in my life forever, Cassie. She came into it when I really needed someone, right after the war. There were other women, but she was closest to me and sometimes it's hard for a person to let go."

"I have no holds on you, Flynn." I was trying to be sophisticated about his relationship with this woman, Faye. "You go out with whom you want and so do I. One thing you need to know though, I'm not sleeping with you —"

Flynn laughed. "Did I ask you to?" I looked away. No longer laughing, Flynn

323

gently ran his forefinger down the side of my face. "Doesn't matter, at least not right now."

I looked at the water, then back at him. "Is that good or bad for us?"

"You're special to me, Cassie, and it's more than your body I want."

"Well, what else do you want?"

"Give it time," Flynn said. "You'll find out."

After that, Flynn began seeing and calling me more often. That night we went to a movie and to dinner afterward. The next weekend we drove down to Tijuana for the day. The weekend following, we drove up the coast. What was left of the Los Angeles winter passed into a Los Angeles spring, hardly different from the Los Angeles winter, and then came the summer and we continued seeing each other. We took long walks along the beach. We went to his land, and we talked. We talked and talked about many things. We also spent a lot of time on Central Avenue. There was always something going on there. Not only did we spend some of our weekend nights at the jazz clubs, we looked for bargains at the record shops, went to the restaurants and, of course, to the theaters. We were even on the Avenue when Joe Louis, the Brown Bomber, fought Jersey Joe Walcott.

It was tradition on Central Avenue that whenever Joe Louis, heavyweight champion of the world, was in a fighting match, the hectic bustle of the street ended and Central Avenue was mostly deserted. Everyone who ordinarily would have been on the street was somewhere huddled near a radio, listening to the fight. This had been going on since 1937, when Joe Louis knocked out James J. Braddock, the world heavyweight champion. James Braddock was white. Joe Louis knocked him out in the eighth round. Mrs. Hendersen talked about how the street had erupted. Everyone had pretty much gone crazy. After the fight, people burst onto Central Avenue yelling and screaming, riding in cars, honking and leaning out windows and shouting in celebration. Down home, we had had the same feeling. Papa, the boys, and I had gathered around the radio for that fight and all the Joe Louis fights after that when we were home. Most of black America had done the same, for when Joe Louis fought, it was a time for joy. He had defended the title numerous times and had kept it. In a country where we as a people were belittled, not recognized for all we had contributed to building it, a country that still denied us equal rights, Joe Louis's victories were our victories. The days that Joe Louis fought were days to be black and proud in America. The fight Flynn and I celebrated together was different from the many previous fights, for Joe Louis was fighting another Negro boxer. But Joe Louis won. He remained our champion, our hero.

He kept us proud.

Flynn began to open up to me about his life. He told me about his life in Puerto Vallarta and British Honduras. He told me about his life with Miguel and Maria Peña. He told me about poverty. He said I knew nothing of what real poverty was like. In my life my family always had food on the table. I had never gone hungry. I always had people to call family. That was not the case for him. After his mother took him and Justine to British Honduras where she had found work, his little family had to survive on their own. He told me about his brothers, both killed by police in Mexico. He told me about the harsh conditions of their lives, how they struggled to make ends meet, how he had worked, how Justine had worked, how his mother had worked. He told me how he had once swum the crocodile-infested waters in an effort to reach his mother and sister after a fire had consumed the land. The hard life they lived, in the end, had killed his mother. That is when Justine took over. For a while there were only the two of them, and they totally depended on each other. Then Justine made the decision to come to the States and send him back to Mexico to live with the Peñas.

Flynn did not speak again of Faye. I wanted to ask him about her, but I thought I shouldn't. I knew he was still seeing her, and probably sleeping with her. He was not sleeping with me, and he made no overtures to do so. That bothered me even though teachings throughout my life forbade me from having sexual relations until I was married. To do so was not only considered a sin, but would have brought disgrace upon the family if it were known. There were weekends when I did not see Flynn and he did not call, and that bothered me even more. I had no real hold on him. We had made no commitments to each other, but I was jealous. I tried not to show it.

In the fall I decided to take a law course at UCLA. The course wasn't toward a degree, just for my own learning, and I relished being on a college campus again. The class invigorated me. After each class I shared what I had learned with Flynn and he was always attentive, asking questions, and he delighted in my enthusiasm. The class was once a week on Friday afternoon, and although I took the bus to the university campus, Flynn came for me after class.

He waited for me outside the class building or, if for some reason he ran late, I would meet him on the walk to his car, which he always parked on the same campus street. I never worried about my safety on campus. After all, this was a university, a place of higher learning and highly educated people, where ethics were taught and moral values were supposed to be intact. One evening in early January after an oral exam I emerged from class and Flynn was not outside the building. It was already dark. I waited for a few minutes, then walked the well-lit pathway toward the street. My mind was on Flynn, on seeing him and telling him about the exam. I paid no attention to the man walking toward me. As I neared the man, he stopped and blocked my path. "You need somebody to walk you home? I could do that."

Startled, I looked directly at the man and did not panic. He was a white man, looked to be in his late thirties, early forties. I had been propositioned before and knew how to respond. "No thanks," I said. "I can see myself home."

"Well, really, I don't mind —"

"Well, I do. I have someone coming for me."

"Oh, really?" said the man, moving

closer. "And just who would that be?"

"That would be me."

I looked past the man and smiled. It was Flynn.

The man turned, and now it was he who was startled. " 'Ey," he said, backing away. "I was just trying to be of help."

"Yeah, I know what you were trying to do," said Flynn.

The man glanced at me, then hurried toward the street and into the night. "My hero," I teased.

"Am I?"

"Well, you always seem to be there when I need you."

A scowl shadowed Flynn's face as he looked after the man. "I should have laid him out."

"He didn't touch me, Flynn. I'm okay." I hooked my arm into his. "Come on and let's do something fun," I coaxed, trying to get him to forget about the man. "I'm feeling so good about my exam, I'm not going to let anything spoil it. I got an "A"! Come on, let's go celebrate! Let's do something special!"

The scowl still on Flynn's face, we walked to the car. I wasn't yet ready to go home. Since we were already in Westwood, close to the wealthy neighborhoods of Beverly Hills and Bel-Air, I suggested we drive through the area and look at the beautiful houses. I wanted to celebrate my "A" and dream of what might be. I also wanted to lighten Flynn's mood and get his mind off the would-be masher. Flynn hesitated at the suggestion and said that might not be a good idea, but I wanted to see the glittering lights of the massive mansions, the places of dreams of the very rich, and he gave in to me. But Flynn was right. It wasn't a good idea.

As soon as we had made our tour of several of the residential streets and turned back onto the main street of Wilshire Boulevard, a police siren blasted behind us. Lights flashing, the police car tailed us until Flynn pulled over and stopped. The police car stopped right behind us and two policemen got out. The headlights, still on, shone through the Mercedes, almost blinding us. One of the policemen stopped at the rear of Flynn's car, looked at the license plate, and took out a pad. The other came to the driver's side of the car. Flynn rolled down his window. The policeman took a moment studying the two of us, and I had no doubt he had realized we were colored before he stopped us. "You're kind of out of your neighborhood, aren't you?" he said to Flynn. "Let's see your license." Flynn pulled his wallet from his jacket and handed the license to the officer. The officer checked it under the boulevard lights. "Registration," he said. Flynn handed him that too. The officer looked at it, then again at Flynn. "This is a mighty fine car you're driving. Foreign, isn't it? Step on out."

"Why?" I asked. "What did he do?"

The officer ignored me. Flynn got out without a word and the officer said, "Hands up against the car." Flynn, as if he had been through all this before, placed his hands against the roof of the car. The officer patted him down.

I was furious. I jumped out of the car. "What are you doing? He didn't do anything!"

"You, girl," said the officer at the back of the car, "you best shut your mouth."

"But he didn't do anything!" I continued to protest. I figured I should be able to speak my mind here in Los Angeles.

"Cassie," said Flynn, "Cassie, be quiet." His voice was calm, but I felt anything but calm.

"Turn around," the officer next to Flynn ordered. "Step away from the car." The other officer at the rear came forward and stood directly behind Flynn. The officer who had checked the license and registration now began to check inside the car. The first place he checked was under the driver's seat.

A gun was beneath the seat.

"All right, cuff him," he said to his partner as he took the gun from the car.

"I've got registration for that too," said Flynn.

"We'll check it at the station."

"I've got it with me."

"We'll check it at the station," the officer repeated. "We'll check the car registration too. Foreign car, could be stolen.

Meantime, the car stays here until we do." The officer pulled the keys from the car as the other officer pulled out his handcuffs and ordered Flynn to put his arms behind him.

I stared in disbelief. This was not Mississippi. This was Los Angeles. Maybe I had been studying the law a little too much, but I pressed them with my frantic questions. "What's he done? What are you charging him with? You need to let him go!"

The officer holding Flynn glanced over at me and said, "Gal, you know, we can take you in too."

Flynn interceded. "Look, she's done nothing! She has nothing to do with this!"

As the policeman clasped handcuffs on Flynn, my blood ran hot and I ran around the car toward Flynn. The officers saw me coming, and the one with Flynn's gun grabbed me and shoved me hard back against the car. At that, Flynn, already handcuffed, wrenched away from the other officer and lurched toward the one holding me. "Get your hands off her!"

The officer holding me turned. "What

you say?"

And the other officer countered, "Nigger, you resisting arrest?" Flynn was given no time to reply. The officer, holding my arm with one hand, lifted the other holding the gun and slammed the side of Flynn's head with the butt of the gun. The other officer, with his hand on the back of Flynn's neck, slammed Flynn's face against the top of the car, jerked his head back, and slammed his head down again.

I stood frozen, horrified.

The one officer pulled Flynn away from the car. Blood was dripping from Flynn's scalp and running down the side of his mouth. His eyes looked dazed as he stared at me. The policeman yanked Flynn toward the police car.

"Flynn!" I cried out, not knowing what to do.

Flynn managed to speak, his voice low, sounding gargled. "Drugstore few blocks down. Call Justine, come get you."

The policeman holding me let me go. Then the two officers pushed Flynn into the back seat of their car. The door slammed and the police car sped away.

I was left alone on the streets of Los Angeles.

CASSIE'S LOVE STORY
CHAPTER III
(1949)

I did as Flynn had instructed. I walked as fast as I could toward the drugstore. I wanted to run, but I didn't want to draw any more attention to myself from passing motorists than I already was doing. After all, I was colored in a white neighborhood. I walked one block, then two. They were long blocks, and I saw no sign of a corner store up ahead. Well into the third block, a car filled with white teenage boys slowed on the other side of the street, then made a U-turn and pulled slowly alongside me. I did not turn to look at them.

"Hey, girlie!" one of them shouted. "Need a lift?"

"We'll take you wherever you want to go," yelled another.

I kept on walking. The car kept pace

with me.

"Yeah, and, hey, we'll give you whatever you need too!"

There was laughter from the car. "Say, maybe what we need to be asking is how much you want for the four of us?"

I wanted to run. I knew I shouldn't run, show my fear. I thought of the white boys on the Mississippi road down home who had followed me years ago. I wanted to cry out, but was afraid to do that too. I wanted to turn and scream into their faces and tell them where they could go, but I knew I shouldn't stop or acknowledge their insults. My face burned hot, but I kept on walking. They continued to follow, laughing and hurling their obscene remarks. I reached the end of the block and was fearful they might turn and cut me off as I crossed the street. They didn't.

In the fourth block now, I searched for lights on the next corner, for any indication that there was a store. Still, I saw nothing, only houses with long rolling lawns set back some distance from the street. I thought about running up to one of them, but what good would that do?

They were all houses occupied by white people.

The car stopped. I guessed the boys were tired of their game of cat and mouse and I feared they were now about to take a different action. As the front passenger door opened, I was about to break into a run when I saw an elderly man and woman emerging from a driveway, walking their dog. I hurried toward them, speaking before I even reached them. "Excuse me. Excuse me, please! Can you tell me where there's a pay phone near here? I understand there's supposed to be a drugstore nearby."

The couple stared at me, I'm sure knowing as well as I that I was out of place here in this Westwood neighborhood. "Do you work near here?" the woman cautiously asked.

"No," I answered, quickly glancing back toward the carload of boys. "My car had trouble and I had to leave it a few blocks down. I need to call someone to pick me up."

The couple's gaze followed my glance. "Well, we're going down that way," the man said, his eyes on the car. "About a block and a half. You can walk along with us."

"Thank you," I said. "Thank you."

The car with its load of boys took off.

At the drugstore I called Justine, and within thirty minutes she and J.D. arrived to get me. The elderly couple stayed at the drugstore while I waited. They sat sipping sodas at the ice cream fountain, and even offered me one. I declined their offer but thanked them profusely for their help. Although I had not spoken of the car following me and they hadn't mentioned it either, I knew that they stayed at the drugstore because of me. I didn't know their names. They didn't give them, and I didn't give mine to them, but I knew on that night, when I was alone in a white world, they had been my guardian angels. I knew now that angels came in all colors.

When Justine arrived she told me that she would go to the police station to see about Flynn, but she figured nothing could be done until Monday morning. I wanted to go with her, but she adamantly said that she was taking me back to Mrs.

Hendersen's. She told me not to worry about Flynn. She would get him out. "You don't know 'bout these things," she said. "You been a protected girl. I'll handle it."

Flynn was in jail for three days.

On Monday evening Flynn arrived at Mrs. Hendersen's. I went right into his arms. His face was terribly bruised and swollen, his lip was cut, and he looked tired, but his first thoughts were of me. "Are you all right, Cassie? Justine told me what you went through."

"I didn't go through anything, not really, nothing like you." I pulled away to look at him again. I gently touched his face. "How are you?"

He enfolded my hand in his. "I'm all right, Cassie. I've been through it before," he said, dismissing the beating he had taken. "But I was worried about you. I should have been there for you. Those boys —"

"I'm all right too. They never even got close to me."

Flynn pulled me back to him. "That's all that matters," he whispered.

341

I asked him about the arrest, about the charges, about his car. He said the police had charged him with resisting arrest. He said he would have to go to court and, like Justine, he said he was taking care of it. He told me not to worry about any of it.

"But I do worry. Your face . . ."

"It'll heal. What I need now is sleep."

"Then you need to go home and sleep."

Flynn cupped my face in his hands and stared into my eyes. "Not without you. We can sleep at Justine's. She says she'll clear out a room for us. She's sending the children over to a friend for the night. Sleep, that's all I mean. Tonight, that's all I need and want . . . and for you to be with me. I don't want to be without you tonight."

"Why Justine's? What about your place?

"It's better for us to be at Justine's."

I was silent.

"Tomorrow, I'll bring you back here before I go to work."

"Flynn —"

"I've hardly slept in three days, Cassie." He held my face. "Will you come with me, Cassie? Everything else, we can talk about tomorrow."

I pulled from his arms and went and told Mrs. Hendersen I would not be spending the night at her house. "He's out there, isn't he? Then you do what your heart — and God — tells you. But you put God first. He won't guide you wrong."

Flynn fell asleep minutes after we lay down. We were fully clothed, not even under the covers except for a blanket that Flynn had thrown over us. For some time after he fell asleep, I studied the outline of his face, shadowed from the moonlight shining in. I studied him and pondered our future. I lay against his chest and wondered if this was what marriage would be like. I felt such warmth and comfort lying next to him. With him, I felt protected and secure. Finally, I too fell asleep and rolled over on my side, but when I did, Flynn stirred and, without a word, pulled me back to him. We both fell back into sleep. We were jolted awake when a voice screeched into the night. "What's that?" I said.

Flynn didn't answer as we heard Justine's voice loudly saying, "Get outta my house! That fool J.D. had no right to let you in!"

And then the voice that had woken us, the voice of a woman screaming, cried out, "I want to see him! I know he's here! His car's out front!"

Suddenly Flynn was out of bed.

"Flynn —" I started.

"Stay here, Cassie," he ordered, but I too got out of bed and followed him to the door. He turned before opening it and looked at me. "Do what I say, please."

Flynn opened the door and closed it behind him. A moment later I heard the woman's voice again. "I knew it! I knew you were here!"

At that, I cracked the door open. The hallway leading to the living room was dark, and only a small lamp was lit there, but I could see Flynn standing beside Justine. I couldn't see the woman.

"See there! You gone and woke him up!" admonished Justine. Then, in a softer voice, she said, "You didn't have to get up, Flynn. I can take care of this. That fool J.D. let this crazy woman in here!" J.D. sat on the sofa, his head lowered, looking chagrined.

"I knew you were here!" the woman cried. "I went to your apartment. Why didn't you come home?"

Justine turned on the woman. "Why don't you just shut up and get outta my house?"

Flynn touched Justine's arm. "It's all right, Justine," he said quietly.

"It's not all right!" exhorted Justine. "You need your sleep!"

"I needed to see you, baby!" the woman exclaimed. "I need you to come home!"

"And we need sleep!" Justine retorted. "You got any idea what time it is?"

"Look, Justine," Flynn said, "you and J.D. go on back to bed. Faye and I'll go outside."

"Not going back to bed 'til that crazy woman's out of my house and you're back there getting yourself some sleep!"

Flynn said nothing else to Justine, but

passed by her and away from where I could see him. I heard the door open, then close. After that, there was only silence as Justine plopped down on the sofa beside the forlorn J.D. For a few minutes I waited quietly beside the cracked door, then finally closed the door and sat down on the side of the bed. I sat there for some time. I glanced at the clock. It was ten past two. I watched the hand on the clock slowly turn as I waited out the minutes for Flynn to return. I wanted to turn on the light, but was afraid that somehow the light would be seen outside, that maybe that woman would see it. I left the light off. At two thirty-six, I got up and sat in the chair beside the bed. At two fifty-six, I heard muffled voices down the hall, then a few minutes later the door to the bedroom opened and Flynn came in.

"Cassie," he said softly.

"I'm here."

Flynn came over to the chair and touched my face with the back of his hand and sat on the bed in front of me. "That was Faye," he said as he turned on the lamp beside the bed.

"I gathered that. Is she why you didn't want to go to your apartment?"

He nodded. "I told her it was over between us, but she's not willing to accept that. She keeps coming by there, calling my friends. One of them told her I was in jail and she wanted to bail me out."

"Did she?"

"No. That was Justine." He sighed. "Look, Cassie, while I was in jail those three days I did a lot of thinking about my life, about us. I've been trying to get things straightened out concerning Faye before I made a commitment to you, but I'm thinking now I've gone about this all wrong." He took both my hands into his. "Cassie, I want us to be married."

I had not expected this, not tonight. I said nothing.

"I've never thought about a woman the way I think about you." He bowed his head and was silent before he looked at me again. "You remember I told you it's more than your body I want and you asked what else I wanted? It's a family I want with you, Cassie. I want us to have children together. You're the only woman

I've ever envisioned being the mother of my children. That's what I wanted. That's what I want. I love you, Cassie."

My voice was barely a whisper. "I love you too, Flynn."

Flynn leaned closer to me. "I want us to get married right now, before the week's out. I don't want to wait."

I pulled from him. *"What?"*

"I don't want you to slip away from me or anything to come between us."

"I'm not going to slip away, Flynn, and what could come between us? Faye?"

"Not if we don't let her. Cassie, a lot of things in my life have slipped away. My brothers in a heartbeat, and being in that war, I learned that we can't count any days beyond the day we're living. In a heartbeat I could have been killed. Getting beaten by the police, being in that jail away from you, not knowing what was happening to you made me do a lot of thinking. I want you now. I don't want to wait. Why should we? I love you and you love me. There's no reason to wait. I want to begin my life with you." His eyes fixed on mine. "Marry me now, Cassie."

"Not without my family!"

He held my hands again. "Cassie, I know it won't be the kind of wedding you want, but I promise I'll work to give you everything else you want. I want to take care of you, to be there for you, to do the best to give you whatever I can. You can trust me on that. You can always trust me."

What Flynn was asking was almost too much to take in at past three o'clock in the morning. A wedding without Mama and Papa, without Big Ma, without my brothers. How could I do that? Flynn was silent, awaiting my answer. His face was so swollen and bruised, and all I could see as I looked at him was how much he was wanting me, and feeling how much I was wanting him. Flynn's hands grew tighter around mine. Uncontrollably, I leaned toward him, knowing that if Flynn were to become my husband he would be all I would ever need. I was in love with this man, and he was what I wanted. I put my arms around his neck, touched my forehead to his, and whispered, "Yes, Flynn, I know I can."

We were married the following Sunday.

CASSIE'S LOVE STORY
CHAPTER IV
(1949–1950)

All my life I had been wrapped in love. I had been blessed with love from my family, from the church, from friends, from others too. Now Flynn wrapped me in love. But this was a new kind of love, a different kind of love, all-consuming and all-giving. It was the kind of love that made me smile just thinking about it. It gave me peace, made me feel safe. It made me want to wake in the mornings and look forward to the nights. It was the kind of love that angered me when others encroached upon it. It possessively wrapped its arms around me and made me fear losing it. It was the kind of love I had dreamed would be mine, but each dawn when I awoke, I was still in wonder that it was.

Flynn had moved from his apartment and we had gotten another apartment in

Los Angeles. It was small, one bedroom, but together we painted it with warm, vibrant colors and made it comfortable. The kitchen and living room were in one room. Also in the room and taking up a great portion of it was a large architect table Flynn had recently bought. I didn't like its being there, but I kept my silence about it. We hung native rugs bought during our trips to Mexico and Arizona on the walls, and I dotted the apartment with greenery. We both loved music, especially jazz. Flynn already had a collection of records and they lined the floor next to his record player. Each evening after work we sat on the sofa, usually in each other's arms, reading or talking, but always listening to the music.

Ours was a sweet life.

Weekdays were pleasant, quiet, and routine. Flynn continued working construction, but I was no longer working as a ticket taker at the Lincoln Theater since more and more I had been asked to work evening hours. Instead, I was working at a weekly Negro community newspaper. It too was on Central Avenue. My job was secretarial and proofreading copy from local contributors. It was low-paying and dull, but it was fine for now. One evening a week, Flynn and I both took noncredit courses at UCLA, Flynn in architecture, and I in law. The weekends were quite different. Sometimes we went to the neighborhood café that had good southern cooking, other times we went to more fashionable restaurants, but my favorite place to dine was at the Peña café. We didn't go there often because the Peñas would not allow us to pay. We began to visit them at their home instead.

After dinner we would either go to a movie or take in a live performance at the Lincoln or a jazz club where we joined Justine and J.D. or others Flynn knew. Flynn didn't much like to dance. He refused to be out there "bouncing around," as he said. But I loved the dancing and so did most of Flynn's friends, so I was never without a dance partner and Flynn didn't object. He sat back and watched me as I danced, a smile on his face. He just wanted me to be happy. He was always proud of me and he liked showing me off. Occasionally I could get him up for a slow dance and he would tease me. "Can't understand it. A Baptist country girl like you loving to dance."

"Baptist country girl like me never got a chance to dance in the country," I replied.

"A lot of things a Baptist country girl didn't get to do."

"I know . . ." I smiled up at him. "But I get to do them now." And he laughed.

Saturday mornings were the best mornings of the week. We slept late, but by midmorning we were up and Flynn took off for the neighborhood basketball court in the park. Sometimes I went with him to watch him play with other young men of the neighborhood or throw a few baskets myself before the game started. Later in the day, we either headed up the coast, enjoying the small towns dotting the road leading to San Francisco, or down the coast to Tijuana, sometimes east to Arizona, or to Flynn's mountain acreage, and sometimes to parts unknown. Flynn liked just to get in the car and drive, and I looked forward to that too. If we came across a place we liked, we explored it and spent the night either in the car out in the open or, if we could afford it, sometimes even at a motor court. We went to fairs and to ball games and to amusement parks and sometimes to pool halls, where Flynn taught me how to play pool.

It was all very exciting to me. I had never felt more free. I was truly a woman now. On Sunday mornings if we were in the city, I went to church. I couldn't get Flynn to go with me. It wasn't that he had never been religious. He had once been a Catholic, but now did not believe in organized religion. On those Sunday mornings I left him at the apartment and took the car. When I returned, he was usually gone, but was back by midday and ready for Sunday dinner at Justine's or at the Peñas'. Sunday evenings we returned home early to ready ourselves for the next week. This was our life as the new decade began in 1950.

In the short days before Flynn and I married, I had written Mama, Papa, and Big Ma and told them about Flynn. I told them that by the time they received the letter I would be married to Flynn. I couldn't call to tell them since they had no telephone, but I did call my cousin Oliver in Jackson and asked him to go to the house on Saturday, so Mama, Papa, and Big Ma would know about the wedding before I married. I also called Toledo. None of my brothers were happy with me. "Why so soon?" Stacey asked. "Can't you wait?"

"Don't worry," I said, knowing what he was asking. "I'm not in trouble."

"Well, then, why are you rushing this? You know Mama and Papa always expected you to get married at home, at Great Faith."

I didn't tell Stacey that the rush toward marriage, despite my first objection to the idea, was now all very exciting to me, for within the week I would be Flynn's wife. Instead, I said, "You didn't get married there. Or at Dee's church either."

"Well, that was different."

"How come?"

"It was wartime," he attested. "I thought I'd have to go to war."

"Well, anyway, you were in love and you got married. Well, I'm in love, so we're getting married because Flynn doesn't want to wait and I don't either. Besides, we can't afford to take off work and make that long trip across country to get married down home. There's no reason to wait. Just be happy for me."

"Can't you just wait long enough for Uncle Hammer and Aunt Loretta to get down there? Have some family there with you."

"I've already called them. They'll be here on Saturday. Uncle Hammer's going to walk me down the aisle and give me away. It'll be a church wedding right after services on Sunday. Aunt Loretta says she has got the perfect dress for me. It'll be floor-length and white."

"Well, at least that's all good." There was quiet on the line, then Stacey said, "You know Moe won't be happy to hear this."

I already knew how Moe would feel and it had weighed heavily on my mind. "Well, I'm sorry about that, Stacey, but I always told Moe he wasn't the one."

I heard Stacey sigh. "You sure you love this man?"

"I'm sure."

"You sure he loves you?"

"I'm sure about that too."

"Then, Cassie," said my brother, "be happy."

I wrote Moe. It wasn't an easy letter to write. Moe did not write back.

After the wedding, when I got the letter from Mama, she said basically the same as Stacey had, and added that they were hurt and disappointed that I had not married there. They had hoped I would marry someone from down home, someone they knew, but they trusted I had good sense about the kind of man I chose. They all wished me happiness and hoped that I would bring Flynn to meet them soon. As always, their letter ended with their love for me. I wrote them back and told them not to worry about me. I told them I was happy. And I was.

The only worry I had during the first days of our marriage was the resisting arrest charge against Flynn. But when Flynn appeared in court with a lawyer and told the circumstances of the arrest and that he had never touched either of the officers, the judge accepted his statement and the charge was dropped. Since then, nothing else had marred our happiness. I was, in fact, gloriously happy. Still, I wanted more. I wanted a place to stretch out, a place bigger than the tiny space of our cramped apartment. I knew it would take a few years to save for a down payment on a house, but I figured we could afford a bigger space than what we had, a place I could make more homelike. I began to look in the classifieds and one day saw an ad describing an apartment I thought we should see. It seemed perfect, both in pricing and in space. I called the number listed and the apartment manager gave more details about it. I was really excited, but when I told Flynn about it, he looked at the paper and shook his head. "We won't get it, Cassie."

"Why not? We can afford it."

"You know where this street is? Westwood."

Westwood was certainly not our neighborhood. Memories of police and the carload of white boys flooded my mind. I looked again at the ad. "It sounds really nice though, and the lady was friendly."

"The lady was friendly . . ." Flynn repeated, "and the lady probably did not realize she was speaking to a black woman. She probably thought you were white. Keep looking, Cassie. We'll find another place."

I stared at the paper. "I want to see this one," I stubbornly insisted. "Woman won't rent it to us, she can just say it to our face."

"It's a waste of time."

"Well, it's our time to waste."

Flynn was right, of course. When the woman opened the door to us, her face changed from pleasant to startled. "I'm afraid you've made a trip for nothing. The apartment's been rented," she said.

"You told me earlier there was no chance of your renting it before we had a chance to see it," I said.

"Well, I was wrong," countered the woman. "Good luck finding a place in your own neighborhood." She shut the door.

I started to knock again, but Flynn stopped me. "Let it be, Cassie."

"I want her to know we know that

apartment's not rented and why she's not renting to us."

"I'm sure she already knows we know. There's nothing that says she has to rent to us."

"Well, there ought to be."

I shouldn't have gotten so upset about not getting the apartment, but I did. Flynn tried to calm me down and promised he would give me a house of my own. "I'll build you a house on the land one day," he said. "But before then, you'll have a house." Soon after he made that promise he began working weekends. He told me that he had gotten a job remodeling a house with a friend in San Bernardino, more than sixty miles away. In order to start working at eight on Saturday morning, he left immediately after work at the construction site on Friday evening and made the drive to San Bernardino, where he spent the night sleeping in his car. He worked full days both Saturday and Sunday but did not drive back on Sunday evening. He said he was too tired to make the drive. Instead, he spent the night in San Bernardino and drove directly to work early Monday morning. It was lonely without him over the days and nights we were apart, but I knew that what he was doing was in the best interest for our future. Flynn said it was for only a few months and we were young and could endure that. He was right. The time we did have together became more precious. Surprisingly to me, the fact that Flynn and I were apart made me feel truly married, maybe for the first time.

I shared this with Justine. Although Justine and I were still not close as friends, we both loved Flynn and that made us family. "He feels the same," Justine said. "He loves you, you know. Never seen my baby brother like this before. You're his wife and he takes that seriously, no matter what. Always remember that."

She was in front of me before I knew it. As I stepped from the newspaper office I saw the woman crossing the street from her car and I knew she was headed for me. She didn't introduce herself. She didn't need to. It was Faye. She got right to what was on her mind. "You think you know where Flynn's been all these weekends, don't you, Mrs. De Baca? Well, Mrs. De Baca, I'm here to tell you what you think you have, you don't have. Flynn isn't yours, never has been and never will be. You think he's been working in San Bernardino all these weekends. Well, he hasn't. He's been with me all these six weekends you thought he was working. What I'm telling you, Mrs. De Baca, is that Flynn's been lying to you so he could be with me. He'll always be with me, always want to be with me, and if you stay with him, he'll always lie to you about it. He belongs to me, Mrs. De Baca, and he always will."

Then the woman turned and crossed back to her car. I hadn't said one word. I was stunned into silence. This woman, Faye, had come into my perfect day, into my perfect world, into my perfect love, into my perfect marriage, and socked me right in the gut. I stood silently on the sidewalk and stared after her as she drove away.

■ ■ ■ ■

When Flynn came home, he encircled me in his arms as he always did and tried to pull me to him. I pushed him away. "What is it?" he asked.

"Your lady friend came to see me today. She stopped me right outside of work."

Flynn's lips parted slightly, but he did not speak. He sat down on the sofa. I sat in the chair beside the sofa and tried to keep my voice calm. "She told me you haven't been working in San Bernardino. She told me you were spending the weekends with her."

"And you believed that?"

"I believed you were working. Were you working?"

"I was working, Cassie."

"Then you weren't with Faye? Why did she say you were?"

"Because she's Faye. The woman's unstable, Cassie."

"She knew exactly how many weekends you'd been away and where you were supposedly working. How would she know that unless you told her or unless she was with you there? Was she there?"

"She was there, Cassie. I saw her unexpectedly."

"And you didn't bother to tell me?" I had always been jealous of Faye, and now that jealousy was red-hot. It was an insanity. Yet I kept my voice steady. "You were spending weekends with Faye, then coming back to me?"

Flynn spoke, his voice as calm as always. "Cassie, I didn't tell you because I was afraid you'd react like this."

"Did you sleep with her?" Flynn just looked at me. "Well?"

"I'm not even going to answer that. Faye did come to San Bernardino. Twice. But it wasn't like what you think. It was all about the car."

"What about the car?" Flynn did not answer. "Flynn," I repeated. "What about the car?"

"She wants it. Faye co-signed the note on the car when I bought it. I missed one payment and she paid it. Now she's using that payment to claim it."

"You mean to tell me all this time I've

been riding around in a car you were able to buy because of her? Why didn't you tell me this before?"

"Cassie, the car belongs to me. I repaid Faye for the payment I missed, but now she's just being vindictive and she wants me to sign the car over to her."

"Then give it to her! I don't want to be riding around in a car she has claim to!"

Flynn's eyes went cold. "That's not going to happen. The car is mine."

"Then I guess that car's more important than I am."

"Now you're just talking foolish, Cassie. You know that's not true."

"Then get rid of the car!"

"I already said no to that."

I rose and went into the bedroom. Flynn did not follow me. I slept alone. The next day things between us were no better. Flynn hadn't told me about Faye's involvement with the car or about her trips to San Bernardino. As far as I was concerned, he had broken the trust between us. I figured as long as he kept the car, Faye would have a hold on him. But Flynn refused to give up the Mercedes. He said it was his. He had paid for it and he was going to keep it. Flynn was stubborn and so was I. I refused to ride in the car. Flynn refused to give it up. It remained a point of contention between us.

During the next weeks we argued constantly about the Mercedes. We also argued about the fact that Flynn continued to go to San Bernardino each weekend. He said he had a contract and he was going to honor it. I continued to sleep in the bedroom; Flynn continued to sleep on the sofa. Finally, I grew tired of the arguing. I told Flynn I was going home. It had been almost three years since I had seen my brothers, Mama, Papa, and Big Ma, and maybe now was the time for me to go. Flynn didn't try to get me to stay. I bought a one-way ticket to Toledo. There was no warmth between us as I left. Justine drove me to the train station.

CASSIE'S LOVE STORY
CHAPTER V
(1950)

The Dorr Street house was full, and I added to it. Rachel was there, tending to Becka, who had recently given birth. Becka had been ill throughout the pregnancy and was still ailing. Rachel had come to help take care of her and the baby; she was sleeping in the upstairs sun parlor. Three of the Davises, Dee's younger brother Zell and two of her cousins, also had come up from Mississippi. Zell slept on the Sunday room plastic-covered sofa, the two cousins on a cot on the dining room floor, where there was just enough room between the wall and the dining room table and chairs to squeeze in a mattress. Man slept on the sofa bed in the living room. As I had done before, I slept with Rie and 'lois in their bedroom.

There were now four single young men

sharing the space downstairs along with Dee and Stacey and the girls. They all also shared the one bathroom. It seemed amazing to me that Dee could keep the house in such order, but she did. The house was always clean and everything in place. Dee saw to that. She had set up housekeeping rules for everybody and they followed them. When all the young men got up, they rolled up the cot, reset the sofa bed, and put away all the bedding. "I might have to work like a mule to get things done," she said, "but I told all of them, they have to work with me or they better find themselves another place to live."

Dee seemed always to be working. With my being back, she decided to clean the wallpaper in the living room, dining room, and Sunday room, a chore she had not tackled since I was last there. Rachel came downstairs to help. With wallpaper cleansing putty, the three of us scrubbed the walls from ceiling to floor, removing the dirt until the wallpaper looked like new again. Dee washed all the curtains in those three rooms as well and had Stacey and Man set up the curtain rack, an eight-feet-long, six-feet-high adjustable frame for drying curtains, which were attached to straight pins embedded all along the frame. The walls and the curtains took several days, but after the walls were cleaned and the newly washed curtains rehung, the floors mopped and waxed, Dee nodded with satisfaction.

"I just don't know how you do it," I told her as I helped hang the wash on lines strung between the house and the ivy-covered garage. "Do all this work and take care of all these people."

Dee laughed. "I'm used to hard work."

"Yeah, I know, but with four single men in the house?"

"Just made it clear to them," Dee said. "There's some things I'll do for them, but other things they have to do for themselves. I've got one husband I'm taking care of, and my girls. I'm not their wife, and I'm not their mother. They need to take care of themselves and help me keep this house clean. I can't stand a filthy house." I laughed; Dee didn't. "I wasn't kidding with them! I've got two little girls to take care of and I'm teaching them how to take care of themselves, so I'm certainly not going to be cleaning up behind a bunch of grown men."

"I admire you," I said. Together we pulled a sheet from the washtub and folded it to pin on the line. It was a sunshine day and there was a soft wind that blew the fresh wet sheet back against us. As I pushed the sheet away and pinned it, without looking at Dee, I said, "Dee, I think I'm pregnant."

Dee, clothespins in her hand, turned toward me. "Really, Cassie? Have you seen a doctor?"

"Did you ever see one when you thought you were?"

"No, never. You want to see one?"

"No. I've pretty much had it with doctors."

"You tell Flynn you thought you were pregnant?"

I finished with the sheet and stared out at all Dee's bright multicolored petunias growing in large flower beds around the house, the garage, and along the fences. "No." I told Dee about Faye and how things were when I had left Flynn.

"You know you have to tell him."

I was silent.

"You know you do. It's not like you don't love him."

"No. It's not like I don't love him."

"You think he's been unfaithful?"

"I just don't know, Dee. He wouldn't say."

Dee finished pinning a pillowcase on the line and turned to me. "From what you've told me about Flynn, you've got a good man, a really good man. Whatever's between you, you need to go back and work it out. Don't throw it away, Cassie. Like they say, a good man is hard to find. Not only that, I've seen a picture of this man and, believe me, he's not hard on the eyes!"

We both laughed, and I felt my heart race at the very thought of Flynn.

When I returned so unexpectedly to Toledo, my brothers and Dee had pretty much guessed there was trouble between Flynn and me. Dee even asked me outright if Flynn had done something to make me leave and Stacey had said, "Dee, it's not our business." It wasn't their business, but I had to tell them something. What I told them was the truth. Flynn and I had had a disagreement. But that was all. Now I had told Dee the full story, but not my brothers. Whether they accepted my explanation or not, they had not questioned me further.

Now, as I sorted out my feelings about Flynn, I settled back into life on Dorr Street. Clayton Chester had a new white Buick convertible, and I teased him about it. "I suppose being so near to getting your engineering degree and working too, you had to splurge on something. Oh, yes, I heard about you riding all around town with your hair blowing in the wind. Dee wrote me. Heard about all these pretty young ladies riding around with you too. I suppose you wouldn't want to be taking your big sister for a ride."

Little Man smiled at my teasing. "I'll do you one better, Cassie." He dug into his pocket, pulled out his keys, and tossed them to me. "Anytime you want to take it out, you got it."

I took him up on that. It was fun driving the Buick, top down, when I wanted to get away from the house and be by myself. Sometimes I took 'lois and Rie with me. Sometimes Rachel went with me too. We always had fun together. I noticed that Rachel also went riding with Man, and Rie and 'lois tagged along with them as well, like little chaperones. But both Clayton Chester and Rachel firmly insisted that they were only friends, just as they had been since childhood. We took them at their word, though we speculated that Rachel would be a perfect fit to the family.

Although I was missing Flynn, I was enjoying my life in Toledo, enjoying the busy days and the family-filled evenings. On some of those late summer evenings when the weather was fine and the house felt stuffy and hot from the heat of the day, all the family both from upstairs and downstairs spilled out onto the tiny back porch and onto the small lawn sandwiched between the house and the garage, and everybody began to talk about back home. Stories that had been told time and time again were now told again, and we all enjoyed the retelling. As Rie and 'lois chased lightning bugs in the soft dusk of the summer evening, I wondered how much of the stories they would remember.

There were new stories, too, to tell. One was about Joe Louis. Christopher-John told the story. "Cassie, you hear about Man here driving around the champ?" Dee had written me about it but I didn't know all the details. Christopher-John filled me in. "Seems there was this real pretty young lady Clayton Chester was seeing and she really liked that Buick of his. Her family liked it too. Now, her family was somehow connected with the champ and heard he was coming to town and needed someone to drive him around. That young lady figured Man and his white convertible would be perfect. So, when the champ came to Toledo, it was our little brother here took him all over town. Worked out well for him. Got to meet a lot of important people and got to drive that pretty girl!"

I turned to Man. "You've been doing big things here in Toledo! You still driving that pretty girl around?"

374

"No."

"No? So, what happened?"

Man glanced over at Rachel sitting on the porch swing. "You're looking at her."

I smiled and so did everyone else as we all turned to look at the shy Rachel. "I thought you two were supposed to be just friends," I said.

"Well, we are friends, always will be." Clayton Chester gazed at Rachel. "But now we're getting married." He got up and went over to his bride-to-be, took her hand, and sat beside her. Rachel was smiling.

The announcement was welcome news, and everybody heartily congratulated them. They said they had decided to wait until next spring to marry. By that time they hoped there would be a room available upstairs. Both of them figured to work until then and for Man to get his degree. It was a good plan. As I watched them sitting together on the swing, I thought of Flynn and me. My brothers were all happy with the women in their lives. Soon we would all be married — as long as I stayed with Flynn. I didn't know if I would.

■ ■ ■ ■

Moe came to visit. Morris was with him.

"Well, it's about time you two came to see me," I said. "I thought you'd forgotten about me."

Moe smiled awkwardly. "Could never forget about you, Cassie."

I returned the smile and asked of Morris, "So, Little Brother Morris, how are you liking Detroit?"

"It's okay."

"Just okay?"

Morris shrugged. "Well, it's a lot bigger than Jackson. Lot dirtier too."

"What about your school?"

"Rather be going to Lanier."

"You don't like your school?"

"Well, here's the thing, Cassie. At Lanier I'd know exactly who I'm supposed to be. I'm colored, everybody else is colored too. I'd run for class president and probably win. I'd play football and likely be captain. I'd take out a pretty girl and she'd probably be homecoming queen. Up in Detroit, Toledo too, I figure, going to school with white folks, I'm not likely to do any of that. White folks won't have it." He smiled wide. "But I'm learning, getting myself a good education."

"You want to go back south?"

"No, I'm not saying that." Morris glanced over at Moe. "I like being here with Moe. Course, I like being home too, being with Daddy and everybody. I miss them. But I'll be staying here. Moe says I can go to college here, maybe Wayne State, if I want."

"Not to a Negro college back home?" I questioned. "Jackson? Alcorn? Tougaloo?"

Moe stepped in and slapped Morris on the shoulder. "He's got plenty of time to decide that, Cassie. For right now, he's just getting himself through high school."

"Not all that much time, Moe," corrected Morris. "I'm going into my senior year. Time I made up my mind about a college. Kind of depends on Daddy and how he's doing. He's been feeling more poorly than usual lately. We're all kind of worried about him. Levis came up in June and took me home and I stayed there for the better part of the summer. Maynard brought me back just last week."

"Course, I would've liked to have gone south with Morris," said Moe. "Really wanted to see Daddy, but we all know I can't." He was silent a moment, his eyes expressing the pain he felt at being so far from home and unable to return. "A lot of things are hard, but I just have to accept them." He looked at me as he spoke. "I have to accept a lot of things."

It was an awkward moment.

When we were alone, Moe said, "I never congratulated you on your marriage. I can't say I was happy about it. I always hoped —"

"Now, Moe, you know I always told you —"

"Yeah, I know. You always told me. But, least you found somebody made your heart rush. This guy you married must be something special for you to marry him."

I was direct with Moe. "He made me feel what no other man has."

"Well, I'm not going to lie and say I'm

happy about that. But I will say I'm glad you're happy." He studied my face. "Are you happy, Cassie?"

I took a moment before answering. "Depends on the moment. Body can't be happy all the time."

Several weeks into my stay, Justine called. "You need to come back here," she announced bluntly. "My brother needs you."

"Did he say that?"

"Naw, he don't even talk about you. Told me you left him after a fight about Faye and where he was spending his time and that's all. Told me that the day you left him and he ain't spoke 'bout you since."

"Then why are you calling?"

" 'Cause I know my brother. He made a commitment to you. He married you. He'd never break that commitment, not for Faye, not for anything, not for anybody."

"Then why didn't he tell me Faye was coming to see him while he was working in San Bernardino?"

" 'Cause he was afraid you wouldn't understand and you'd leave him, but then you up and left him anyway. Cassie, he wasn't sleeping with Faye, I know that much. Look, this here's a person-to-person call. I gotta hang up."

"All right . . . but, Justine, wait . . . is he all right?"

"You need to come back here and see for yourself, else somebody like that Faye will move right on in and try to make him all right. I gotta go. Bye."

There was a click on the phone and she was gone. I heard nothing further from Justine, but soon after her call I received a letter from Flynn. The letter was only two sentences long. "Justine told me she spoke to you. I want you to come home." A train ticket was enclosed.

It was early September when I received Flynn's letter. I decided to go back to Los Angeles. I supposed I had always intended to go back. The draw to Flynn was too intense for me not to go back. I was certain now I was pregnant and I couldn't deny him that. I told Stacey I was returning to Los Angeles. "You sure?" he asked. "I don't know what's going on, not my business what's going on between husband and wife, but I want you to be sure. Are you?"

I nodded. "I'm sure. One thing, though, before I go back, I need to go down home. It'll be a while before I get this close to home again."

Stacey said he would take me down. "Less traveling by train the better," he said. "I'll get Man or Christopher-John to go with us."

I wrote Mama and Papa to let them know I was coming. I also wrote Flynn and told him I would be coming back to Los Angeles, but I didn't know when. I was going to Mississippi first.

It was good for me to be home again. It was good to go to bed early and rise in early morning long before dawn to take care of the animals, to feed the cows and the hogs, the chickens and the guineas, to milk the cows and gather the eggs. It felt good to carry wood from the log pile to the wood-burning stove, and to tend the fireplaces before bed on a chilly night. It felt good to ride the new horse, named Lady, after the horse of my childhood, and even ride old Jack, the mule of my childhood. It felt good to walk through the forest down to the pond, take off my shoes and slip my bare feet into the cool water, and wonder at the dear, dear old trees all around. It felt good to walk the land. It felt good to sit at the long table, even though it felt empty without the boys, and to rejoice in Big Ma's cooking, to sit in front of the fire at night or on the front porch on warmer evenings, to talk about the day, to talk about the past, and even to venture into the future.

I told Mama I thought I was pregnant.

She smiled wide. "Oh, that's good," she said.

I shook my head. "I don't know. Flynn hasn't been truthful with me."

Mama gave me a look. "Then make him be. You love him, right?"

I conceded to that. There was no denying that I loved Flynn.

"Then whatever you think he's done, you talk it out with him and, between you, make it right. I did that with your papa when we were young, married, and separated, and I've never regretted it."

I looked incredulously at Mama. I had never heard this before. "What? You mean to tell me, you and Papa . . . What was it about? Why'd you separate?"

"Not your business," Mama stated curtly. "Point is, we both got past it. So, whatever's going on between you and Flynn, you've got to get past it, and not just for the baby's sake, but for the two of you in this union."

Big Ma agreed. I didn't have to tell Big Ma I was pregnant. She had already guessed. "No matter what, Cassie. Long's he's a good man, you need to figure a way to keep yo' family. Ain't nobody ever said it was gonna be easy. Long's he ain't hittin' on you, disrespectin' you, or doin' some ungodly thing, you need to stand by this man. You love this man, he love you, y'all gotta work to make this marriage sound. Ain't nothin' worthwhile come without work and that's the same in marriage, same's anything else." Now Mama knew and Big Ma knew. I was waiting for the right time to tell Papa.

I lingered for several weeks at home

and felt my clothes getting tighter. I couldn't zip my skirts all the way up, and there was no point in trying to button up a dress. I wore cardigan sweaters to cover the gaps. I should have gone shopping for maternity clothes while still in Toledo but I had put it off, thinking I would not need to go shopping until I was back in Los Angeles. Now I had to get some new clothes, and as much as I hated it, I decided to go shopping in Jackson. I asked Papa to take me. I went first to look for dresses on Farish Street, but couldn't find anything I liked. I decided to look for something on Capitol Street. At one of the department stores I found several dresses that suited me. They were not maternity dresses, just larger sizes. I did not want to show up at the train station in Los Angeles and meet Flynn in maternity clothes before actually telling him my news. I took the dresses over to the saleslady.

"You ready to buy those?" she asked.

"No. I'd like to try them on first."

The woman's look was condescending. "You know our policy."

Yes, I did know their policy. Colored

folks could buy clothes, our money was welcomed, but we could not try on the clothes. I had known the policy since I was a child, but it was now 1950, not 1933. A war had been fought and colored men had fought in that war and colored women had served in that war. I thought maybe, just maybe, there could have been some changes made about policy. But nothing was changing here, not in Mississippi.

"Well, you buying these?"

I handed the saleswoman the dresses. "Not without trying them on I'm not. You keep your dresses and I'll just keep my money."

On the way home, I told Papa about the baby.

Papa smiled. " 'Bout time you said something. Your mama's already told me." I smiled, knowing I should have figured she would. "Told me too that you and Flynn been having some problems. Course she didn't have to tell me that, long as you been away from him." Papa looked at me for a moment, then back to the road. "Now, I ain't ever met Flynn, but if you chose him, I figure your good sense was all I needed to know he's a good man. He was mistreating you, I'd take a shotgun to him, but you say he ain't, so you gotta figure a way for him to make whatever's wrong, right. It's been long enough, Cassie. Time you went home."

"But, Papa, I am home," I said.

"No, Cassie girl. This ain't home no more for you. Your home is with your husband, wherever he is and where y'all make your family. If you're gonna stay married to this man, you need to go home to him. Much as I'd like for you to stay here and in my care, it ain't the right thing. Now, you'll always be my baby girl, but you're his wife now and your place is with him. Like I said, time you went home, back to your husband."

I looked at Papa. They all had spoken.

Soon after, I took a train, segregated out of Jackson, and traveled through Louisiana, Texas, New Mexico, and Arizona, back to California, back to Los Angeles, back to my husband, back to Flynn.

CASSIE'S LOVE STORY
CHAPTER VI
(1950–1951)

It was evening when I arrived in Los Angeles. Flynn met me at the station. I was nervous about seeing him again, nervous about what I had to tell him. As we walked to the car, I took a deep breath knowing I would have to ride in the Mercedes. But the car Flynn led me to was not the Mercedes. It was a Pontiac. "Where's the Mercedes?" I asked.

"Sold it" was all Flynn said. I asked nothing further. I was saving all my talking for later. Flynn opened the door for me, touching me for the first time, his hand on the center of my back, as was his habit whenever he helped me into a car. I fought to control my trembling. For a while as Flynn drove through the streets of Los Angeles we said nothing, even though there was so much that needed to be said. Then I realized we were not headed for the apartment and I broke the silence. "Flynn, where are we going? This isn't the way home."

"Are you sure?" Flynn returned. "As I recall, you don't know L.A. all that well."

"I know it well enough to know this isn't the way to the apartment."

"No, you're right, it's not. But I have something I want to show you —"

"Oh, Flynn, not tonight! I'm so tired! I just want to get home!"

Flynn glanced over at me. "You're so eager to get there, once we're there, what do you want to do?"

I looked at him. He was smiling and I knew he was teasing me. "I just want to sleep, Flynn," I replied, feeling exasperated with him. "I feel like I haven't slept for days. I don't even want to talk tonight. I just want to sleep."

The smile gone, he said, "Then that's what you'll do . . . as long as you sleep in our bed, beside me." His eyes were on the street. I said nothing else.

When Flynn slowed the car, we were on a tree-lined street with deep lawns and deeper walkways. He pulled into a driveway and stopped. There were lights shining from the house. I looked at him and he nodded toward the house. "We're home, Cassie." Without giving me time to respond, he got out of the car, walked around, and opened my door. I just looked at him, then back to the house. Flynn took my hand as I stepped from the car and we walked to the front door. He unlocked the door and ushered me in. The front hallway was bathed in golden light. "Welcome home, Cassie," Flynn said.

I shook my head in silent disbelief. Flynn led me through the house, first into a living room with a fireplace and bookshelves on either side of it. Our sofa and chairs were in front of the fireplace. On the wall opposite the fireplace, two sets of sliding doors opened onto a patio and a backyard garden. Then he led me into a kitchen equipped with a separate pantry room, then to a bathroom and a small room unfurnished except for Flynn's architect table. The final room he showed me was a large bedroom that had its own bathroom. Our bed was in the room, and a vase full of yellow roses accentuated with blooms of baby's breath was on the nightstand next to it. Also on the bed was the nightgown I had last worn when we were together. It was laid out newly laundered and pressed. I stared at the bed, beautifully made and waiting for us. Finally, I spoke. "What is all this?"

"What does it look like?" said Flynn. "It's our home. It's where we're going to live."

"But . . . how did you do it?"

"Well, have to admit it's not quite all ours yet. It's only leased for now, but if you like it, it could be ours. It's called rent to buy, but it's only if you like it."

I looked around the room. "Like it? I love it!"

"Then that's all that matters. It's ours."

Flynn came to me and, cupping my chin in his hands, gently held my face. "When you wrote saying you were coming back, I just wanted you to come back to a promise I made to you, that I'd give you everything I possibly could, everything you wanted, and from the beginning, I knew you wanted a house of your own."

I was awestruck by all Flynn had presented to me. I pulled away from him and simply gazed around the room. I looked at the bed, so perfectly made, everything so elegant, sunlit sheets already turned back over a golden comforter, fluffy pillows in bright yellow pillowcases, flowers. "You did all this?"

"Some of it. Some of it Justine did."

"Justine?" I questioned. "I'm surprised about that. I never saw her place looking this good —"

"Well, Mrs. Hendersen had a hand in it too. She brought the ladies from her house to help."

I laughed. "Then that explains it."

Flynn smiled. "She's a romantic."

I gently touched the edging of the comforter. "Well, it's just beautiful." Then I touched the petals of a rose. "You chose these?" I glanced at him for his answer.

"You always loved yellow roses," he said.

I sat down wearily on the side of the bed. I still had on my coat.

"I know you're tired, Cassie," Flynn

said. "Why don't you just get changed and get into bed."

"I'm so tired I don't even feel like changing."

"You'll feel better if you do." Then unexpectedly Flynn kneeled down and gently took off my shoes and set them beside the bed.

"I suppose you're right," I said, standing again. "I think I'll shower too." I picked up the gown and went into the bathroom. When I returned, Flynn had pulled the covers back for me. I lay down. Flynn lay beside me. He held me and we slept.

As the morning sunlight poured into our new bedroom, Flynn sat up and leaned against the headboard. "I know I was wrong, Cassie, not to tell you everything, but you and I both know I was never unfaithful to you. I just was embarrassed to tell you about the car. That means nothing now." He was silent before he added, "Faye found out I was working in San Bernardino and she followed me there. I never slept with her."

Pulling the covers with me, I sat up too

and took him in. "I know." I thought of the weeks without him. "But you should have told me. Main thing is, you finally got rid of the car."

"Well, it wasn't worth it to me to try to hang on to it." He smiled wryly down at me. "Especially since I couldn't get you to ride in the car with me."

I felt somewhat guilty. "Do you regret selling it?"

"No," he answered. "You ought to know that it was Faye who bought it."

I thought of the irony of it all. "So, now she's driving around in your car, the car you drove me in?"

Flynn shrugged. "Least I have no further ties to her. You do believe me, don't you, Cassie?"

I was touched by his confession. I was touched by his nearness. "Yes," I softly answered. I laid my hand on his chest and met his eyes. "Flynn . . ." I waited a moment, then said, "Flynn . . . I'm pregnant."

Flynn was silent.

"Did you hear me?"

Flynn chuckled. "You think I didn't

already know that? You think I didn't see your fat belly?"

"Why didn't you say anything?"

He smiled that golden smile. "I was waiting for you to tell me."

At that, I smiled too and snuggled close to him, my head against his chest. "Well, now you know," I said. Flynn tilted my face upward and kissed me.

Before Christmas I lost the baby. I was devastated and so was Flynn. The holidays came and went. The days that we had looked forward to with such hope and joy were now all emptiness. In the days and weeks of 1951 following our loss, Flynn's love was all-enveloping. His love became the other half of me. I poured out every thought to Flynn. I held nothing back. I cried a lot, and my sadness washed over us both. Once, Flynn softly said after one of my crying spells, "You know I hurt too, Cassie. I lost our baby too." I couldn't seem to get over it, and as time passed, Flynn said maybe I should go back to Mississippi, go home to be with Mama and Papa and Big Ma or maybe go back to Toledo and be with my brothers and Dee and the girls. He said he wanted to keep me with him, but maybe I should go home to heal. But I chose not to go. Flynn was now my home.

Flynn coaxed me out of the house, got me to leave the comfort of that warm haven. On the weekends, he began taking me with him to the park basketball court, and I sat watching him play basketball with the other young men gathered. Other times he got me to play with him one on one. I hadn't played basketball before I met him, but I enjoyed the game and I was pretty good at shooting baskets. I was good at shooting pool too, and we began spending some of our Saturday afternoons at Jake's Place, the local pool hall. We also spent more time with the Peñas at their home. On Sunday mornings Flynn persuaded me to dress for church and he even went with me. On warmer weekend days we walked along the sands of Venice Beach. I didn't swim, but Flynn did. Sometimes he stripped off his shirt and dove into the cold waiting water. He wanted me to go with him. He wanted to teach me, to make me unafraid of the water, but I wouldn't go. Instead I sat on the beach and waited, watching his strokes, his perfect form. Once when he came out of the water, he plopped onto the sand beside me and, despite my objections, pulled me against his wet body and enveloped me in his arms. "Warm me up," he said.

I laughed and tried to pull away.

"Un-unh," he said. "I'm not letting you go. Ever."

He kissed me.

I leaned my back against his chest and we gazed out at the azure sky against azure water. "Papá Miguel is thinking about getting a boat," Flynn said. "A motorboat. Maybe I'll go in with him to buy it. Maybe that way I can get you out onto the water."

"You don't have to buy a boat," I said.

"I want you to sail with me. I want you to enjoy the water with me."

"Okay, if Señor Peña buys a boat, I'll sail with you. But I'm not going in the water."

"I won't let you drown. Trust me. I'll always take care of you."

I turned to face him. "I do trust you,

396

Flynn. You're my beautiful, absolutely gorgeous husband! You're my love! Sweetheart, I trust you with all my being!" His lips were waiting, and as always I was drawn to kiss him. I closed up tight against him, my breasts against his chest. I put my arms over his shoulders and clasped my hands behind his neck and succumbed, kissing him long, then I pulled away and got up quickly from the sand. "But you're not getting me in that water!"

Flynn too jumped up, and I ran away laughing. He caught me, picked me up, carried me to the water, and I screamed. "Don't you throw me in there!"

He laughed. "I promise I won't let you go."

And he didn't. He didn't throw me in, but he carried me into the ocean until he was waist-deep and I was wet as well; then, laughing still, he brought me back to shore. I pretended to be angry. He pretended to care that I was. He put me down and we walked back to the car, drove back to our little house, and spent the rest of the day loving each other. We talked about having another baby.

■ ■ ■ ■

Señor Peña bought the boat. I persuaded Flynn not to take on the debt, not right now with my not working. Despite that, we knew we were always welcome on the boat, and in April, during one of its early voyages, Flynn and I were on board, along with Jorge, Justine, and J.D., with Señor Peña at the helm. Señor Peña christened the boat for the second time in honor of Flynn and me, then we set sail on a crystal-clear Saturday morning.

"To *mi amado hijo* Flynn and his beautiful wife!" Señor Peña proclaimed, saluting us with morning champagne. "To them, the beauty of love and family!" He took my hands. "There will be a time for children, Cassie, the greatest blessings of life. In the meantime, just enjoy young love, being together, and then the children will come." Now he laughed. Everyone on board did.

It was a glorious morning. The sky was clear, brilliant blue and cloudless. The waters were calm, and we sped far from shore before Señor Peña stopped the boat, threw down the anchor, and announced it was time for the fishing to begin. Fishing rods were in holders fixed to the stern, and Señor Peña insisted I take a rod and give it a try. I was feeling a bit queasy being on the water and I really didn't want to stand near the boat's edge with a fishing rod in hand, but I got up anyway and went over. I didn't want to spoil the morning with my complaints. As I reached for the rod, Flynn, always so attuned to my feelings, met my eyes and said, "Cassie, are you all right?"

I managed a smile. "I'm fine."

"How's your stomach? First time on the water, you might feel sick."

"I said I'm fine, Flynn. Now give me the rod."

Flynn smiled. "Yes, ma'am."

Flynn handed me the rod and I took it, expecting the feel of it to be the same as when I fished back home on the Rosa Lee, but the swaying of the waters gave it a different feel. I don't know how long I stood there, just holding on to the rod, before Señor Peña advised me to sit in the chair in front of the holders, but to keep a steady hold. "Once you feel something tugging, that's when you'll need to jump into action. Then your work begins!" He laughed, and I sat down, waiting for a tug on the line.

While I waited, Flynn and Señor Peña and Jorge swapped stories about fishing in Mexico when Flynn and Jorge were growing up. Both of them had taken up rods and were waiting for a bite, but neither Justine nor J.D. wanted anything to do with fishing; they both felt seasick. I still felt the queasiness myself, but I fought it as I held on to the rod and the boat began to rock.

By now the weather was changing. The bright sunshine that had ushered us onto the water was gone, and dark, ominous clouds were gathering. A wind had kicked up and it looked as if it was going to storm. Señor Peña said that there had been no forecast for rain. It was supposed to be a sunshiny day, all day. He figured the clouds would pass. Yet still the clouds gathered and darkened.

"I think I'm going to be sick," Justine announced.

"Then stop drinking the damn champagne!" J.D. admonished.

"That's the only thing keeping me from

throwing up," retorted Justine, and, champagne bottle in hand, went over to the side of the boat and leaned over.

"Don't get so close, Justine," Flynn warned.

"Oh, I'm all right. Just go on with your fishing."

"Justine, you want a rod?" asked Señor Peña. "You want to give it a try now?"

"You kidding? Naw, I just want to get off this damn boat."

Señor Peña chuckled. "That'll be soon enough. The sun will come out soon and all this will pass. For now, just try to settle back and enjoy the water. You lie down there on the seat. You'll feel just like a baby being rocked to sleep."

"Well, this baby feels like throwing up, so I best stay right where I am, case I do."

Flynn said, "Looking down at the water, Justine, will only make it worse."

"What I tell you?" Justine quipped irritably. "You tend to your wife. Let me tend to me."

"Have it your way," Flynn replied, then

turned to J.D. "Why don't you go stand with her?"

"Ah, shoot, man, naw. I'm sick to death myself," said J.D.

"Maybe you'd better take a bucket then," advised Señor Peña as he waved over to Jorge to pass an empty bait bucket to J.D.

I felt a tug on the line and jumped up. It had just begun to rain. Excited, I ignored the rain as I watched the line tugged downward. I tried to reel it in, but the tension was too great. I cried out to Flynn. "Help me!"

Flynn slipped his rod back into its holder and quickly came over. "Keep a firm grip on the rod, Cassie," he ordered as he stood behind me. He wrapped his arms around me and placed his hands over mine.

Señor Peña came rushing over. "If it's a big one, you might be in for a long fight."

"Could be," said Flynn. His hands pressed down upon mine as I reeled in my catch.

"Flynn, you're hurting my hand!" I

protested. "Why don't you just take the rod?"

"Because," he said, "it's your catch, Cassie." And he kissed the side of my face. I turned to look at him. He was smiling that glorious, golden smile down at me.

Then the scream came.

We both quickly turned.

"Oh, my God!" cried J.D. "She's gone overboard! Justine's gone overboard!"

I felt the pressure of Flynn's hand leave mine as he let go of the rod and ran over to the side of the boat. Without hesitation, he tossed off his shoes and jumped into the water after Justine. The rod, now belonging to whatever was towing it, was torn from my grasp, and as the rain pounded down, I stood frozen, waiting for Flynn to come back over the side of the boat. Señor Peña and Jorge were already at the side, tow lines in hand, peering over. J.D. was as useless as I was, muttering over and over again, incoherent words.

I managed to move. The boat was rocking.

"Get back, Cassie!" ordered Señor Peña.

I ignored him and hurried to the side of the boat and looked over. I could see Flynn in the rush of foamy waters swimming with one arm over his sister's chest, towing her back to the boat, the other treading the waves. Jorge, with a line tied around his waist, climbed over the side, rope in hand, splashed into the water, and looped the rope around Justine. Jorge pushed Justine upward from underneath. Señor Peña pulled from the deck. "J.D., help me!" yelled Señor Peña. But J.D. remained useless. I ran over, caught the line, and together we managed to get Justine's heaving and water-weighted body back onto the deck of the boat, knocking both Señor Peña and me down. As Justine lay on the deck she coughed up water and blurted out, "My brother! My brother! Where's my brother?"

I jumped up and looked over the side. I didn't see Flynn. "Where is he?" I screamed. Jorge, wild-eyed and still on the boat's lifeline, looked around in dismay. *"Where is he?"*

Jorge dove back into the water.

"Oh, my God! Oh, my God! Oh, my God!" I found myself screaming, crying, as Jorge dove repeatedly and each time came up alone.

Then, from some distant place, I heard Señor Peña order his son back onto the boat, and I heard someone whose voice was mine cry out, "No!" And a body that was mine leapt over the side of the boat into the freezing water.

I had to find Flynn. I had to find my husband.

This man.

GOING HOME
(1951–1952)

I was in Colorado.

I had come in the spring through the Colorado Rockies on a bus from L.A. I had witnessed the majestic peaks of the Rockies still capped with snow, the emerald plush grasses of the mountain meadows dotted with bluebells and yellow lilies, and even a late spring snowstorm that coated the pines and brought even more splendor to the land. After three years of sunshine or occasional rain in Los Angeles, with no hope of snow, and, before that, two years in the flatland of Toledo, the high peaks of the Rockies, the crisp air, the altitude, and the prospect of snow were welcome to me. When the bus pulled into Denver for a rest stop, I got off, and although I had a ticket all the way to Toledo, with a change of buses in Chicago, I did not get back on.

I had not made any plans to stop in Colorado, but I didn't think twice about my decision. I saw a colored woman cleaning the station restroom and asked her if she knew a good place I could stay. "You got the money, the Rossonian Hotel. It's a colored hotel over in Five Points, that's where I live, most other colored folks too. Lots of famous colored folks stayed at that hotel — Ella Fitzgerald, Nat King Cole, Duke Ellington. Couldn't get rooms at the white hotels downtown. Could play there, but couldn't stay there." She laughed. "You know how it is."

I thanked the woman and took a taxi to the Rossonian. That evening I studied the brochures about Colorado I had picked up at the bus station, and the next morning I walked the Five Points neighborhood, then took a bus to downtown Denver and walked it too. I passed the bus station, walked to the train station, then back toward Civic Park and the gold-domed capitol. I took in the mountains west of Denver that I had come through the day before. I wanted to be nearer to them. The following morning I boarded a bus and headed to the university town of Boulder, nestled at the foot of the Rocky Mountains. The bus rolled through the countryside of the plains dotted with ranch houses, horses and cattle roaming freely. As the snowcapped mountain range spreading from north to south as far as the eye could see drew nearer, the bus driver announced that we were approaching the scenic overview of Boulder Valley. The bus was on an incline and only the mountains were in view, not the town. Then the bus reached the peak of the hill and began to descend. The town of Boulder lay below. The bold red-tiled roofs of the University of Colorado at the immediate entry of the town were striking in the distance.

It was all spectacular.

The bus driver pointed toward the mountains known as the Flatirons, which were now so close it seemed as if I could reach out and touch them. Above, the sky was cloudless, a cobalt blue. As I stared out at the beauty before me, at the pristine town, the cobalt sky, the rugged Flatirons, the infinite mountain range, for a few moments, I forgot my sorrow.

■ ■ ■ ■

After the boating trip, Uncle Hammer and Aunt Loretta had been called, and they had come to Los Angeles. I hardly spoke during the days following. Uncle Hammer took charge of things. It was Uncle Hammer who called all the family to let them know what had happened. It was Uncle Hammer who claimed Flynn's body when it was recovered after Señor Peña and Jorge had pulled me, crazed and delirious, from the water. Another boat had approached, and divers, along with Jorge, had assisted in bringing Flynn from the water. At the time I knew nothing of this. Flynn had been taken to the other boat.

I had been taken to Flynn's and my house, the house that was supposed to be our home for years to come. Mrs. Hendersen had come with all her ladies, and they had sat with me through the night. The next day Uncle Hammer and Aunt Loretta had arrived. I moved in a daze. Uncle Hammer, along with Señor and Señora Peña and Mrs. Hendersen, arranged the services. Neither Justine nor

I was in any condition to do it. I attended the services, but I never looked on Flynn again. My beautiful husband, gone. His body, dragged down by the sea.

I just couldn't bear it.

With the services over, Uncle Hammer and Aunt Loretta tried to get me to return to Oakland with them, but I refused. Mama and Papa called from Jackson and told me to come on back home, back home to Mississippi, and Big Ma said, "Come on, baby, come back home to the land," and calls came from Stacey and Dee, and they said, "Come on home to Toledo, be with us," and calls and letters too came from Christopher-John and Man, who said, "Come on home, back to us." But I couldn't go home, not yet. Not back to Toledo, not back to the land, not back to the family. I was too empty, too filled with grief. I knew everyone who loved me wanted to wrap their love around me, but I was not ready for that, not yet. I wanted to grieve on my own. The love I wanted was gone.

And, in the end, Uncle Hammer let me be alone. He looked at me and said, "You're my blood, and I know you're strong, Cassie. You always were. You have to do this thing the way you figure you have to do it. You going to hurt like hell for a long time, but in the end you'll be stronger because of it. You deal with this the way you figure you've got to. You need me, you let me know. I won't be far away."

I assured him I would. After that, Uncle Hammer and Aunt Loretta left. Aunt Loretta wanted to stay longer to help me heal but Uncle Hammer said no. He understood me. He understood I did not want anyone to help me heal. I just wanted to be alone.

And I was.

There was no describing the loneliness, no way to expel it. It was a shroud that enwrapped me and cast doubt of living over my whole being, but somehow deep inside me I knew I had to go on. Less than a month after the boat trip, I packed up my few belongings and left Los Angeles, leaving the household items to Justine and the leased house to its owners. I boarded a bus and headed home to those I loved, but not really wanting to see them yet. I knew I wasn't ready, and when I arrived in the Rocky Mountains of Colorado I felt that I had been given a haven for my grief, at least for a while.

I stayed in Colorado through the summer. I got a room in a boarding house near the university campus and enrolled in two political science courses. I registered under my maiden name of Logan. I did not want to talk about Flynn or explain to anyone about him or think about his drowning. I spoke to no one at all about my husband. I figured to keep my mind busy. With my political science professor's help, I was able to get a part-time job at the university doing clerical work. It didn't pay much, but it helped with my expenses and occupied my time. It also helped keep my mind off Flynn.

When I wasn't in class or at work, I often walked to Chautauqua Park situated right at the foot of the Flatirons. Sometimes I would take a sandwich and eat there alone and envision Flynn and the dream of his land. Sometimes I would hike partway up the trail that led to the top of the Flatirons or the road close to the trail leading up Flagstaff

Mountain, but I never walked all the way up. I promised myself I would do it someday, go all the way up to the top of Flagstaff and the Flatirons, but I wasn't ready for that yet, not without Flynn. In fact, I wasn't ready for much of anything without Flynn, but I knew I had to go on, so, as much as I could, I blocked out thoughts of him. To think of Flynn, to dwell on him, was too painful. When thoughts of Flynn came rushing in, I pushed them out again. I tried to concentrate on what was now.

In the evenings I turned to my studies, reading the assigned books and articles, and writing papers. While writing one of those papers, I felt a sharp pain in my wrist. At first, I paid no attention to it, but then felt the pain again and rubbed my wrist. Right beneath the skin was a lump. I didn't think much of it, but a few days later when I awoke, my wrist was throbbing and the bump was no longer concealed beneath the skin, but clearly visible. It made writing difficult. It also made typing difficult, and a couple of days after it protruded, another clerk in the office noticed it.

"You ought to get that checked, Cassie," she said.

I glanced at the lump and shrugged it off. "It's okay. It doesn't hurt that much."

"I'm serious. You can go over to the medical center. It's right off campus. They shouldn't charge that much."

Initially, I didn't take her advice, but when the lump seemed to expand and the pain in my wrist intensified, I went to the clinic. The doctor looked at my wrist and felt the lump, which rotated almost like a ball underneath my skin as he probed it. "It seems to be a ganglion," he said. "Nothing serious, just some fatty tissue that's popped up, but it could become awkward and more painful to your wrist if it continues to grow."

"So what should I do about it?"

"Well," the doctor said, releasing my arm and leaning back in his chair, "we could just slam a book on it to flatten it out." He smiled. "People have done that. Unfortunately, though, the lump usually grows back, so I don't recommend that option. What I suggest is that we remove it surgically. There is little chance that it will regrow. However, if it's not removed, it could keep growing and be quite painful."

The following week I had the ganglion removed. I stayed overnight at the hospital, but was out the next day. Although my wrist was bandaged and my fingers were swollen, within a few days my hand began to return to normal and the pain in my wrist subsided. After a few days the doctor removed the bandage and said everything looked fine, but he wanted to see me again in a few weeks. When I received the bill for medical services thus far, I paid it in full, but when I returned to the center for the follow-up appointment, a secretary checked my name in the files, then, looking uneasy, told me that the doctor I wished to see was no longer at the center. When I asked to see another doctor, she told me that wouldn't be possible.

"I don't understand," I said. "Why can't I see another doctor?"

The secretary shoved my name card back into the file. "It's just not possible. You'll be receiving a letter." Then, dismissing me, she swiveled in her chair and turned her back on me. The next day I received the letter from the medical center administrator stating that the medical center's services were no longer available to me. No reason was given why.

I again went to the medical center. I demanded to see the director, the man who had written the letter. A different secretary told me he was not available. I asked when the director would be available. I was told I would have to call and make an appointment, that she couldn't make one for me until she checked with him. Each day after that I called the medical center, and each day the director was not available. I was told his appointment schedule was full. I was getting nowhere. Finally, I stopped calling, but this thing really bothered me. It was not only the exclusion that bothered me, but even more the fact that they had given me no reason. It was more a matter of "because we said so." Of course, in the back of my mind, I suspected what that reason was. I needed for them to say it to my face. I wrote a letter to the medical center, outlined all that had happened, and requested an explanation. Within the week I received a letter in reply and was told that they had reviewed my file and their decision to exclude me was final. They stood firm on their decision. I could no longer be treated at the center. Again, they offered no explanation why.

I decided on a different approach to get the answers I needed. I went to see my political science professor. Dr. Skurnik was somewhat of an intimidating man and demanded full concentration from every student in his seminars. He was from Germany and had immigrated to the United States before the war. I was put off by his gruff manner at first, by his German accent, but for some reason, maybe because I was the only colored person in the class, he extended his hand to me. After Rowland Tomlinson, I was wary concerning older men who took a seemingly helpful interest in me, but Dr. Skurnik had never asked or even suggested in his actions that he wanted anything in return, except that I be a good student.

"So, this is all of it?" Dr. Skurnik asked after reading the letters from the medical center. "And what do you want now,

Miss Logan? What do you want to happen?"

"I want to know why they will no longer give me medical care."

"Do you believe you know why?"

"Yes, I believe it's because of my race. Everyone there had always been pleasant to me before. They did the operation on my wrist and they were fine then too. There was no reason for them not to see me. I'd paid my bill. I don't know where all this other nonsense came from. I mean, it was out of the blue. I hadn't felt this way in Colorado before. It's an insult in a place I thought maybe was different. . . ."

"Colorado, with all its clean air and brilliant blue skies and all its mountain beauty?" There was mocking in Dr. Skurnik's tone. I didn't respond, and he went on. "So, what else do you want besides knowing why you are no longer welcome there? Do you want them to include you again, for you to be able to get medical treatment there at the center?"

"I think more than that, Dr. Skurnik, I want an apology."

"An apology," Dr. Skurnik repeated. "Maybe that's what the world wants too." He was silent for several moments, then suddenly stood. "Please, you stay here, Miss Logan." He picked up the letters. "I need to see an acquaintance down the hall. I'll bring these back to you." He waved the letters as he went out the door.

While I waited for Dr. Skurnik to return I went to the window and gazed out at the grandeur of the mountains. I reflected on the hope they brought me when I first came through them, how I felt when I had seen them from the plains of Denver. I wanted to believe there was a promise of hope in them still. There was such splendor in this place, and a fairness in people like Dr. Skurnik, or so I thought; I also reminded myself that here I was, totally enmeshed in a white world. All around me, the people I had met in Boulder were white. There were Negroes in Denver, but I was in Boulder, a truly white town, where I wasn't sure if there was even a handful of colored people, and I had reached out to a person from former Nazi Germany. I reminded myself that I had come to Dr. Skurnik for help, just as Mama and Papa and Big Ma had done with Mr. Wade Jamison. It was a matter of trust, and I had to trust someone in this matter.

When Dr. Skurnik returned, he was not alone. With him was a gray-haired gentleman whom Dr. Skurnik introduced as his colleague, Brad Buchanan. He invited us both to sit, then continued. "Don't think badly of him, but he's a lawyer."

I smiled at that, and as we all sat, Dr. Skurnik behind his desk, and Brad Buchanan and I in chairs in front of it, Brad Buchanan turned to me and said, "I've looked at the correspondence —"

"I took the liberty," Dr. Skurnik interrupted. "I thought maybe we needed a legal mind to advise about this matter."

I looked from Dr. Skurnik to Brad Buchanon. "I didn't say I wanted a lawyer."

"I know, but whatever advice he offers will be gratis. He knows you're a student."

"Unfortunately," Brad Buchanan went on, "the medical center is a private professional corporation and they can contend that they have a right to exclude or accept as patients anyone they choose."

"So, there's nothing I can do to find out why they excluded me or get an apology from them?"

"An apology is important to you?" asked the lawyer.

"Yes. And the reason why I was excluded. I can guess, but I want them to say it."

"And what do you think that reason was?"

"I'm a Negro."

Brad Buchanan rubbed his chin and took a moment before speaking again. "I'll tell you what I'll do, Miss Logan. I'll write a letter to the center, to this director, and if he'll see me, I'll meet with him. Maybe they'll tell me, but don't get your hopes up about anything. I don't know how far we can get with this, but I'll surely do my best to represent you and your sentiments. All I need is your okay to proceed."

"And that's all gratis too, right, Brad?" Dr. Skurnik clarified.

Brad Buchanan nodded. "Yes. I'd like

to get to the bottom of this myself and find out why they refused you."

I studied these two white men sitting opposite me, awaiting my decision, and said, "All right, Mr. Buchanan, thank you. Go ahead. Write the letter."

It was more than two weeks before I heard back from Brad Buchanan. He met with me in Dr. Skurnik's office and showed us the letter he had written to the medical center. He had met with the director of the center, along with the center's lawyer, who said that the center was under no obligation to include me as a client and also was under no obligation to tell me why. They would not render an apology. The center's lawyer had written a letter to that effect. Brad Buchanan told me, "You'll be receiving a letter directly from the center concerning all this. I am truly sorry, Miss Logan, that this matter has not turned out as we all had hoped, but after you receive the letter, you let me know what you want my office to do."

I looked at Dr. Skurnik for advice, but he offered none. I then looked back to

Brad Buchanan. "What else could you do?"

"Honestly, I don't know, Miss Logan, but new ground is being broken every day. Maybe nothing can be done, but who knows? Possibly you could sue on the grounds of discrimination, but that costs money and you most likely wouldn't win. Just let me know."

I nodded and we left it at that. When the final letter came from the medical center, it said what had been said before, "In review, we stand by all former decisions. You will not be allowed the services of this medical center."

Short. Curt. As painful as before. I read the letter over and over again, thought about it, was infuriated by it, frustrated by it, insulted by it, despondent about it, but in the end I decided to let it be. For now. For now, I couldn't deal with it. Too much devastation was in my life right now to deal with it. I had to get on with my life, whatever it was to be, and it was clear to me it was not to be in Colorado, what I had seen as a promised golden land. For all its grandeur, all its promise, the people of Colorado were treating me the same as those in Wyoming, in California, in Iowa, in Ohio, in Mississippi, and in all the states up and down the Dixie Highway. Colorado, which in the short time I had been here I had grown to love, had put another dagger in my heart, which was already wounded from the loss of Flynn and our baby. Whatever had been revitalized by my being here, by some of the good people I had met here, was dissipated by the medical center's actions toward me. It seemed I couldn't win. I had long ago come to the realization that being colored was a full-time job in America, and I knew now it was a full-time fight, one I couldn't win alone.

I stayed into the fall, but I enrolled in no more classes. In October I said good-bye to Dr. Skurnik, to my fellow workers in the political science office, and to this land that had filled me with such hope. I took a bus from Boulder to Denver. In Denver, I continued on my way east, back to Toledo, back to my family. They were waiting for me.

■ ■ ■

The house on Dorr Street was crowded, even more than before, but no matter what Dee or Stacey said about there being no more room for even one more person, they seemed always to find room. This time, I was the one more person. I slept on the Sunday room sofa. I could not sleep in the room with Rie and 'lois since that room was being temporarily occupied by two of Dee's cousins, Verlene and Mayetta, visiting from Mississippi, and the girls were sleeping on a mattress on the floor in the dining room. Sleeping on the sofa bed in the living room were Clayton Chester and his bride, Rachel. They were waiting for a room on the second floor. I didn't figure for Clayton Chester and Rachel to sleep in the living room long. There was no privacy for them, not the way the house was laid out.

There was no privacy in any of the common rooms, which flowed into each other. The Sunday room opened into the living room through a large archway, large enough for two doors, but there

425

were no doors. The living room, with a door leading into Rie and 'lois's room on one side, opened into the dining room through double sliding doors that were never closed. A door to one side of the dining room led into Stacey and Dee's bedroom. Another door, following the flow of traffic through the common rooms, led into the kitchen at the back of the house. Along the farthest wall of the kitchen, overlooking the backyard, was a door off to the right. That door opened to the bathroom. Initially, after their marriage in the spring, Clayton Chester and Rachel had roomed at the apartment hotel down the street but, hoping a family from upstairs would be moving soon, they had recently moved into the house to save money. The three of us added to the congestion of the house.

We were not the only ones.

In the basement were the Davises. They were now here in full force. There were seven of them — Dee's brother Zell and six of the long-legged cousins I had met when visiting with Dee's family. They had come, one by one, hitching rides with other family members or friends headed this way. Zell and one of the cousins had actually come back with Stacey and Dee after one of their trips south. As more of the cousins arrived, there were no rooms for them and the sofas used as beds were already taken. Stacey and Dee told them they would have to find another place to live. But then the Davises discovered the basement, which comprised a large wash-room where Dee and the other women of the house washed their clothes and hung their laundry in winter, and a coal room that was no longer used since the house had been converted to gas heating. The coal room, now empty of coal, was perfect for them, they said. Dee and Sta-cey said it wasn't suitable, but the Da-vises pleaded that it was. They said they would paint it, get furniture for it, make it livable, and finally Stacey and Dee gave in, and so the Davises stayed.

As it turned out, the Davises hardly were in that basement room except to sleep. Mostly they stayed on the first floor with Stacey, Dee, and the girls, and Dee took charge of them as if she were their mother. She cooked for them, washed for them, ironed their clothes, packed their lunches, and treated them as her own. Although they all found jobs and paid weekly rent, I saw how much Dee did for them and knew that the money she received hardly compensated for all her work or what both she and Stacey had sacrificed for them to stay in the house. The way the house was configured, the interior basement stairs were accessible only from Stacey and Dee's bedroom, so to get to their coal room in the basement, all the young men had to go through Stacey and Dee's bedroom. But Stacey and Dee put up with that for a while because they were family. We all were family — three families, really — melding into one.

Although the married couples on the second floor took care of their own cooking and had their own living space, at any given time they joined all the family on the first floor. We saw them daily. At dinnertime there were at least thirteen folks sitting at the kitchen and the dining room tables, along with any travelers coming through from down home or folks coming over from Detroit or Chicago, Peoria or Muncie. My staying at the house increased the number to fourteen. After dinner the living room was full as well, and there was usually some form of entertainment going on. Some evenings one of "the boys," as Dee and Stacey referred to the Davises, plucked at his guitar or the radio was on and we all listened to one of the mystery dramas. In addition to the music and the radio, there was now the television Dee and Stacey had bought last Christmas. It was the only television in the house.

Encased in a mahogany console, which was a grand piece of furniture that also included a radio and phonograph and doors that hid them all when closed, the television was the focal point of the Sunday room. Christopher-John and Becka, with the baby, often joined everybody downstairs in watching it. So did the other folks from upstairs. They would stand in the sun parlor doorway opening into the Sunday room to watch favorite programs like *I Love Lucy, The Ed Sullivan Show,* and *Amos 'n' Andy.* On the nights national fighting bouts were broadcast, the men of the house totally took over the Sunday room. Fortunately, television programming was limited to a

429

few hours a day, with a break of several hours following the afternoon programs, so Stacey and Dee did not have everyone crowding the downstairs throughout the day and night.

Most evenings Dee set up her ironing board along with her new electric iron in the living room so that she could join in listening to the radio or the music or watching the television. After the ironing and the programs were over and most of the family had retired for the night, she returned to her kitchen to make lunches for the next day. I helped her. "Don't you get tired of all these people?" I asked as I wrapped two of the chicken salad sandwiches Dee had prepared, and put them in a paper sack along with an apple and a thick slice of pound cake Dee had baked. "And that includes me," I added.

Dee shrugged. "Everybody's family."

"Well, still . . ."

Dee spread mayonnaise over several slices of bread she had placed on the table. "I've got to admit sometimes I don't know how I can get through another day with everything that has to be done, but it's okay for now. At least I don't have to cook breakfast every day, just Saturdays and Sundays, and those are late morning, so I don't have to get up at the crack of dawn. The boys get their own cereal or whatever in the mornings and even Robert gets his own breakfast. You know, they all leave here by six thirty, so that gives me a little time before I have to get up to take care of Rie and 'lois."

"Yeah, well, still a lot of work."

"Oh, don't tell me. I know it," Dee said. "But things at least are not like before you all left for California, when we didn't know how we were going to make the next mortgage payment. Now, with the jobs back and everybody working, the rent money is more than enough to pay the mortgage each month, and Rob and I can actually save for another house — one that will be a single-family house."

"One for just you two and Rie and 'lois."

She nodded. "I dream of that, for one day. But for now, I can deal with this one. It's a blessing."

"Even with all these people traipsing in and out of your bedroom to go down to wash or get to their room?"

Dee laughed. "Well, I've got to admit Robert is getting pretty tired of that. Me too. But Robert is about to take care of that. He's going to rebuild that broken set of stairs that leads from the basement washroom to the backyard. He and Christopher-John and Clayton already put in a sink and toilet and a small shower down there, so the boys don't have to come through our room to use the bathroom."

"I don't know how you've stood it this long," I said. "I know Flynn and I certainly wouldn't have put up with all this traffic."

Dee scooped up another big spoonful of chicken salad to spread, then paused to look at me. "You know, Cassie, that's the first time you've mentioned Flynn since the day you arrived."

I hesitated. "I don't talk about him . . . because I can't."

Dee sighed. "Well, maybe I'd feel that way too if something happened to Rob. But like we all told you that first night, you can always talk to us, to me, your brothers."

"I know."

Dee stopped with the sandwiches and looked at me. "Robert's really worried about you." I was silent. "They all are."

I took up the next sandwich. "I know. But, Dee, I still can't talk about him."

Dee nodded in understanding and spread the chicken salad across another slice of bread.

When Moe first saw me after my return, he expressed words of sympathy. "I know you said you don't want to talk about it, Cassie, about what happened to your husband, but if you ever want to, I'll always listen." Later, as the weeks passed, he said, "I know it's probably too soon, but when you're ready, Cassie . . . I want you to know I'm here . . . waiting."

"Waiting? For what, Moe?"

"For you to be my wife."

I looked at Moe, unbelieving, and shook my head. "Don't. Don't wait, Moe, not for me. You find yourself somebody else to love." Moe started to speak, but before he could, I held up my hands and repeated, "I mean it, Moe. I don't want to talk about this. Don't wait for me. I don't plan to marry again." Then I turned and walked away. There was no point in trying to tell him, to tell any of them, that there could never be another man like Flynn in my life. There could never be, and I didn't want any other.

"Have you decided what you're going to do?" Stacey asked. It was a Saturday afternoon and we were the only two seated at the kitchen table. Clayton and Rachel were out, the Davis boys too. Dee's cousins, Verlene and Mayetta, had moved on to Chicago, and Dee had taken the girls shopping downtown. The house was quiet.

"Decided about what?"

"Your life."

I smiled. "Oh, that. No."

"Don't you think it's time you did? If you're going to stay here in Toledo, you can get a teaching job. Your certificate should still be good. Maybe you ought to go ahead and apply."

"Stacey, you know how I feel about teaching."

"Then what do you want to do?"

"That's just it. I really don't know. A year ago when I left here I had my life pretty much figured out. I was pregnant. I was going back to Flynn. I was going to have our baby and make a life with him. I wrapped my whole head around that. Now there's nothing." I glanced over at Stacey, who just looked at me. "I suppose I'll have to get a teaching job. I'll have to support myself some way."

"When are you planning on going home?"

"I'm not ready yet."

"You need to go, you know. They're worried about you too." Stacey paused. "I never met Flynn, just talked to him a couple times on the phone, but from what you told me about him, I think he'd want you to go. Cassie, I know you miss him. If I was in your place, I know I'd be going crazy if something happened to Dee." He studied me, and his voice was full of caring. "I think going home will help you with your healing."

I sighed. "Mama and Papa and Big Ma will be asking me the same questions you're asking and, Stacey, I don't have answers for them."

"Maybe they can help you figure some things out. They're pretty good at that."

"I guess, but they might want me to stay there."

"And that's not what you want either?"

"What? Move back to Mississippi?" I laughed. "You crazy? I don't think so!"

Stacey rose from the table. "Well, whenever you make up your mind to go, let me know. I'll drive you down." He headed for the dining room, then turned back. "Oh, by the way, I ran into Lawyer Tate today at the barbershop. He asked about you. Asked what you were doing. Told me to tell you to come by his office. He'd like to see you."

"He did? Why?"

"Don't know. Just told me he wanted to talk to you. He knows a lot of people, Cassie. Maybe he can give you a lead on a job."

"Maybe," I agreed. "I'll go see him next week."

■ ■ ■ ■

"How have you been doing, Cassie?" asked Lawyer Tate as he ushered me to a chair. He did not sit at his desk, but in a chair opposite me. "I was sorry to hear about your husband."

"Thank you, Mr. Tate. I'm doing all right."

"Well, so you're back in Toledo. Does that mean you're here to stay?"

"I'm back here because my family is here. Whether or not I'm going to stay, I don't know yet."

"Why not stay in California? It's a mighty pretty place, state of opportunity, so they say."

My voice went low as I replied. "I couldn't stay there."

"He was never here in Toledo, was he? Your husband?"

"No, he wasn't." I lowered my eyes, then looked directly at Lawyer Tate. "Mr. Tate, was that why you wanted to see me? To talk about my husband? I'll tell you right now, I don't want to talk about him."

"Just in part, Cassie, I wanted to ask about him. I wanted to know how you're dealing with your loss. I know it's a difficult time."

"I'm managing."

"But you don't know where you're going." I was silent. "Robert told me that on your way to Toledo, you spent time in Colorado. Said you had even enrolled in some summer courses and had a part-time job for a while. How'd you like it?"

"It was all right. I loved the mountains."

"What kind of courses were you taking?"

"Political science," I answered, now wondering about his interest. "But why are you asking me about them?"

"I assume you did well in those courses. Did you like them?"

"Yes, I did, but —"

"So, why didn't you stay in Colorado? Not many colored folks there, but it's beautiful country, so I hear. A job. Coursework you like. Was there a possibility you could have stayed there?"

"There was . . . at first."

"But you didn't stay. You plan on going back?"

"I don't think so. There's no reason to go back. My family's here."

"And what do you plan on doing here?"

"I don't know yet."

"So, you're drifting." I stared at Lawyer Tate, then looked away without answering. He allowed the silence before he spoke again. "I know you're probably thinking the kind of questions I'm asking are none of my business, but if you'll bear with me, I'll explain my interest. Now, Robert told me that you ran into a bit of a legal problem while you were in Colorado and that is one of the reasons you left —"

"He told you that? He shouldn't have —"

The attorney held up his hand in defense of Stacey. "Please. All he said was one of the reasons you left was because of a legal matter that should have been resolved in your favor but wasn't, and that you figured it could have been racial."

I looked at him cautiously. "That's all

he told you?"

Lawyer Tate nodded. "If it's extremely personal, Cassie, and you don't want to talk about it, I won't question you further."

"You can't do anything about it."

"Don't plan to. I've got enough cases on my desk. I just thought you might want to talk about it to another colored person who has a legal background."

I wasn't clear what Mr. Tate's interest was in my story, but I told him what had happened. "In the end, there seemed to be nothing I could do. The medical center is a private professional corporation and I'm told they can choose to treat or not treat anyone they choose."

"And how did that make you feel?"

"How do you think it made me feel?" I retorted, my anger rising again at the thought of how I had been banned. "I paid my bill. I was told I needed to see the doctor again, then they wouldn't see me, and on top of that, they refused to give me a reason. It was just because they said so."

"And you've heard that all your life,

440

right? From places in Mississippi, all throughout the South."

"All throughout these United States."

Lawyer Tate crossed his long legs, pulled off his glasses, and rubbed his eyes before putting the glasses on again. For several moments he seemed deep in thought. I remained quiet, waiting for him to speak. "Cassie, several years ago at that movie theater downtown I was quite impressed by the way you took a stand. It was risky and it was foolish, but you took a stand."

"Didn't get me anywhere."

"No . . ." he agreed. "Not then. But like I told you, things are going to change. With all our boys being back from the war and more opportunities opening up, there can be big, big changes coming, some on the legal front."

"Like what? I mean, really, Mr. Tate, it's nineteen fifty-one and what's changed since Clayton and Christopher-John got back? Down south we still can't drink from a water fountain unless it's marked 'colored,' and most times those fountains are rusted and dirty and run-offs from the 'white' fountains. We still have to go

441

to back doors at restaurants to get served, and we still can't try on clothes when we go shopping in the department stores. We go to separate schools and on and on, and — well, I don't need to tell you. You know how it is. And here in Toledo and all across this place, it's just as bad sometimes. My brothers told me when Nat King Cole came not too long ago, it was a real mess when colored folks were still expected to sit in the balcony to hear him sing, while the white folks sat downstairs. Maybe theaters around here might be opening up some with their seating, but other places aren't. Some hospitals right here in Toledo are even segregated. So, you tell me, what change is going to come?"

"Changes we need to fight for, Cassie. Changes in our school system. Changes in race laws all across this land. Changes that could affect your being banned from treatment at that medical center in Colorado."

"So, why are we talking about all this right now? It's not like we're at an NAACP meeting."

Lawyer Tate smiled. "No, we're not.

But the reason we're talking about it, Cassie, is because I believe you can be part of the change that's coming. I believe you can help make that change. You've got a degree in education but you said you didn't know what you wanted to do yet. How about the law?"

"What?"

"Certainly being a lawyer isn't a new idea to you. You yourself told me how your white friend in Mississippi — a Mr. Jamison, as I recall — had affected your life and the lives of the people in your community. We discussed the possibility once before. You've got the head for it. You've got the fire for it, and if you want it enough, I can help you get started toward it. I know a number of well-placed people in some very excellent law schools, and I believe if you applied, you would be accepted."

"Really? But, Lawyer Tate, I'm twenty-seven years old. Don't most law students start right after college?"

"Your age, that bothers you? Listen, Cassie, I know plenty of lawyers who got their degrees later than that. Even if you haven't made a decision about your next step in life, it won't hurt to fill out the applications, to apply to these schools, to see what they offer and then make your decision. You have the time. You have nothing to lose. Think on it, Cassie. Doors are opening, and one of those doors could be yours."

In the weeks that followed, I decided to take Lawyer Tate's advice. I applied to the handful of black law schools in the country, the most prestigious and oldest being Howard University School of Law. Lawyer Tate had graduated from Howard. I also applied to northern schools that had graduated black lawyers. Mr. Tate wrote recommendations for me. Community leaders did as well, including the Roman brothers. Mr. Tate suggested I request recommendations from Dr. Skurnik and Brad Buchanan. He said it would look good on my applications to receive recommendations from outside Ohio. I did as he suggested, and both Dr. Skurnik and Brad Buchanan complied. They sent letters to the schools and copies of their letters to me. They were very complimentary.

After all my applications were sent, I finally decided to go south, back home to Mississippi. It was high time I faced Mama, Papa, and Big Ma. With the possibility of law school looming in my future, I figured I was strong enough to keep them from worrying about me. I stayed in Toledo through Christmas. In the week between Christmas and New Year's, my brothers drove me south. The plant, as usual, was shut down during the holidays, so it was a good time for them. They stayed several days, then left in time to be back in Toledo for New Year's Day.

"You sure this is what you want to do?" asked Papa after the boys were gone. "Go into law?"

I answered honestly. "No, sir, I'm not, but I've got to do something."

"You know I was hoping you'd go into teaching," Mama said, persisting in her dream for me.

I just shook my head and smiled.

"Well, still . . . I know you'd be a good teacher."

"Child be good at anything she do," asserted Big Ma.

Mama didn't dispute that. "But a lawyer . . . that's a high undertaking. You know of any colored women lawyers?"

"I don't even know of any white women lawyers," I admitted.

"It's a hard course," said Mama, "for anybody."

"You saying I can't do it, Mama?"

"No, Cassie, I'm not saying that. You know Papa and I have always said you can do anything you set your mind to do. Only thing I worry about is your state of mind right now and if you're strong enough to take on all that studying."

I considered Mama's words. "Maybe that's what I need, Mama. Something difficult to concentrate on."

Mama said nothing else. I glanced at Papa, who remained silent.

During that first week of the new year, I asked Papa to take me to see Mr. Wade Jamison. We went to his office in Strawberry, and as always, Mr. Jamison seemed pleased to see us. I told Mr. Jamison about my applications to law schools and he said, "Well, I'm happy to hear that, Cassie."

"You asked me to let you know if I decided to become a lawyer. I want you to know you helped to inspire me to this decision. I believe that knowing the law can help change things, and there certainly are things needing to be changed."

Papa glanced my way, but said nothing. Mr. Jamison nodded without speaking. I knew he understood what I meant.

I went on. "I wanted you to know about my applications and ask if you would write a recommendation for me. I have several already from Colorado and Toledo, but I believe a recommendation from a lawyer in my home state could carry a lot of weight. You've known me since I was a child and you know so much of what people in my community have been through. You could give a character recommendation about who I am through the eyes of a Mississippi lawyer, something none of the other people writing recommendations can do. Yours would be going in later than the others, but it can still be submitted." I paused, waiting for his reply. "Will you write one for me, Mr. Jamison?"

Mr. Jamison looked at Papa, then again at me. "I'd be most pleased to do that, Cassie." He smiled. "Very pleased."

Returning home, Papa said, "I'm right proud of you, Cassie. Always have been. I'm proud of your decision and how you're going on with your life. But there's something I need to know. You tell me, baby girl, how you're really doing. Your Uncle Hammer wrote about how things were right after your husband died."

"I'm fine, Papa."

"Are you?"

"I miss Flynn. I'm always going to miss him and what we could have had. But I'm all right, Papa. Don't worry about me."

"Don't tell me not to worry. You've been through a lot this past year. Now you're talking about going off to some northern state where you've got no family, nobody you know, to study in a field where few black folks have gone and, yes, I am gonna worry about you. Your mama and your grandma are gonna worry too. I'm always gonna worry about you. No matter you get to be sixty years old and I'm still around, I'm gonna worry."

I grinned at the thought. "I know, Papa, but believe me, I'll be fine."

"In time, find a good man, Cassie, marry again. You need a partner in life. Don't go through it alone."

I repeated, "I promise, Papa, I'll be all right. I'm your daughter, so take my word for it. I'll be fine."

Both Mama and Big Ma talked to me about the loss of my baby and the loss of Flynn. "I know your heart has to be crying," Mama said. "My heart is crying for you, for you losing your husband, for you not going through your lives together, growing old together. When a woman loves a man, loves her husband like you loved Flynn, it's a loss that can't be measured. I know it's too soon now to be thinking on it, marrying again and having children, but you're young. Even after you graduate law school you'll be young. Find yourself a good man. Maybe he won't be like your Flynn, but a good man like him. Make yourself a family. Have children. It'll take time . . . and there is time."

Big Ma pretty much had the same advice. "You go ahead and grieve for this man of yours. You grieve for this boy Flynn. You grieve for yo' husband like you s'pose to. But then, child, you get on with yo' life like God meant for you t' do. You find yo'self another love and give yo'self to that love. Have yo'self another child. I done it, and that's what you gotta do too."

They were all saying the same thing to me. Big Ma, Mama, Papa. But I wasn't ready to hear any of it. I walked the land with them and alone, and when I was alone, that was the only time I let the tears come. I sat on one of the fallen trees by the pond and cried, screamed up to heaven, and felt unable to stop. I felt raw inside. I missed Flynn's touch. I missed his touch in the morning, his touch at night. His loving me. I missed his laughter, his beautiful face, his beautiful body, his golden smile. I missed the safety of his arms.

No man could ever give me that again.

■ ■ ■ ■

Letters from the law schools arrived in early spring. I had been accepted at each school. The schools that interested me most were Howard University School of Law and Boston University School of Law. Now I had to choose. If I went to Howard — the oldest Negro law school, established only years after slavery in 1869, a law school with an impeccable reputation but an all-Negro student body — I could be comfortable in classes with other Negro students, facing the same challenges together. Or I could go to Boston University School of Law, which had graduated its first Negro student in 1877 and opened its doors to all. As when I took classes at the University of Toledo, at UCLA, and at the University of Colorado, at Boston University School of Law I would be in an interracial setting, learning side by side with white students, interacting with them on all levels, and being challenged by them.

I stayed on with Mama, Papa, and Big Ma throughout the remainder of the spring and most of the summer. In Au-

451

gust, when Stacey, Christopher-John, and Clayton Chester came to revival with their families, I packed my bags and returned to Toledo with them. A few days later, I was on a train headed east to Boston.

PART II

Part II

A DIFFERENT WORLD

(1959)

"Moe's in trouble, Cassie. You need to come home."

I stared at Stacey, who had come knocking on my door in the middle of the night. He had left Toledo after work and driven straight through to Boston. I poured coffee into his cup. "What kind of trouble?"

"They're trying to extradite him back to Mississippi."

"Oh, Lord." I placed the pot on the coffee table and, still in my housecoat and pajamas, sat on the sofa across from Stacey. "After all this time?"

"We all figured it was bound to happen someday. Well, yesterday was the day. Police came to Moe's house in Detroit searching for Moe with an arrest warrant on charges from Mississippi."

"They arrest him?"

"He wasn't there. But they'd found out where he worked and under what name. They went over to the Ford plant, but Myrtis managed to get word to Moe through her brother, and Moe was gone before they got there." Myrtis was Moe's wife. He had married her shortly after I moved to Boston.

"Where is Moe now?"

Stacey shook his head. "Don't know exactly. Haven't heard from him, but Moe and I talked about where he'd go if he thought he might be arrested. Most likely he's in Canada."

I nodded, thinking that was the best place for him. Many of our people had fled to Canada seeking freedom during slavery. Now Moe might have done the same thing. It was easy enough to get into Canada. "That makes sense," I said. "He could drive over as long as he showed a driver's license."

"And he has more than one of those. Showed me." Stacey took a gulp of his coffee. "Figured he might need a new identity if all this came up."

"Well, he was right about that." I

frowned. "So, what next?"

"That's why we want you to come home, Cassie, to help figure that out. If they catch him in Michigan, then he'll soon be on his way to Mississippi. If you get together with Lawyer Tate, maybe you can find a way to stop the extradition."

"I doubt that," I said. "Extraditions are usually granted. You tell Lawyer Tate about Moe?"

"Not yet. Wanted to talk to you first."

"What did they charge Moe with?"

"Murder."

"Murder?" I echoed.

Stacey set down his cup. "That's what Myrtis said. She saw the warrant. Moe's charged with the murder of Troy Aames."

"But one could argue that was aggravated assault! Not murder! At the most the charge should be manslaughter!"

"Maybe you can argue that, but Mississippi is charging murder. They're saying Troy died as a result of injuries inflicted by Moe."

I felt floored. "Murder. That could be

the death penalty." My body seemed to go numb, and I couldn't speak.

Stacey watched me and allowed the silence to settle before he spoke again. "Moe's extradition, that's not all the bad news. Got a call from Levis. Hertesene's dead." Hertesene was Moe's sister. She was the eldest girl of the Turner siblings. "Got killed on the Natchez Trace. Car crash. Morris already on his way down."

It was difficult for me to take it all in. Stacey poured himself another cup of coffee. "So, are you coming back with me?"

"Back with you? Now?"

"Cassie, who knows? They could already have Moe by now. If they do, we need you there to help him. We need you in Toledo to work with Lawyer Tate."

"I know that's what you said, but you could have called me instead of driving all the way from Toledo to Boston. Could've saved time and money. You didn't even let me know you were coming. I could have been away."

"Had to come because I wanted to tell you in person." Stacey took a swallow of coffee and stared pointedly at me. "I figured maybe you wouldn't come, not even for Moe, unless I came and got you. Question still stands. Are you coming back with me?"

My hair was hanging long, partially covering my face. I pushed it back behind my ears, giving myself a moment to think. "I'll be in Toledo in another three weeks. I requested a week's vacation with my law firm for Christmas week and I don't see how I can go before then."

"Moe could be in a Mississippi jail by then. Do you even care about Moe?"

"If Moe's in Canada, that's not hardly likely, and of course I care. But I've got cases here I need to tend to."

"Cases more important than Moe?"

"I didn't say that. The truth is there's nothing I can do for Moe — if I can do anything at all — in Toledo that I can't do from here."

Stacey just looked at me. Then he said, "You'll be in Toledo Christmas week. Will you be there the whole time Mama, Papa, and Big Ma are there?"

"Most of it. I'll arrive a day or two after

they come. That's my plan."

Stacey nodded his approval. At least I had that much from him. "We got sleeper berths for them on the train. Cost more, but Christopher-John, Man, and I figured them to be comfortable."

"That's good," I said. I was looking forward to the trip to Toledo. It was the first time Mama and Papa would be in Toledo together. They had always said one of them had to stay at home with Big Ma to take care of the animals and the land. As for Big Ma, this was her first time traveling north. The train would be segregated as far as Chicago, where they would change trains for Toledo. At least with the sleeper berths, they would get a good night's sleep. Maynard and Levis had said they would take care of the house and the animals while they were away. "I want to pay my share for the tickets and the berths. For Maynard and Levis taking care of the place too."

Stacey shrugged. "Up to you."

I didn't like his tone. "You left me out of it?"

"Didn't think you wanted to be in it."

"Well, last time I looked I am still part

of this family."

"Well, you could've fooled me."

I gave him a look. "Now what's that supposed to mean?"

"Sometimes, Cassie, you don't act like it."

Stacey set his empty cup on the table and leaned forward in his chair, an elbow on each knee. "You know how long it's been since you've been home, Cassie? Not just Toledo, but really down home?"

"Oh, please, don't get into that again."

"Can't help but get into it."

"You know my work —"

"Two years."

"I've been busy," I said. I knew it was a weak defense.

"Yeah, I know," Stacey said. "Busy living a life that has nothing to do with where you're from."

"Now, wait just a minute —"

"Think about it. Think about just how long it's been since you've seen Mama and Papa and Big Ma. I think one of the main reasons they are coming is so they can see all of us gathered in one place.

461

They're not getting any younger, you know —"

"None of us are," I retorted.

Stacey ignored my comment. "Rest of us go down couple times a year. You haven't shown your face down there for two years."

"Don't get on me about that. They understand about this law business and what it takes for me to deal with it. I write them every month and send them something too."

"Well, I'm sure they appreciate all that, but you haven't been home. Why is that, Cassie?"

"Go ahead and tell me, you seem to think you know so much."

"Because I figure you're doing something you don't want them to know about."

I raised my hands in exasperation. "All I've been trying to do is make a living and do what I'm supposed to do as a lawyer. You know it's not easy."

"Never was supposed to be. You knew that going in."

"Yeah, I knew, all right. But I did it,

didn't I? I got my degree. I passed the bar. Now I'm just trying to live my life."

"Without us?"

I sighed, shook my head, got up, and went over to the window. I pushed back the curtain and stared at the snow-covered street below. Boston was not yet awake. No one was on the street.

"You need to come home," Stacey said again.

I rubbed my forehead and tried to calm myself. The lawyer in me did not want to say the wrong words, even to my brother. I turned back to him. "I'll need to think on it, call Lawyer Tate, see what he thinks about the situation Moe's in."

Stacey didn't say anything.

I decided not to discuss it any further right now. "You must be tired, what with that long drive. I can make up the sofa."

Stacey nodded wearily. "All right."

"You want something to eat first? I can fix something."

"No. Just sleep. Come Sunday morning early, I need to head back to Toledo."

"You've got to leave that soon?"

"You know how it is, Cassie. Got to be at work come Monday morning. You'll have all day Saturday to make up your mind about whether you're going back with me or not. Just remember, Moe's life is on the line."

I stared at Stacey and he stared back. I looked away first and headed for the closet. "I'll get your bedding," I said. "Bathroom's down the hall."

Stacey slept until midmorning. When he woke I cooked breakfast and we sat down to eat together. As we ate, Stacey looked around the room. "I like your place, Cassie," he said. I smiled, pleased to have his approval. I loved this room. It was large and open with the kitchen at one end and the living area at the other. There was no fireplace, but that didn't matter. It was an older building with thick walls and high-quality wood, and the living room/kitchen had ceiling-to-floor windows that lined most of its eastern wall. The bedroom, down a short hallway off the living area, was small and so was the bathroom, but it was the expansive space of the great room that had immediately at-

464

tracted me to the apartment. A sofa, draped with one of Big Ma's handmade quilts, a comfortable chair, a coffee table, and a desk, all bought secondhand, were in the living area. A round dining table made of pine with four matching chairs, and a smaller oblong kitchen table without chairs, which sat directly in front of the kitchen counter, were at the other end of the room.

I had painted the far end of the living area wall a brilliant orange and hung drums and spears and African paintings. The other walls I had left the original Navajo white, but above the kitchen cabinets I had hung an assortment of brightly colored African baskets. The wall opposite the windows was divided by the entry door to the apartment. On the living room side of the door hung Native American rugs, which I had bought with Flynn, as well as other items I had collected while in the West. On the kitchen side of the wall were family photographs. At the center was an enlarged photograph of Grandpa Paul-Edward and Big Ma standing with all their sons in front of our house in 1901, shortly after it was built. Surrounding it were photographs of Mama and Papa, of Dee and the girls, of the family on Dorr Street, and of the boys and me taken before Clayton Chester and Christopher-John went overseas. The only photograph that wasn't there was one of Flynn. I kept his image forever engraved in my mind and my heart. Each morning as I sat at the table drinking my coffee with sunlight flooding the wall or when a winter's day darkened the room, I always felt warmth from that wall of family photographs. It kept the family with me, and I was glad I could share it with Stacey.

We stayed at the table talking for more than two hours. We had much catching up to do. Stacey did not press me on going back with him. Both of us had decided to give that decision a rest until later. Earlier I had called Lawyer Tate but was unable to reach him. After breakfast, Stacey said he was going to gas up the car and also have a mechanic look under the hood. He had heard a pinging noise on his way here. He also said he wanted to walk around a bit before dark and get a better look at Boston. He had been here only once before and that was for my graduation. He asked me to come along, but I declined. I had legal papers to study and I wanted to call Lawyer Tate again. When Stacey was gone I sat at my desk to study cases, though I could hardly keep my mind on them. Shortly after Stacey left, there was a knock on the apartment door and I figured it was Stacey coming back for something.

But it wasn't Stacey. It was Guy.

"Hey, beautiful," Guy said, and handed me a bouquet of mixed flowers accented with baby's breath. He bent his head toward mine and kissed me lightly on the lips and pushed past me into the room. He was carrying a large bag of groceries with a couple of French baguettes poking out the top.

"What are you doing here?" I asked, closing the door. "I thought you'd be in Brewster through tomorrow."

Guy went straight to the kitchen table and set the bag on it. "Client changed his mind. Got him to settle this morning. I couldn't do without you and came back soon as I could." He came over to me. "Miss me?" he asked. He slipped his arms around my waist, pulled me to him, and kissed me again, this time without hurry. I allowed the kiss, then pulled away. Guy took off his coat and tossed it on the sofa. "Thought we could have the rest of the weekend together."

I gave him a placid smile as I went to the table and checked the bag of groceries. "Seems like you've got quite a weekend planned."

"Look further," said Guy.

I did. There were paper-wrapped packages of steak and frozen lobsters. There were potatoes and asparagus and fruit, lemons, strawberries and blueberries, and a pineapple. Two bottles of wine were also in the bag.

"And guess what?" Guy went on. "I'm going to do all the cooking. You don't have to lift a finger." He came to the table and again slipped his arms around me.

I allowed him to hold me, but after a moment I said, "It's not going to happen."

Guy nuzzled his face close to my ear. "What? What's not going to happen? This dinner? Oh, I think it is."

"No . . . it's not. . . . My brother's here."

Guy immediately released me. "What?"

"You heard me. Stacey came last night. Actually early this morning, like about three o'clock."

Guy took a step backward. "Were you expecting him?"

"Don't you think I would have told you if I were?"

"He came without letting you know? Why is he here?"

"A friend of ours is in trouble and Stacey wants me to go back with him on Sunday to help him."

"What kind of trouble?"

I hesitated, reluctant to go into it. As much as I trusted Guy, I had never told him about Moe or his flight from Mississippi and why he had to run. "Look, I don't have time to talk about it now. You have to go."

Guy was silent, then shook his head. "I want to meet your brother, Cassie. He's got to know sometime. They all do."

I stared at him. "But not today."

"Today is as good a day as any."

"I don't think so. I wasn't planning on any of this, and I'm not ready for you to meet my brother —"

"Would you ever be ready?"

"Look, Guy —"

"Would you ever be ready for me to meet any of them?"

I put my hands up. "I told you I don't want to talk about this right now, and I do not want a fight about it. You need to understand, I can't deal with your being here and Stacey too. You need to go."

"No, I think I'll stay," Guy said quietly, then went to a cabinet and pulled out a large pot.

I was angry, but I didn't want to fight with him. I just wanted him out of here. He couldn't meet Stacey, but when Guy got stubborn like this, it was hard to dissuade him. I left Guy in the kitchen and went to the bedroom. I sat on the bed, pulled my legs up against my chest, and slumped my head against them. I was shaking. I was not ready for this.

I stayed in the room for more than an hour, expecting Guy to come in to say he was leaving; he didn't. I smelled cooking. I glanced outside. The winter sky was almost dark. I got up and went into the living room. Guy was at the kitchen stove, stirring something in the skillet. The lobster pot was on the stove and steaming. A smaller pot was opposite it. Guy glanced over at me and smiled. "Still here, I see," I said.

He nodded in affirmation. "Still here."

I went to the stove and stood beside him. He had minced the garlic and onions and was stirring them in butter along with oregano. "Smells good," I admitted.

"Already got the potatoes ready to go into the oven. The steak is seasoned, ready to broil. Pot here has all the spices and some butter ready for the lobster, and the asparagus is ready for a quick dip. Hollandaise sauce is waiting on the asparagus."

"You've gone to a lot of trouble."

471

"Why not? Special dinner for a special lady."

I walked away. "It won't be special, not with my brother here. It'll be a disaster."

"No need for it to be," Guy said, turning off the fire and removing the skillet and setting it on the counter. "I'm sure he's a reasonable man."

"You don't know my brother, not when it comes to matters like this. You have no idea."

Guy looked at me, then covered the skillet. He wiped his hands on a towel and came over to me. He put his hands on my shoulders. "Then you tell me," he said.

"There's not time. Stacey will be back soon."

Guy took my hand. "Cassie, talk to me."

"I told you before, Guy, I really want you to go. Please do that for me. I really want you out of here before Stacey gets back."

"You feel that strongly about it?"

"Thought I made that clear."

Guy looked away, then back again. "Cassie, what do you want for us?"

"Right now, Guy, there is no us."

"I suppose not. Not until you face up to your family and your feelings."

"Will you please go? Do this one thing for me."

"This one thing." Guy looked at me long, sighed, then went to the sofa and got his coat.

"And you might as well take some of this food with you."

Guy glanced at the food-laden table. "No, Cassie. I brought it for you. It stays. Maybe your brother will enjoy it. Hope you will too." He headed for the door, but before his hand was on the knob, there was a knock.

"Oh, Lord," I moaned. I knew it was Stacey.

Guy opened the door.

Stacey stood in the hallway. He looked from Guy to me in silence. Guy extended his hand. "You must be Stacey, Cassie's brother. I'm Guy Hallis. I work with your sister at the law office."

473

Stacey looked again at Guy, then hesitantly shook his hand.

"I was just leaving," said Guy. "Brought by some paperwork for Cassie from the office. Also brought in a little food for you and Cassie from the corner store after I heard you were here. I knew Cassie would probably be too busy to go grocery shopping, what with all the casework she has this weekend. Well, I've got to run." Guy glanced back at me. "See you at the office Monday, Cassie." Turning back to Stacey, he said, "Nice to meet you, Stacey. Hope we get a chance to talk next time you're here." Stacey did not respond as Guy slipped out the doorway and past him. Stacey remained in the hallway, staring after him.

"Well, are you coming in?" I asked, and returned to the kitchen table.

Stacey came into the room and closed the door behind him. I glanced at him as he stood silent by the door, then occupied myself with the food still to be cooked. "You get everything done you wanted?"

Stacey came over to the table. "Gassed up. Got the car checked. Did a little shopping for Dee. I'm set to go."

"Good," I said, keeping myself busy and my look directed at the table.

Stacey watched me. "Looks like quite a feast here."

I nodded. "Lobster. Steak. Potatoes."

Stacey picked up one of the wine bottles, looked it over, and set it down. "Uh-huh, quite a feast."

His mood was darkening. I tried to dispel it. "Remember when we went to see Uncle Hammer and that was the first time we had lobster? And Uncle Hammer and Aunt Loretta said we needed to have some prime rib with it too. One of the best meals I can remember."

"This white man know about all that?"

I stopped my busywork. "Look, Stacey, I don't know what you're thinking, but —"

"Cassie, you know perfectly well what I'm thinking. No man brings over this kind of food to a woman unless something's going on."

"Maybe what's going on is a friend caring enough to provide some food for another friend and her brother."

"And this is what he chose to bring? Did you ask him to bring it? Did you pay him for it?"

"No, it's just what he brought. Stacey, I've known Guy since law school. He was in my group that went overseas. We work in the same law firm. He's a good and considerate person. He wanted us to have this dinner."

Stacey stared at me, then said, "Are you going to Toledo with me?"

"I thought I had until tomorrow to decide."

"Did you reach Lawyer Tate?"

"No, not yet —"

"Are you going back or not? Give me your answer."

I placed my hands flat on the table and took a moment before replying. "I can't give you an answer right now, Stacey, and I won't let you pressure me into giving you one. I still want to talk to Lawyer Tate first. I've got a lot going on here —"

"Yes, I can see."

"And just what do you mean by that?"

476

I was no longer sounding apologetic.

"Cassie, you know exactly what I mean."

I rounded the table to face Stacey close up. "Look, Stacey, this is my life here. I have friends, and not every one of them is colored. A lot of people in Boston have been good to me, and not every one of them is colored either. I haven't done anything wrong, so don't come judging me on anything."

"You didn't answer my question."

"Which one you want me to answer? Your first question or all your insinuations?"

"Are you going back with me?"

I took a deep breath. I didn't like Stacey putting me in this position. I put my hands on my hips and, defiantly, I issued an adamant "No." Without another word Stacey turned, walked over, and picked up his suitcase from behind the sofa. My arms slipped to my sides. "What are you doing?"

"Going back to Toledo."

"But . . . you said you were going to stay until Sunday!"

"What's the point? I came to get you. You said you're not going with me. I leave now I can be back with Dee and the girls before morning."

"But I don't want you to leave right now. I want you to stay. I've got all this food —"

Stacey glanced at the table. "Maybe your good, considerate friend can come back and enjoy it with you." He turned to go.

"Stacey, listen —"

Stacey stopped at the door. "No, you listen, Cassie. You're moving into some very dangerous territory here. You've moved away from your family, and now you're moving away from your people too."

I walked toward him. "What are you talking about?"

"You're living in a white world, Cassie. Look at this apartment building, this white neighborhood. I was almost afraid to park my car out front the way people were staring at me. But you're comfortable here, aren't you? How'd you get this place anyway?"

I didn't say anything.

"That friend of yours help you get it?"

I kept my silence. I did not want to lose my temper.

Stacey now took the time to lecture me. "Cassie, we've been slaves to white men since our people were first thrown on those ships and dragged here in chains. White men could do whatever they wanted to our colored women, our men too. Think about it, Cassie. You know all the stories as well as I do, and now you're willing to be with a white man? You're willing to turn your back on your family and your race too?"

I grabbed at his wrist. "Stacey, don't you dare say that to me! That's not what's happening!"

Stacey's look was cold. "Isn't it?"

"Look here, I'm a woman grown, many years over! You can't come in here telling me what to do!"

"I'm not telling you what to do, Cassie. I'm just telling you what you already know. You're a good-looking woman, Cassie. You're smart, highly educated. You're the best of the best. You've got all this going for you and that white man sees it. Like I said, you need to come home, Cassie. This white man, he's taking you away, taking you into that white world of his."

"What if I told you he wants me to marry him?"

Stacey's jaw set and he stared icily at me. "Do you think I give a damn if he wants to or not? You'd still be a black woman choosing to go with a white man! Too many of our women gone with them! Forced to go with them, our blood included! Now, you've got choices and this is what you're choosing to do? You don't go sleeping with a white man, Cassie, no matter what, marriage or no marriage." He sucked in his breath and his voice grew quiet. "You do, you turn your back on all of us. I won't even call you my sister."

"Stacey —"

"Like I said, it's time to come home, Cassie." He shook his head, visibly disappointed in me, then looked down at my hand, still clutching his wrist. After one last look at me, he yanked away, opened the door, and went out.

"Stacey!" I called after him.

My brother did not answer as he walked down the hall, turned the corner, and disappeared down the stairs.

It had been seven years since I had come to Boston. I had received my law degree and passed the bar examination on my first attempt. Being a lone woman of color on many occasions, I had stood out and come to the attention of people with influence, who pointed me out as an example of what a colored person could achieve. After my first semester at Boston University School of Law, I had been offered a scholarship, full tuition and board. I had been given a part-time job. After graduation and the bar, I was offered the opportunity to travel to Europe and Africa with a program funded by a philanthropic group associated with colleges in the region whose purpose was fact-finding and improving relations with emerging African nations. The program was for one year. It was something very few Negroes had the opportunity to do, and I reveled in it. Before heading to Africa I went to England and France and

Germany, up to the Scandinavian countries, Denmark and Sweden, down to Greece and Italy too. With the group in Africa, I traveled to Egypt and down into Kenya and Uganda, Tanganyika, and Ethiopia.

Each African country where I went, people stared at me, studied me in silence, then welcomed me even more than they welcomed others in my group. They told me I was not what they had expected. In Europe, the people had seen our colored soldiers during the war and the ones still stationed in Germany. But in Africa it was a different story. Many of the people in the villages had never seen an American Negro before. All many of them had seen of the American Negro was what was presented in American films, and most of those films certainly did not flatter American Negroes. They were movies depicting the American Negro as enslaved, shiftless, ignorant, usually following behind or at the will of some white person. Few showed the Negro as heroic. Very few showed the Negro as standing up for herself or himself, educated, with a mind of her or his own. Few showed the Negro as handsome or beautiful or with an intellect equal to a white person. Although Negro filmmakers had produced films showing these qualities, such films were not widely distributed. In recent years, a handful of Hollywood movies had begun to depict these qualities too, but still the widespread concept of the American Negro was of a people enslaved, and maybe that was because in many ways we still were. As the lone Negro in a group of twenty Americans, I fit none of these stereotypes, and everywhere I went people seemed amazed that I didn't. I was welcomed, and that amazed me.

Upon my return to the States I had gone first to Toledo, then with Stacey and Dee and the girls back home to Mississippi. Christopher-John and Becka, with Clayton Chester and Rachel, had followed with their children. We all went home to celebrate my being back. It was 1957, the first time all of us had been together in five years.

Some things at home had changed. Some things had not.

For our family house, some of the

changes were major. The old outhouse was gone. We now had an indoor bathroom. The boys had built it themselves, walling off a section of their old room to install it. They had done all the work — the carpentry, the drywalling, the painting, even the plumbing, which was now in both the bathroom and the kitchen. We no longer had to draw water from the well, though that didn't keep us from doing so. A bucket of well water with a ladle handy for anyone who wanted a drink still hung from a giant hook on the back porch. Electricity was now available in the community, and it had been installed throughout the house. The kerosene lamps were no longer needed, but were kept nearby in case the electricity went out. The boys bought an electric stove and a refrigerator for the kitchen. Big Ma balked at having to give up her wood-burning stove, but she liked the idea of the refrigerator, which kept her foods from spoiling. Telephone lines were also strung in the area, and Stacey, Man, and Christopher-John had insisted that Mama and Papa have a telephone in the house. Neither Papa nor Mama much cared for the idea. Mama still believed letters were the best means of communication, and Papa, who never wrote letters, figured there was nothing like face-to-face communication. Finally, they were persuaded that a telephone would allow the family to keep in contact more easily, and they relented. The boys even bought them a television. While I was going to law school and traveling, Mama, Papa, and Big Ma had allowed the modern world into the house.

There were changes in the community too.

Although Great Faith Church remained the same, there was no longer a Great Faith School. A new school built by the county for Negro students in the area was located several miles away. The old class buildings, which had been built by the church, not the county, still stood. Many of the families I had always known remained in the community. Moe's brothers and sisters, most with families of their own, were all still in the area. So were the Averys, Claude and the others, and most of the Wigginses, although Little Willie and his wife, Dora, with their five children had moved to Jackson.

Some things had changed. Some things had not.

Mostly things remained the same. This was still Mississippi, and Mississippi at its core, despite some attempts at modernization, had not changed. When I went into Vicksburg and into Jackson, life was still the same. I still could not eat in the white restaurants. I still could not try on clothes I wanted to buy in the department stores. I still had to go to the back door to buy ice cream or a hamburger from a fast-food parlor. I still could not go to the "white only" library. I still had to drink from nasty-looking water fountains marked "colored" in public places. I still had to sit at the back of the bus. And, of course, the signs all were still there. Signs, signs everywhere you looked.

Whites Only. Colored Not Allowed.

The racial divide in Mississippi had not changed. But I was different, and much of the world was different, and I expected Mississippi to be different too. I stayed with Mama, Papa, and Big Ma for three weeks, then returned to Boston. I had not been back since.

Stacey was right about more than one thing. I did live mostly in a white world. The law firm at which I worked was all white except for me. The neighborhood in which I lived was all white except for me. The building in which I lived, all white except for me. I had managed to get the apartment through my connections with the law firm. Guy had helped me get it, but I couldn't admit that to Stacey. Although I was the only colored person in the building, I refused to let that bother me. At first there had been odd looks and hostile stares from the other tenants. I was reminded of the apartment Flynn and I were denied in Westwood, and I put up with their hostility. The apartment was worth it.

I worked at a law firm owned by Guy's father and uncle. I had come to the attention of the firm in part because of Guy, but also because of my own merits at the law school. Before the trip to Europe and Africa, several law firms, impressed by my scholastic record, had approached me, but I had chosen Guy's firm. It was another opportunity to advance. Opportunities always seemed to be coming my way, opportunities so many other colored folks didn't have. I was fortunate. Most Negro lawyers could not get into such a firm, into any kind of white firm, so they established their own individual law offices or partnered with another Negro attorney. I knew the opportunities offered to me were because of my youth, my mind, even my looks. I knew also that I was accepted in part because I was the "only one." In a white world, a few black folks could be tolerated, even welcomed, but if it was more than a few, that worried white people. I knew that too, and I snatched every opportunity presented to me, as the "only one."

Despite the white world in which I lived, I kept connected to the Negro community. Each Sunday morning I took a bus across town to Roxbury, to the Baptist church I had attended since my return from Africa. I knew the congregation well and they knew me. They knew I was a lawyer, and some of them came to me for advice about their legal problems.

Mostly their problems stemmed from landlord issues, such as people about to be evicted from their homes because they couldn't pay the rent, or from a husband or child who was being charged with some misdemeanor and the family had no money for bail or anyone to represent them in court. I offered them advice and did not charge them for it, but I did not become fully involved in any of their problems until a woman came to me about a medical issue. She had been denied services at a doctor's office in Boston. Her situation was similar to mine when I had been rejected by the Boulder medical office.

I talked to Guy about it. Guy was hesitant about taking the case. "This doctor works for a professional corporation. Unless you can prove the woman was denied medical care because of her race — and that might be hard to do — you'll have no case. According to law, he has a right to accept or reject anyone he chooses."

"I know. But I plan to file a complaint with the Massachusetts Commission Against Discrimination."

"Could take a lot of time, and you won't be able to bill for it," Guy cautioned.

"It'll be my time," I said. "I need to help this woman."

Guy offered me his help if I needed it, but I forged on alone. I filed a complaint with the Commission which investigated the matter, but discrimination could not be proved. I chose not to give up, and I told the woman I represented not to give up either. We would bide our time and we would file again. I told several people who came to me much the same thing. We had to wait for another day.

I did not see Guy again until Monday morning at the law office. He had not called or come by after Stacey left, and I chose not to call him. "Your brother get off okay?" he asked.

"He left shortly after you did."

"I thought he wasn't leaving until Sunday."

"Changed his mind."

"What about that friend of yours who's in trouble?"

490

I did not want to talk about Moe with Guy, although Moe had been constantly on my mind since Stacey left. I had called Lawyer Tate throughout the weekend and finally reached him at home late Sunday night. He told me what I already knew about extradition laws. "If Moe is in Canada and they arrest him there," Lawyer Tate said, "they'll send him back to Mississippi. If he's still in the States, same thing. Now, we can fight the extradition, but most likely either way he'll be on his way to Mississippi. There's really nothing to be done until then. Let's talk about it when you come home for Christmas."

In answer to Guy's question, I said, "He still is."

Guy knew me well enough not to press the matter. "Well, I assume since you didn't leave with your brother, you won't be going early to Toledo. That means you can come up to Maine for my parents' Christmas party." Although Guy's parents had a house in Boston, they also had what they called a vacation house in Maine and Guy said they usually spent their holidays there.

491

"Guy, I told you before I don't know about that."

"And I told you before they'd be happy to have you. Several other people from the office are going up. A couple of them will be staying at the house too. My parents know about you and they're getting a room ready."

I smiled. "They know all about me?"

Guy smiled too. "Well, I didn't want them to be shocked when you arrived."

"No, wouldn't want that," I laughed.

Guy grew serious. "Look, Cassie, they're not stupid people. My dad and my uncle have seen us together, and they're experienced enough to know a relationship when they see it."

"Have they said anything?"

Guy shook his head. "Not to me. I know they'd rather I'd be with my ex-wife or someone like her, but so far, they've said nothing."

I didn't respond.

Guy put his finger under my chin and lifted my face upward. "So are you coming to Maine?"

"If I do, I don't want it to be like that other time we ventured out together." On that occasion Guy and a married couple who had gone on the trip abroad with us and to Africa had persuaded me to go to a Boston nightclub. The club was white, and although the entertainers onstage were colored, I was asked to leave. We had already been seated when the manager told us we were not welcome. The next day Guy had filed a discrimination suit against the club, but the suit went nowhere, which did not surprise either of us.

The club claimed it was a private club, for members only. We knew that it was not, just an excuse to deny me admission. It mattered to me that Guy had cared enough to file a suit against the club, but that was the last time I had gone to a public place with him. "Don't worry, it won't be anything like that," Guy said. "You know I'm still sorry about that."

"Yeah, I know you are. I am too."

493

I had met Guy Hallis during my first year of law school. I was the only colored person in the class, and he had come right over and sat beside me and said, "Is this seat taken?"

I had looked around. Other empty seats were available, and I answered, "Guess not, just like all the others sitting there unoccupied."

Guy had laughed, sat down, and opened his notebook as the professor approached the podium. He had said nothing else to me, not even when the class was over, but twice a week when the class met he sat in the chair beside mine, even when I sat in a chair different from the previous class. He always spoke pleasantly and with a smile. I always returned his greeting, minus the smile. He made me feel awkward, and silently I questioned why he was always sitting next to me, although I knew of course that it had nothing to do with the available seating. I knew that he was trying to befriend me. I didn't know why. Maybe it was just because I was the lone Negro in the class.

Maybe he thought I needed a friend.

I didn't.

I went my lone way and was accustomed to it. Since arriving in Boston I had met few people outside the law school. I had no real friends, no need for friends, and I preferred it that way. I had come here to study law. I wasn't interested in friendships. But Guy Hallis was. At the end of one of the winter class sessions he asked if I would join him for coffee. As I gathered my books, I shook my head. "Can't," I said. "I've got other plans."

"It's just coffee, Miss Logan, nothing else. I'm not the enemy and I won't bite. I promise." I thought of Flynn's words to me.

"Why do you want to have coffee with me?" I asked outright.

Guy hesitated, then slowly said, "I think you know why. You look all alone here."

"Maybe that's what I want. Because I am."

"You don't have to be," Guy said.

"Well, maybe I prefer it that way."

"Like I said, it's just coffee."

I headed for the classroom door. Guy followed me. We walked in silence until we reached the library, where I stopped. I decided not to take Guy's hand of friendship, if that was truly what it was. "I'll see you in class," I said, and walked away.

"It's just coffee, Cassie!" he called after me.

I didn't respond. I just kept on walking.

Guy didn't give up. I thought at the next class he would choose to sit elsewhere. He didn't. As always, he came right over and sat next to me. As always, he smiled and spoke pleasantly. As always, I returned his greeting without a smile. He didn't invite me to coffee again.

It was at a law school Christmas party that I finally accepted Guy's friendship. I hadn't planned to attend. I felt awkward since I was the only Negro who would be attending and I had no one to invite to go with me. I had decided not to go to the party until another student warned that not to attend was frowned upon by the staff and possibly it could affect job

496

recommendations down the line; I had to be able to socialize within the legal community. So, at the last minute, against my better judgment, I went.

The party was at one of the professors' houses. It was an early evening party, so I took the bus over. I planned to get back the same way. I intended to make my appearance and stay for only a short while. The fact that some of the faculty were late in arriving persuaded me to stay longer since I believed it was in my best interest to be present when they arrived. I stood quietly by as the law students arrived and made merry. A few of them came over to speak to me and made polite conversation for a few minutes, then were gone. I was totally uncomfortable.

Then Santa Claus arrived.

It was one of the law students, and from the sound of him, he was already inebriated. He called for all "good little boys and girls" to come over. The partygoers gathered around. I happened to be standing by the table where he plunked the huge red sack he was carrying. He then announced, "You good little boys

497

stay where you are. I want to see these good little girls first . . . and . . . they don't all have to be so good." He winked. "They can be as bad as they want to be."

The crowd roared with laughter. I started to back away, but I was penned in at the front of the circle by people surrounding the jolly law student.

"Now," said Santa, sitting down with a grunt, "who's the first naughty little girl wants to sit on Santa's lap?"

Someone pushed a young woman toward Santa. I recognized her from one of my classes. Her name was Maureen. She had dark hair, block-cut at chin level, very dark eyes, and wore movie star red lipstick. She was quite pretty. Drink in hand, she went over to Santa. Santa patted his thigh. "Have a seat," he said, "and let me see what you're drinking there." Maureen giggled, sat down on Santa's lap, and handed her glass to him. Santa took a sip. "Owww, good stuff," proclaimed Santa. "Bourbon. This tells me you must be a mighty good girl!"

Maureen laughed and so did the rest of the partygoers.

"Now, tell Santa what you want for

Christmas," ordered Santa. "You don't have to tell everybody, just put your sweet lips next to my ear and whisper your wish to me."

Maureen complied; leaning seductively close to the Santa and cupping her hand to one side of her mouth, she whispered into his ear. Santa's eyes went big in mock surprise as Maureen made her wish known, then Santa nodded profoundly and said, "Well, I sure will try to do my best, little girl! I am sure I'm the man for the job!"

More laughter.

"Now, hang on before you get down from Santa's lap. Got a little present for you." He reached into his sack and pulled out a neatly wrapped box with golden ribbon. "This is because you've been such a good little naughty girl! Now give Santa a kiss."

Maureen complied, kissing him full on the lips. As she got up, two more young women were summoned to Santa. One sat on each knee. They were given much the same Santa treatment as Maureen. Then someone shouted out, " 'Ey, Santa! What about Miss Logan here?" Someone grabbed me from behind. "Don't want to discriminate!" I was pushed forward and down on Santa's knee. I tried to get up, but strong hands on my shoulders kept me down.

"Ah, come on now," said Santa, "you figure you've been too naughty to sit on Santa's lap?"

"I figure," I said, "this is something I don't do." Again I tried to rise. Some in the crowd laughed, but the laughter was not as raucous as before. There was a nervousness to it. I thrust my arms back hard, jabbing the person holding me. The grip slipped away and I jumped up. "You might think this is funny," I said, "but I don't."

"Ah, look here," said Santa, grabbing my arm, "it's all just in fun. Be a good girl and sit back down here on Santa's knee."

That was when Guy Hallis suddenly stepped forward. "Let go of her arm, Sean. She said she wants no part of this. Let her go."

The red-faced Santa looked up at Guy and released his hold. "Neither one of you is any fun. You two, expect to get lumps of coal in your stockings!" A few people laughed, but mostly there was quiet as I finally was allowed to turn and make my way through the crowd. Guy followed.

"Sorry about that," Guy said when we were out of the crowd and into the next room.

"It wasn't your doing." I looked around. "What did they do with the coats?"

"You're leaving?"

"I think so."

"You have a car?"

"No. I'll take the bus."

"I can take you home."

"I can make it fine on the bus," I said, heading for the pile of coats on one of the settees.

Guy went with me. "It's dark already. I'd feel better if you'd let me take you. Believe me, I'm nothing like Santa."

I studied his face. Guy had always been kind to me, kind and considerate. I decided to trust him. That was the beginning of our friendship.

■ ■ ■ ■

Guy Hallis learned early on in our newly formed friendship that I was widowed and the circumstances of it. He also learned that I did not want to talk about my husband. The pain was still too great. I learned about Guy too. His Christian name was Augustus, but everyone called him Guy. He had been drafted after graduation from college in 1943 and served in the Pacific as a Navy officer. When the war was over, he came home for a short while, then went to Europe. He wanted to see what five years of war had done. He stayed on in Europe for several years, and when he returned to the States he enrolled in Boston University School of Law.

Guy accepted the friendship that was forging between us on my terms, but as a woman I knew he wanted more. When that didn't happen, he went his own way with another law student, Maureen from the Christmas party. It was obvious to everyone that she had eyes for him. Their relationship didn't bother me, for I felt nothing for Guy in that way. Although

Guy was seeing Maureen, we remained friends, and I was close to no one except Guy. There were things I could talk to him about, although not everything. He was a good listener. He had his own opinions too and I listened to those, although not as intently as he listened to mine. There were times when I needed to be held, just to feel a human touch, and he held me. Guy married Maureen in the third year of law school, and after that I no longer saw him except in the classes we shared. The marriage did not last long. By the time Guy and I were selected for the trip to Europe and Africa, they were divorced, and he called me again. Our renewed relationship was all about friendship, as it always had been. It wasn't until we traveled through Europe and Africa together that things began to change between us. Guy was no longer content to be just a listener. He wanted to be a greater part of my life.

I decided to go to Maine. I took the bus. Guy drove. He had wanted me to drive up with him, but I wasn't about to consider it, a Negro woman driving alone with a white man, sitting up front beside him at that, even in the North.

"It isn't the South, Cassie," Guy said.

"No. But it is the United States," I countered. "So what's the difference?"

I had my way. Guy met me at the bus station in Portland. As he picked up my bag, he said, "Hope you don't mind riding with me far as my parents' house."

"You can joke about it," I said, "but I still figure it's a mistake. I don't even know what I'm doing here."

"Look, Cassie, I told you what I told my parents. I invited you along with some others from the law firm. They're expecting you. They've got a room ready. They're great people, believe me."

"I'm sure they are, but I only know your father professionally, not socially. He's hardly ever spoken to me."

"Take my word for it. He'll speak to you this weekend."

"They won't approve of us."

"We'll have to wait and see about that. Like I said, they're great people."

"My folks are great people too," I said,

"but they'd never accept something like this."

By the time we got to Guy's family house, others from the firm had already arrived, as well as some of our classmates from the law school. As Guy said, his parents were warm and welcoming. Upon entering the Hallis house, I was impressed by it, but not overwhelmed. During my stay in New England, I had been invited to a number of homes owned by prominent New Englanders. The houses were always attractive, well-appointed, and the kind of houses Americans of all races could only dream of having. The difference I immediately recognized from the other New England houses I had visited was the location of the Hallis house. As I stepped from the heart of the house to what the family called their backyard, I found myself facing the Atlantic Ocean.

Guy hadn't told me.

The lawn, brownish now, rolled down unencumbered to a rocky cliff. There were no fences. On either side of the Hallis house, several hundred yards away, were houses just as grand, all looking toward the ocean. One belonged to a former governor. On the ocean, great ships passed slowly by. I had never seen such a sight, not up close, not so personal.

"You didn't tell me," I said softly to Guy.

"I know." He took my arm. "I want to show you something."

He led me down the long sloping lawn to the cliffs, then we wove our way down a trail to the water. There was a wooden cage at the edge, several feet beneath the ocean surface. Guy lifted it out. The cage was filled with lobster.

"So," I said, meeting his eyes, "you get fresh lobster whenever you want."

"Only in season." He smiled and returned the cage to its waters. He straightened and looked at me again. "You want me to apologize? I know you like lobster as much as I do. Would you object to having lobster anytime you wanted during the season if you could have it? Just like fishing, Cassie, down on the Rosa Lee you told me about. You could have fish anytime you wanted, just as long as you were willing to put in the time to get it.

It's the same with the lobster. No difference."

I just looked at him. Maybe he was right about that, but I didn't know any colored folks who could just walk out to their backyard and get themselves a cage full of lobster.

The festivities began soon after dark with holiday partygoers arriving in great spirits with good wishes and gifts. All were well-dressed, all seemed merry, all were white. Once again, I found myself the only one. As on previous occasions, people took note and a number of them went out of their way to start a conversation with me. These were well-educated, world-traveled, sophisticated people. Some tried to engage me in casual conversation about how I liked Maine. I told them I liked it just fine. Some tried to engage me in conversation about the New England weather. I told them I liked it just fine. Some tried to engage me in conversation about Boston and the law office there. I liked them just fine too. Then there were those keeping up with current events who pointedly asked my views as a Negro about race relations in our country, about ongoing attempts at desegregation in the South. I looked at each of them directly and said, "It's way past due."

By the end of the evening I had had my fill of all the people with their polite but curious conversations with me. I went onto the stone patio and stood shivering, staring at the ocean, at the glimmering lights of the ships as they passed, and at the sky laden with thousands of bright stars, and was in awe at the meeting of God's sky and the earth's waters. Guy soon joined me. He took off his jacket and put it around my shoulders. He leaned his elbows on the stone ledge of the half wall that separated the patio from the lawn and stared at the ocean too. "Are you about tired of these people now?"

I laughed. "What makes you think that?"

"Because after seven years, I think I know you a little bit." He turned and looked at me. "Do you think you'll ever feel comfortable with them?"

"Probably not," I answered honestly.

"Different world."

"They're not bad people, Cassie. Different from the world you grew up in, but decent and willing to accept new ideas." He took my hand and kept hold. "But you're comfortable with me."

"You, I've gotten used to."

"It took a while," he said. "But you do trust me now, don't you?"

I smiled. "As much as I can."

Guy didn't smile back. "I want you to trust me, Cassie. I've told you that before. All this time I've been trying to earn your trust, and I think it's time that you do trust me."

I sighed. "Why is it so important to you, Guy?"

He turned again toward the ocean. "Because I want you to marry me, Cassie. I've told you that before. I want you to be my wife." He did not look at me for some time. Finally, he pulled from the ledge, his eyes on mine. I just stared at him. Guy let go of my hand. "Something to think about for the new year."

Several of the houseguests joined us on the patio, and the conversation between

Guy and me was ended, but not before his eyes met mine again. I knew he wanted an answer. I had none to give him. The next day I took the bus back to Boston. A few days later I boarded a train for Toledo. I told Guy I would see him in the new year.

FAMILY REUNION CHRISTMAS
(1959)

The family no longer lived on Dorr Street.

Dee had finally realized her dream of having a single-family house. She and Stacey had lived in the Dorr Street house for eight years and it had served them well, but in the fall of 1953 they found their dream home. In a neighborhood where real estate was opening up to people of color, they were able to buy a house from an elderly white couple who, like a number of other residents on the elm-lined street, were moving from the changing neighborhood. A decade before, when Stacey and Dee had first come to Toledo, this neighborhood would not have been open to them. Now Negro professional people — doctors, lawyers, teachers, even a judge — lived on the three-block street, along with business owners and factory workers like Stacey and the Davises. It was the best neighborhood in the city for colored people; other areas were still off-limits to us.

Stacey and Dee's house was fabulous, huge and majestic, with a brick chimney running up its front porch to its roof of red Spanish tiles. A long driveway ran along the side of the house to the two-car garage, also roofed in red tile, which restricted the view of what lay to the south of it. In front of the garage was an expansive concrete turnaround space, in front of the house was a deep lawn, and beyond the garage and the turnaround space was an even deeper back lawn that extended to a tall woven wooden fence. A stately blue spruce towered high above the garage and grounds and stood like a sentinel guarding the back gate.

All of us were in awe of this new house, bigger and finer than any our family had owned. The living room was impressive, much larger than other living rooms in the area, and had a sizeable fireplace. Two entries led from the living room to the kitchen, one through the dining room, the other through a short hallway that passed stairways going to the second floor, and to the basement. There were oak beams in the ceiling of the dining room, and ceiling-to-floor beveled-glass cabinets lined the back wall. Beveled glass also was in living room cabinets and the French doors opening from the living room into the sun parlor, the front entry room into the house. Brass wall light fixtures shaped like long-tapered candlesticks adorned the walls of every room throughout the house. A tiered chandelier hung from the dining room ceiling and another hung in the breakfast nook.

Adjoining the breakfast nook through an archway was a spacious kitchen. Cabinets and counters and appliances lined three of its walls. Tucked into an alcove of the fourth wall was the refrigerator. Also on the wall was a rectangular box, designed like a clock. In the box were the numbers one through four lined up vertically, with an arrow next to each number. When the doorbells at the front door, side door, or back door were rung, an arrow turned to the number, indicating which had been rung. The fourth number was to ring the maid. None of us had seen such a thing. Built in 1918, the house was large enough to have a maid, and during its early days, a maid had stayed in the attic, two rooms of which were completely finished with a living area, a bedroom, and a closet. The attic became a playroom for Rie and 'lois.

In addition to the fireplace in the living room, there were fireplaces in the master bedroom and the recreation room, located in the basement. Also in the basement were a large washroom and an even larger furnace room, where Stacy kept his workshop. It was a grand, grand house, and like the Dorr Street house, it became the family gathering place for the Logans and the Davises. Through Dee and the girls, we were melded into one family now, and the house was a source of pride for all of us.

Stacey and Dee did not sell the house on Dorr Street. One of the Davises had married and the couple with their two boys moved downstairs, where Stacey, Dee, and the girls had been, while an elderly gentleman from Mississippi took over two of the upstairs rooms and a young married Mississippi couple with a paraplegic daughter moved into another. All the unmarried Davises had moved right along with Stacey, Dee, and the girls and immediately claimed the recreation room as their bedroom. Dee and Stacey were all right with that. Zell and the Davises had become like older brothers to Rie and 'lois and were protective of them, just like Stacey, Christopher-John, and Clayton Chester. Now they were all married and had places of their own, so only Stacey and Dee and the girls lived in the house. It was just the four of them now. It had been a long time coming.

By the time I arrived in Toledo, Mama, Papa, and Big Ma were already there and the house was filled with the aromas of Christmas. Dee, of course, had all the cooking under control and I continued to be amazed by how she managed to get everything done. Once the girls were in high school Dee had gone to nursing school and was now working full-time as a licensed practical nurse, an LPN, at a Toledo hospital, yet she kept the house operating smoothly and, as expected, was totally organized concerning all the Christmas cooking. Rie and 'lois were preparing the food along with Dee. Teenagers now, both girls looked like Stacey. They had his skin coloring and his features, and Dee wryly said, "Robert couldn't deny those girls if he wanted to, they're so much like him."

Throughout the week Dee and the girls had cooked coconut pies and apple and sweet potato pies, two of each. Dee had made two of her special raisin-nut pecan pies as well, but was holding back until Christmas Day to top them off with whipped cream. The same was true of the icebox lemon pies still to be made and topped with meringue. 'lois would make them and some scrumptious homemade rolls, while Rie was preparing German chocolate cake, which had become her specialty. Dee still planned on making an old-fashioned pound cake topped with a lemon glaze. She would also be making a coconut cake. She didn't even think about making a red velvet cake, knowing that Rachel would be bringing one and no one could top Rachel's red velvet cake. Becka would be bringing one of her specialty cakes, moist and soaked in rum. No one could bake cakes better than the two sisters. Their mother had taught them well. Dee still planned to make a chocolate cake, though. There would be many of us for Christmas dinner and she intended to have plenty of food on hand.

Stacey, as he always did, kept popping in and out of the kitchen, worrying if there would be enough food. He always wanted to have plenty, and Dee, as she always did, assured him there would be more than plenty. "Believe me, Robert, there will be enough," she said with the patience she showed every Thanksgiving and Christmas, when Stacey started worrying about something he knew little about. Christmas dinner was Dee's department and she firmly, though sweetly, let Stacey know that. "You ever known me not to have more than enough food on the table? Like I've always said, a little of this and a little of that and everyone will have more than enough for seconds and thirds and leftovers for tomorrow and days after that."

There seemed very little for me to do

except take orders and accept all the menial cooking assignments such as chopping celery, onions, and green peppers to simmer along with the turkey while it cooked, and chopping the same for the potato salad, as well as peeling and dicing the potatoes. The ham was already cooked; so was the cornbread for the dressing. Still to be cooked were dishes of macaroni and cheese, a broccoli-cheese-rice casserole, and all the vegetables, baby English peas and a pot of string beans laden with bits of ham and bacon and onions, as well as a fruit salad mix of canned fruit, sour cream, and marshmallows. I figured maybe I could handle some of that. Rie would stir up a combination of collard greens, cabbages, and onions too. Dee had everything in order as to what would be prepared before Christmas and what would be prepared Christmas morning before the Christmas feast.

One thing that was not on Dee's list of fabulous foods for the Christmas dinner was hog-head souse. That was Stacey's specialty. He prepared it not for Christmas Day but for New Year's Day. Since the hog-head souse had to set a few days for the flavor to seep in, Stacey always prepared it at the same time as all the Christmas cooking was going on. He cooked it every year.

But not in Dee's kitchen.

Being a southern woman, Dee cooked chit'lings, calves' brains, neck bones, tripe, and the like, but she could not abide the thought of a hog head, coon, or pig's feet simmering on her beautiful new stove in her newly remodeled, modernized, immaculate kitchen, so she relegated Stacey to the basement washroom to cook his hog head and all the other southern delicacies, such as coon, which he annually brought back from his hunting trips to the woods of Upper Michigan. There was no coon baking during the days before Christmas, but there was coon meat in Stacey's basement freezer that was on the menu for New Year's Day. I don't think Dee could have stood for both the coon and the hog head being cooked at once. The hog head was bad enough. When first put on to simmer, it had a distracting smell, so Dee closed doors, both to the kitchen and to the living room, to ward off the odor rising from the basement cooking, and she insisted that Stacey keep the washroom door closed as well so that the smell would not waft so strongly up the stairway and mix with the more traditional aromas of her kitchen.

Stacey had set up his own cooking station in the basement washroom. It worked out well for them both. The washroom was quite spacious, with a washer and dryer, huge double laundry sinks, and an old-fashioned ringer-washer Dee still used for large items such as rugs and quilts. Stacey's kitchen was set up in a corner of the room and had a full-size refrigerator, a small stove, and a chopping table. During the holidays the washroom was as active and as full of people as the kitchen. Christopher-John and Man always were there, and the Davis boys dropped by, as well as some of Stacey's friends, all hailing from the South. They all enjoyed hog-head souse.

Hog-head souse. It was one of those delicacies born in slavery. Like so many foods now rooted in our culture — meats like chit'lings and tripe, neck bones and pig's feet, calves' brains and hog head — they were the leavings of the slaughter. While the white folks got the choice cuts, steaks and roasts, ham and bacon, ribs, pork chops, and such, colored folks took the leavings, every bit of what the white folks didn't want, and made a feast of them. Not allowed guns, colored folks also trapped whatever they could to add meat to their meals, and that included raccoon. Now all these foods had become tradition. They were part of our heritage.

All the men contributed to the preparation of the souse in chopping the vegetables and checking on the hog head before pulling the tender, succulent meat from the bone. They all shared in the laughter and the storytelling too. With Papa here, the cooking of the souse became even more festive, for Papa also made souse. Although the room was always filled with men of the family, the women were certainly welcome. Dee didn't set foot down there while the cooking was going on and neither did Rie, but I enjoyed being down with the men, and so did 'lois, who loved their stories. This year, Big Ma joined them too.

"I wanna know what's goin' on down there!" Big Ma announced before she was even down the stairs. Stacey and I both stepped from the washroom and there was Big Ma, standing on the landing by the side door, cane in one hand, her other hand on her hip.

"Big Ma!" Stacey exclaimed with a grin. "Come on down!"

He hurried up the steps to help her. "Get out of my way, boy!" she ordered, holding up her cane slightly to shoo him back. "I can make it!" But when Stacey remained standing on the step below her, his hand extended, she changed her mind. "Well, all right then. Come on then, give me a hand, you figure you jus' gotta." As Stacey led her down the stairs, Big Ma was beaming. She was so proud of Stacey, of his being the first to come to Toledo, of all he had achieved here, and especially of his beautiful house. Mama and Papa, who had been to the house before, had told her all about it; still, Big Ma was awed at the wonder of the house and kept repeating, "Lord, sho am proud. My Paul-Edward, wish he could've done seen this. He was always a man workin' to have somethin'. Now his grandson got a house like this! He sho 'nough would be proud!"

By the time Big Ma got down the stairs to the landing, both Christopher-John and Man had come from the washroom. "We've been waiting on you, Big Ma," said Clayton.

"Then why ain't ya come up to get me?" fussed Big Ma. "Been smelling somethin' cookin' down here for the longest time!"

"Cooking souse," announced Christopher-John.

"Could use your help," said Stacey.

"Well, let me see it," demanded Big Ma as she pushed past all of us into the washroom. A chair was quickly brought for her, but Big Ma ignored it as she went over to the stove, picked up a dishcloth, and lifted the top from the giant pot. She then picked up the cooking fork next to the pot and poked at the head. She grunted.

"What do you think, Mama?" asked Papa. "I can make souse, but not like you."

"Still got some cookin' to do," she surmised. "See y'all got your onions and such in there. Got your salt in the pot, your pepper, your vinegar? Got your sausages, your sage, your red pepper ready?"

"Yes, ma'am, all there," said Stacey. Big Ma nodded with approval. She put the fork down and re-covered the pot. "But like for you to help me with the souse, Big Ma. Get it seasoned right."

"Ain't you been doin' this every year without me?"

"Had to, you weren't here."

"S'pose you right about that, boy. But you been doin' fine enough without me. What you need me for now?"

"Always need you, Big Ma, and tell you the truth, I might make some good souse, but somehow it's never been good as yours."

Big Ma cocked her head at the flattery and looked up at Stacey. "I done taught you how to make it, oughta be good as mine!"

"Well, it's not!" Stacey declared.

"I know what you doin'! You just tryin'

to get me to do your work for ya!" she teased, then laughed, and everybody else did too. Big Ma sat down. "All right then, meat get tender and y'all get it off them bones, I sit right here and season it for ya."

"Ah, man!" Christopher-John exclaimed. "This here's going to be some kind of good souse this year!" We all watched Big Ma as we gathered round, and she grinned with pleasure at all the praise.

On Christmas Day, it was like being down home again. We woke to Christmas prayers, the singing of hymns, and calls from Christopher-John and Man wishing us all a merry Christmas. Then we gathered around the Christmas tree set in front of the sun parlor windows, its lights burning bright, and began opening our presents. It was a joyful time filled with much surprise and happiness at the gifts given and received. But the greatest gift of all was having Mama, Papa, and Big Ma with us. Later, when all the family gathered with the arrival of Christopher-John and Clayton Chester with their families, we all felt truly blessed.

In addition to Rie and 'lois, there were now ten more children in the Logan family. As soon as the children entered the house they saw the towering Christmas tree and the many presents still unopened. Their eyes grew big. Rie and 'lois, wearing Santa Claus caps and sitting on the floor in front of the tree, gave the children their presents. All the adults gathered around and watched the children's glee as they unceremoniously ripped away wrapping of red and green and gold paper, of Santa Claus and angels, to reveal bright shiny toys, trucks and trains, dolls and games. The children's laughter and their joy touched us all. I pictured my child with all the others. It did not sadden me. I was touched by their joy as much as everyone else. We thought the day couldn't get any better.

We were wrong.

Just as Dee was beginning to set food on the table, the doorbell rang. Stacey answered it. Those of us in the living and dining rooms heard an elated shout from Stacey and a familiar voice responding.

Papa, Christopher-John, Clayton, and I all hurried to the sun parlor. Standing at the front door was Uncle Hammer. Aunt Loretta was with him.

"Man, what you doing here?" cried Papa as they stepped inside.

"Heard you was going to be here, brother. You expect me not to come?"

Papa laughed and wrapped Uncle Hammer in a big bear hug before turning to Aunt Loretta and hugging her too. "This sure is a surprise!"

"Surprise to me too," said Aunt Loretta. "But this brother of yours, you know how he is. When he found out all y'all was going to be here, he said to me, 'Loretta, I'm going to Toledo for Christmas,' and I said to him, 'Not without me you ain't!'" She laughed her raucous laugh. "So we jumped on a train and come on."

"Why didn't you let us know you were coming?" questioned Stacey. "We could have picked you up at the station."

"Didn't come here all the way on the train, just far as Chicago," said Uncle Hammer, taking off his coat. "Got a car from one of Loretta's boys in Chicago and drove over. It's sitting out front there. Where's Mama?"

Papa smiled. "She's in the kitchen, where else?"

Aunt Loretta took the time to hug each of us, but not Uncle Hammer. We would have to get our hugs later. Right now, he wanted to see Big Ma. Stacey led the way through the living room and dining room to the kitchen. The rest of us followed. We all wanted to see Big Ma's face when she saw Uncle Hammer. Stacey stopped at the kitchen door. Big Ma and Mama with Dee, Rachel, and Becka were at the counters, transferring food from cooking dishes to dishes to be set on the table. Their backs were to us.

"Mama," said Papa, "look who's here."

Mama turned first. "Oh, dear Lord, I don't believe it!"

"Better believe it, sister," said Uncle Hammer. "I'm standing right here."

At that, Big Ma turned, a ladling spoon in her hand. She just stood there for a moment looking stunned before she said, "Hammer, that you? What you doing here?"

"Come to see about you, Mama. Aren't you glad to see me?" Uncle Hammer then went to Big Ma as tears streamed down her face, slipped his arms around her, and held her close. All Big Ma could do was cry.

For us, there had never been a Christmas like it. It was the first time all the family was together in Toledo. There were too many of us to sit at the dining room table, which had been expanded to accommodate twelve, so some sat at the table in the breakfast nook and others ate from trays in the living room or just from plates set on laps. It didn't matter where we ate. The food was just as good. We feasted and laughed and talked and enjoyed the celebration of the day and of our family. After we all had seconds and thirds, we were so full we finally had to turn away from the platters of food to give our bodies a rest until later in the day, when we would all be back to get another taste of this or that.

When all the eating was done, the children hurried down to the rec room with their new toys, and Rie and 'lois went with them to watch over their play. The men folded up the trays and put them away while the women cleared the food from the dining room and breakfast nook tables and stacked the dishes, which would all be washed by hand. One thing Dee did not have in her splendid new kitchen was a dishwasher. She refused to get one. She figured she could do the dishes better herself. I helped with all the clearing, then joined Mama, Papa, Big Ma, Uncle Hammer, and my brothers in the living room. I figured there were enough women taking care of things in the kitchen. I would do my part later, in the next round of dishwashing.

Throughout dinner Mama, Papa, and Big Ma had filled in Uncle Hammer about all the people down home. Now, as we sat with the gas fire burning through artificial logs, Uncle Hammer wanted to know about what else was going on. Papa told him, and he was blunt about it. "Things as bad as they always been."

"Or worse," interjected Mama.

"Can't get no worse," said Uncle Hammer with a glance her way. He turned his attention back to Papa. "What's going on down there?"

"You hear 'bout that Clemens boy got killed few weeks back, lived far side of the Rosa Lee?"

"Lemoine Clemens's boy?" questioned Uncle Hammer. "You know we don't get that kind of news unless it comes direct from somebody down home."

"Well, we certainly can't write you about it," Mama said.

"Wouldn't expect you to, sister."

"No telling who reads that mail," said Big Ma. "Course now, son, you come home more often, you'd be knowin' what's goin' on."

Uncle Hammer released a slow smile. "Now, that ain't much of a reason to go back down there, Mama, to hear news about another lynching. Only reason I even set foot in that state is to come see about you, Mary, and David."

"Boy wasn't lynched," corrected Big Ma. "He was shot in the head. Well, anyways, I sho hope you plannin' to come back down home when it's time to put me in the ground —"

"Ah, Mama, now —"

"Time ain't that far away. You gonna come, ain't you?"

"Now, Mama, how'd we get on that?" chided Papa. "We were talking about that Clemens boy."

"Got on it 'cause I wanna know! I want both my boys there when I go meet my Maker!"

Papa started to speak again, but Uncle Hammer waved his hand, stopping him, and said, "I'm still in this life myself, Mama, I promise you I'll be there."

"All right then." Big Ma now sounded satisfied and settled back in her chair. "Go on 'bout that boy."

Uncle Hammer turned back to Papa. "What happened?"

"Boy come back from Germany, still in uniform. Was walking down the street in Strawberry and maybe he thought he was still in Germany, but he refused to move over on the sidewalk to let a white man pass. Bunch of men followed him out of town, shot him, then dumped him in the Rosa Lee. Like I said, things as bad as they always been. We might be a week from the year nineteen sixty, but things ain't changed."

"You expecting they would?" asked a cynical Uncle Hammer. "Only change coming to a black man down there in Mississippi is getting put in the ground."

"We had a meeting up at Great Faith about what happened," Mama said.

"And what good that do? Y'all collect some new clothes for that Clemens boy to be buried in?"

"Yes, Hammer, as a matter of fact, we did," Mama replied. "Collected a little money for his family too. We also listened to a man from the National Association for the Advancement of Colored People, the NAACP. I even went to an NAACP meeting up in Jackson and heard the young man who's leading it in Mississippi. His name is Medgar Evers. He's from Decatur. Worked in the Delta selling insurance for a while, but he's been working with the NAACP for about eight years now, and I heard from Little Willie that he did investigative work for the NAACP checking on so-called accidents whenever colored people were killed. He even did investigative work up around

Money, town where that poor Emmett Till boy was murdered. He said they're organizing for some real protests in Mississippi."

"To do what?"

Mama leveled her gaze at Uncle Hammer. "To deal with what's happened to all the young men like Clay Clemens. To deal with all the killings and the mutilations and the burnings, with all the injustice. There was another young man too recently, roped and dragged along the road because he didn't address a white woman with the kind of respect they demanded. He was so torn up his own family couldn't even recognize him. We've got to stop it, Hammer. You know if we organize, take a chapter from the Montgomery boycott, we might be able to get some change."

"And you believe that?"

"I have to believe something's going to change things, Hammer."

Uncle Hammer sneered. "Haven't long as I've lived. Our folks been in this country how long now? Went from slavery to so-called freedom. What freedom? Still got to kowtow to those white folks down there, other parts of the country too. Can't vote down there. Can't drink from their water fountains. Can't eat in their restaurants, except at the back door. Can't sleep in their hotels, though they don't mind us cleaning them for them. Still got to sit at the back of the bus. Still got to step aside when they come walking."

"What you said about riding at the back of the bus, that's no longer the case in Montgomery," contested Mama. "After that boycott in fifty-six, colored folks can sit wherever they choose on the bus. They don't have to sit in the back any longer. They got that through a boycott and the protest movement. Now, from what I understand, it was the Supreme Court that ended the boycott, banning segregation on the city buses. Said it was unconstitutional, but Negroes hurt the city with the boycott. We hit the white businesses where it counted, in their pocketbooks."

"Yeah, well . . . you let me know how that goes in Mississippi," retorted Uncle Hammer.

"I'll just do that, Hammer," Mama

countered. She smiled at Uncle Hammer's disillusionment. "Got to start somewhere, Hammer."

Uncle Hammer laughed. "Well, you just keep on believing, Mary. I'm going to keep on believing too, believing things don't ever change much with these white people. Just think about it. Right here in Toledo just year before last, wasn't it, white folks got all upset because a colored girl was voted queen of the high school? First colored queen in the city? From what you said, they hung an effigy from a tree right there on the school grounds. They doing that stuff up here, you know it's a whole lot worse down there." He turned to Papa. "Remember Cousin Thad?"

Papa nodded. "Course."

"Went to work one morning, came home early and found that white sheriff on his wife. Cousin Thad yanked that white man off her and beat him near to death. White folks put him in jail for life."

"Wonder they didn't lynch that boy," said Big Ma.

"Only reason they didn't," Papa said, "was because that sheriff didn't die."

"Might as well have," concluded Uncle Hammer. "Thad, he still down there serving time at Parchman. Been there going on more than thirty-some years."

Big Ma sighed heavily. "Crying shame," she said. "Thad, he was a first cousin of mine."

"Point is," said Uncle Hammer, "same thing happening today."

Big Ma nodded agreement. "Just blessed that ain't happened to that boy Moe."

"What about Moe? What's going on with him?" We told Uncle Hammer about the arrest warrant and extradition request from Mississippi. "Where is he now?" Uncle Hammer was looking at Stacey, but it was Papa who replied.

"Hear he's in Canada."

"Better stay there," said Uncle Hammer.

After that the evening was full of stories, long-ago stories told over and over again. There was the story about our friend Mr. Tom Bee and how the white store owner John Wallace had shot him because Mr.

Tom Bee refused to address him as "Mister." There were stories from Big Ma's childhood, stories of her first husband Mitchell, and stories of Grandpa Paul-Edward. There were stories of Uncle Hammer and Papa when they were boys, stories about their mischief, stories about their older brothers, Uncle Mitchell and Uncle Kevin, stories of laughter and good times. Stacey, Christopher-John, Man, and I had our stories to tell too. Stacey had gotten to be a master storyteller and we all deferred to him, calling on him to recount the events as we all remembered them, and he did so with great gusto, acting out the parts of all persons involved, standing up to show their action and mimicking their voices. We laughed as hilariously as when I was a child hearing the stories in front of the fire down home.

Most of the children did not hear the stories. They were still downstairs in the rec room. There was plenty of room to run and play down there; also, there was an old standup piano they could bang on, games, and a phonograph, as well as all of Rie's and 'lois's childhood toys. Of course they had taken their new Christmas toys downstairs too. We had not seen them since they disappeared and figured we wouldn't see them again until they were called to come upstairs.

Rie and two of her girlfriends were in the recreation room with the children, along with a gangly young man who had come courting Rie on this Christmas Day. He was captain of her high school basketball team. Rie always had some boy courting her and they were good boys. Stacey saw to that. He drilled them like an Army sergeant when they came to call. All boys who ventured to see Rie knew the protocol and they adhered to it. They knew they could only visit on Sunday or a holiday, knew they had to be wearing a suit and tie, and knew above all else that Rie was to be treated with respect. She was a gregarious girl, high-spirited, as beautiful now as she had been as a baby, and the boys flocked around her. They were always the popular boys, on the football and basketball teams; shyer boys were too mesmerized to approach her, though Rie had no airs about herself. She treated everyone the same; yet there was a magnetism to her, and girls and boys alike enjoyed being around her. With 'lois, though, it was different. She pretty much kept to herself. While all the other children entertained themselves in the adult-free rec room, 'lois had come back upstairs to sit with the "old" folks. She was listening to the stories. She was always listening to the stories.

Late that night, when Aunt Loretta and I were alone in the kitchen washing the last of the dishes from the second round of Christmas dinner eating, Aunt Loretta, her hands in soapy water, suddenly said to me, "Cassie, you got a man in your life?"

"What?" I asked, startled by the unexpected question.

"It's time, Cassie. Past time. Woman needs a man. Now, you had a good one, fine-looking one at that. But he's been gone a good long while now and you need to be with somebody."

I laughed. "You know who you sound like, Aunt Loretta? Big Ma."

Aunt Loretta nodded at the comparison. "Couldn't be compared to a finer woman, but getting back to what I was saying, you're not getting any younger, you know. Fact, you getting old, girl!"

I laughed again. "Well, thank you very much!"

Aunt Loretta reached out a soapy hand and squeezed mine. "Serious now, Cassie, don't you want children? It still ain't too late."

I pulled away and dried the casserole dish I was holding. I turned my back to Aunt Loretta and put the dish away before turning to her again. "I lost my child, and the only man I wanted."

Aunt Loretta's hands were back in the dishwater. "You're wrong, Cassie, to talk that way. I had a no-good man. Fact to business, I had two no-count men. They was good for only one thing and you know what that is. Come to think of it, they wasn't always good at that neither, but you better not tell them that. Thought they was God's gift!" She shook her head and went on. "Didn't treat me right. Ran around with other women. Beat me when it suited them, even though I gave almost good as I got. Both those men, each of them, they gave me a child and I couldn't love those children any more than I do. Mostly, I had to raise them by myself. Then I met Hammer. My children were near to grown and he was good to them. Hammer didn't give me a child. I was already too late for that. Wish I hadn't been, but that's just the way it was. Still, he's the best man's ever come into my life. Now, he's got his ways, you know that, but the man has never raised a hand to me, never cheated on me, and he's totally honest with me. If he doesn't like a thing he sure enough lets me know about it. You know how direct he can be. Me, I don't want to think about growing old, but each day I look in the mirror and face the fact that I'm doing just that, and I thank the good Lord I've got Hammer." She looked at me again. "You need to have that too, Cassie, a man who loves you as you grow old. Every woman needs that." She gave me a studied look. "Just don't wait too long."

I thought of Guy and took up another dish to dry. As I did, Aunt Loretta looked at me hard. "Saw something in your face just now. Is there somebody?"

I shook my head and smiled. "No one I

could ever bring home."

"And you don't want to tell me about him?"

I continued to smile, but said nothing.

"All right, nosy me," said Aunt Loretta, turning back to the dishes. "I'll butt out of it then."

During the Christmas week, I went to see Lawyer Tate. He was in the same office, wore pretty much the same kind of clothes, and had the same personality. "How's my old block?" he asked as he ushered me in.

"Just like you left it," I said.

He laughed. "It's good then. Hated to leave it."

"But you did."

"Had the opportunity. Had to take it."

I figured he did. Lawyer Tate and his wife had bought the house next door to Stacey and Dee about two years after Stacey and Dee bought their house. Then, a year ago, the Tates had seen a house that they liked in wealthy, all-white, exclusive Ottawa Hills. The house

543

was for sale. They were politely shown the house, but their offer was rejected. The rejection was clearly racial. The white realtor admitted it. "No way are they going to let you in there," the realtor said. "Only reason I could show you the place was because of all your political connections. They didn't want an uproar about it." Lawyer Tate was not dissuaded. He went to a man for whom he had great regard, a man he trusted, a white lawyer and a friend, and made a deal with him. The white lawyer, with impeccable credentials and sizeable wealth, bought the house, then turned right around and, at the same price for which he had bought it, sold it to Charles Tate.

"So, Mrs. De Baca," Lawyer Tate said, "I understand you have really made it now! You're a big-shot lawyer in Boston."

I reacted with a smirk. "What?"

"All the talk. Miss Cassie Logan, also known as Mrs. Flynn de Baca, one of a handful of colored lawyers in all these United States employed by a very highly respected white law firm."

Still smiling, I shook my head. "Well, in my case, that's overexaggerated. All I am is a glorified paper pusher."

"Maybe. But a paper pusher who's made a dent, maybe an indelible impression."

"I don't think that's the case."

Lawyer Tate came from behind his desk and sat beside me on the sofa. "Look, Cassie, not only are you a person of color, you are a woman of color, so you are knocking down walls on two fronts. Tell me, how did you get into a firm like that anyway? You must have had some powerful recommendations."

I thought of Guy. "I did," I answered honestly.

"Well, however you got there, you're in a position to deal with some important issues. You know, Cassie, in years to come we're going to need powerful lawyers like our Thurgood Marshall and Charles Houston. And let's not forget Constance Baker Motley, backbone of the NAACP Legal Defense Fund. Lawyers who can fight the fight on a legal front to turn back all these laws that are keeping us down. You're young, you're of that generation that can do it."

I shrugged that off. "Not me. I'm not

here to deal with all our issues, Lawyer Tate, just with Moe's."

"All right then, let's talk about our friend Moe. It's public knowledge that Mississippi is trying to arrest him and get him extradited back to Mississippi. They haven't been able to do so thus far, since they can't find him. What we should be talking about is what we can do if they find Moe and if he chooses to challenge the extradition. Somehow, we've got to figure out how to save him."

Moe did not remain in Canada. The same day I talked to Lawyer Tate, Moe showed up at the house. His wife, Myrtis, was with him, along with Myrtis's brother, Dwayne. We were all shocked to see Moe and berated him for risking coming back into the States. He was unapologetic. "I knew you'd all be here and I needed to be with folks from home. Been eighteen years this month since I left from down there and I wanted to see Miz Caroline, wanted to see Mr. and Miz Logan. It's worth the risk. Besides, I figure the police got better things to do than worry about me at Christmastime."

Moe had been staying in Toronto. He had gotten word to Dwayne that he planned to be in Toledo during Christmas week. Myrtis and Dwayne drove from Detroit and met Moe here. Moe had parked his car near a church and come to the house with Myrtis and Dwayne in Dwayne's car. It was odd seeing Moe without Morris at his side. Since Morris had gone to live with Moe, they had always come to Toledo together, and even after Morris became a student at Wayne State, they always made the trip together. When Morris graduated from Wayne State with a degree in business administration, he had stayed on in Detroit to be with Moe. The death of Hertesene had taken him back south and he had not yet returned. With Moe's flight to Canada, we didn't know if Morris would be coming back.

"No need for him to come back now," said Moe when we asked about Morris. "Least not 'til I know where this mess is going to take me. He might as well stay south with Daddy."

Soon after their arrival, we all sat down for dinner. During dinner I noticed Myrtis watching me, but as soon as I looked at her, she looked away. I had met Moe's wife only once before. She also was from Mississippi, from around Greenwood. She was a quiet woman and somewhat skittish. She had heard about me and seemed particularly shy when I spoke to her. Her words were awkward and few. She seemed so shy that I mostly left her alone. She and Moe had no children. After dinner I told Moe I needed to talk to him about the arrest warrant and extradition request. We decided to go outside. Moe let Myrtis know and we left by the breakfast room door. Walking along the stone pavers that led to the back gate, I asked Moe, "Myrtis know you once had feelings for me?"

"Once had?" questioned Moe, and smiled.

I nudged him with my elbow as I had done in younger days. "You know what I mean."

"She knows. Once when Levis was up here, he let it slip. Then she asked me about you and I told her I'd asked you to marry me, but you were having none of that from me. Told her you ran off to

California and married some exotic fellow from Central America."

I laughed. "Well, it wasn't quite like that."

Moe laughed too. "Well, seemed that way to me. Why are you asking about Myrtis now?"

"It's just that she seems so uncomfortable around me. I've tried to talk to her, but she pretty much has nothing to say."

"She's intimidated by you, Cassie, and why shouldn't she be? She's heard a lot about you."

"Good things, I hope."

"Always good from me."

We reached the towering blue spruce and stopped. The tree's branches were laden with the morning's snow. I walked around the tree, touching the softness of its new, blue-green needles. "I love this old tree," I said. "Reminds me of trees down home. Not the same kind, but just that feeling of beauty, of something grand."

"I know what you mean," said Moe.

I rejoined Moe, still standing on the

walkway. "You know you were stupid to come back here. You can't keep taking these risks, Moe."

"So I've been told."

"You have any idea how they tracked you down?"

"I've been thinking a lot on that. Back when Maynard and Levis were here in the summer, they ran into this fella they knew from Strawberry who was up in Detroit visiting some of his people. Ran into him right in my neighborhood. Fella asked them what they were doing in Detroit and they told him they were doing same as him, visiting folks they knew. They told me about it and that they didn't know this fella too well, but they'd heard he's one of these Negroes likes to talk a bit too much to white folks. Well, I didn't think much about it at the time, but I'm thinking since then that this fella might have gone back and told some of those white folks in Strawberry about Maynard and Levis being here and whereabout he had seen them. Police down there could have contacted police here, and they got to checking around the neighborhood, found out about me and where I work." Moe's brow wrinkled to a frown. "You know, I changed my last name, Cassie, when I came up here, but I never changed my name from Moe. . . ." He was silent a moment. "That was stupid."

"Well, it's too late to fix what's already done," I said. "Hope you're not going by Moe in Canada."

"No. Least I've learned that much. Cassie, if they find me, arrest me in Canada, do I have to come back? Is there any way to fight the extradition?"

"Well, we can try to fight it, Moe, but there are international treaties on extradition and if there's an arrest warrant for you in Canada, Canada is supposed to turn you over."

Moe shook his head in despair. "Murder. That's what they charged me with, Cassie. I didn't murder anybody."

"Mississippi can charge whatever it wants, Moe! You beat Statler, Leon, and Troy pretty bad and now they're claiming Troy died because of the injuries you inflicted on him."

"They had it coming!" Moe's voice was

hard and the look in his eyes harder still.

"I don't dispute that, but the state of Mississippi will. We could contend that Troy's death was aggravated assault, a result of the beating, at the worst manslaughter, but not murder, and if you have to go back to Mississippi, that's what we'll argue. We all know you can't get a fair trial in Mississippi." Lawyer Tate and I had discussed this at some length. There had been a number of cases in which blacks were accused of attacking whites, and in the outcome of each case, the black defendants were convicted and sentenced either to life or death row. In addition, there was the whole matter of Moe not having the opportunity of a trial before a jury of his peers. Any jury selected would be all white. I told Moe this. "We'll use these facts to fight the extradition and the charges. There are also charges for hitting Statler and Leon with the crowbar. We'll fight those charges too."

"I'd have to go back to Mississippi to change the charges?"

I was honest with Moe. "More than likely."

Moe looked to the peak of the pine. "I can't go back to jail, Cassie. I was jailed when Stacey and I ran off to work the cane fields. Now, I'm sorry about Troy, I truly am, but I can't go back."

"You keep taking risks like coming here, you will."

Moe kept looking at the tree. "Thing is, I want to go home. I want to see my daddy. He can't travel, but I still can."

"Don't even think about going down there, Moe. The best thing for now is just staying in Canada and not drawing attention to yourself. That means not crossing that border again. Let Mississippi make the next move. If they issue an international extradition request on you and you're arrested in Canada, we'll fight the extradition on the grounds that you can't get a fair trial in Mississippi since you won't be facing trial before your peers, but in front of a white jury. But like I said, most likely Canada will still turn you over."

Moe now looked at me. "New year, new decade coming up, Cassie. They say change is coming. Hope it's good change for me."

We walked back to the house, and I saw Big Ma standing at the breakfast room window, watching us. As we entered the house she turned and gave Moe a nod, then called to me. Moe smiled at her, crossed the kitchen, and went into the living room. "It's too late now, Cassie," Big Ma said when we were alone.

"What do you mean?"

"He taken now. You waited too long."

"Big Ma, what did I tell you before? I never wanted Moe."

"Well, you sho ain't gonna have him now. You know I don't hold with comin' 'tween husband and wife."

"Well, I don't hold with it either. Moe and I were just talking about the arrest warrant and extradition."

Big Ma grunted. "Make sho that's all y'all talkin' 'bout. That boy, he ain't over you yet. Maybe never will be."

"Ah, Big Ma," I said, taking off my coat. "Don't worry about it."

"Gotta worry," countered Big Ma. "You

need to be married again."

Stacey had called Christopher-John and Man to come over. Their families weren't with them. All of us sat talking late into the night. It was past midnight when Moe and his wife and Dwayne left. If it hadn't been for Myrtis and Dwayne being with him, I believe Moe would have stayed the night. He did not want to leave.

I had waited for Stacey to say something about Guy, but it was Dee who brought up the subject. "Robert told me about that friend of yours in Boston," she said when we had a few minutes alone in the kitchen. "You serious about him?"

I ignored her question. "What did Stacey tell you?"

"Said that he figured something was going on between you two. Something outside of marriage."

I became defensive. "Stacey wasn't there long enough to know anything. He just jumped to conclusions because he saw a white man in my apartment. He just got angry and left."

"Well, what did you expect? You know

how he feels about colored women being with white men. You know how they all feel."

I took a moment before responding. "He tell Christopher-John and Man?"

Dee shook her head. "No, just me. Told me to talk to you."

"What? He can't talk to me himself?"

"Says he'd get too angry."

"Well, Dee, you can tell him you did talk to me. You can tell him too that I know plenty of white people in Boston. I work with them every day. Sometimes I go to their houses, sometimes they come to my place. We go out together, we enjoy each other. That's my life in Boston."

"And the man who was in your apartment, he's a special part of it?"

"He's a good friend."

"Good friend, huh? Don't hedge with me, Cassie. Give me more credit than that."

I was silent, then I said, "Dee, did Stacey tell you that man he met wants to marry me?"

Now it was Dee who was silent before

she said, "No, Stacey didn't tell me. But if you don't want this family torn apart, you better make sure that a friend is all this white man stays."

Stacey didn't say one word to me about Guy, but he did speak to me about Rie. "She wants to go south to school. She says she wants to go to one of the Negro schools, not one of the schools up here. She talk to you?"

We were seated at the breakfast nook table. I pushed my empty coffee cup back a bit and folded my arms on the table. "She did, some."

"I don't understand it," Stacey admitted. "All I wanted to do was get away from down there, and here she is wanting to go back down there to school."

"And you don't want her to go?"

"It's not that I don't want her to go. It's that I'm afraid for her to go."

"You'll always be afraid for her, Stacey."

"But going south?" Stacey shook his head. "I just don't understand it. She wants to go to a Negro school so bad, she could go to Wilberforce or Central State right here in Ohio. She doesn't have to go all the way down to Georgia or South Carolina or Tennessee. She's even talked about Mississippi. She's applied to all those schools down there — Tuskegee, Alcorn, Tougaloo, even Jackson State."

"I know."

Stacey fingered his cup. "I don't know what to do, Cassie. What if she's accepted?"

I smiled. "You know she will be."

Stacey acknowledged that with a glance. "I don't know if I can let her go to the South without me, Cassie, not without me there to make sure she's all right."

I understood my brother. He watched over his two girls with the strength of a lion and the magnitude of his father's heart, just as Papa had watched over me. He wanted always to protect them and keep them safe. Everyone who came to live at the Dorr Street house, everyone who came to live in their new house, Stacey had let them know how Rie and 'lois were to be treated. He would never tolerate disrespect to them in any way, and everyone adhered to his words. Stacey once confided to me that when the girls were little, before they got so grown that they wouldn't have wanted him doing so, he had always opened their door at night with Dee, just to check on them, just to make sure they were all right. He said that during those moments, he wondered how he could have fathered such beautiful, talented, and vivacious daughters.

I reached over and laid my hand over his. "Stacey, you're going to have to let Rie go at some point. You're going to have to let both of them go, sooner or later." Stacey looked at me, then out the back window to the snow-flocked spruce. I knew Stacey was not about to give up his mantle as protector of his girls.

In the days following Christmas, the family had gathered first at Christopher-John and Becka's house for another huge dinner and then, on the following day, at Clayton Chester and Rachel's. Both sisters had spread out more fabulous meals for all to enjoy. In addition to all the Logans at the post-Christmas dinners were Becka and Rachel's four nephews and their young families. All the nephews had followed their aunts from Mississippi, lived in their houses with them, and married Toledo women. Dee's brother Zell and the Davises had married Toledo women as well, so their Christmas dinners were with their wives' families, but during the holiday week, they all made their way back over to Stacey and Dee's with their families and enjoyed some of the holiday cheer, so everybody in the family saw everybody else during the holidays. I couldn't help but reflect on the fact that all this extended family was in Toledo because Stacey, the first one to come, had made the abrupt decision to leave Mississippi.

It was a good time.

On New Year's Day, all of the Logan family gathered one last time at Stacey and Dee's. In celebration of the new year, hog-head souse was on the table, along with chit'lings, baked coon with sides of sweet potatoes, collard greens, cornbread, and black-eyed peas, a New Year's Day good luck tradition. It was a real down-home meal. Later, as we sat around the evening fire, we talked and laughed some more, squeezing in as much as we could before we had to part. While the adults talked, the younger children played way beyond their bedtime, but no one worried about that. We took comfort in just being together. Tomorrow Uncle Hammer and Aunt Loretta would be leaving, heading back to Chicago, then to Oakland. The day after that, Papa, Mama, and Big Ma would be taking the train south, and I would be heading back to Boston. We did not know when we would all be together again.

As the first day of the new year wound to a close and the younger children lay asleep covered by blankets on the carpeted floor, we sat talking quietly, reminiscing about what had been and projecting what was to come and dreading the thought that at some point, the day and our time together would have to end. Midnight neared, the older children yawned sleepily, and Becka and Rachel insisted they had to get the children home to bed. Finally, we had to part.

As always before a journey, we held hands and formed a circle and the children who were still awake joined in, and we prayed, each person in turn. Papa's words were the final words, and in closing the family circle of prayer, he said, "Dear Lord, please bless us now and forever, and please watch over each and every one of us while we're apart, one from another." And with those words, amidst hugs and kisses, we said good night and wished each other a happy new year.

A new decade had begun.

TIME OF CHANGE
(1960–1961)

It was 1960. The year had hardly begun when Negro college students down in North Carolina decided to sit at the lunch counter of the local five-and-dime store. This was unheard of. Five-and-dime lunch counters in the South were for whites only. In fact, all stores owned by whites in the South that had lunch counters were for "whites only." Yet students from North Carolina sat down at the lunch counter anyway. All the students wanted was to be served. They were not served. The North Carolina students weren't the only ones who chose to sit down at "white only" lunch counters. Negro college students in South Carolina, Virginia, Missouri, and Georgia sat down at those exclusive "white only" lunch counters. They, too, were not served. Students were now being arrested, but more kept coming, again and again, to the lunch counters. Each day it seemed there was a new demonstration, not only in North Carolina but in other states that had "white only" signs. In Nashville, the police arrested some one hundred students for sit-ins. In Chattanooga, a riot broke out because of the sit-ins. White citizens clashed with the demonstrators, and the white police kept on arresting the peaceful sit-in students and hauling them off to jail.

The nightly news reported it all.

The students did not let up. They even challenged the Deep South. In Alabama hundreds of students from the Negro college Alabama State marched on the capital in protest of Alabama's racist laws. Students participating in the demonstration were expelled. Across the South from Florida west to Texas, the sit-ins and the demonstrations were going on. Students were being jailed and high-velocity water hoses and police dogs were being used to dispel them, but mostly the hard line of segregation held, though now the world was beginning to pay attention. In September, Rie enrolled at Spellman College in Atlanta, and our family got worried. At Rie's request, I went with Stacey and Dee and 'lois when they took Rie to the school.

"Now, I don't want you getting into these demonstrations down here," Stacey told Rie, not for the first time.

"I know, Daddy, you told me."

"You're at this school to study, not get yourself put in jail."

"Daddy, wasn't planning on getting myself put in jail."

"Then stay out of trouble."

"Seems like good trouble to me," Rie said.

"You think it's such good trouble, you can just get in the car and go back to Toledo and go to the University of Toledo. We let you come here, but we don't have to let you stay here."

Rie was wisely silent.

Later Rie said to me, "Just think, Aunt Cass, we're breaking the chains." Excitement was in her voice and her face was lit in full anticipation at the prospect of helping to break those chains.

"Be careful those chains don't break you," I warned.

Rie laughed. "Oh, Aunt Cassie, you know if you were my age, you'd be in this fight. All of us need to be in it."

"Your daddy's worried about you. It's hard for him to let you go."

"I know," Rie said.

After we left Atlanta, Stacey, Dee, 'lois, and I went on to Mississippi. From Toledo to Atlanta and now from Atlanta to Mississippi, we were frequently stopped, running into road construction all along the way. The federal government was building an interstate highway system across the country. The construction had been going on for several years and would continue for many more. It was tiresome waiting at the many stops as the big machinery took over the roads, not letting any vehicles through for many minutes at a time, sometimes thirty or more, but as wearing as it was to wait we all were happy to see the highways being built. Once they were finished, we would no longer have to drive the rural roads going south. We would no longer have to go through small towns to get to Jackson. It would lessen our fear and make us feel safer.

Once we were in Spokane County, we rolled on toward home, going first through the town of Strawberry. Soon after leaving Strawberry the paved road ended and we continued the drive on the narrow rusty road. As we neared home we passed the new Negro school, built of cinder blocks and ranging from grades one through eight. Soon after passing it, we approached the crossroads. The Wallace store still dominated one corner of the crossroads. Several trucks, a wagon, and a couple of cars were parked in front of it. Some white men sat on the store porch playing checkers. Other white men stood near the vehicles. Statler and Leon Aames and their uncle, Charlie Simms, were among them. They all stared at us. Stacey came to a full stop, then turned west toward home.

The day after our arrival, Stacey took Dee and 'lois down to Dee's family, stayed one night, then returned home for an evening meeting at Great Faith. A man from the Jackson NAACP was speaking. Little Willie had urged Stacey and me to be there. Mama went with us, but Papa and Big Ma stayed at home. Papa didn't put much faith in any changes coming and Big Ma didn't much either. Many people felt the same as they did, so when we drove onto the church grounds we were not surprised to see few vehicles parked in front.

The old classrooms and the small building that had once housed the principal's office were vacant now, except for occasional church and community meetings and activities. The buildings looked quite lonely standing there. There had been talk of tearing them down, but the congregation couldn't agree to it, so they remained standing. All the buildings faced the expansive lawn where children of the Great Faith School had once run and played. The church, set apart from the class buildings, also faced the lawn, but not the road. Beyond and behind both the church and the class buildings was the forest, still dense with growth. Forest also loomed on the other side of the road.

Little Willie Wiggins greeted the gathering as the meeting began. "Now, all y'all know me," said Little Willie. "We all know what's going on out there. We all know a lotta our young people are fighting to change things. And not just young people. Got older folks too putting their hands in this. We all know what it's like down here and there's not a one of us ain't been touched by it. Now, we got a young man name of Medgar Evers who's leading our fight in Jackson. He's head of the Mississippi NAACP. He was a soldier over there in World War II, served along with fellas like me, some of you. He even applied to the University of Mississippi. Can you believe that! Ain't been accepted, of course, but that's how courageous he is! Anyways, I ain't up here to preach. I'll leave that to Brother Adams here. He's real involved up in Jackson and he's come to tell us a few things and get our support. Okay, I'm done." Little Willie then turned to the man from Jackson. "All right, Brother Adams, all yours."

Brother Adams from Jackson talked about the protests taking place across the country. He talked about all the college students and their sit-ins at restaurants and stores and movie theaters throughout the South. He talked about a man being beaten for having the audacity to insist on his voting rights. He talked about Negroes going to a public beach down in Biloxi and wading in the waters. He said it was being called a wade-in. More than seventy-one people had been arrested during several of those wade-ins. Nothing "public" in Mississippi was meant for black folks, only whites. He said we were going to change all that. It didn't all make the newspapers, he said, but through word of mouth local folks had heard about all this just the same. The stranglehold and the hammer of the white man was fierce, but change, little by little, inch by inch was coming.

He talked about what was to come and said everybody needed to get involved with this movement. "Don't just be sitting back, waiting for somebody else to do it. We're all in this fight together, and whether we want to be or not, each and every one of us is a part of it." He said money was needed to keep going forward, and even more important than that, body support in the protests. "If you can't actively participate, then give money, or if you can, give both. This is all of our fight and when we win it, each and every one of us can claim the freedom and victory." He also urged us to come to the NAACP meetings in Jackson.

When he sat down, Morris got up. Morris talked about the need to vote and how things could be changed with the vote. He talked about how to get registered to vote and about classes to teach people to prepare for the registration. "Everybody needs to know from the get-go that we don't get to vote in the primaries. Right now, that's just for the whites only, but we'll deal with that later. We're going to concentrate just on getting registered so we can vote. Now, the white folks got to register too," he said. "They're supposed to know the state constitution and be able to interpret those 285 sections of it just like us in order for them to vote. Got to take a literacy test, just like us. Thing is, for the most part, white folks don't even take that literacy test, and if they do, registrar gives them easy sections to explain, and when they give their interpretation, whether they got a notion of the constitution or not, it's always right as far as the registrar's concerned. Well, we don't have that luxury. We've got to know that constitution backward and forward to get the vote. Not only that, we got to fill out a questionnaire before we register with some twenty-one questions and there can be no kind of mistakes whatsoever! No spelling mistakes, no misspelling your name, your address, or the state of Mississippi! And how many of you know how to spell that one without messing up?"

There was an acknowledgment of laughter. "Now, the state of Mississippi requires a poll tax to be paid before a body can register to vote. Most folks around here can't afford to pay it, but don't worry about that. We're raising money to cover that tax, so anybody go to register can pay the poll tax. We've got to do everything just right, but if we do and we get the vote, then we get to help elect people like the sheriff, people like the county registrar, people like the governor. The vote is power and the white folks know it. There was a time they didn't even want us to learn how to read or write, because they know knowledge is power. That's the same with the vote. The vote is power and getting it won't be easy, but nothing worthwhile ever is."

After the meeting I spoke to Morris. Morris, now in his mid-twenties, was a confident young man, smart and affable and tall — six and a half feet of tall. "So, Little Brother Morris," I said, "looks like you've decided to stay down here."

"Well, there's no reason to be in Detroit now that Moe's gone. Besides," he grinned — "you see that pretty young woman over talking to your mama? Teaches at the school. She's plenty of reason for me to stay, her and my daddy."

"Denise Thomas," I said as I looked over. "Good reason."

"I think so."

I turned back to Morris. "About this voter registration, when do you expect to start classes?"

"Right now, we're thinking not until next year. We've got to get organized."

"I know the Mississippi constitution," I

said. "Maybe I can help."

"Guess you do, being a lawyer and all."

"That's not why I know it. Long time ago I studied it with Mrs. Lee Annie Lees."

Morris nodded knowingly. "Mrs. Lee Annie," he repeated. "Heard about her."

I knew he had to have heard about Mrs. Lee Annie, even though he was too young to have known her. Most people around here knew her story. Mrs. Lee Annie was an elderly woman who decided she wanted to vote and she asked me to help her with reading the constitution. I was only eleven at the time. When interpreting the constitution became difficult for both of us, Mama joined us in our studies. Mrs. Lee Annie and her family lived on the Granger plantation and she was told by Mr. Harlan Granger himself not to try to register to vote. She went to register anyway. Mama and I went with her. She failed the test, but that made no difference to Harlan Granger. He put Mrs. Lee Annie and all her family off his land.

"Well, that's what folks are afraid of now, same thing," said Morris. "Folks in some counties already got put off their places just this year for trying to vote. These white people intend to stop registration if they can. They know once we get the vote, we can outvote them in a number of counties. We got more black folks in Mississippi than any other state, and if we can outvote them, we can begin to change some things. Problem is though, getting folks to come to classes and learn that constitution. Even then, if folks learn it, you know as well as I do, it's up to the county registrar to choose the section he'll question them on and then it's up to him to decide whether or not he approves of the interpretation of the section. It'll be a slow process and not always a rewarding one."

"Well, you let me know when you get started. I can't do much from Boston, but maybe I can lend some ideas and raise some money too."

"That'll be a big help, Cassie. What would be a bigger help is if you come down and teach in the drive —"

"Now, I don't know about that."

"Think on it. Fact, why don't you come to a meeting we're having in Jackson this weekend? We'll be discussing organizing drives here in the state. Won't be a big meeting, but we'll have some speakers there."

"Maybe I will," I said.

"You'd be surprised to know who's offered to help." Morris didn't give me chance to respond. "Mr. Wade Jamison. Saw him in Strawberry the other day and he stopped me right there on the street and asked me into his office. He wanted to talk to me about the sit-ins. He asked me if there were any plans for sit-ins in Vicksburg or Jackson. Fact is, I didn't know and I wouldn't have told him if I had, but he was genuinely interested. He went so far as to say he supported the sit-ins. Said he understood the need for them."

"I'm not surprised."

"Well, I was."

"Little Brother, he knows the constitution backward and forward. Wouldn't hurt to have him on our side."

"Maybe. Anyway, he said his door was always open if he could be of help." Morris glanced around, then took my arm and led me away from anyone else's hearing. In a low voice he said, "What do you hear from Moe? Nobody down here's heard a thing."

"He's all right," I quietly replied. "Stacey and I went up to see him a couple of weeks ago. We knew you all would want to know how he's doing."

"And how is he doing?"

"He's still in Toronto, managed to get himself a little job under another name. He sent a letter by us to your daddy. Stacey'll take it over tomorrow."

"Good. Daddy'll be happy to get it." Morris frowned. "You think Mississippi knows Moe's in Canada?"

"I really don't know, Morris. Only thing I do know is that the arrest warrant and extradition request are still in effect in Michigan. But as long as Moe stays in Canada, I think he'll be okay. Thing I worry about though is Moe taking risks like he did at Christmas, coming back into the country."

"I worry about that too," said Morris. "He better not come back here again. I don't want him to be a dead man."

Mama and I went with Morris to the organizational meeting in Jackson. The meeting was at Little Willie and Dora's house. Little Willie and Dora owned a dry cleaners on Farish Street and were doing well. They had even bought a house in what many considered an exclusive neighborhood for coloreds. It was a middle-class neighborhood occupied mostly by professional people, educators, lawyers, business owners, and the like. The street was only a block, but it was a long block, curving at one point and going up a slight incline. Situated right in the middle of a white neighborhood, the houses had been designed by a black architect and built by a black builder. They designed the houses for Negro veterans like themselves, and Little Willie and Dora had gotten the house under a VA loan. Living at the other end of the block from them was Medgar Evers, field secretary of the NAACP and also a veteran. Both he and his brother had fought in World War II, but unlike Christopher-John and Clayton and many other returning Negro soldiers who could no longer tolerate the racial injustices of the South and had left, Medgar Evers, his brother Charles, and men like Little Willie had stayed. Many of them were now in the fight for equal rights.

The meeting was informal. Before the call to order, I was introduced around by Little Willie and Dora as the lawyer from Boston. I didn't meet everybody. As the meeting began, several people scheduled to speak were seated in wooden chairs in front of the fireplace. One of the men looked very familiar to me. I tried to place him. I searched my memory, knowing I had seen that face in a younger time. It was a face now different, but echoing of the past. It was not until his name was announced that I recognized who he was.

Solomon Bradley.

Solomon Bradley had been my first love. My Memphis prince. I had met him when Stacey, Little Willie, and I had fled Mississippi to get Moe on a Memphis train headed north. Solomon Bradley had been in his twenties then and was publishing his own newspaper. At the meeting he was introduced as an active member of both the NAACP and CORE, the Congress of Racial Equality, and as publisher of a weekly Negro newspaper up in Memphis. When he began speaking, his voice was as I remembered, deep and resonating.

"There's a lot of talk now about voter registration," he said. "The NAACP is talking about it and CORE is talking about it. Now, there's some might think we've got no chance to get our people registered to vote, but we've overcome hurdles just as big during this last decade alone. We put pressure on the government and now we've gotten the end of segregation in our armed forces. President Truman ordered desegregation back in forty-eight, didn't get it though until we were deep into the Korean War, but now our colored soldiers fight side by side with white soldiers. In fifty-four, the Supreme Court ruled racial segregation in public schools unconstitutional, under Brown versus Board of Education, that separate but equal no longer stands since there is no 'equal' when it comes to segregation. We've already moved forward with school integration in Baltimore and Washington, D.C., and, of course, down in Little Rock at Central High School — other cities too. We've gotten integrated city buses in some cities. Just look at Montgomery. Supreme Court ruled segregation on those buses was unconstitutional.

"Supreme Court also ruled way back in forty-six that segregation in interstate travel is unconstitutional, and the Interstate Commerce Commission has banned segregation on all interstate travel, and that includes trains and buses — waiting rooms too. But these southern states still enforce their own segregationist laws while the federal government just looks the other way and lets them do it. Well, now we could change all that. If we continue to organize in Mississippi, we take our fight right to the heart of the beast. We change things in Mississippi, we break the backbone of segregation.

"Now, we all know Mississippi is going to be a tough nut to crack," Solomon said. "No state in this union is harder on black folks than Mississippi, and more than likely it'll be the last state to go down before we finally get the equal rights we're fighting for. Just saying the word 'Mississippi' strikes terror in the heart of the strongest black man alive. Sure does me! But the time has come for us to face the terror, to face the fear. The time has come for all of us to stand up, stand up and be heard."

During his talk, I noticed Solomon Bradley's look more than once directed my way. It was as if he was trying to place me too. After the meeting was adjourned, I watched as people crowded around him, but I did not join them. I remained with Mama, Little Willie, and Dora and those encircling us. Soon, however, with everyone enjoying coffee and sandwiches and homemade sweets, a soft voice from the past spoke over my shoulder. With my mouth full of sweet potato pie, I turned.

Solomon Bradley was standing in front of me.

"Cassie Logan," he said, then he smiled his big smile.

I gulped, held up my hand to let him know that at the moment I could not speak, and swallowed my pie.

Solomon laughed. "Hot-shot lawyer from Boston can't find her words! Ah, yeah, I heard about you!"

I laughed as well. "I don't think of myself as a hot-shot lawyer," I declared as I studied him. Solomon was heavier now and he was balding, but once, when I was seventeen, I had thought him the most handsome man I had ever met. "I can't believe it!" I exclaimed. "I'm standing in the presence of Mr. Solomon Bradley!"

"And I've sure heard plenty about you, Miss Logan," he responded. "Little Willie and Dora been talking you up. They're mighty proud of you."

I patted my lips with a napkin. "Well, they're pretty much family. What do you expect?"

"You know, Cassie, at seventeen you were a very pretty girl, and now you are a woman. A beautiful one." I let him know that I had heard that line before. Solomon smiled. "So, what are you doing here in Mississippi, Miss Cassie Logan?"

"The name's Cassie Logan de Baca, Mr. Bradley, and I'm just here visiting my family."

"De Baca? That's your husband's name?"

"It was. He's gone now." I cleared my throat. "He passed."

"My condolences."

"No need," I said. "It was a long time ago. What about you? Are you married?"

"Happily, with four worrisome teenagers." I laughed. So did Solomon, then he said, "All right, Mrs. De Baca, what do you do after your visit with your family? Do you go back to Boston?"

I put down my empty pie plate. "Well, that's my plan."

"Not joining in the fight?"

He caught me off guard. "Here in Mississippi? I don't think so!"

"You know you're needed here. You could make a big difference. You're a lawyer. You could challenge the Mississippi laws. A lot is being planned for this state and change is coming. It's coming sooner than a lot of folks think."

"To Mississippi?" I was doubtful.

"All over. Even Mississippi. It's coming

— as sure as the sun rises, it's coming. Won't be overnight, but we've already put in close to three hundred fifty years of slavery and inequality and it's high time for a change. Come nineteen sixty-three, we'll be facing a hundred years since the so-called emancipation that was supposed to set us free, but we still don't have equal rights. We're still second-class citizens. We've got to get those rights, Cassie, and the time is now."

I stared at him. "You know you're preaching to the choir."

"Sorry. Wasn't meaning to talk down to you. But thing is, Cassie, we'll need lawyers like you when things begin to break here. Some people even been talking about taking interracial bus rides all across the South, even into Mississippi. We'll sure need lawyers then."

"What!" I exclaimed. "Lord, these white folks down here'll kill them!"

"Maybe," Solomon said. "But if the rides happen, they'll get the attention of the whole country. They'll help show just how bad things are down here."

"It'll get attention all right," I agreed. "Could get folks killed too."

"Well, everything we take on could get us killed, Cassie. As you probably know, back in forty-seven when there was that interracial bus ride through part of the South — the Journey of Reconciliation, it was called — those riders were arrested; some even served on chain gangs. Back then, we pretty much only had radios and newspapers and word of mouth about things. Now we've got television and we've got national networks following what's happening. This time if we start this, it will have to be more than just one bus that comes down here. There'll have to be bus after bus, buses that keep on coming so people don't just go and dismiss it. Buses have to keep coming until things get changed, just like the students sitting in at the lunch counters have to keep on doing what they're doing. One sit-in wouldn't have done it, but now we're beginning to see some change. If the bus rides come about, all we'll be doing is forcing the federal government to enforce the laws already on the books and override the state laws preventing integrated seating and putting colored folks at the back of the bus. And if we do this thing, lawyers like you'll be needed. If these riders don't get killed, they will get jailed."

"And you expect me to come back down here to help take care of that?"

"You could do that . . . or if you're really brave, you could ride one of the buses yourself. In fact, I recommend it."

I stared at him. "You plan to ride one?"

"Now, what kind of journalist would I be if I didn't take the ride at least once? Course now, I'd be scared shitless, but if I'm telling other people to do it, I can't hardly not do it myself, can I?" He leaned toward me and spoke close to my ear. "We need to do this thing, Cassie. You need to ride too. You need to be on the bus."

I figured Solomon was right. I figured Rie was right too in what she had said about all of us needing to be in the fight. Stacey and I at Rie's age would have taken on the fight. There was that much anger in us, that much that needed to be done. I thought about all the times I had put my pride aside, had tolerated the insults of whites, had been denied the rights all the white folks had just because of the color of my skin. I thought often of the time Charlie Simms had shoved me off the sidewalk in Strawberry when I was nine years old. I thought often of when we were on the road to Memphis to take Moe to the train to escape Mississippi and how I wanted to use the restroom at a gas station, a restroom for white women. I thought often of how I was so frightened by white men when they saw me standing in front of that restroom door that I fled in fear, slipped, and fell into the mud. I thought often of the white children taunting us as their school bus passed by my brothers and me, splashing muddy water over us, and how we had to scamper up the banks of the roadside to avoid being soaked. I thought often about all the insults, about all the days of humiliation. Every colored person in the South, every colored person in Mississippi, had memories of humiliation and anger.

Rie was definitely right. If I were her age, I would go join the fight. But I wasn't her age any longer. Neither were Stacey, Christopher-John, or Little Man.

My brothers had their families to look after. They couldn't just take off and go south to sit-ins and demonstrations. As for me, I had my job and all my legal responsibilities — not the same as family, but still a responsibility. So I sent money instead to the organizations fighting the fight, NAACP and CORE and the Southern Christian Leadership Conference. I watched the daily news, saw the students and the arrests, listened to Rie when she called, harbored my guilt for not being there too, and stayed on in Boston.

"You're looking mighty comfortable," Guy said as he stopped in the hallway outside my open office door.

I laughed. I was seated at my desk with my feet propped upon it as I perused a stack of papers. My office was no larger than a sizeable broom closet, with only room enough for a desk, two file cabinets, two straight-back wooden chairs in front of the desk, a swivel wooden chair at the desk, and a narrow space for people to walk in and sit. There were no windows. I didn't feel bad about the office. Everyone low in the office hierarchy had similar offices, even Guy, although his office did have windows. I took my feet from the desk and said, "Come in."

Guy entered smiling and sat down on the edge of the desk. He was dressed in jeans and a shirt. I was dressed in jeans too. It was a Saturday and the office was closed. Everyone who came to do catch-up work dressed casually. There were usually only low-level people in the office on Saturday, none of the brass, so everything was more relaxed. During the week, when a professional appearance was required, I wore clothing more suitable for my position. There were two other women attorneys in the firm and they always wore suits. I chose to be different. I wore dresses, mostly A-line cuts. I had a couple of jackets that matched the dresses very nicely in case a more formal look was needed. The pumps I wore were practical for long standing or walking and were never flashy. Whenever I saw shoes or clothes I liked, I bought two or more in the same style, but different colors. That way I didn't have to go shopping for a while. I hated shopping.

Because I didn't like dressing up, as soon as the workday was done, I slipped into a pair of jeans and a loose-fitting top and flat shoes. I felt more comfortable that way.

I tossed a set of papers to Guy. "Take a look and tell me what you think." It was a case about a colored woman who had been forcedly removed from a white doctor's office by the medical staff and had suffered injuries during the removal. The reason given for the removal was that the woman had no appointment and had become belligerent when she was told she had to leave. The woman said she had made an appointment over the phone, that her voice had not been recognized as being Negro, and the address she had given was in a white neighborhood. She believed she was denied the appointment because she was colored. There had been only white patients in the doctor's waiting room. All medical complaints involving colored people and white doctors caught my eye, and I worked them all pro bono.

Guy read through the papers. "Obviously, there's a strong case here. The woman needs to sue. But tell me, Cassie, are you billing for any of this, or is this another one of your pro bono causes?"

"Does this woman look as if she has any money to pay me or anybody else? We go to the same church, so she came to me. This case is personal to me, Guy."

"All your pro bono cases are."

"Well, some of the things in this case are similar to things that happened to me. I plan to win this one."

Guy handed back the papers. "My dad and my uncle aren't going to like this, all these pro bono cases of yours."

"It's a Saturday and I'm on my own time."

"In the law firm's office."

"What they don't know . . ." I took another look at the papers and asked Guy, "Have they said anything about my pro bono work?"

"You know they don't talk about that sort of thing to me. I'm as low on the totem pole as you are. They'll talk to you before they talk to me. But frankly I think you're safe. They're totally satisfied with all the cases they've assigned to you, and besides, as you've told me often, you're our lone token in the office. As long as you do the assigned work well, they're not about to get rid of you." He smiled and got up. "So, what time shall I come this evening?"

"Anytime you want, after seven."

Guy leaned over the desk and lightly kissed me. "All right then. One minute after the hour. You can tell me about all the similarities in your life to this case."

"I'll do that," I said as he left the office, then put my feet back on the desk.

Although Guy had an apartment in the city that was almost totally bare, he also had a small farmhouse in the countryside. The house was secluded on thirty acres, set back far from the road and screened from view by towering sycamore trees. The house was nothing much to look at, but it was warm and comfortable and I helped Guy paint it inside and out. A barn much larger than the house was on the property and although there were no animals, Guy found other uses for it and invited me to do the same. He had discovered welding and loved collecting junk metal, which he transformed into intricate shapes that he used to decorate his house and his yard. Following his lead, I developed a penchant for making jewelry, mostly out of beads and organic material found in the forest surrounding Guy's house. Although we didn't go out much to public places together, we both enjoyed going to markets and scrapyards and secondhand stores looking for treasures that we could use.

Guy spent as many weekends as he could at his house, and I spent many of those weekends with him. Much of our time there we worked in the barn, but we also took long walks in the forest and sometimes Guy borrowed horses from a nearby neighbor and we rode along the trails. A small pond was on the property and Guy stocked it with fish, mainly for me. I loved fishing and I taught Guy. On summer weekends after hours at the pond, we usually had a big enough catch for at least one meal, and sometimes Guy even invited a few friends over to join us. They were friends who knew about us and had no problem with our relationship.

■ ■ ■

Despite how good we were together, I
knew from the beginning that I could
never marry Guy. But once back in
Boston, I let down my guard about all
the reasons I couldn't. Guy was sweet
and caring toward me. We talked and
laughed easily together. We had explored
the big cities of Europe together, Paris
and London, Rome and Athens, Stock-
holm and Berlin. We had walked the lush
green mountains of Ethiopia and explored the glories of Tanganyika and felt
the warm sands of Mombasa together as
we walked along the shore, with the
waters of the Indian Ocean lapping over
our bare feet. Guy understood my work
and I understood his. We were more alike
than we were different. Mostly, it was our
race that defined our difference. Guy's
mind-set was similar to mine in more
than one aspect of our lives, but in
particular our dedication to the law in
finding the means to apply it equally for
every breathing person. When I finally
had told Guy about Moe and what had
happened in Mississippi, Guy had be-

come as passionate as I about defending Moe if he were arrested. I told Guy that an arrest warrant had been issued for Moe in Michigan, but Moe had fled. I hadn't told Guy that I knew where Moe was and Guy hadn't asked me, but I suspected he knew.

As we both became more and more involved in finding a legal argument for Moe in case he was arrested, Guy teasingly said, "You're sure I shouldn't be jealous of him?"

"I've told you how close Moe and I are and what's between us. That won't ever change."

Guy was silent, his gaze on me. We were in his office. He rose from his desk and came over to me. "Cassie, I wish you'd let me more into that part of your life." His voice was now serious.

I laughed curtly. "I don't think so."

"Why not? Look at all that's going on around us. Things are changing."

"Well, not that fast," I said. "We can hardly step out here in Boston without people staring. Back with my family, back with people at the church, everybody at home, there would be no way we could live like we're living now."

"I took you to be with my family, Cassie, and you're still working here in my father's law firm. My family might not like our marriage any more than yours will, but I took that risk. Why can't you?"

I hesitated, then said, "You are whiter than white, Guy. Blond, blue eyes, well-to-do. I just am not as brave as you, not when it comes to my family."

Guy went back to his desk, then turned to face me again. "So, what about marrying me, Cassie? I've been waiting almost a year for you to say yes, but you don't even address the subject."

"Now's not the time, Guy."

"Well, when will be the time?"

I didn't answer.

"Cassie, maybe I can never expect you to love me like you loved Flynn, but can you ever get over our racial divide and simply just love me for who I am? I am a man who fell in love with this beautiful woman with a brilliant mind and a laughing spirit. Color didn't have anything to do with it. Despite our world, it shouldn't."

"Oh, please," I said, "of course color had everything to do with it. You saw me sitting there by myself and you took pity on me. You figured I was sitting alone in that lecture hall because of my color. Well, truth is I was. But truth is too you have a good and compassionate heart, and that's why you came over to sit by me. Don't tell me if I had been sitting there with that whole row filled with other students that you would have noticed me, that you would have come over?"

"Who knows? But it wasn't that way, was it? You were sitting alone for a reason . . . and for that reason I noticed you." He sighed. "And, Cassie Logan de Baca, I haven't been able to take my eyes off you since."

I wasn't being totally honest with Guy. Certainly, I wasn't being honest with my family, and I wasn't even being honest with myself. I looked at my life. It was slipping away. All the girls who had been in my class were married. Mary Lou Wellever, Gracey Pearson, and Alma

Scott — all were mothers of teenagers or children even older. Some were even grandmothers. They had married the sweet boys of our Great Faith community, had stayed on working their sharecropped farmland, attempting to improve their lives as best they could. As the white landowners began to mechanize their farming methods and fewer workers were needed, some in the community had moved to Jackson or elsewhere with their families and seemed to be doing well. They all had something worthwhile in their lives. They all had their own little families, security in the men they loved. I knew their worlds weren't perfect. Some of the men had strayed. Some of the women had as well, but for the most part they seemed to come back to each other, to embrace whatever they had built together and just get on with their lives, imperfect as they were. In comparison, I felt my life empty.

If I married Guy, he could help fill it. But whenever he pressed about our getting married, I put him off, not wanting to discuss it. Despite his liberal outlook and supposed understanding of what I experienced as a black person, I knew he could have no true understanding of my world. He had never walked in a black person's shoes. He did not understand that my concern was not only about marrying him, but having children with him, children who would be mixed-race. My cousin Suzella had been mixed-race. Her father was Mama's nephew and her mother was a white woman, mostly an unheard-of thing to me when I was a child. Things had been tough for Suzella, and more than once she denied her own heritage. I didn't want that for my child.

I spoke to a colored woman married to a white lawyer in the firm. He was British, she was from Alabama, and they had four children. I asked her how having parents of two races affected their children. She was straightforward about it. "Sometimes it's harder than hell," she said. "Sometimes when they make a white friend at their school, the white parents don't want their children socializing with them. They get along better with colored children most of the time, but then there are those times when colored children turn on them too, beat them up, say they're acting uppity, think they're better than the rest of the colored kids because they look so white, straight hair, light skin. It's not an easy road, Cassie. You have to be willing to sacrifice for a marriage like mine, and your children will have to sacrifice right along with you. You have to be mighty in love to take it on. My advice? Don't marry this man unless you're willing to take it on."

That was the thing. I didn't know if I could take it on. The family would not have understood. Even though our family was racially mixed, that racial mixing had come during the days of slavery, when black people had little to no say about what happened to our bodies. We had no choice with whom we had relations; sexual relations were forced upon us. Both Papa's father and Mama's father had white fathers. Grandpa Paul-Edward's mother, Deborah, was the child of a black slave woman, Emmaline, and a Choctaw Indian, Kanati. There was black-Indian heritage on Mama's side of the family too. But now, despite all this racial mixing, we were expected to stick to our own race, and Stacey had made

601

that very clear. I had so-called succeeded in a white world, but if I stepped outside the bounds of what the family and the community expected of me, I would betray them both. I would be a traitor to all the values they taught.

In addition to all the problems involved with interracial marriage, marriage between the races was illegal in the Deep South states, and a person could be jailed for it. So, I vacillated between making a commitment to Guy and totally breaking off the relationship. But I didn't want to lose Guy. Since I had come to Boston, Guy had been such an important part of my life; it was difficult for me to imagine it without him. There had been a time I could not have imagined life without Flynn either, but when he died, somehow I managed to live. Still, every time Guy asked me about marrying him, I told him it would have to wait; for now, I just wanted to continue as we were. Reluctantly, he accepted that.

■ ■ ■ ■

It was almost midnight when Stacey called. "Cassie," he said, "Rie's in jail."

"What?"

"That sit-in today, you hear about it?"

"No . . . I was tied up at the office all day working on a case. Didn't get home 'til late. What happened?"

"Hundreds of college students were protesting down there in Atlanta. Police came, arrested a bunch of them. Rie was one. I'm headed down there now. Man's going with me to help on the drive. Need you to meet me there, help get her out."

Without hesitation, I said, "I'll check the planes. I'll be down in the morning." Stacey told me where they were holding Rie. "See you down there."

All across the South, Negroes could not sit at lunch counters in department stores or try on clothing at those stores. Students in Atlanta had begun to protest. They came from the black colleges in the area — from Spellman, from Morehouse, from Atlanta University, from Clark, from Morris Brown. There was even a

603

sprinkling of white students too from the white colleges — Emory and Georgia Tech. They all came together in sit-ins and protests against the big stores of Atlanta. Many protested, many demonstrated, and on October 19, many were arrested, charged with "trespass and refusing to leave private facilities." That was how Rie was charged, along with more than fifty others. Among those arrested was Dr. Martin Luther King.

Stacey was already at the jail by the time I arrived. He looked angry and distraught. "Did you see her?" I asked. "Did they set bail?"

"They set it."

"You have the money for it? I've got some."

"I've got it, but the girl wants to stay here."

"What!"

"They're saying jail, no bail to protest the jailing. Supposed to bring more attention to what's going on down here."

I considered. "Well, I suppose it

would." I looked around. "Where's Man?"

"Seeing to the car." We both were silent. Then, in a sudden outburst, Stacey proclaimed, "I'm not going to have it, Cassie! I'm not going to have Rie stay in this white man's jail! I've been in jail. I won't have it!"

I said nothing.

Stacey despondently shook his head, almost in surrender to his daughter's will. "I should never have let her come down here, Cassie. I can't protect her anymore."

"But you did let her come. You knew the risks . . . and you knew Rie."

Stacey looked away. "I can't believe it, Cassie. My baby in jail."

I felt my brother's pain and touched his arm. "But think why she's in here, Stacey. Just think about that."

Stacey turned back to look at me. "I'd rather be in jail myself, Cassie, than have Rie here."

"But you're not. Fact is, Stacey, you and Dee, you done good. Rie is right where she's supposed to be."

In the end, Rie did not stay in jail. Fourteen others did, along with Dr. King. They remained there for six days, until October 24, when Atlanta's white mayor ordered their release, except for Dr. King. He was to remain. Eventually, the protest charge against Dr. King was dropped, but a judge sentenced him to four months in jail for violating a traffic ticket probation. It was said that Dr. King didn't even know about the ticket. It was a misdemeanor charge, but the judge refused to set bail. We all kept anxiously tuned to the radio and television news, trying to learn what was happening to Dr. King. Then word came that he had been secretly moved from the Atlanta jail to Georgia's Reidsville State Penitentiary. Reidsville. It was a dangerous place known for its brutal chain gangs and the questionable deaths of its Negro inmates.

People in high places were contacted to try to get Dr. King out, people like John F. Kennedy and Richard Nixon, who were in the middle of an election year as they ran for the presidency of the United States. Richard Nixon did nothing to help Dr. King; he made no response to the pleas for help. But word spread that John F. Kennedy personally called Mrs. King, and that his brother Robert Kennedy called the judge who had sentenced Dr. King and questioned the judge as to why bail had been denied to Dr. King; after all, a traffic violation was simply a misdemeanor. Following that call, the judge changed his mind about the bail and granted it.

Dr. King was released.

On election day, John F. Kennedy defeated Richard M. Nixon by the narrowest of margins, and it was said that the Negro vote helped put him in the presidency. John F. Kennedy had reached out a helping hand to Dr. King and we, as a people, did not forget that. In January of 1961, John F. Kennedy was sworn in as the thirty-fifth president of the United States. We now had a new president, one we thought would be sympathetic to our struggle, and the fight went on.

Spring came. Solomon Bradley called. "It's happening, Mrs. De Baca," he said.

"What's happening?"

"Freedom rides."

"When?"

"Not sure yet, soon though. There'll be both black and white riders to integrate the buses, sit side by side all through the bus, front to back. You going to go?"

"You?" I countered.

"Not on the first one, but if they keep the buses rolling, then I'm going to try like hell to get up my nerve." He paused. "So, you with me?"

I hesitated. "I don't know. I'd have to get up an awful lot of nerve too."

"Well, think about it. Call me."

Before I had a chance to really think about it, let alone get up my nerve, Morris called. "It's on, Cassie, voter registration drive in several counties, including Spokane. Come the summer, we're starting things up."

"Why the summer?" I questioned.

"Folks'll be working the fields. Why not wait 'til winter?"

"Can't wait," contended Morris. "We've got to strike on all sides, keep the irons hot and our fight in the national consciousness. You hear there's supposed to be freedom rides coming soon, along with the sit-ins?"

"I heard."

"Well, that'll get headlines, but you know as well as I do, we've got to get people educated to vote for long-term political gain. Like we talked about, we'll have to teach folks the constitution and how to interpret it. We need people like you, Cassie. Wait a minute, I didn't say that right. We need you, Cassie. Can you come?"

"Let me think about it."

I had a lot to think about. If I chose to board an interstate bus and ride it across the South, across Alabama and into Mississippi and try to use a white restroom or sit at a white lunch counter, I was in for real trouble. The same could be true if I went teaching the constitution and trying to get black folks to the courthouse in Strawberry to register to vote. I knew what could happen. As if it were yesterday, the memory of Mrs. Lee Annie was fresh in my mind. But I also knew I would not be in as much peril as the people who actually lived in Spokane County, people who depended on white folks for just about every dollar they made, for the land they lived on, for their very existence. If I were to teach in the drive, I still could go back to Boston and find some employment. Folks brave enough to go against white folks upon whom they depended in Spokane County would truly be putting their lives on the line. That's what Mrs. Lee Annie had done, and her whole family had paid the price for it.

I talked it over with Guy. "Not only all that," I said, "but I'd have to give up my job here. I know I couldn't take that much time off and still have a job when I got back. Besides that, I have bills to pay and if I were to do the registration drive, it would be strictly voluntary."

"But you could stay with your family. You won't have to worry about food or a place to stay," said Guy.

"True. But I still would have bills to

pay here . . . my rent, my car, utilities."

"You know, I could pay all that for you."

"I don't think so!"

"Okay. Sorry, said the wrong thing." Guy looked appropriately contrite, then said, "I think you're wrong about not having a job if you took the time. My dad and uncle are sympathetic to civil rights. You ought to talk to them about a leave of absence. They might just give you the time. If you do the registration, how long do you think you'd be gone?"

"Morris wants me to commit to at least two months. He says once people get to know me, to trust me, he doesn't want to switch out to another teacher. He wants each teacher to take a class through the learning of the constitution and go with them to Strawberry and walk up the courthouse steps with them to try to register to vote."

"Well, that makes sense," said Guy. He looked pointedly at me. "And what if you were to go on one of the buses? That's a commitment of what? Just a few days?"

"Maybe it would be if everything went smoothly, which I doubt it will. Riders are bound to be arrested."

Guy shrugged. "Well, then, we'll get you out on bail."

"A friend of mine told me everybody on those rides is committing to jail time. The rides will get the nation's attention that way. It's going to be scary, Guy, very dangerous. You've seen what's happened with the student sit-ins. You think those white folks down south are about to let people take an integrated bus ride through there with black folks sitting next to white folks and sitting up front in the bus, not in the back? You've never been down there."

Guy smiled. "Been to Florida."

"Yeah, right. On a train or plane, then a limousine to an exclusive white resort and back. If you'd even left that exclusive white world you're in, you'd have discovered Florida's hands aren't clean either. They discriminate there too. You don't know how bad these people are. They can be savage!"

Guy was silent as he looked long at me. Finally, he said, "Then give me a chance to know how they are, how things really are down there. What if I come with you?

We'll go together."

I sighed and turned away. "Oh, Lord, that's the last thing I need."

Guy pulled me back. "I mean it, Cassie. It's time I got in this fight too, whichever you choose to do, ride the buses or the registration. We can do this thing together. Like in the Book of Ruth, your people will be my people. Cassie, whatever you want, I'll follow you anywhere."

I was consternated at the thought. "I don't want you in it, Guy. It's my decision and I'd rather do it alone. You being a part of it would just make it more difficult for me. I'd have to be worrying about how folks would see us. I can't deal with it. I couldn't deal with it with the white folks down there and I couldn't deal with it with colored folks, and I certainly couldn't deal with it with my family."

Guy placed his arms across my shoulders and leaned his forehead against mine. "You forget, Cassie: I'm a big boy and it's not just your decision to make. If you get in this fight, I get in it too."

"No, not around me you won't."

Guy's eyes questioned me. He looked hurt, but I didn't care. The last thing I needed was for Guy Hallis to be in race-torn Mississippi with me.

The news in May was riveting. Beginning on May 4, the first Freedom Riders, as they were called, left Washington, D.C., on a perilous route through the South. They were sponsored by CORE. There were thirteen of them, each one battle-tested and with impeccable reputations. Seven were black, six were white, and among the white riders was a man named Jim Peck, who had been on the 1947 Journey of Reconciliation. Another rider was John Lewis, a young black man about the same age as Morris, who had been in sit-ins up in Nashville. Both names were broadcast on the national news. The networks were covering the news about the Freedom Riders, but I learned even more from Solomon Bradley, who, with his close ties to CORE, kept me informed about what was happening. Solomon told me the plan was that, after leaving Washington, D.C., the riders would travel through Virginia,

North Carolina, South Carolina, then on into the dreaded Deep South states of Georgia, Alabama, and Mississippi, arriving in New Orleans, Louisiana, on May 17. The white riders would sit in the back seats relegated to black passengers, and black riders along with some of the white riders would sit up front in seats reserved for whites, and in those states that chose to enforce their segregationist laws, all would refuse to move from their seats. At each rest stop, the colored riders would attempt to use "white only" restrooms and sit at the "white only" lunch counters, while the white riders would go to "colored" waiting rooms and use "colored" restrooms. Everybody knew sooner or later there would be a confrontation with the segregationists. In fact, the riders and CORE were counting on it.

The first part of the ride through Virginia, North Carolina, and South Carolina went relatively smoothly, except for a few minor interactions with whites determined that the riders not use the bus terminals' all-white restrooms or sit at the lunch counters. In Atlanta, the riders split into two groups to travel on to

Birmingham, Alabama, some on a Greyhound bus, the others on a Trailways bus. The only scheduled stop for the group on the Greyhound bus headed to Birmingham was Anniston, Alabama. At the Anniston bus station, the bus was stoned and its tires slashed by a white mob. The white bus driver got the bus out of the depot as quickly as he could and sped out of town, where he stopped to try to fix the tires.

The mob followed.

Whites encircled the bus and threw in a firebomb. The Freedom Riders and all the other passengers managed to escape, but the bus exploded into flames. The mob savagely attacked the Freedom Riders. Another white mob was waiting at the Birmingham depot for the second group of riders on the Trailways bus. They too were attacked. There were no police to protect them.

These attacks were reported all over the newspapers, in all the national television broadcasts, and in international news too. The government suggested that the Freedom Riders give up their rides for now, to let things cool down. But the

Freedom Riders refused the request for a cooling-off period. They kept right on with their plans to continue their ride. The problem was that now the bus companies were refusing to take them. They did not want their buses destroyed. On top of that, all their drivers were white, and they refused to drive buses for the Freedom Riders. They feared for their lives.

Solomon said black college students experienced in the sit-ins began to arrive in Birmingham to carry out the ride. Before they could even try to arrange for a bus to take them on their journey, the students were arrested, supposedly placed in protective custody, or so they were told, "for their own well-being." They were put in jail on a Wednesday night, and in the darkness of early Friday morning, around two o'clock a.m., they were packed into police cars and taken to the Tennessee state line, where they were forced out of the police cars and left by the side of the highway. Once the students got someone to pick them up, they headed right back to Birmingham to get a bus to Montgomery to continue the ride, but they could not get a driver to take them.

Finally, the Kennedy administration became involved. Attorney General Robert Kennedy contacted the Greyhound bus company directly to secure buses for the Freedom Riders, and a week after the riders had been stopped in Anniston and Birmingham, the ride resumed. On this second leg of the trip all was calm from Birmingham to Montgomery. As the bus carrying the riders pulled into the bus terminal in Montgomery, things still seemed quiet.

Then all hell broke loose.

Hundreds of whites were suddenly everywhere, carrying sticks, bricks, baseball bats, pipes, any kind of weapon they could find. Spewing words of hate and wielding their weapons, they cried, "Kill the niggers!" The riders, black and white, were beaten, as well as a white federal agent who ended up in critical condition. He and several of the injured riders who at first were denied medical attention by ambulances eventually were taken to a hospital. The remaining riders fled. The following night the riders gathered at a

Montgomery church. As the black congregation celebrated the riders, several thousand whites surrounded the church, putting it under siege. By this time, more than fifteen hundred people were in the church. Solomon was there.

So was Dr. King.

When President Kennedy had heard about the attacks on the riders, he had sent federal marshals to protect them. But the several hundred marshals were no match for the thousands in the mob who attacked them and lobbed bricks, breaking church windows. The marshals responded with tear gas, which wafted into the church, but churchgoers feared the marshals would be overwhelmed. After talks between Dr. King, in the church, and the attorney general, in Washington, pressure was put on the governor of Alabama, who finally declared martial law and ordered the state police and National Guard to the church. They dispersed the white crowd, but did not allow the churchgoers to leave until early the next morning. Two days later, the Freedom Riders, twenty-seven of them now, left Montgomery on two buses to continue their ride to New Orleans. But they had to get through Mississippi first.

They didn't make it.

At the Jackson bus terminal, the riders were not greeted by a white mob, but by white police. They were arrested and taken directly to jail. Mississippi had decided not to put up with any violence in its streets. The day after their arrest, after a trial of sorts, all the riders were sentenced to sixty days at Mississippi's maximum-security penitentiary, Parchman, the most dreaded prison in Mississippi. Our childhood friend T.J. Avery had been sentenced to Parchman when he was only fifteen. We had never seen him again. He died there.

At the end of May, I went to Toledo. I had been sickened by the savage attack on the riders. Even more, I was angry. I had to do something. I left on a Friday evening and planned to take a plane back to Boston Sunday night. It was to be a short trip, but that didn't matter. I needed to talk to my brothers. "I've made a decision," I announced as we sat at the table in the breakfast nook. Dee and 'lois were there as well. "I've decided to work in the voter registration drive down home."

They all looked at me in silence.

I went on. "Morris called me back in April, wants me there in July. He's gotten Pastor Hubbard to agree to let us teach classes at Great Faith, and he'll be announcing that to the congregation. We'll be going around to see folks there too, trying to get them to take part."

Again there was silence, then Christopher-John said, "Won't you be putting your job on the line, you do that?"

"Well, I was thinking maybe I would, but someone at the firm suggested I could take a leave of absence." I didn't mention that someone was Guy. "I wouldn't get paid, but the firm would hold my position. I've done good work and they like having me, if only as a token."

"Still, you go down there to teach," Stacey said, "it could be dangerous."

"You know as well as I do, anything we

do down there is dangerous."

"So, you've pretty much made up your mind?"

"I figure I can be of help and I've got to do something. You know, people are protesting in all kinds of ways, putting themselves at risk down there. Look at those students from Tougaloo who went to the main public library in Jackson a few weeks ago and got arrested for disturbing the peace. Just imagine that! Colored college students sitting quietly in the white library and they were the ones charged with breach of the peace! On top of that, they got expelled! Whatever I do, other folks have done just as much — or more."

Christopher-John looked worried. "I can understand you wanting to go, Cassie. I'd like to do more myself, but you know what can happen." He was silent, then asked, "You going to talk it over with Mama and Papa first? It'll affect them too, you know."

"I'll talk to them, but they're not going to change my mind about it."

"You stay with them, you could be putting them at risk too."

"Maybe I can stay somewhere else."

"Where?" questioned Dee. "You know they'll want you at home with them."

"There'll be some other workers coming from different parts of Mississippi and outside of Mississippi to teach. Morris'll be asking folks at Great Faith to put them up, feed them, but if they don't, he was thinking maybe we can all stay at Great Faith in one of the old class buildings. We can get some foldaway beds. It's only for a couple of months." I looked at Man. He had been uncharacteristically quiet. "What do you think, Clayton?"

Man's eyes were downcast. Without looking at me, he said, "Least you'll be doing something, Cassie." He was again silent. He was in one of his moods.

"You're mighty quiet," I observed. "What is it?"

Man's eyes were still downcast, looking at the table. "Remember that friend of mine, Ray Wallace, served in the Army with me? Got killed back in forty-nine because he refused to move to the back of the bus."

I nodded. "I remember."

"They dragged him off that bus, kicked him, beat him over the head with baseball bats. Police stood there and watched it all. Everybody who wasn't beating on him just stood there and watched it. They killed him because he wouldn't move to the back of the bus. He served this country. He fought in their war and they killed him." Man paused, then looked up. "Ray and I always watched out for each other. Once I got into it with some white soldiers and Ray came right over and joined up with me to fight them. He didn't even know what the fight was about, he just jumped in. He didn't stop one moment to think about the trouble we were about to be in either. He never let me down. Now, I've been thinking, maybe I need to do the same for him."

Christopher-John leaned forward. "So, what are you thinking, Man?"

Little Man looked around the table at each of us. "We all know how they used to do us when we were walking to school, how those white school buses used to pass us spewing that red road dust and splashing all that muddy water over us."

Dee, who had experienced the same

where she grew up, said, "How could any of us forget?"

"That's right," said Man. "How could we forget? Well, I'm thinking maybe it's time for me to take one of those freedom rides right into Mississippi. Maybe it's time for me to get on the bus."

"You know what this could mean, don't you?" asked Stacey. "You would go to jail. You thought this through?"

Little Man looked at Stacey with a wry smile. "When you know me not to think things through? I've talked to Rachel. She knows the risks. She'll go along with what I decide to do. We've already figured it out, how we'll get along. We've got those two rental houses that'll bring in some money. We've got a little savings and we've got the gas station."

Yes, they did have all that. Man had been very good about investing his money. Like Stacey and Christopher-John, he had bought houses that he rented. He also had bought a small gas station on the corner of his block. It was a quiet street of residential houses. Several blocks around were all residential too, and the little gas station on the corner was a bonus to the residents of the neighborhood. People stopped there in the early morning on their way to work or when they returned in the evening. Clayton, always hardworking, opened the station at five in the morning and worked there until he left for his job at the factory. A part-time worker took over after that.

"Clayton," I said, "you know anybody going on a freedom ride has to be prepared to stay in jail for thirty-nine days, and not post bail until after that. In Mississippi, sentencing is usually for sixty days, but to stay any longer would mean giving up any right to appeal. Are you ready to be in prison that long?"

Man's eyes met mine. "If you were going, wouldn't you be?"

I shook my head, doubtful about my own perseverance. "It'll be hard. It'll mean Parchman. That's where they're sending all the riders, men and women."

Man nodded in acceptance and for several minutes we all were silent; then Christopher-John said, "What about your job?"

"I'll do like Cassie and apply for a leave

of absence. I'm hoping that time will cover some of my jail time. Of course, I won't tell them what the leave is for, just that it's personal, and it is. If they find out, if it gets on the news and they have a problem with it, I figure I can find work somewhere else." Clayton spoke as if unconcerned about his job; being a mechanical engineer, he had more security than workers like Stacey and Christopher-John. "I've talked to the children, tried to explain to them what I plan to do, tried to explain that this is for them and their future. But they're so young, it's a difficult thing for them to understand."

"But one day they will," I said.

"I hope I'll be around when they do. I've updated my will just in case. I want Rachel and the children to be taken care of."

"Ah, Man," sighed Christopher-John.

"You bound to take that ride," said Stacey, "don't worry about anything here. We'll watch out for Rachel and the children and take care of the gas station, your houses too." He looked across at Christopher-John, who, without a word, nodded in affirmation. Then we all looked at Man, knowing what could happen.

We made a plan. Man would go on the bus ride, but Stacey, Christopher-John, and I would follow him all the way; others were doing the same to give some protection to the riders. I put Clayton in contact with Solomon Bradley, and the two of them made arrangements to ride together. Since that first ride, which had brought so much national attention, a number of rides had taken place, originating from different cities with destinations throughout the South. Clayton Chester and Solomon were assigned to a bus going from Nashville to Jackson. They knew they would be jailed once they reached the bus terminal in Jackson. They would not post bail. Not posting bail and staying in jail brought continued media attention both nationwide and around the world, and that international attention was important. Communist countries were now using the injustices here against the United States in their international dealings, and emerging

African nations were turning a skeptical eye on the so-called democracy preached by a United States that denied equal rights to black people within its own borders. With every civil rights stand we took — every sit-in, every bus ride, every kneel-in, every demonstration — the white backlash of terror that followed gave a black eye to America and embarrassed the government.

The Kennedy administration was up against it. It was politics. Most black folks thought of John and Robert Kennedy with affection and as being friendly to the movement, but in reality the Kennedy administration was concerned with how the protests made the United States look, both at home and abroad. The Kennedys also needed the white Democratic vote that dominated the political South. They were caught in the middle.

In June, Stacey, Christopher-John, Clayton Chester, and I drove to Nashville. We arrived early enough before the ride so that Man could meet with the other riders and be briefed on what to expect and how to react. There were both black and white riders. Solomon was already there. He greeted Stacey, met Clayton and Christopher-John, and said to me, "So, you're not making the ride this time."

"No, not this time. We'll be following along though."

"Good. We'll need witnesses."

"You'll have plenty. How are you doing?"

Solomon smiled. "I'm scared, like everybody else. I'd be lying if I said I wasn't."

"I know the feeling. I'm not even going to be on the bus and already I've got a knot in the pit of my stomach."

After the meeting we went to a motel, where we got little sleep. The next day we all met at the bus station. Before getting on the bus, Man said, "Well, I guess I'll be seeing you next month sometime."

"You be careful," cautioned Christopher-John. "Don't do anything I wouldn't do."

Man smiled. "Just watch out for Rachel and the children."

"Anything they need, we'll take care

of," Stacey assured him, "and soon as you're out of jail, we'll be down to pick you up."

Man looked at me. "Guess by the time I get out, Cassie, you'll be back home doing the voter registration."

"More than likely," I said as I put my arms around him and hugged him tight. "You be careful." I heard myself repeating what Christopher-John had said. I didn't want to let him go. I was more afraid for him now than when I had said good-bye to him as he headed overseas to fight in the war. The world war had been far away, fighting against a massive, faceless enemy for whom I had felt nothing. Now this war was at home and we were fighting an adversary we knew all too well.

Little Man hugged all of us and got on the bus. We watched as he gave his ticket to the driver, walked down the aisle, and sat beside one of the white riders right up front. Stacey, Christopher-John, and I went to our car parked on the street. We waited as the bus pulled from the station. Then we followed.

The ride from Nashville to Jackson was

uneventful. When the bus reached the terminal, all was quiet. There were no crowds, no boisterous demonstrators protesting the arrival of the Freedom Riders. Stacey parked the car and we hurried to the terminal. Standing outside where the bus was parked, we waited. The riders were still on the bus. Finally, the bus door opened. We saw Solomon step out, and then Clayton Chester. The riders had been instructed that if they made it to the terminal, they were to go immediately to the white waiting room. Doing this, they would surely be arrested. The riders never got the opportunity to go to the white waiting room. As soon as they stepped off the bus, the police lined up on either side, creating an aisle for them to walk through straight to waiting police paddy wagons. They were being taken directly to jail. Stacey, Christopher-John, and I watched Man go, then made our own decision to protest. We sat down at the lunch counter. Several other people joined us.

We were all arrested.

Voter Registration Drive

(1961)

I arrived back in Mississippi in late July to teach in the voter registration drive. Man was out of Parchman prison and in Toledo. Stacey, Christopher-John, and I were released from Hinds County jail located in Jackson after an overnight stay. The jail was overflowing with protesters. I went home first to see about Mama, Papa, and Big Ma. All three were worried about the boys and me, but they did not try to dissuade us from what we were doing. I had already told them I would be staying at Great Faith with the other registration workers. One building would house the men working in the drive, another the women, and the third would be used for the classes. Mama, Papa, and Big Ma did not like the idea of my not staying at the house with them, but I pointed out it was better for all of us who were teaching to be together so that we could drive to the different farms to contact people for classes and, if needed, take them to and from the classes. Also, teachers needed to be in one place for training and planning. I did not mention I was concerned for their safety and that was the main reason I was not staying at home, but I think they knew that anyway.

"You just be careful out there, Cassie," Papa said when Morris came to get me, "and you call if you need us."

"And you make sho you get here for Sunday dinner," ordered Big Ma.

I smiled and hugged them all. "See you at church."

Morris had already laid the groundwork for the voter registration classes. He had made announcements not only at Great Faith Church but at the other local black churches in the area. He, along with a few others, had visited many of the families working the farms, many of them still living on the Granger and Montier and Harrison plantations. Some of the people still sharecropped, although not as many as when I was a child. The plantations over the years had mechanized and now needed fewer workers to produce crops, especially cotton, for market. Some of the smaller farms had mechanized as well. Also, since the war, many of the younger people had left their farms for better lives in Jackson or cities in the North and West. Still, those who remained on the plantations were dependent on their white landlords for their livelihood and for being able to keep their homes.

The first week I was back, I went with Morris to several families. They were mostly families I knew and they greeted us warmly, but when Morris and I got down to our reason for coming, most people shook their heads and said, "Naw, can't do that. Admire y'all for puttin' in the time, but we been told already, we go takin' classes and tryin' to vote, we gotta start lookin' for another place to live."

"Who told you that?" asked Morris.

The answer was always the same. The plantation owners — the Montiers, the Harrisons, and the Grangers. That was the same thing the Montiers, the Harrisons, and Harlan Granger had threatened years before, when Mama had organized the boycott against the Wallace store. That was what they always threatened whenever the colored folks of the community tried to exert their rights for equality. Despite that, when classes began, there were a few stalwart souls who turned up, and the hard work of teaching the Mississippi constitution began.

Our Great Faith community wasn't the only one undertaking the difficult task of pursuing the right to vote in Mississippi. Several counties were involved in the voter registration drive, among them Pike County. At the center of the Pike County drive was McComb, the largest town in the county and a former railroad center. Unlike in Spokane and many other counties, colored workers living near McComb were not so much dependent on sharecropping as on jobs provided by the railroad. Still, some of the colored folks in the county had small farms or lived on white-owned land and, like most other colored folks, were hesitant to go against centuries of tradition and white rule.

The drive in Pike County was staffed

by a number of people who had come from outside the county, from outside Mississippi. Mainly, they were from CORE or were members of the Student Nonviolent Coordinating Committee, known as SNCC. SNCC workers had started teaching in August, about the same time we had. Morris knew some of the people in McComb who were working in the drive and who had helped in getting the SNCC workers to come. He had also worked with them in setting up our program. Morris and I along with Denise, now Morris's fiancée, decided to go to McComb. First, we went to visit Aunt Callie. Several of her family were studying to register to vote. They took us around the area and introduced us to some of the people working in the drive. We spent the day in McComb observing their program. Among those local people leading the drive and working with SNCC were Reverend C.C. Bryant and Mr. Herbert Lee. Together and with others, they canvassed the black community for food donations, money for the drive, and housing for the SNCC workers. They seemed tireless.

They inspired us.

By the end of August four people in the Great Faith community were prepared to take the test. Both Morris and I went with them to face the county registrar in Strawberry. I had last climbed the stairs of the courthouse when I was eleven years old, walking with Mama and Mrs. Lee Annie Lees when Mrs. Lee Annie defiantly had gone to register to vote. Now, as I walked up the steps, I felt eleven years old again, and even more afraid than I had been back then. I knew more now and understood how risky it was for us. Morris and I and the four brave souls taking the test stepped into the registrar's office. They filled out the registration questionnaire, paid the poll tax, and answered the constitutional questions. The result was no different than the result had been for Mrs. Lee Annie.

That wasn't surprising. Although it was disappointing, we all figured this would be the case. In some counties, recent attempts at registration had resulted in a few colored people being registered, but not many folks who attempted to register had been successful. Judgment was still up to the white county registrar and his interpretation of the Mississippi constitution. In addition to filling out the form to register without any mistakes and interpreting a section of the constitution to the satisfaction of the registrar, the Mississippi legislature had added another hurdle to keep black folks from registering. In November of 1960 legislators had passed a morals clause and added it to the list of qualifications for any prospective registrant, stating that the person had to be of good moral character to vote. Judging the morals of anyone attempting to vote was, of course, also left to the county registrar. Still, as Morris pointed out, each solitary registration of a black voter made a dent in the racist armor of the state and gave hope to every black woman, man, and child that one day they could be registered to vote too.

"Now, we all knew this would happen," said Morris, trying to keep discouragement from settling in as we drove back to Great Faith. "We just have to keep going back, time and time again, until we get one of you registered, then all of you."

There was silence in the car.

Morris let his words sink in. After several minutes he suddenly began to sing. It was a song instilled in all of us, a song we all knew: "Free at Last." "Day we get registered," said Morris, "this here'll be the song we'll be singing." Hesitantly everybody in the car joined in. By the time we reached Great Faith we had sung the song over and over again, and we were all inspired. "Thank God A-Mighty, we're free at last!"

As we got out of the car everybody was in a joyful mood and pledging to take the test again. Despite the letdown of the day, I was feeling good about our commitment as I crossed the lawn to the class building. Before I reached the building, Flora Johnson, another teacher in the registration drive, shouted out to me. She was standing by the old well talking to another teacher, but now hurried to meet me. "Cassie," she said. She paused, looked out to the road as if worried someone was watching, then back at me. "There's someone here to see you."

I could feel her distress. "Who?"

Her voice lowered. "A white man. He's inside, waiting on you." Flora then hurried away without giving me a chance to question her further. I looked after her and walked with foreboding to the building. At the door I stopped, took a deep breath, and opened it. Across the room, standing by the old potbellied stove, was Guy. I sighed.

"Cassie, I had to come," he said softly.

"I told you not to come."

Guy came toward me. "I had to, Cassie."

I was angry, but I spoke with measured words. "No, you didn't. You just did what you chose to do."

Guy didn't come any closer. "Listen, Cassie, I knew how you felt, how you feel, but I figure this is my fight too —"

I looked past him to the potbellied stove from another time, from the days of my childhood when I was a student in this very room. "You could never understand." My voice was almost a whisper.

"Maybe not." His tone was contrite. I didn't say anything, and he went on. "But dammit, Cassie, I want to understand!

I'm not the only one who wants to understand. There are other white people feeling the same as I do."

"But you're the only white person I know standing up here in my old classroom, standing here where I never wanted you to be."

Guy argued his case for coming. "I couldn't have you putting your life on the line and my doing nothing. I don't want you fighting this thing without me. It affects us both and our future together. You're my world, Cassie. You have no idea how you've affected my life. I had to join you here."

I kept looking at the stove. Guy stood in silence. Finally, I looked at him. "Do you have any idea what you've done, what you're doing? I'm trying to help get the vote for my folks here, people I know, people who've known me since I was born, people I grew up with, old people who took care of me when I was little, people who never thought they'd have a chance to vote. This is *my* world. These are *my* people. You have no place in it."

Guy shook his head in denial. "I'll make a place. I'll do whatever it takes.

I'll teach, I'll drive and go pick up people, take them to the courthouse, run errands, whatever. I'm here to learn, Cassie, to support you in any way I can. I'll do whatever it takes."

I froze out his words. "I won't forgive you for this."

"I think you will." Guy took another step toward me and stopped again. "I managed to get some time off from the office." He smiled. "You know I've got pull there."

I didn't smile back. "Well, it's your choice. I told you I didn't want you down here, but you came anyway. You're this smart white Boston lawyer, so I suppose you figured you knew better than I do about how things are and what was best, and you could totally disregard my wishes. Well, it's done now. You stay or you go, but if you stay, there'll be nothing between us. I'll let people know we're from the same law firm and that's it. There's nothing else."

Guy stared at me. "You're ashamed of me, Cassie? Afraid to face up to what we have together?"

I stared back. "You're so smart, you

figure it out." With that being said, I turned and left the room.

I kept my word and kept my distance from Guy. I was polite to him and professional, but I allowed no overtures from him and refused to be alone with him. The other workers were all aware that Guy and I worked together in Boston, but only Morris connected the two of us to a closer relationship. "You sure you don't want to tell Mr. and Miz Logan about Guy?" he said.

"Tell them what?"

"That he's more than just a co-worker?"

I scoffed off the suggestion. "What makes you say that?"

"By just looking at the two of you. Body language, Cassie, body language. Better watch it."

I just shook my head at that and refused to acknowledge that Morris's assertion had any validity, but I knew he knew he was right; yet he kept my secret.

At Sunday morning church service, Guy was introduced to the congregation, as all the registration workers were when they arrived. Guy was the only white worker in the drive, but he was welcomed. Pastor Hubbard made a point of announcing that Guy and I worked together as attorneys in Boston. I had already told Mama, Papa, and Big Ma that a member of my law firm had arrived to work in the registration, but of course I told them nothing else about the relationship, and Stacey hadn't either. Mama suggested maybe having Guy over for Sunday dinner, but I discouraged it, saying that wasn't necessary since the church was celebrating all the workers with a picnic dinner. I really didn't want Guy getting any closer to the family, coming onto our land, into our house, into our lives.

I wasn't strong enough for that. I felt like a hypocrite.

At the picnic dinner, when all church members brought dishes of food to share with the registration workers, Guy took the occasion to stand close to me and whisper, "I like your folks. I think they like me too."

"Well, don't get too comfortable with that notion."

"Anyway, glad I could finally meet them. I'd like to get to know them better."

"Don't plan on it."

Guy shook his head at my retort, then moved even closer. We talked a few minutes longer, the first personal talk we'd had since that first day he had arrived, then I saw Papa watching and I moved away.

It was on that picnic Sunday when we first noticed the white men on the road parked in their cars and trucks watching us. After that, there were often days when small groups of white men and teenage boys gathered on the road in front of the church. Charlie Simms and his boys and his nephews, Statler and Leon Aames among them. They did not come on the grounds, but they spewed their obscenities and taunted us. When they realized Guy was with us, they singled him out and were especially hard on him. " 'Ey, white boy! What you doin' with these niggers? You think you helpin', tryin' to teach them how to go vote when we all know they ain't got the sense for it!"

"You ain't nothin' but another nigger-lovin' outside agitator!"

"What kinda white man are you, workin' with these here niggers?"

"Ain't nothin' worse than a nigger lover!"

"Go on home, white boy, back up north where you come from!"

The taunts kept coming, but Guy took them in stride and never responded to them. I was proud of him.

I also was proud of the fact that Guy not only immersed himself in the drive but in the Great Faith community. He said he was there to learn as well as to teach, and it did not seem to bother him that he, for the first time, was the "only one." He attended the church services and offered help to those in need of transportation for medical appointments to Strawberry, or even to Jackson or Vicksburg. He also volunteered to help a couple of families with work on their farms, and even though I had discouraged Mama from inviting him to dinner, some of the other families did, and Guy happily accepted their invitations.

Best of all about Guy was how he

interacted with the children. Just about everybody at Great Faith, young and old, loved baseball. Morris had organized two Saturday games at the school, one game played by the men, another by the children, both boys and girls. Guy participated as one of the coaches to the children. He taught them how to swing a bat, tossed balls with them, and even ran the bases with some of the younger players. He was very empathetic to their needs and the children loved him for it. Once, when the school field became crowded with Great Faith spectators, a little boy was trying hard to see the game in which his daddy was playing but couldn't get through the crowd. Guy, with the permission of the boy's mother, picked him up and placed him on his shoulders, allowing him to tower above the crowd. The boy beamed. So did I. Guy had endeared himself to the children and to me. He would have made a good father.

One afternoon when the white men were parked on the road, Mr. Wade Jamison came to the church. He parked on the grounds and spoke to the small group of people gathered in the classroom. Morris had invited him. Mr. Jamison spoke only briefly about the Mississippi constitution. He said he knew that everyone had been receiving instruction about its meaning and its intricacies and the possible questions they could face before the county registrar and how to answer them. What he chose to speak about was how he felt about the laws and the changes he wanted to see.

"Not all white people in Mississippi are against you in this," he said. "I've been around a long time now, more than eighty years. As I grow older, it's very difficult to face change, but change is always a reality. My father and his father and his father before him were all slave owners. None of them wanted to give up that way of life, but that change came. My father and my grandfather were forced to give up slavery and start a new way of life. I didn't have to make that choice, but I did have to choose how to go forward after that and how to see the world. I had to decide if I would see people — black and white — as separate and unequal, separate and equal, or just plain equal. It's taken me a while to reach the conclusion of just plain equal. That's what all you are fighting for, and from my perspective, I want you to know there are white people here in Mississippi who understand and support you."

After the class Morris, Guy, and I walked outside with Mr. Jamison. Mr. Jamison glanced at the white men across the road. "You know," he said to Guy, "you're taking quite a chance being here. You stick out like a sore thumb."

"No more than you."

Mr. Jamison smiled and said wryly, "Oh, they won't mess with me. They've tried to in the past, but I've been around too long now for them to do me any harm. But all of you young people, you know what the risks are. Morris, you know better than anybody." Morris only nodded. Mr. Jamison looked at me. "Cassie, glad to see you here. Looks like that law degree is coming in handy now."

"Hope so," I said.

Mr. Jamison then said good-bye, got into his car, and drove off the grounds. The men on the road stared after him as he passed, but said nothing to him.

■ ■ ■ ■

With the white men watching the com-
ings and goings of people attending the
classes, an uneasy feeling descended
upon the church and the classes. Threats
were made against Pastor Hubbard and
all of us teaching. Some people chose not
to return to the classes after the threats,
but most stayed on, and in the early
weeks of September several members of
the Great Faith community, all of them
elderly, decided they were ready to take
the test again. Both Morris and I were
going with them, but Guy also wanted to
come. Neither Morris nor I thought that
was a good idea. "You best stay out of
it," Morris told him. "It's going to be
tough enough when all colored folks walk
into that white registrar's office, but having a northern white man with us, helping us, is just going to make it tougher."

"Well, maybe I could follow you in, just
as a precaution, as an observer, in case
something doesn't go right and a witness
is needed. I won't be with you, just waiting outside." He looked at me. "All right
with you?"

I stared at Guy for a moment, then turned to Morris. "Perhaps he's right. Who knows what could happen, and maybe we'll need help from an outside source."

Morris agreed and we headed out for Strawberry. Morris drove his car, and Ted Sanders, a Great Faith deacon, drove his. Guy trailed us. Once in Strawberry, we parked near the courthouse and all of us except Guy walked to the courthouse steps. At the top of the stairs, Morris opened the door and we all walked in. When we walked out again, not one person was registered to vote.

Everybody failed the test.

A white crowd was now gathered on the sidewalk at the bottom of the courthouse steps. They shouted obscenities at us. Some moved close and shoved all of us, including the old people. They spat on us. A sheriff's deputy stood by doing nothing. I wanted to lash out, but we were taught to accept these white people's anger and move on. Always we were to keep our goals in mind and not stoop to their level. The ugliness of their vitriolic hatred drenched over us, their vile spittle ran down our faces, and we kept on walking, saying not a word, keeping to our teachings. But at that moment, I hated these people as much as they hated me; there was no love in my heart. We pushed our way through the crowd. Some of the crowd followed us to our cars. We continued to ignore them. Deacon Sanders and his group immediately got into their car and left Strawberry. Mr. and Mrs. Steptoe had already gotten into Morris's car, when Mrs. Batie whispered to me, "Cassie, I've got to go to the pot."

I looked at her and understood. There were no restrooms for "colored" in the courthouse. I told Morris, and he decided we would go to the lone Negro café in town. Mr. Don Beasley, though, said he didn't have to go. "I tell you what," he said, "I'll just go on with this boy here and keep him company." He pointed his finger at Guy. "That be all right with you, young man?"

"Fine with me," Guy said.

"All right then! Y'all go 'head, relieve yo'selves," ordered Mr. Beasley. "See ya back at Great Faith!"

Guy helped Mr. Beasley into his car

and they left. The rest of us headed for the café. The white crowd watched us go. Some thirty minutes later Morris and our group also left Strawberry. On the trip back to Great Faith, both Morris and I were upbeat, trying to keep the Steptoes and Mrs. Batie from being discouraged. "It's going to take time," Morris reminded them. "We couldn't hardly expect to knock down the walls of Jericho in a day, but we'll get there, be assured of that. We'll get there." As we traveled along the dirt road, Morris continued to talk about the next registration attempt, but soon after we passed the Wallace store and the road straightened toward Great Faith, he jammed on the brakes. In the middle of the road were Mr. Don Beasley and Guy. Mr. Beasley was seated on the ground, bent over Guy, who lay flat on his back, unmoving. At the side of the road was Guy's car, the back end of it caved in and its front end in the ditch that ran along the road. Morris and I hurried from the car. I dropped to my knees beside Guy and reached out to him. His face was badly bruised and bleeding. His forehead had a gash across it. His eyes were closed. I cried out his name.

"He can't hear you, Cassie," mumbled Mr. Don Beasley. "He can't hear nothin'."

Morris hunched beside me and placed his fingers on Guy's neck, just under his jawline. "He's still breathing," I said, my hand on Guy's chest.

"Barely got a pulse though." Morris looked over at Mr. Beasley. "What happened?"

"White men," answered Mr. Beasley, his voice in a whisper. "Four white men. Ain't know'd who they was. Come along in two trucks, shoved us off the road into that ditch yonder. Boy here helped get me out the car and them white men, they got outta their trucks, standing all around, and they hollered at this boy, 'What kinda white man are you, helpin' these niggers?' Then they started beatin' on him something terrible. Told me, 'Uncle, you stay outta this.' Told me I wasn't worth foolin' with, being old and ignorant and all." Mr. Beasley's voice rose angrily. "But I ain't stayed outta it! I'm a man still and I tried to help, but I couldn't do nothin'. They knocked me down and I couldn't get up. They kept beatin' on this boy and all I could do was pray the boy was all right and drag myself over to him when they stopped beatin' on him." Mr. Beasley looked at Morris and me with searching eyes and lowered his voice again. "He gon' be all right?"

We gave him no answer. I just looked at Mr. Beasley, then back to Guy, and Morris said, "Come on. We've got to get him to the hospital."

By this time Mrs. Batie and the Steptoes had joined us. They helped up Mr. Beasley as Morris brought his car as close to Guy as he could, then we lifted Guy onto the back seat. Guy was too tall to lie totally prone, so I got in and we lifted his upper body so that I could hold him in a sitting position to my chest with his legs outstretched on the seat. Morris started the car, and the Steptoes, Mrs. Batie, and Mr. Beasley all stepped back, silently watching as Morris turned the car around and we headed back toward Strawberry. They would have to walk the last half mile to Great Faith.

■ ■ ■ ■

At the hospital, Morris and I explained that we had found Guy in the middle of the road. We gave them Guy's name and how to contact his family. The white doctors listened, asked a few questions, and took Guy away. We had come through the white entrance and they had allowed us to do so since Guy was white, but now, with Guy gone, we were relegated to the colored waiting room. Right after that I found a pay phone, called the law firm, and spoke directly to Guy's father. I told him that Guy had been beaten and was now in the hospital. I told him Guy was unconscious, but I didn't go into detail. I didn't know who could be listening in on the call. Mr. Hallis said he would be taking the earliest flight he could get. I also called home to let Mama and Papa know Morris and I had taken Guy to the hospital. I told them no more than that and they asked no questions. They understood questions would have to wait until I was home. After that, Morris and I waited. We waited for several hours but no one came to tell us anything. Finally we asked at the desk about Guy. The nurse looked at her chart, then back at us. "He's not on here," she said.

"He's white," said Morris.

The nurse looked skeptical. "White? You work for him?"

"We brought him in," Morris replied. "We'd like to know how he's doing."

The nurse was wary. "Well, I wouldn't know. He's in the white wing of the hospital."

"Can't you find out?" I asked.

"Now, why would I do that?" questioned the nurse. "You're not family."

"Never can tell," I said. The nurse gave me an irritated look. "Well, can you tell us anything?"

"What did I just say?" demanded the nurse.

I felt like going around that desk and yanking her. "Lady, I didn't ask you about what you just said! I asked you if you can tell us anything about how Guy Hallis is doing!"

Morris interceded. "Ma'am, can you at least check for us to see about his condition? We've been waiting some time now to find out how he is."

The nurse turned her back on us without answering Morris. I started toward her, but Morris, his hand grasping my arm, led me away. "Come on, Cassie, that's not going to help anything for you to go off on her. There's nothing we can do but wait."

So, that's what we did. We waited.

Morris and I waited all night long. We asked several more times about Guy but still got no answers. The night passed and the morning came. The shift changed and the new nurse on duty was a bit more cordial. She made some inquiries about Guy, but learned nothing concerning his condition. She said she had left word for Mr. Hallis when he arrived that we were waiting. It was not until early afternoon that we received word about Guy. It came directly from Mr. Hallis. "They told me you were here," he said as he entered the waiting room.

I rushed over to him. "How is he? They wouldn't tell us anything."

"Still unconscious, Cassie. He's got

broken ribs, some internal injuries —"

"Did they operate?"

Mr. Hallis shook his head. He glanced at Morris and gave a nod in greeting, but did not speak to him. "And they're not going to." He hesitated. "There could be some brain injury. . . ."

I was silent.

"After you called, I called down here and talked to these doctors directly and then called my own physician. I've decided to take Guy back to Boston."

"What?"

"I've hired a medical plane. They're moving Guy to an ambulance now to take him to the airport."

"Well, wait — can't I see him?"

"Afraid not. There's not time. I have to go. I'm riding in the ambulance with him."

"But I need to see him —"

"No, Cassie . . . this is not the right time. I'll be filing a report and talking with the local police about what happened. I'll see to his car too. Now, I've got to go. I'll keep in touch." He gently

660

touched my arm. "I'll call you, Cassie. I believe the office has a number for you down here. We'll get back to you." Mr. Hallis then turned and left the waiting room.

Before going home, Morris and I went to Great Faith. We passed Guy's car, still in the ditch. At Great Faith we let the other registration workers know about Guy, then Morris took me home. We both needed sleep, but I stayed up for a while telling Mama, Papa, and Big Ma all that had happened.

"And that's all you know about Mr. Hallis's condition?" asked Mama.

"His father has your number. He or someone will call to let us know how Guy is doing when they know. If they don't call before night, I'll call them. Right now, I'm going to get some sleep."

"And no one got registered?" Mama said as I turned toward Big Ma's room.

I looked back at her. "No, ma'am. Not one person."

Mama, Papa, and Big Ma looked at each other and were silent. That was what was expected. I went to bed, but as exhausted as I was, I couldn't sleep. I kept seeing Guy bloodied on our Mississippi road, Guy who had hardly known pain in his privileged life, Guy who had come down here so optimistic and innocent, unaware of how brutal these people could be, Guy who put his life on the line because of his feelings for me. When evening came and there was no word yet from Boston, I called the Hallis house. Neither Mr. Hallis nor Mrs. Hallis was available, but the word on Guy was that he was now conscious. Little else was known. I thought about returning to Boston.

"You're very worried about this young man, aren't you?" Papa asked when I stepped onto the front porch. Papa was sitting alone on the steps, looking out across the land to the forest. I sat down beside him.

"Yes, sir, I am."

"He special to you?"

I didn't hesitate. "Well, I've known him for years. We went through law school together, traveled on that group project through Europe and Africa together. He's been a good friend."

Papa was silent a moment, then, still gazing out at the forest, said, "Any more than that?"

Now I hesitated. "Sir?"

Eyes still on the forest, unexpectedly Papa said, "I don't want you marrying white."

"Sir?"

"You know what I mean, and why."

I was silent.

Papa now looked at me. With his eyes on me, I started to protest. "Papa, what makes you think —"

Papa stopped me. "You think I ain't seen how y'all been looking at each other? My own papa was half white, looked white, and he always said, 'You have daughters, don't ever let them go with a white man.' "

I looked away.

"Years ago, there could be no thinking about marriage. Now we're in this new world and some folks do marry white, like your Cousin Bud, but it ain't something I want for you. I don't want you with a white man, Cassie. I don't want you marrying white. Now, you know 'bout your grandpa. You've heard the story often enough. I've told you and your grandmama's told you too. Now, my white grandpa was a decent enough man for his times. He treated my papa and my papa's sister almost the same as his white children. He took care of them, made his white sons share their books with them and teach them each day whatever they learned in school. He even treated my papa's mama all right too, I suppose, but that didn't take away from the fact that she was his slave and first time they were together as man and woman was because she had to do whatever he said because he was her master. Both my papa and his sister were born out of that union, born their daddy's slaves, and as much as my papa loved his daddy, he hated what his mother had to do for that man not because she wanted to, but because she had to. It wore at my papa all his life, and he always taught my brothers and me, 'You ever have daughters, don't y'all let them debase themselves at the feet of a white man.' "

Now Papa was silent, and I said quietly without looking at him, "I haven't debased myself, Papa."

Papa said nothing to that, and we both looked out at the forest without another word.

Mama was now contributing to the registration drive. Although she didn't teach a class at Great Faith, she taught people what was needed to register when she made her teaching rounds in the community. She also expressed an interest in registering to vote herself. She knew the 285 sections of the Mississippi constitution as well as I did, but Papa had never studied the constitution and had no interest in doing so. "I'm not about to waste my time studying on rules these white men have set down, then march up to another white man who's going to judge me as to whether or not I've got the same way of thinking about them as he has."

"But, Papa," I said, "for now, that's about the only way to get to vote down here."

"Then I won't be voting. Besides, even if I could vote, who'd I vote for? More white folks?"

"Maybe," Mama said, "one day we'll get some white people running for office who'll think twice about their politics and do what's good for colored folks as well as whites because they'll want our vote. We don't like how they're doing us, we'll help vote them out."

"And maybe one day," I added, "there'll even be some colored folks running for office and we can vote for them."

Papa laughed. "Well, maybe then I'll see about trying to vote. 'Til then, they just gonna have to do without me." He sounded like Uncle Hammer, and both Mama and I told him so, but we understood. A lot of people felt the same.

I told Mama and Papa I needed to return to Boston for a few days to take care of some casework. I told Morris the same, but Morris knew I was going to see about Guy and I didn't deny it. Probably Mama and Papa knew that too, but they said nothing. Each day I had called the Boston office to check on Guy. He was still in the hospital. There had been some swelling on the brain, but the swelling had gone down and the prognosis was that he would fully recover and that there would be no brain damage. As soon as I arrived in Boston, I went to see him. His mother was at the hospital when I arrived and she did not leave. When I went again, he was alone, but there was an awkwardness between us. He didn't have much to say. I didn't know how he was feeling toward me. I didn't know how I was feeling toward him either.

I was in Boston less than a week, but while I was there, Morris was arrested. He had taken Mrs. Batie and the Steptoes back to the county registrar. As before, white people had gathered in front of the courthouse and were waiting when he, Mrs. Batie, and the Steptoes came out. The sheriff was waiting too. As the white folks jeered at Morris, Mrs. Batie, and the Steptoes, the crowd became animated and the sheriff stepped forward and arrested Morris. He handcuffed him and took him to jail, saying Morris was "inciting folks toward riot." I returned to Mississippi and got Morris out on bail. Although paying bail was discouraged, many in the movement did pay bail for expedience. As head of the Spokane registration drive, Morris was needed, not in jail, but to continue the drive. He still had to appear before a judge, and most likely he would have to serve more jail time. He would be standing before a white judge, and we all understood what that meant.

Mama decided to take the test. On the next trip to the registrar's office, Papa drove her to Strawberry and I went with them. Morris drove his car with a group, and Deacon Sanders also drove a group. Once more we walked the long flight of stairs to the courthouse doors and once more no one's answers suited the registrar's interpretation of the articles. No one passed the test, not even Mama, and we all knew if anyone, black or white, was qualified to pass that literacy test, it was Mama, and she was clearly upset about it. "So, what happens if folks keep failing the test according to the registrar?" Mama demanded to know on our way back.

"Well, there are already lawsuits against county registrars. We'll probably do the same here. Over in Pike County and a couple other counties, the registrars have allowed a few colored people to pass the test, mainly doctors, college professors, and leading Negro business people, so they can point out in a lawsuit how qualified the people they let pass are, not like all the other colored people who are attempting to register. Course now, only a handful of colored people voting won't change anything and these white people know that. Thing is, here in Spokane County no one has passed."

"And with these white folks around here," Papa said, "no one will."

I turned to Papa. "Then eventually we'll file a lawsuit against them."

Coming from Strawberry the sky was clear, but halfway to home we noticed haze settling in. As we neared the Wallace store we smelled smoke. "Something's burning," Mama said. The pungent smell of smoke grew stronger as we approached the crossroads. Then we saw the black plumes rising above the trees.

"Great Faith!" I cried.

Papa pressed his foot flat to the gas. Morris was right behind. When we reached Great Faith, we saw several people already on the grounds running to and from the church toward the old well, buckets in hand. Others held hoses that were connected to the building, spraying water onto the fire. Mama, Papa, and I rushed to join them. Morris and the folks in his car did the same. Papa and Morris went over to help with the hoses. Mama and I and those able-bodied enough took up buckets and ran to join the brigade of people at the well. Already the fire had burned through a portion of the roof and smoke was spewing from broken windows. No one rang the bell; no one could get to the belfry to summon the community for help, but more folks were coming anyway. They had smelled the smoke.

More people joined the line at the well. Another line formed all the way to the creek as folks passed along bucket after bucket of water in a frenzied effort to save the church. Others took up wet blankets and attacked the fire directly to try to beat it down. The men with their hoses at the front and back of the church sent water rushing onto the building. The elderly people, unable to lift buckets or swat the fire with blankets, stood back and prayed. We all fought the fire as best we could, coughing as the smoke filled our lungs, enduring the rising heat, the filth of the soot, and the burning embers that scorched our skin as the flames leapt toward us. Night settled over the grounds of Great Faith, but the light of the fire reddened the night.

The fire kept growing. We couldn't stop it.

The fire could be seen in the belly of the church sanctuary. It consumed the pulpit and the altar and the benches. There was no longer hope of saving the building. Finally, as the roof of the church totally caved and the walls began to crumble, we put down our buckets and our hoses and our blankets and stood in horrified silence, watching Great Faith burn.

A HUNDRED YEARS
(1961–1963)

I went back to Boston. Morris stayed in the fight. After Great Faith burned, people turned away from trying to register to vote, but once Morris was out of jail, he became more defiant and went to each person who had previously attempted to register and tried to persuade them that this was not the time to quit. He told them that quitting was what the people who had burned Great Faith wanted, for the drive to end. Still, people were frustrated by their attempts to register, for despite all their efforts no one was registered, and they were sorrow-stricken by the burning of the church. The church could be rebuilt, but they figured they would never be allowed to vote. The teachers who had come from other parts of the state returned home, just as I had done, and only Morris was left in the Great Faith community to carry on the drive.

The Great Faith drive in Spokane County wasn't the only one to falter. In other counties, teachers were also going home, but that didn't mean protests were over. In late September we learned that Mr. Herbert Lee of Amite County had been killed by his white neighbor, who had ordered him to stop working in the drive. Mr. Herbert Lee refused. The white neighbor, a Mississippi legislator and relative to the sheriff, pulled out a gun and shot Mr. Herbert Lee right in front of more than ten other people. That white neighbor went before a coroner's jury that same day and was acquitted. County law officials dismissed all charges. But the death of Mr. Herbert Lee sparked the black community to action and people took to the streets in protest. Some of the SNCC workers were arrested. High school students were arrested. Then, right around Christmastime, a bus carrying Freedom Riders arrived in McComb and the riders were brutally attacked and arrested too.

Soon after the freedom ride into Mc-

Comb, Morris stopped in Toledo on his way to see Moe. It was the holidays and I was in Toledo. Since the burning of Great Faith, all of us had been raising money to rebuild the church. I had managed to raise more than a thousand dollars in Boston. Stacey, Christopher-John, and Clayton had done the same in Toledo. Across the country people who had been part of the Great Faith community, but had fled from Mississippi, were raising money. That included Uncle Hammer in Oakland. All of us were going to the churches and businesses in our communities and telling them what the church meant to our Mississippi community and why it was so important to rebuild. None of us knew the names of those who had burned Great Faith. Other churches throughout the South had been burned, but mostly under darkness. The people who burned Great Faith had come during the day, but no one had seen them. No one had been at the church.

Back home, plans were already under way for the rebuilding. Papa and other elders of the church had met with banks in Jackson and Vicksburg to see about getting a loan. They wanted the rebuilding to begin by the next revival, and the money we were raising would lower the amount of the loan needed. The banks, however, denied the loan. Great Faith Church had allowed the registration drive, and the banks were not about to forget that. Great Faith would have to raise all the money needed to rebuild. The Great Faith community remained undaunted. They wanted a building kickoff that would involve people coming home for the week of the revival to labor along with the community. In the meanwhile, church services were being held in one of the vacated school buildings.

"So, here's the thing," said Morris as we sat in Stacey and Dee's living room strategizing about our next moves for Great Faith. "We get enough money raised and start rebuilding, we've got to make sure another burning doesn't happen. You know a lot of the younger people have left over the years, but we've still got enough able-bodied men, women too, who could watch over the grounds, both during the rebuilding and after. We want to recruit those people coming for the revival and the rebuilding to stay on at night as well and watch out for the place."

We were all in agreement with that.

Later, Stacey and I went with Morris to Canada. Morris told Moe about plans for the rebuilding of Great Faith. Moe was somber as he listened, knowing he could never be a part of it. Morris, reading Moe's mind, slapped his eldest brother on the shoulder.

"One of these days, Moe, you're going to get a fair hearing from up here. One day you'll be able to come home."

Moe didn't respond. His look said it all.

When I had taken my leave from the firm, it was understood that I would return. I had committed to that. Also, I was committed to seeing Guy again. There was so much unresolved between us. By the beginning of 1962, Guy was back in the office, and by the spring he was fully recovered and working full-time. That he had gone to Mississippi and had put his life on the line made me care for him even more, but what he had done had not made things easier for us. Mama and Papa were both aware of why he had come to Mississippi. They knew I was the reason. They admired Guy and respected him, but that didn't change their minds about my having a relationship with him. Just like Stacey, they were unrelenting in their thinking. Any union with Guy, even if it were a legal one through marriage, would mean betrayal as far as they were concerned. I tried again to explain that to Guy. "I can't go against them in this, Guy. I just can't do it. I'm not tough enough or brave enough."

Guy shook his head and was momentarily silent. "You'd be brave enough if you loved me enough."

Now it was I who was silent. Maybe that was so.

"What do I need to do, Cassie?" We were in his office. He walked over to the window and looked out. He sighed heavily. "I don't know how else to show you I'm up to whatever we would have to face. I've gone into the heartland of Mississippi, seen your life and felt its brutality. What else can I do?"

I stared at his back. Guy turned from the window to look at me. "What?"

And I answered, "Nothing."

It was over, and we both knew it. I had never loved Guy the way I had loved Flynn. If I had, maybe despite the racial divide, I would have stayed with him. If Guy had been colored, most likely I would have stayed with him. But neither was the case. Guy had been in my life for so long and had become so ingrained in it through some of the toughest and loneliest times. The thought of losing him broke my heart, but there was no path for us. Guy wanted me to commit to him, but in the world in which I lived, my commitment had to be to my family. It had to be to my race. Before the summer came, I quit the firm, left Boston, and moved to Toledo.

I planned to stay in Toledo only for a short time until I could figure out the next steps in my life. Lawyer Tate gave space to me in his office, but it was up to me to get my own cases. I had some money saved from my years of working in Boston and I figured that would last me through the year. By that time, I hoped I could move on, although I didn't know to where. In the meanwhile, I stayed with Dee and Stacey. They had three bedrooms, one of which was used as a guest room, but I chose instead to live in the attic.

The attic was a great space.

The two fully finished rooms were quite spacious and there was plenty of natural light throughout the day. I furnished the rooms with used furniture. The space was warm and comfortable and gave me privacy. I paid Stacey and Dee a small rent, chipped in for living expenses, helped with the housework, and we were back to living as a family.

Shortly after my return to Toledo, I went to visit Moe. I went alone. Moe looked fine, but there was something in his voice that told me he was worn out by all the uncertainty in his life. "I'm tired, Cassie," he said. "I'm just tired, sick of worrying about being found. Sick of worrying about Mississippi getting me back down there. They do, I'm as good as dead."

I studied my old friend for a few moments before I responded. "What can I tell you, Moe? I can't say I know how you feel, because this arrest warrant and extradition aren't hanging over my head. But I can tell you that I know something close to how you feel. You, Stacey, and me — Little Willie too — we've been in this thing from the beginning, from that day back in Strawberry."

Moe heaved a sigh and looked away from me. "You know it wears on me, Cassie. Every day I think about Troy and the fact that what I did caused his death. I feel real bad about that, sorry for it, Lord knows." He paused, then turned back to me. "What was I thinking, Cassie? I keep wondering, what was I thinking? If I'd just let those Aames boys rub my head like they done Clarence, we all could've gotten out of there and all this wouldn't be happening. I could be walking free."

"Walking free? Really? You think you could've?" I shook my head. "You know as well as I do, Moe, you couldn't live with yourself if you hadn't stood up. I admire you for standing up. If Stacey had been out there with you instead of over to Mr. Jamison's office, he would've done the same thing."

"Good thing he wasn't," said Moe. "I wouldn't want anybody else to be in my shoes."

"Well, plenty are, and you know it. Maybe not fighting arrest and extradition, but going through the same hell every day, getting all bloodied up and going to jail just for wanting to be treated like a human being. Just for trying to have the same rights as these white people."

"You think I'm feeling sorry for myself?"

"Aren't you? Course now, everybody's allowed a 'poor, poor pitiful me' day every now and again. I know I take mine about once a month."

Moe laughed. "Cassie, you always could cheer me up."

"Good," I said. "But I wasn't trying to cheer you up. It's just the truth."

"You ever think, Cassie, how our lives would've been if you'd taken a chance on me, maybe married me even without having the same feelings for me as I had for you? We would have been good together. We come from the same place, have a lot of the same memories. We know each other."

"Yes, we do know each other, Moe. Maybe too well. No sense in looking back at what-ifs. It's done now."

"You're right," Moe said with resignation. "It is done." Then he looked at me hard, a long, dwelling look. "I've thrown my life away, Cassie."

"You haven't thrown your life away, Moe —"

"And I'm alone."

"You're not alone. You've got your family and you've got us. You've got Myrtis."

Moe scoffed. "She won't even move here to be with me. Says she needs to stay in Detroit, be with her family there. I don't fault her for that. She feels about her family like I do about mine." Moe looked away, then again to me. "Myrtis is putting in for divorce. She said she can't live her life like this."

"Ah, Moe . . ."

"There were times I felt alone in Detroit, but I always had all of you nearby, then I had Morris and later on Myrtis. Now I don't have any of you."

"That's not so, Moe. We're still here for you."

Moe looked at me for a long moment. "Sometimes, Cassie, I think I ought to just take my chances and go see my family. Hertesene's dead, who knows who's next?" Moe sighed and looked away. "You know there were seven of us children when Mama died. Course Morris had just been born and my daddy was beside himself in grief and worrying about all of us and how he was going to make it. I was thinking along with Levis and Maynard and Hertesene, maybe he'd take himself another wife, but he never did. Instead he just kept on going, trying to make the crops each year on Montier's place, and when Aunt Josephine and Uncle Homer up and died within a couple months of each other, Daddy took their four little boys in too. They became brothers to us and we called them that, but I saw Daddy wear down, making himself sick working so hard trying to take care of everybody. Me being the eldest, I figured I needed to do whatever I could to help him keep that place going and take care of all the younguns."

"Well, you did that, Moe, and you went to school. Lot of boys wouldn't have."

Moe grinned. "Yeah, I wanted my education, and Daddy wanted me to have it too. Insisted on it even when I said I'd stay on at the house to help do the work instead of going. He told me, 'You get yourself on to school, boy, 'fore I lay a whip on you!' And you know how long it took to walk those roads to Great Faith and back."

"Yeah, I know."

"Course, like Stacey, I never did finish school. Stacey went on to Jim Hill in Jackson for a year, but I decided to stay on with Daddy to help him, things were so bad. And you know how things turned out after that."

I nodded.

"Cassie, I want to see my daddy again. I want to see my daddy before he's gone."

I reached over and laid my hand over Moe's, but said nothing else, and Moe just looked at me in silence.

The summer of 1962 turned out to be a hot one. National news broadcasts from CBS, NBC and ABC reported church burnings in Georgia and sit-ins in North Carolina. Since the beginning of the year, there had been demonstrations in Georgia and Louisiana. There were demonstrations, boycotts, and sit-ins all along the Eastern seaboard from Maryland to Florida as protesters attempted to integrate white establishments. There were demonstrations in the North as well. The whole country was heaving with unrest and we all felt it. The sit-ins, the freedom rides, the boycotts — every single act of civil disobedience was bringing attention to all the injustices black people endured daily. In some states, high-pressure water hoses were used to disperse the demonstrators, as were police dogs and tear gas. Each time there was a protest, the hammer of white law slammed down even harder to keep the old line of segregation and bigotry intact. In Mississippi, it was commonly known that the white Citizens' Council, which had been formed to prevent integration of the schools, worked hand in hand with the mayor of Jackson and with the governor and state legislature to prevent all integration. Television programs that promoted integration were not aired, and physical violence was always threatened against blacks who participated in any protests.

News about the battle for equality came daily, not only from the national broadcast networks but also from our local colored newspapers, from NAACP publications, and from *Jet* and *Ebony,* national magazines published by and about people of color. News also came from our churches, from people who were greatly involved in the movement and went around speaking to church congregations and Negro civic groups, raising money for the cause and arousing our communities to action. What was happening around the country was uniting Negroes as a people, and making us proud. News also came directly from down home. Mama wrote weekly in her long letters of what was happening there. She cautioned us to be forever vigilant, both in Toledo and certainly when we ventured back to

Mississippi. It was a troubling time and a dangerous time and she worried for all of us.

News came too about a new group rising. They were known as the Black Muslims. Unlike the peaceful protesters around the country, the Black Muslims wanted nothing to do with white people and advocated total separation of the races, as well as a separate state to be governed by blacks. Their leader and founder, the Honorable Elijah Muhammad, had organized the religious group in the 1930s, but most black folks had never heard of them until now. Few of us knew either that long ago in Africa, before our ancestors were snatched away, captured and thrown onto slave ships to the Americas, many of them had been Muslims. The Honorable Elijah Muhammad and the Black Muslims' most vocal minister, Malcolm X, taught us that.

Many of the Black Muslims changed their last name to a simple "X" to eradicate the taint of white slave owners whose last names so many of us carried. They lived by a strict religious code, the men always wearing suits, the women dressed in traditional Muslim clothing, with their heads covered. They were a disciplined people organizing their own businesses. They set a good example for black folks, but they advocated a militant stance that made white folks even more uneasy than did the peaceful protesters who were demonstrating daily. The fiery Malcolm X did not hold back feelings about white people, calling them "white devils" and warning them that they had better deal with the nonviolent blacks, because dealing with groups like the Black Muslims would not offer the same peaceful alternative. Much of what the Black Muslims said made sense and many were drawn to the group. But most black people still held on to the promise of America, and continued to fight nonviolently for the end of segregation.

So much was happening, and each time a new event arose, news that took over the headlines, I wanted to call Guy and talk about it. I was accustomed to talking to him about everything, speaking to him several times each day, and I missed that. I wanted to talk to him about Moe's situation, about what was happening in the country and in the world, about what was happening in my life, about my cases. I wanted to talk to him about the little things that were going on in the church and in the neighborhood and in my family. I just wanted to talk to Guy, but I resisted calling him. I had to learn to do without him, as I learned to do without Flynn. There was no other choice for me.

August. Hot and sweltering. It was time for revival.

We would all be going home, including Uncle Hammer — but without Aunt Loretta, who said Mississippi had seen the last of her in the heat of an August summer. I was the first to arrive. Mama and Big Ma had asked me to come a few days early to help with the cooking. Mama, as a professional lady, had never cared that much for cooking. Her days and evenings had always been devoted to teaching her students and preparing for the next day of studies. Besides, she had Big Ma, and Big Ma, no matter how old she got, still loved to cook. In addition, the kitchen had always been Big Ma's domain, and even though Big Ma had signed the land over to Papa and Uncle Hammer many years ago, she still proclaimed the kitchen as her own and declared that it would be until the day she was gone. Although Big Ma allowed others in from time to time, she was totally the boss of the kitchen and she let everybody know it. Now in her nineties, her sight failing and her movements slower, her mind was as sharp as ever and her hold on the kitchen stronger still, but she knew when to ask for help and wasn't too proud to do it.

"Now, your mama's got to make a speech coming up during the revival," Big Ma said as I sat at the table, cooling myself with some freshly made lemonade, "so she's got her hands full workin' on that. 'Sides, she ain't never been much hand in the kitchen anyways."

I smiled, knowing that was true.

"So, you and me, we've got a lot of work to do."

"Well, that's why I'm here, Big Ma. You know, though, Dee, Becka, and Rachel all are cooking something to bring."

"Course I know that. But they can only bring so much that ain't gonna spoil on the way down here. Told them to bring cakes and pies and such, maybe some of them rolls they make so good. Rest, we'll cook up here."

"There's a lot of us to feed."

"Girl, don't you think I know that? Already got some of the food ready." Big Ma rattled off a list of meats smoked and ready for the stove. "We'll get your papa to take care of a couple of them chickens so we can roast them for dressing and cook with dumplings. Course, I don't want to ask your papa to do too much though. He ain't been feeling quite hisself lately."

I put down my lemonade. "What do you mean, Big Ma?"

Big Ma waved her hand in dismissal, as if waving away a fly. "Ah, ain't nothin' much. You know your papa, girl. Strong as a bull. Just comin' down with a cold or some such. He'll be all right. Now, what was I sayin'? Ah, yeah, the chickens. We'll fry up some for Saturday so we'll have something ready for the boys and their families to eat when they get here." Big Ma had thought of everything. She always did when it came to preparing food for the revival.

Big Ma let me rest the remainder of my first day home, but the next day she had me up before dawn. After the morning chores and before the sun settled in to overheat the land, Big Ma, Mama, and I went to the garden, where we gathered collard greens, turnip greens, tomatoes, green peppers, onions, squash, and other vegetables for the coming days of cooking. Once the vegetables were gathered, Mama went back to working on her speech and Big Ma and I spent the next days in the kitchen. We cooked a lot, sweated a lot, laughed and talked a lot, but by Saturday, when the rest of the family began to arrive, we had all the food prepared, from turnip greens mixed with collards and onions and chunks of ham hocks to roasted chicken and cornbread dressing, as well as chicken and dumplings and desserts of coconut, pecan, and sweet potato pies and cobblers, both sweet potato and blueberry. As much of the food as we could, we jammed into the refrigerator; the rest we put in storage boxes filled with ice Papa had brought. As when I had been a child,

I could hardly wait for Revival Sunday and all the good eating to begin.

On Sunday morning the grounds of Great Faith Church were overflowing. We got there early. It seemed everybody who had moved on to the cities of Jackson or Memphis and beyond had decided to come home. Everybody knew it was a time of change and everybody wanted to be home. Also, we were rebuilding the church and everyone wanted to be a part of it. As many people as possible packed into the old school building where most of us had once been students. Walls had been removed to open up the space, but still more space was needed for all the people. Papa, as a deacon, had his work cut out for him. He and the other eleven deacons took care of trying to get as many people as possible seated in the building. As the elderly arrived, they helped them in and, as was the custom, every young, able-bodied person gave up his or her seat without being asked. This is just what folks did. It was understood.

Extra chairs were brought in, and churchgoers lined the walls of the school building, spilling outside the doors and onto the lawn. Windows were open and people outside gathered in front of them. As electric fan blades whirled, cardboard fans were handed out, and churchgoers waved them furiously, trying to cool themselves. Although the building had electricity, there was no air conditioning, but most folks could endure that. Most people, even those living north, did not enjoy that luxury either. No one complained. We had come to hear the sermon, to join together in community. We had come because no matter where we now lived, this was home and always would be. The heat didn't matter. The comfort didn't matter. So, we took our fans, cooled ourselves as best we could, and awaited the words of the Lord.

After services, the eating began. Pots and trays of food were set out on the tailgates of trucks and wagons. Long tables had been brought from all over and set up across the lawn. Chairs that had lined the school walls were brought to the tables, along with benches, and as many as could sat, but many folks stood, plates heaped with food in hand, and enjoyed the tremendous feast. Others, mostly the young folks and children, plopped down on the ground, shaded by the huge pines, and ate voraciously, then hurried back to the pots and trays for more. Once the family food had been tasted, people moved from truck to truck, wagon to wagon to sample a neighbor's food and enjoy their neighbor's camaraderie. Our family sat with the Turners and the Wigginses. Little Willie, Dora, and all their family were at the revival, and so were most of the Turners. I thought about Guy. He would have loved all this.

"So, how y'all doing?" asked Morris, holding a plate of food piled high as he swung his long legs over the bench to sit between his father and me. He had come late to the table after having made the rounds to as many people as he could to get them enrolled in this year's summer registration drive.

"Question is," I said, "how are you doing, Little Brother? Getting any people registered?"

"Few. But far as that Strawberry registrar is concerned, it's all show so the county can say to Washington that it's got Negroes registered to vote. But they know and we know just a couple Negroes voting can't help bring the change we need."

"What about people coming to the classes? Any increase from last year?"

"Little down, but hoping it'll pick up after this week. Wish you were teaching again this year, Cassie. We could sure use the help."

"Like to, but I've got to work."

"Well, want you to do that too, especially for Moe." He bit into a chunk of sweet potato pie. Like a lot of folks, he started with his sweets first. I waited for him to swallow. "Umph!" he said, once he did. "You make this, Cassie? Got it from your truck there. It sure is good!"

"No, I'm not much of a cook. That's Big Ma's cooking you're tasting."

"Should've known." Morris looked down the table to Big Ma. "Miz Caroline!" he called. Big Ma turned to look at him. Morris pointed to his plate with his fork. "Great food! You sure you don't want to marry me?"

Big Ma laughed. "You get on 'way from here, boy! I was twenty years younger maybe, but I ain't, so you just enjoy your food and think on that wedding you got comin' up here with Denise. Hope she still gonna have you!"

Morris smiled and glanced at Denise sitting across the table. "Are you?" he asked.

Denise shrugged. "I guess so, seeing Miz Logan don't want you."

Everybody near laughed, including Morris; then he got up. "I gotta get me another piece of that sweet potato pie before it's all gone. Can I get you something, Daddy?" he asked of his father.

"Naw, son," said Mr. Turner, smiling toothlessly up. "You just go 'head, eat all you want. Eat some for me too."

"I'll do just that, Daddy," promised Morris.

As Morris left the table, Uncle Hammer said to Papa, "You don't look so good, brother."

I was seated next to Papa. Uncle Hammer was across the table, next to Denise. I turned to Papa. Sweat was pouring down his face.

Papa grunted. "Well, what you expect, Hammer? It's hot out here."

"Yeah, course it is. But you don't see me sweating like you." Uncle Hammer, as always, was blunt.

Papa gave him a look. "Body just different, that's all."

"Maybe. But I never seen you sweating like this, no matter how hot it got."

I hadn't either. I touched Papa's arm. His shirt was damp. "Papa, you sure you're all right?"

Papa looked at me. "Just fine, baby girl. Do something for me now. Go get me some of that nice cold ice cream we just churned. It'll cool me down."

"Better cool you down," said Uncle Hammer. "Got a lot of work to do on this church these next few days."

"Don't worry, Hammer," said Papa. "We'll get it done. Can't afford not to."

On Monday morning Stacey drove Dee, Rie, and 'lois down to the Davises. Stacey stayed the night and returned the

698

next morning to begin working on the church. Both Rie and 'lois wanted to help with the rebuilding so they arranged for one of their Davis cousins to bring them back on Wednesday. Another one of the Davises would bring Dee on Friday, and we would all be leaving, along with Christopher-John and Man and their families, on Saturday. All day Monday I worked at the church with Christopher-John, Man, Papa, and Uncle Hammer. Stacey joined us on Tuesday. On both days in late afternoon, we went back home, washed up, had an early supper, and returned to the church grounds for the evening revival service.

After the Tuesday service the boys and I sat with Mama, Papa, Big Ma, and Uncle Hammer around the dining table. Becka and Rachel and the children were staying with a couple of the sisters and their families and they had been since their arrival. There were just too many family members to stay here in the house. With the windows open wide as a thunderstorm approached, we enjoyed some cornbread mixed in clabbered milk and some of Big Ma's coconut pies. We talked about the night's sermon, about what was happening all around Mississippi, about our land, and about what the future could hold for us all. Stacey, however, said very little. He had sat quietly throughout with a scowl on his face, looking as if his thoughts were elsewhere.

"You've been mighty quiet there, Stacey," said Papa after a while. "Something on your mind?"

Stacey thumped the table with his fingers and looked at Papa. "Yes, sir, as a matter of fact, there is. It's 'lois."

" 'lois?" questioned Mama. "That child's never given you a moment's worry."

"Not until now," said Stacey.

I smiled, knowing what this was all about. Both 'lois and Stacey had told me. 'lois was now a student at the University of Toledo, and although she was studying to be a teacher, she planned not to teach in the States when she graduated. She wanted to teach in Africa. She had applied to the Peace Corps, John F. Kennedy's new international program to aid developing nations. This was most upsetting to Stacey, who couldn't fathom his daughter being so far away that he could offer her no protection. He told everybody about 'lois's plan. "On top of that, she's saying she wants to be a writer, not a teacher. Now, how is she going to make a living being a writer?"

"She's a Logan," Uncle Hammer said. "That's what she wants, she'll figure it out."

Stacey stared at Uncle Hammer, as if not understanding why he wasn't supporting him in his opposition to 'lois's plans. But Uncle Hammer wasn't the only one supporting 'lois. "The Peace Corps?" Mama said thoughtfully. "Oh, the opportunities these young people have these days!"

Stacey, looking stunned, turned to Mama. "You support her in this?"

"I do. Young woman can broaden her horizons, learn so much about the world. I would have liked to have had that opportunity myself when I was her age."

"But, Mama, she might go over there, get married, then she'll never come home!"

"Well, what does Dee have to say about

all this?" asked Papa.

"You know Dee. She's scared for 'lois, like she was scared for Rie in those sit-ins, but all she'll say is long as 'lois is happy and figures she's doing the right thing for herself, then Dee's all right with it. She can say that, but I'm not going to have it!" The scowl etched deeper into his face. This was not the plan he had for his daughters, Rie following her own mind, protesting and getting put in jail, and 'lois going off to faraway Africa. "All I want is for them to get married to some good men and give me and Dee some grandchildren and stop all this other stuff. Maybe then I'll stop worrying about them."

Both Mama and Papa smiled know-ingly, and Papa said, "Believe me, son, you never will. Long as you're on this earth and they're here on it with you, you never will stop worrying. They can be as old as me, and you're still going to worry."

"Ain't that the truth!" exclaimed Big Ma with a burst of laughter. Mama and Papa laughed too.

Stacey just looked at them and did not

laugh. He found nothing funny about his daughters' rebellious actions, nothing humorous at all. He had brought up Rie and 'lois in his own image and now they were going off on their own paths. He had done his job well, but right now we all knew he was regretting it. I figured though in time Stacey would get over it and be proud of the daughters he had raised. They were the new generation.

Big Ma sighed heavily. "That child go off to Africa, then I s'pose that's one more I can't count on to be on this land."

"What you mean, Mama?" said Papa.

Big Ma shared her worries. "I don't mind tellin' y'all, I'm real worried 'bout what's gonna happen to this land. I mean, after I'm gone. Ain't got much time left here on this earth —"

"Ah, Big Ma," I said, cutting her off, not liking to hear her talk like this.

"Hush, child! It's the truth. The Bible says three score and ten, that's all that can be expected if we're so blessed. The good Lord, though, done seen fit to keep me here way longer than that, and I know He got His reasons for doin' it, and I thank Him for allowin' me to be here with my children and my grandchildren and seein' my great-grands all growin' up, but I know I ain't gonna always be here." She took a moment, then looked from Uncle Hammer to Papa. "For that matter, my boys won't always be here either. Once they're gone, then what comes of this land?"

"Now, Mama, I've told you not to be worrying 'bout that," Papa chided.

"I know what you told me! But that don't mean I'm not gonna worry! Somethin' happen to you, then who's gonna be here? Hammer? He's way off in California!"

Uncle Hammer cocked his head in attention. "I'm here now, aren't I? Something happens and you need me, we'll figure it out."

"What?" countered Big Ma. "You comin' back here to live?"

"Now, I didn't say that, Mama."

Big Ma grumped and turned her head. "That's what I thought. Then who's gonna be here? All my grandchildren and all their children way up north. Land'll just be sittin' here empty. Land my Paul-

Edward and me worked hard for, sacrificed for, just sittin' empty waitin' for these white folks to take it over."

"Big Ma, that won't happen, I promise you that," Stacey said. "You don't have to worry about white folks taking the land over. The taxes will always be paid." Christopher-John seconded that.

Big Ma nodded in recognition that the taxes would be paid, then said, "Well, that's all well and good, but what I wanna know is who's gonna live on this land? It ain't just the taxes I'm worryin' 'bout. I want to know who's gonna be here taking care of it, keepin' it from all going back to weeds and woods. Who's gonna keep life on this land? Just about everybody round here still got some young folks on their places to take care of it for them, but here our family got all our young folks gone."

The boys and I looked at each other. We all felt guilty about leaving Big Ma, Papa, and Mama alone on the land.

"You know, Big Ma," said Man, "things are better for us up there."

"Boy, don't you think I know that? I ain't faultin' none of y'all for moving up north, not a one of you. Y'all doin' well up there for yourselves and for your children and I'm happy 'bout all that. Still, I can't help worryin'."

We were all silent, pondering Big Ma's words, then Stacey said, "Well, Big Ma, if things were different here, maybe we'd be coming back. Fact is, Christopher-John, Man, and me, we've all talked about just that. Things ever change down here, we'd want to come back and build houses on the land, enjoy the rest of our days here. Course that would be years away, after we retire."

"But that's only if change comes," clarified Clayton Chester, so there was no misunderstanding. "I'm not about to come back down here to live the way things are now, way they've always been."

Now Mama spoke up. "We all know there's some hope for change. Just look at that freedom ride you were on and that sit-in Rie was in —"

"And look what happened to them," grumbled Uncle Hammer. "Both Rie and Man sat in jail and nothing was changed when they got out, so what the hell did they accomplish?"

"They accomplished a lot," contested Mama. "In some states, colored folks can now sit at the lunch counters, sit where they want at movie theaters, and the signs have come down —"

"Not here in Mississippi," interrupted Uncle Hammer.

"— and on interstate buses," Mama continued, "colored folks now can sit where they want —"

"Yeah, federal government finally stood up and enforced their own laws like they should've been doing for years."

"Well, they're doing it now."

" 'Bout time," said Uncle Hammer, not totally conceding the point. "But what happened to that voter registration drive Cassie was in? Still can't vote down here. Look what happened to Great Faith. Still got the same laws in place, still got the same signs, staring us in the face, still got the same old rednecks running things. I don't see these Mississippi white folks about to change voting laws or anything else anytime soon. Remember how colored folks used to have to qualify to vote? By guessing how many jelly beans were in a jar and all sorts of fool nonsense like that!" Uncle Hammer waved his hand in disgust. "That's about how much they think of us. It'll be a cold day in hell before these white folks change around here."

Mama smiled at Uncle Hammer. "Well, that cold day could be coming sooner than you think, Hammer."

Uncle Hammer was unbending. "Can't see it."

"Little changes, Hammer," Mama reminded him. "Little changes — in the end, they become big ones. Everybody knew Mississippi would be the last state to go down in this fight. Alabama and Mississippi. The hardest-line states in the country. Be patient, Hammer. Be patient."

Uncle Hammer snorted. "Been patient long enough. Three hundred and more years of patient."

Papa agreed with him. "Change ain't hardly coming here, Mary, not in our lifetime, least not mine. All we can do is hold on to what we've got, hold on to this land. That's what we fight for."

"But how we gonna do that, son, if

nobody's here?"

All eyes again turned to Big Ma. She looked around the table at the boys and me, and I felt weighed down by my guilt.

Papa defended us. "Well, the boys said maybe they'd be coming back, Mama, that's something."

Big Ma's face was grim. "Maybe." She turned and looked directly at me. "But what 'bout you, Cassie? You ain't said. Ain't heard you say nothin'."

I met Big Ma's look, but I didn't know what to say to her. I couldn't tell Big Ma that no way in the world would I ever come back to live in Mississippi, land or no land.

Before I left for Toledo, Mama spoke to me about Guy. "How is that nice Mr. Hallis doing?" she asked.

Mama's look was guarded and so was mine. "He was doing fine last time I saw him."

Mama was at her desk. She glanced down at her papers before looking at me again. "Is it over?"

"What?"

"Your personal relationship."

"We're still friends," I acknowledged.

Mama nodded. "Good. As long as that's what it is, friendship." She emphasized the word "friendship." Then she reiterated, "That Mr. Hallis was a nice man." That is all she said about Guy.

Papa talked to me too. On the morning I was to leave, Papa and I walked the forest trail to the pond. We sat on one of the fallen logs, as we had done so many times before. Papa coughed, and I asked if he was all right. "Course I am, sugar. Just got this cold I can't seem to shake. Your grandmama's fixing me something for it that'll knock it right out, so don't you worry about it. The worry ought to be on my end about you."

"Sir? Why?"

"The boys, they all got their families and here you are, still alone. Flynn's been gone a long time now, Cassie, and your mama and me, we worry about you."

"Oh, Papa, I've told you before, don't worry about me. No need. I'm fine."

"I know you keep telling us that, but

you know that don't stop us from worrying —"

"And I also keep telling you, I've got
my work."

"Well, work, that might keep you busy,
but I don't see how it keeps you company, 'specially come nightfall when the
workday's done." Papa fell into silence.
When he spoke again, he was looking up
at the trees, not at me. "You know how
your mama and me thought about Mr.
Hallis. He was a nice man . . . but you
know how we felt." I didn't say anything.
I was feeling guilty that I was not being
honest about my feelings for Guy. Papa
looked back to me and went on. "Your
mama and me, we don't want you to be
alone, Cassie. There's still time for you
to find somebody, somebody to love,
maybe even have children. Love to see a
grandchild from my baby girl. We want
you to be happy, honey. Are you happy,
Cassie?"

I placed my hand in Papa's calloused
hand. "When I'm here, in this place,
Papa, with all of you, I am. I'm very
happy." Papa squeezed my hand, and
together, we looked up into the trees.

■ ■ ■ ■

September came, and Mississippi head-
lined the news. A young black man
named James Meredith was attempting
to enroll at the all-white University of
Mississippi. James Meredith was twenty-
seven years old, a student at all-black
Jackson State and an Air Force veteran.
He was denied admission. With the help
of the NAACP and its Mississippi field
secretary, Medgar Evers, who had also
once applied to the university and been
denied, James Meredith filed a lawsuit
against the University of Mississippi, stating that he was denied admission based
on his race. A federal court, supported
by a Supreme Court ruling, ordered the
University of Mississippi to admit James
Meredith.

On September 20, James Meredith,
with the backing of the court order, went
to the university campus to register at
"Ole Miss," as the university was af-
fectionately called by white Mississippi,
but he was denied admission by the
governor himself, one Ross R. Barnett.
Governor Barnett had gone on statewide

television and proclaimed that a Negro would never be admitted to the University of Mississippi. Many whites considered the university a white sanctuary, a bastion of white purity, and they wanted it to remain that way. They said keeping the school all-white would protect the white race. James Meredith did not give up. On September 25 he again attempted to enroll at the University of Mississippi. Again he was denied admission by the governor, Ross Barnett.

That wasn't the end of it.

On September 26 James Meredith once more attempted to register. This time it was the lieutenant governor, Paul Johnson, who blocked him and denied his admission. By now the Kennedys had become involved. The state of Mississippi had defied a federal court order, and President Kennedy and his brother Attorney General Robert Kennedy had no choice but to enforce that order. A war had been fought a hundred years before that decided federal law superseded state law, and Mississippi had to comply with the federal order. It was understood that James Meredith again would attempt to register; this time he would have the full backing of the Kennedy administration and, if necessary, federal troops. The date set for the next attempt at enrollment was Monday, October 1.

On Saturday, September 29, at an Ole Miss–Kentucky football game, Governor Barnett appeared before the all-white stadium crowd and cried, "Never!" and the aroused crowd responded in kind, chanting "Never!" Late Sunday afternoon September 30, the news reported that hundreds of federal armed guards had arrived outside the administration building at Ole Miss. A white crowd had begun to gather on the campus, and before the sun was down a riot broke out as the crowd challenged the guards. Governor Barnett went on Mississippi television and urged calm. He said he had been told by Attorney General Robert Kennedy that James Meredith was already on the Ole Miss campus. Later that night, he assured his fellow white Mississippians that the state of Mississippi would never surrender to the court order.

The rioting grew fierce.

President Kennedy addressed the nation. He said, "No man is entitled to defy a court of law." He too called for calm. He called for rational thinking.

Christopher-John and Clayton Chester with their families had come over to Stacey and Dee's during the afternoon, and we all watched the television news, transfixed, as the rioting, out of control now, raged on and the standoff between the state of Mississippi and the federal government continued. Not only were the white students rioting to keep James Meredith from registering, but also hundreds of whites from around the state and elsewhere were pouring into the university town of Oxford to combat the guards and prevent the enrollment. We watched until after the nightly news. The fierce rioting was still going on.

The next morning we learned just how bad things had gotten down in Oxford. Two people had been killed and more than one hundred wounded, including federal marshals. Several hundred people had been arrested. The white rioters had thrown rocks and bottles, overturned and burned cars, and smashed windows as they raged against the admission of James Meredith. During the night President Kennedy had ordered in thousands of Army troops from Tennessee to quell the violence, and the soldiers had put a stop to all the mayhem. Before eight o'clock on Monday morning, James H. Meredith was enrolled as the first black student at the University of Mississippi.

We could hardly believe it.

The South's racist's armor was starting to fracture. Voting registration was now allowed in some states. Interstate buses now allowed integrated seating. Lunch counters in South Carolina and North Carolina, Georgia and Virginia were now integrated. It looked as if we were actually beginning to win this fight. So much was happening, even in hard-line Mississippi, but we knew that not everything was about to change, at least not right away. Racism and bigotry had been centuries in the making and were not about to disappear without a trace overnight. We had not yet gotten all we were fighting for, but we were making inroads. In October, Mississippi had its state fair.

As always, the first week of the fair was for whites only. The following three days were for blacks. Medgar Evers of the NAACP called for a boycott of the fair. Black folks mostly stayed away. We were, as Mama said, hitting the white powers in Mississippi in their pocketbooks.

As Christmas and the new year approached, 'lois wrote one of her long letters to Mama, giving her all the details to pass along to Papa and Big Ma about the family and how we all were doing. 'lois always wrote long letters. She had gotten that from Mama, and Mama always responded with a long letter of her own. Everybody else in the family, including me, wrote a page or two and were done, but not 'lois and Mama. When Mama wrote back, 'lois shared her Christmas letter with the rest of us. Mama wrote about the boycott of Jackson stores recently begun by Medgar Evers and the NAACP. It was hitting downtown merchants hard right before Christmas. Demands were for the end of segregation in the stores, the right to first come, first served service, as well as for Negroes to be addressed with respect by all store personnel as Mr. or Mrs. or Miss, the same as white patrons. Mama also wrote that there had been more trouble in the area. Hooded riders had driven through Strawberry and throughout the country-side. Pastor Hubbard had asked that no Christmas lights be displayed, in support of the Jackson boycott and to protest for our demand for equal rights. We did not need lights to celebrate the birth of the Christ child. In Toledo, at our church, we asked that the lights be darkened too.

The new year started quietly enough. It was 1963, and the hundred-year anniversary of the Emancipation Proclamation. All of us working in the Movement knew the quiet would not last. There were big plans in the works as we pushed for equality in this centennial year. There was even talk about a grand march for civil rights on Washington. In the spring, demonstrations continued across the South, in Greenwood, Mississippi, and in Birmingham, Alabama. The boys and I talked about going home, not just because of all the unrest but because

Papa was still not feeling as strong as he should. Mama wrote that Papa couldn't shake the cold which had lingered since the revival and throughout the winter. She said he had finally given in and gone to a doctor in Jackson, but the doctor said it was simply a cold and needed to be treated that way. Papa had been given vitamins and he ate well, had all the nutritious food he needed what with Big Ma's cooking and the preserved vegetables from last year's garden, but his strength still seemed to be waning. "You know Papa, strong as a bull," said Christopher-John, "but last time we were home, he got winded just chopping firewood."

I tried to rationalize Papa's diminishing strength. "Well, he is older now. We have to expect he can't be the same as ten years ago."

"But at the revival he still had plenty of stamina," contended Man. "He was fine working on the church."

Stacey pointed out that was several months ago. "Maybe we've all got to accept the fact that Papa's starting to go down, like Cassie said, just because of his age."

None of us wanted to accept that Papa was not as strong as he once had been, but we knew it was true. In early April, Stacey decided to go south. "I'll go before Easter and see for myself how Papa's doing." Before Stacey left, he and I went to see Moe.

"Wish I could go with you," Moe said.

"Well, you can't," said Stacey.

"Ought to go anyway."

"I'd knock you out before I'd let you go," Stacey threatened.

Moe sighed. "Well, anyway, here's something I want you to take down." He gave Stacey a package, then reached into his wallet and pulled out an envelope. "Some shirts and some money for my daddy." Stacey nodded and took the envelope. "Give my love to him, to all of them, and tell that hardheaded Morris to be careful down there. I don't want him getting on the wrong side of Mississippi law the way I am."

"He already has been," I reminded Moe. "Long as he's working in that voter registration drive, he's going to be on the wrong side of Mississippi law."

"Yeah, I know . . . that's what I'm afraid of. . . ."

When Stacey returned from his trip south, he told us news we did not want to hear. "Papa's got a blood disease." He waited a moment, but Christopher-John, Clayton Chester, and I said nothing. We were too stunned to speak. "I persuaded Papa to let me take him to Jackson again, to a different doctor, to have some testing done. This is what they found."

After moments of silence I muttered, "What can they do about it?"

Stacey was somber. "They've got him on some medications, but I'll be honest with you. It doesn't look good, and you know how stubborn Papa is. He already said he's not about to spend his days in a hospital when there's work to be done on the land." We all nodded, knowing that was Papa. "Thing is, Papa looks good, same as always. Lost a few pounds, hardly noticeable, but I could tell his strength isn't the same."

We all were silent, not wanting to believe that Papa was really ill.

Christopher-John broke the silence. "Look, Stacey, we'll each go down, stay a few weeks. I just hate that they're down there without us."

"I'll go down next," volunteered Man.

So it was settled. Little Man drove south in late April and stayed into May. Christopher-John went down in early June. Uncle Hammer joined him there. Stacey and I would go together in July, and I, with the most flexible schedule, would stay on for a while. All of us figured to be home in August for the revival. That was our plan. But then, in the second week of June, while Christopher-John was already in Mississippi, our plans changed. Myrtis suddenly called from Detroit. I answered the phone. She was frantic. "Tell Stacey, he's got to stop him!"

"Stop who? What are you talking about, Myrtis?"

"Moe!" she cried. "They done killed Morris, and Moe, he's gone back to Mississippi!"

LET THE CIRCLE BE UNBROKEN

(1963)

It was late night Mississippi when we reached Jackson. Stacey, Man, and I had gotten on the road shortly after Myrtis called. Our hearts were heavy. We all loved Morris. We all loved Moe too and we had to do what we could to stop him. We didn't know if we could reach Moe before he was caught or he did something stupid like go after whoever killed Morris. We didn't know if there was anything we could do, but we had to try. As always when we drove south, there was the anticipation of being back home again, of being with people we loved most in this life, but there was also, as we drew closer and closer to home, the mounting dread that came with setting foot again on Mississippi soil. The tension had always been there since our first trip back from the North, but in these recent years, with racial unrest and white folks on the alert for every wave of protest against their social order, the dread was more pronounced and the fear mounted.

On the way down the radio news reported that two Negroes had been admitted as students to the all-white University of Alabama. Their names were Vivian Malone and James Hood. The governor of Alabama, George Wallace, who earlier in the year had proclaimed, "Segregation now, segregation tomorrow, segregation forever," at first had stood at the door of the university auditorium to deny them admission. There was a federal court order to integrate the university, but the governor continued to block the entry. Then, after a presidential order demanding the governor step aside, and with federal marshals as well as the federalized Alabama National Guard standing by, the Negro students were admitted peaceably. There had been no riots. President Kennedy again addressed the nation and said that segregation was morally wrong and that it was time for Congress to act to ensure equal rights. Still, the events of the day, no matter how celebratory they were to our cause, knotted our stomachs as we approached home. We knew most Mississippi white folks did not like hearing this news; it was another stone dislodged from their foundation of inequality and white superiority.

When we arrived in Jackson, we went straight to Little Willie's. We needed to know if Moe had contacted him. He hadn't. "You mean to tell me that scound' gone and come back here after all the trouble we gone through just getting him north?" exclaimed Little Willie.

"After what happened with Morris, what you expect?" countered Stacey as Dora brought a tray of cold lemonade for us.

Little Willie shook his head. "Yeah, guess you right. Lord, that's a terrible thing! Dora and me, we been crying 'bout it since we heard. They killed that boy because of all that voter registration business!"

"Well, just what happened?" I asked. "All Myrtis could tell us was that Moe came to Detroit, got Dwayne's car, and said Morris was dead, that they'd killed him. That's it, nothing else."

"Well, from what I hear," said Little Willie, "Morris's car gone off into the Creek Rosa Lee. That's where they found him."

"He just went off the road?" questioned Clayton incredulously, his voice muffled with emotion he was trying to hold back. "How's that?"

Little Willie shrugged. "That's what the sheriff said. Seems Morris had been up to the courthouse in Strawberry, had taken folks there to try to register. That was on Friday. When they came back from Strawberry, he dropped them off and that was the last anybody seen him until they pulled his car out of the Rosa Lee. It was over there where the creek runs along one of them back roads. Now, here's the thing. What's today? Tuesday? Well, the sheriff down there already done ruled Morris's death an accident. We don't know if the boy drowned or what. Talked to Maynard. They seen Morris's body, they ain't seen his car. Sheriff got it. Might not be a bullet in that boy or a rope around his neck, but we figure Morris was forced off that road. Wasn't no accident."

"Any way to prove that?" I said.

Little Willie looked hard at me. "Late at night. Nobody around. What you think?"

There were no words to speak what we all felt.

Little Willie cleared his throat. "Crying shame. And his wife just had that baby, not even a week ago."

I bowed my head thinking of Denise and how much in love she and Morris had been. "How is she doing?" I asked softly.

Dora answered. " 'Bout as you'd expect. She loved that boy. Morris was her world."

"What I want to know," said Willie, "is how did Moe find out?"

"Levis," Stacey said. "He called him from Jackson. Figured Moe needed to know."

"Fool!" cried Willie. "Didn't he know what Moe might do?"

"Guess he wasn't thinking. Time like this, a body doesn't always think straight.

Soon as Moe heard, he jumped in his car and headed for Detroit, that's what Myrtis said. Myrtis couldn't stop him from going. Said if Dwayne didn't give him his car, he'd drive his own, and he was talking about finishing what he'd started."

Little Willie looked wild-eyed at Stacey. "What you mean?"

"What you think I mean?"

"Ah, naw! Ah, naw! He ain't fool enough to think he could go kill them white boys!"

"Well, that's what started it all," I declared. "Statler, Leon, and Troy all those years ago."

"Who said it was them?" retorted Little Willie. "Can't be sure about that! Plenty of white folks hated Morris because of that voter registration business! Heard some white folks say Morris like driving folks around to register so much, maybe they'd just give him a ride. And remember now, the sheriff already ruled Morris's death an accident. So far, nobody got proof otherwise."

Stacey lowered his head and rubbed his forehead in thought. Looking up again, he gazed across at Willie. "If Moe didn't get stopped, he has to be down here by now. We thought he might contact you for help."

"Wish he had've. I would've done told the boy to go on back to Canada. Ain't nothing he can do down here dead."

We all stared at Little Willie.

"It's the truth! He end up dead, just like Morris! If they ain't picked him up, he probably went straight on down to his daddy's." Little Willie took swallows of his lemonade and looked around at us. "So, what y'all planning on doing? Y'all come all the way down here to see 'bout Moe, keep him from getting caught, what you got in mind?"

"Tell the truth, I don't know what we can do," said Stacey. "May already be too late."

"It was too late," surmised Little Willie, "soon's Moe got in his car and headed down here."

We all had to agree.

Man asked about the funeral. "They set a date yet?"

"Heard day after tomorrow. It'll be a

sorrowful thing, young man like that."
Little Willie shook his head. "These white
folks ain't hardly letting up. You heard
what they done to our young people up
at Woolworth's the other day when they
did that sit-in? Threw pepper spray in
their eyes, sprayed them with paint too.
Then come that night, somebody gone
and thrown a bomb at the Evers house.
Shook the whole neighborhood. Heard it
myself. Then, right after that, couple days
later, some high school students, several
hundred of them over at Lanier, got to
singing protest songs, and white folks got
all upset. Police come in with their dogs
and beat those children all upside the
head with clubs. My boy Calvin, he's a
freshman over there, he was one of
them."

"How's Calvin doing?" I asked. "Was
he hurt bad?"

"Boy's got a hard head just like me.
That ain't sayin' I sit easy though with
my son gettin' clubbed like that."

Dora sat on the arm of Little Willie's
chair. "Thought I was gonna hafta call
some of my folks to keep Willie in this
house he was so mad. I didn't want him

going after these white folks and getting hisself killed about this thing."

"Everybody was mad," said Little Willie. "Brother Evers down the street called the Justice Department up in Washington, told them how these white police down here done treated our children. 'Fore Washington done anything about it, the young folks gone and done a protest march right downtown. Yeah, right here in Jackson! Can you believe it? Now, y'all know these white folks really was mad now! Police come in again, clubbed the children and they got arrested. Took them to the state fairground to this here what they called an open-air jail. Fenced them in like cattle."

Dora gently rubbed his shoulder. "They know all that, baby."

"Calvin one of them?" asked Stacey.

Little Willie sighed wearily, but there was pride in his voice when he spoke. "Yeah, he was. They're all out now. Just glad it ain't no worse. Just look what they done to our children in Birmingham! Water-hosing them and setting their dogs on them! Course, we're all thinking it's gonna get worse here too, what with that white Citizens' Council and the mayor saying ain't no more things 'bout to change down here. Things seem to be going from bad to worse with these people since last fall, when James Meredith got into Ole Miss and the white folks gone crazy, rioting and all. We was all proud of our man James Meredith getting into Ole Miss, and it made our young folks stand up. You know what I'm sayin'? If James Meredith could do this thing, then they could too.

"Now, I'm gonna be fair about the thing. I heard there was some white folks right here in Mississippi done supported James Meredith getting into Ole Miss. That speech Medgar Evers gave on television too, some of them took what he said to heart. Made them think, maybe colored folks ain't had it so good. Maybe there was something to this equal rights business. Maybe things need to change. Some of them, they sure did say that. Minds got changed 'cause of that speech."

"Well, I guess we've got the mayor to thank for that," said Dora. "He hadn't gone on television first and made his speech, Medgar wouldn't have gotten to make his."

Stacey, Clayton Chester, and I all knew about Medgar Evers's speech. It had come about because Mayor Allen Thompson of Jackson had gone on television in early May and talked to the Negroes of Jackson. Patronizingly he said that the NAACP and other groups coming from the North were out to fool Jackson's Negroes and that they should not be cooperating with these organizations or with NAACP's field secretary, Medgar Evers. He said that whites and coloreds in Jackson had had a good relationship for a hundred years and warned Negroes not to destroy the relationship by listening to Medgar Evers and outside agitators.

Negroes were outraged at the speech.

A week later Medgar Evers went on television to refute what Mayor Thompson had said. Since segregationists controlled the television stations, Medgar Evers had gone directly to the Federal Communications Commission to get airtime, and he told all of Jackson, all of Mississippi, the truth of the matter. He

733

told all listening that things were not as rosy as the mayor said. He told all listening that Negroes in Jackson could not eat at lunch counters in stores where we spent our money or go to the main public library or to tax-supported parks or playgrounds or to downtown movie theaters. He told all listening that there was not one black person on the police force, not one Negro fireman, not one Negro working in government offices, except those employed in segregated facilities. He told all listening that when colored people got sick, we were segregated into colored spaces in hospital. As for the Jackson police, which the mayor said were giving Negroes twenty-four hours of protection, Medgar Evers stated that he believed the police were giving twenty-four hours of harassment instead. He said the Negroes of Jackson wanted all that to change. The Negroes of Jackson wanted the same opportunities as those afforded the white citizens of Jackson.

"I was here at the time and I heard that speech," Clayton Chester said. "Who would have ever thought a colored man would get the chance to speak to the white people of Mississippi like that? Made me proud."

Dora too confirmed that the speech was something all right. "Had us glued to our seats. Willie and me and all our children. Everybody in the neighborhood was talking about it."

"Soon after that speech," said Little Willie, "that's when our young people began to take up the cause again." He was quiet a moment before his face suddenly erupted into a wide grin. "Y'all hear the Horne was here? Just last week! Come to help raise money for the cause. I'm telling you, that's one beautiful woman!"

Stacey smiled. "Watch it, Willie. Your wife's sitting right here."

"Ah, Dora knows how I feel 'bout the Horne." Little Willie looked up at his wife. "Don't you, baby?"

Dora laughed good-naturedly, knowing that Lena Horne, Negro actress and singer celebrated for her great beauty, was idolized by many men, black and white. "Thanks for taking my part, Stacey, but men like my Willie here like to dream, and a woman like Lena Horne is just a dream."

Little Willie laughed too and placed his hand on her knee. "Ah, baby, you know you more'n enough woman for me. You know you my dream."

"Better be," said Dora, "after all these years and all these children."

"Anyways," Little Willie continued, "Lena spoke at a rally, then later on that same day, she sang. It was golden music from the heavens above!" Little Willie looked upward in sweet remembrance. "Beautiful moment."

Stacey nodded in acceptance of that fact and stood. "We'd better be getting on home. You let us know if —"

The sound of gunfire blasted the night.

Dora jumped up. "Lord have mercy! What in the world —"

And Little Willie cried, "What the hell!" and rushed across the room, swung open the screen door, and dashed onto the porch. The rest of us followed. There was more gunfire. Across the street a door opened and Little Willie hollered over to his neighbor. "You hear that? What happened?" The neighbor answered he was wondering the same thing. Little Willie and Dora's children came sleepily onto the porch, questioning their parents about what was going on. None of us knew. Other doors on the block opened, and a hush settled over the neighborhood. We all just stood there waiting. Then a man came running up the street. Little Willie leaned over the porch rail and yelled at him. "Henry! Henry, that you? What's going on, man?"

"It's Medgar!" the man yelled back, continuing to run. "It's Medgar! They done shot him! Right in his driveway! They done shot our Medgar Evers!"

After we learned that Medgar Evers had been shot, like much of the neighborhood, we went down the street to gather in front of the Evers house and silently waited for any news. Folks already gathered there said Medgar Evers had been taken to the hospital. They said a white man hiding in the bushes across the street from the Evers house had shot Medgar Evers as he stepped from his car. Whites from the surrounding blocks came and stood with us. Through the night we waited and we prayed, but when the news came, it was what we all had feared.

Medgar Evers was dead.

It was light before we left Jackson. We had already called home to let everyone know we had made it in and to tell them about the killing of Medgar Evers. When we got to the house, Big Ma had breakfast waiting. No one had eaten, so we all sat down together. As always, Papa was at the head of the table and asked the blessing. Papa didn't look sick at all, at least not to me. "So, what are your plans for the day?" he asked as he passed the bowl of grits to Stacey.

"Figured first to go see Mr. Turner, see how they're all doing, and find out if they've heard from Moe," Stacey said.

"You think he could've made it home all right?" questioned Big Ma.

Uncle Hammer grunted. "Dangerous, foolish thing for him to come down here."

Papa smiled at Uncle Hammer. "Yeah, look who's talking. You know you would've done the same, you'd been in his shoes." Uncle Hammer just looked at Papa, then speared himself some ham from the meat tray of ham and sausages and bacon.

Big Ma concurred. "He sho 'nough would've done it all right."

"He has done it," added Mama, "time and time again."

Big Ma gave Uncle Hammer a motherly look. "Well, thank the Lord, he ain't had to here lately." Uncle Hammer continued eating, with no acknowledgment of their words. Big Ma looked down the table at Papa. Papa had hardly touched his food. Big Ma picked up the biscuit platter and held it out toward Papa. "Have another biscuit, son."

Papa declined. "Haven't finished this one yet, Mama."

Disappointed, Big Ma set the dish back on the table. "Well, eat what's on your plate," she admonished.

Papa stirred his grits absentmindedly, but did not lift his fork. His other hand rested on the table. Mama was watching him, as we all were. Sitting next to him, she placed her hand lightly over his and looked around at all of us. "I just keep thinking how blessed we are, having everybody home, although I'm sick about the reason for it."

Big Ma shook her head mournfully. "Well, I'm grievin' jus' much for Denise, that poor girl, and that baby of hers as I am for that boy Morris. Much as I seen in this life, still can't believe it. Life jus' stole away from all of them."

Papa looked at Big Ma, then asked the boys and me, "How long y'all planning to stay?"

"Little Willie said he'd heard the funeral's planned for Thursday," said Stacey. "That still the case?"

"Yesterday when we were over there, that's what they said," Papa replied. "Wake'll be tonight."

"You felt well enough to go over to the Turners, Papa?" I asked.

Papa gave me an irritated look. "I might not be feeling the best, but I ain't dead yet."

"Well, I didn't mean —"

"Orris Turner and me been friends since we were boys going to school up at

Great Faith. Day I can't get myself out of bed and go see my friend grieving his son, that's the day I am dead."

Stacey glanced my way, aware of Papa's curt response to me, and got back to Papa's question about how long we were staying. "We'll be going to the funeral and then most likely be staying until the funeral for Medgar Evers if it's this week. There'll be a lot of people at Medgar Evers's funeral so we might not get into the church, but we want to go pay our respects."

"I'd like to go myself," said Mama. "I met him once. He was a fine man, a brave man. Took a brave man to do all he did, take all those risks. Most of us couldn't have done it." Her voice went soft. "I admired him so much. Everybody in the community did."

Stacey acknowledged Mama's words with a solemn nod, then said, "Christopher-John, Man, and I'll be headed back to Toledo right after his funeral. Cassie, though, she'll be staying awhile."

"How come?" Papa sipped his coffee. "You know, y'all don't have to be down

741

here all the time. Hammer's here and he'll be staying — how long you say, Hammer?"

Uncle Hammer sopped up his breakfast gravy with his last remaining biscuit. "Long's you need me."

"Well, that won't be too long. I figure to be able to work again soon."

I felt encouraged. "You getting your strength back, Papa?"

"I expect I will soon, Cassie girl, now that you all come home. But like I was saying, y'all don't have to keep coming down. Y'all got your jobs, your own lives to live, families to take care of —"

I stopped Papa right there. "What family do I have to take care of outside of the family sitting right here? I'm on my own, Papa, nobody to take care of but the people I love around this table." Right after I said that, I knew it was the wrong thing. I knew how Papa felt about my being alone. I knew the fact that I was without a family of my own worried him. It worried Mama also, and sometimes it worried me too.

■ ■ ■ ■

Stacey, Man, and I went to pay our respects to Mr. Turner and the rest of Morris's family. Although Christopher-John had gone over with Uncle Hammer, Mama, Papa, and Big Ma the day before, he went with us. Mr. Turner had given up his place where the family had share-cropped for most of the century and now lived with Levis and his family, who had gone into dairy farming. When we arrived at Levis's farm, several trucks and cars were parked in front of the house, along with a couple of wagons. We greeted all the people standing around the house, then went inside. Mr. Turner's bed was in the living room, and as we entered, he tried to sit up. One of his granddaughters rushed over to help him. Stacey shook Mr. Turner's bony hand, then leaned down and gently hugged him. Christopher-John, Man, and I did the same. Mr. Turner waved his arm toward all his family gathered in the dark room. "Well, y'all get on up, give them some chairs and bring them chairs up close, so's I can see 'em." The Turners quickly obeyed, and chairs were brought. Levis was there; Maynard wasn't. He was in Vicksburg at a funeral home with one of the sisters, seeing to Morris's body.

Levis brought his chair close to the bed and sat with us. "Good of y'all to come," he said.

"Had to," said Stacey. "Morris was family to us too."

"We know that," said Mr. Turner. "Y'all been family to both my boys, and I'm mighty thankful y'all been there for them all these years." Mr. Turner dabbed at cataract-covered eyes with a damp cloth. "Never thought my baby boy would be the one I'd lose."

"Well, Daddy," said Levis, reaching out a consoling hand to his father, "baby brother wouldn't give up that voter registration drive for nothing. We all know that's what got him killed." Mr. Turner nodded in acceptance and Levis added, "But we got no proof of that."

Both Mr. Turner and Levis were mournfully silent. Then I said, "Could have, perhaps, if you had the car. You ask the sheriff about getting it back?"

"Course we did," said Levis, "but the

sheriff said he was impounding it as evidence that Morris was at fault for going off that road."

"Seems though you have a right to see it," said Christopher-John. "Cassie, couldn't they get a subpoena, force the sheriff to show it to them?"

"A subpoena? From who?" snapped Levis. "What white judge down here is gonna give us a subpoena to tell the sheriff what to do?"

"We couldn't get a subpoena anyway," I said. "If according to the sheriff the car is evidence, then he has a right to hold it. He doesn't have to show it to you."

"Besides that," said Levis, sounding discouraged, "that car'll be all beat up. It'll show Morris was forced off the road." He shook his head, as if all were useless, and turned to Stacey. His voice low, he asked, "You talk to Moe before you come down?"

Stacey looked around the dark room at all the people gathered and cautiously said, "No. Was going to ask if you'd heard from him since you told him about Morris?"

"Naw," said Mr. Turner right off. "The

boy was all broke up 'bout Morris. Sho wish Moe could be here, but we know he can't."

"We know it's hard on you, Mr. Turner," Stacey empathized, "losing Morris like this and not having Moe here."

"It's hard all right. Can't deny it. That Moe was my rock, but he been gone from here now more'n twenty years. Don't 'spect I'll see him again before they lay me in my grave."

We sat talking softly for some minutes longer, then Stacey asked Levis to join him outside. I went with them. After taking a few minutes to speak to those who had just come to the house, Levis, Stacey, and I headed over to the fencing that separated the lawn from the fields. There was no cotton growing. The field was planted in corn.

"Corn looks good," I said.

"Maybe it'll feed us," said Levis, who then turned to Stacey. "I'm thinking you've got word from Moe."

Stacey sighed. "More than word, Levis. Moe's on his way down here."

Levis, his arms resting on top of the

fence, looked away. He did not seem surprised. "When did he leave from there?"

"Came before us," said Stacey. "Myrtis called, told us what had happened and that Moe was already gone."

"Well, she ain't called here to tell us that."

"Told her not to. You've got a party line and word could've gotten out." Stacey hesitated. "I hate to tell you this, but I think Moe might be out to get whoever caused Morris's death."

Levis took that with a moment's silence. "Wouldn't doubt it. He been in touch with anybody since he left? Little Willie, maybe?"

"Not far as we know, and Little Willie hasn't heard from him. He had a few hours on us, and soon as we got here, we went to see Willie. If Moe would get in touch with anybody down here outside of your family, it would be Little Willie."

Levis looked back at us and nodded. "The boy's lyin' low. Good thing too."

"He'll show up," I said. "Unless the police get him first, he'll show up by the funeral."

"Hope not," said Levis, then turned and gazed across the road toward the forest. "Look yonder."

Stacey and I both looked. Standing just inside the forest was a group of white men.

"There's been some of them watching since this morning. Ain't told Daddy. Couple of them come up to the house and said man could've been Moe was seen walking the woods up near Strawberry. Wanted to check the place. Moe come here, they'll have him in jail or dead before we even lay Morris in the ground."

I called Guy and told him about Morris. For a moment, there was only silence on the line, then Guy said, "I'm coming down."

"No. Please don't do that. There are other things going on and your being here will just complicate matters."

"You mean about Medgar Evers?"

"Well, that's not all of it."

"Cassie, I want to be there."

"I know that, Guy, and that means a lot to me. But Papa's ill and other things are happening too and it wouldn't be a good time for any of us for you to be down here."

"I'm sorry to hear about your father, Cassie. Is he very ill?"

"The doctors say he has a blood disease. . . ."

"Oh, Cassie —"

"He looks good though. All my brothers are here; so is my uncle. Papa's not in the hospital. He's at home, but things are hard right now, what with what happened with Morris. We're all trying to deal with it."

Again Guy was silent. "All right, Cassie," he finally said. "I'll abide by your wishes, but know I'll be thinking about all of you. Call me if I can do anything."

When we hung up, I walked the forest, trying to clear my head of thoughts of Guy and thoughts of Moe. I had told Guy about Papa, but I had not told him about Moe. I couldn't risk it, not on a party line. If things were different, Guy would have been with me through the days ahead, and I longed for him to be.

We all went to the wake. In earlier days, folks who passed were laid out for mourning in their homes and people went there to pay their respects. Now the dead were sent to a Negro funeral home in Jackson or Vicksburg and were brought back to the church for the wake the evening before the burial. Morris's body was brought during the late afternoon, and folks began arriving soon after to say their good-byes. Throughout the afternoon and early evening, white men watched the church from their cars and trucks parked on the side of the road. Like the old building, the new church faced toward the old school grounds and not the road itself, so the white men were able to see both the front and rear of the church. They were there when our family arrived; we just looked at them and went on in.

At first the casket in which Morris lay was open, and there was great emotion as people approached the casket to look upon him. I didn't go to the casket. I never looked upon the dead. Throughout the first hours of the wake, folks talked softly, reminiscing about Morris and comforting the family, then we all sat through words and prayer by the pastor. After the prayer services the casket was closed and Moe's father, in a wheelchair, was taken out by two of his granddaughters. With his departure, many of the wake-goers left too. We had come over to the church in Stacey's Oldsmobile and Christopher-John's Ford. Uncle Hammer took the Ford and drove back home with Mama, Papa, and Big Ma. The boys and I stayed on with members of the Turner family who did not leave with Mr. Turner. After a while, the church emptied and only we were left to sit with Levis and Maynard and the four Turner cousins raised by Mr. Turner and called brothers by all of Mr. Turner's children. They would stay in the church throughout the night to watch over Morris until the services tomorrow. Now the lights in the church were dimmed and the shades were drawn. Outside, the night was black, clouds covered the moon, and only one truck remained on the road.

■ ■ ■ ■

Finally, it was near midnight, and I said to Stacey, "We need to go."

Christopher-John stood and stretched. "It's late, Stacey. Folks'll be getting worried."

Stacey looked around the darkened church. "Just a while longer," he said.

I looked around too. Levis and Maynard were seated on the front pew, right in front of the coffin. The other brothers had found pews near the back of the church and were lying down. "You think he's coming, don't you?"

"If he's coming," Man said in a low voice, "it'll be tonight. Only chance to say good-bye to Morris."

Stacey got up without answering me and went to the front pew and spoke to Levis. Then the two of them walked past the pulpit and left the sanctuary through the rear door. They were gone some time before Stacey returned alone. "Where'd you go?" I asked as he sat back down.

"To find Moe" was all he said.

Christopher-John, Man, and I just

looked at him. Then the rear door opened again and a man came in.

It was Moe.

He had made his way as far as Jackson driving Dwayne's car. Once in Jackson, he went to the family of a man who had worked at the plant with him in Detroit, and the man's father had driven him as far as the outskirts of Strawberry. Moe had walked the woods to Great Faith, arriving late in the night. He had been hiding in the church crawl space ever since. It was a crawl space not shown on any of the plans submitted to the county and that was for a reason. It was meant to be a place for secret shelter. When the church was rebuilt after the fire, Papa and some of the other men had insisted on such a space, and Stacey and Levis and Morris, among others, had carved it out of the ground. Both Stacey and Levis had shared information about the space with Moe, and they figured if Moe was in hiding, that was where he would be. He was.

■ ■ ■

When Moe entered the sanctuary, he just stood by the door for several moments, his hat in his hands, then, slowly, he approached the casket. Levis came behind him. Maynard stood up, watching Moe, but did not go to him. Moe reached the coffin, stood there a moment, his head bowed, and gingerly placed one hand flat on top of the coffin. Then he fell to his knees, leaned his head against the side of the coffin, and cried.

His sobs echoed through the church. The brothers lying in the back pews sat up. Levis and Maynard just stood respectfully by, their heads lowered too. The other brothers came slowly up the aisle to the front and stood with Levis and Maynard, gazing upon their eldest brother as he wept for their youngest. They did not go to comfort him. They waited for Moe to be ready. Finally, there was an audible gasp from Moe as his sobbing ceased. Slowly, he raised himself from his knees and stood, still facing the coffin. Then he turned, and all his brothers rushed to him. The boys and I waited as the brothers reunited before we went to join them. I hugged Moe, kissed his cheek, then, holding tight on to his arm, I said, "You're all right. You're all right."

Moe's smile was faint. "Yeah, Cassie, I'm all right."

"You know you can't stay long," said Stacey. "Those men are still outside."

"But the doors are locked," Levis told Moe. "I don't think they'll try coming in. Far as they know, you didn't come into the church. Pastor said the sheriff's deputy was here early yesterday morning and walked all through the church, and they've been watching the front and back all the day since. There's time to sit a spell."

Moe shook his head. "I need to get home and see Daddy."

"How are you going to get over there?" I asked. I glanced at Levis. "You going to take him?"

"Levis, you can't leave," objected Stacey. "Those men'll be expecting all of you to stay in here with Morris. I can take him over."

I questioned that. "And how you plan

to do that? The car's out front, church lights on. How's Moe supposed to get to the car without being seen? Can't hardly turn the church lights off after all this time. They'd get suspicious."

"Not only that," said Christopher-John, "they've probably got men over that way watching Levis's house. You drive that road, they'll see you coming."

"No need for anybody to drive me anywhere," said Moe. "I'll walk the woods."

"I'll walk with you then," said Levis.

I put another question to Moe. "And how you plan to get back to Jackson? You going to walk there too? What if somebody recognizes you?"

"I'm not worried about that. It's been more than twenty years since I've been home. I don't figure most folks to recognize me."

"Someone maybe already has," submitted Levis.

Moe ignored that. "Well, anyway, I've got it planned how to get around."

"What else do you have planned?" I asked. "If you're planning to go after somebody about Morris, don't do it, Moe. Don't do it!"

Moe just looked at me. Stacey glanced from me to Moe. "Cassie, let it be. I've already talked to Moe about all this, that it could have been any of these white people caused Morris's death. Levis, Maynard, you talk sense to him. Moe, when you're ready to go to Jackson, we'll take you."

"No," said Moe.

"Moe, you can't walk all the way back to Jackson. Your brothers will take you or we will."

"I said no! None of you are taking me anywhere. You've done enough, Stacey. All of you have, and I don't want any of you facing any more trouble because of me. I got down here on my own and I'll get back on my own."

Moe was adamant. He wasn't changing his mind.

It was decided. Moe and Levis would leave by the rear door. The lights were off at the rear of the church, and all lights in the hallway leading to that back door were off. Outside, there were decorative bushes on either side of the door that would give them some cover. From the hallway they would belly-crawl the steps and across the lawn to the woods. Levis said he had done that during the war and figured they could make it to the woods without being seen. We talked for a short while longer, held hands, and prayed. Then Moe asked Levis to lift the lid to the coffin. He wanted to see Morris. I stepped away. The coffin was opened, and for several minutes Moe stood there gazing down at Morris, saying his final good-bye. Moe himself closed the coffin and, turning from it, hugged each of his brothers, Christopher-John, Man, and Stacey. I was the last one he hugged. Then he and Levis left the sanctuary.

As they left, Stacey, Christopher-John, Man, and I went out the front door. We talked softly as we headed for the car, hoping that the men on the road kept their eyes on us as Moe and Levis slipped out the back door. We got into the Oldsmobile and drove off the church grounds. As Stacey turned onto the road, headlights from the truck flooded the car. Stacey kept on driving. The truck did not follow.

At the funeral the casket for Morris was closed. That at least kept some of the emotions at bay. Still, with death having come the way it had, there was no restraint about what was felt. Women wailed and flailed their arms as they marched past the casket. Morris's sisters flung their arms over the coffin, as if holding to them Morris himself, and Denise, with her newborn baby in her arms, just dropped to her knees in front of it and sobbed uncontrollably. There was no containing the sorrow or the rage that we all felt.

Outside the church, standing near the old school buildings, a group of white men gathered. Some of the church men went over and asked the group to leave. They didn't. The county law was among them. Two of the men wore badges, and all of them were waiting for the services to be over and for Moe to make an appearance. One white man was inside the church. That was Mr. Wade Jamison. He sat with us throughout the services and grieved for Morris.

As we emerged from the church, following the coffin borne by the Turner brothers, we all saw clearly who the white men were, and no one was surprised that Statler and Leon Aames and Charlie Simms were among them. The funeral procession walked slowly toward the cemetery that bordered the back side of the church. All of us were acutely aware of the white men watching us. Mr. Turner, looking more frail than ever, was wheeled to the gravesite. Everybody else followed. The white men moved closer. Several of the men spread out and walked along the forest line, peering into the brush.

As the gravesite services began, I looked at Stacey and wondered where Moe was. I knew Stacey was wondering the same as he looked away from the gravesite, into the forest. My gaze followed his. Levis had told us Moe had seen their father and his sisters, and he and Moe had left the house before dawn. He also said he and his father had talked to Moe through the remaining night, trying to persuade him not to go after Statler and Leon.

They argued there was no way to know if they were the ones who had caused Morris's death, and even if they had, causing them harm would not bring Morris back. The last Levis had seen of Moe was in the forest, when they said good-bye. Moe had told him that he wanted to see Morris lowered into his grave, then he would leave. As Stacey and I gazed out to the forest, we both knew Moe was out there, watching from its depths, blending into it, hidden by the density of bushes and grasses and trees. We didn't see him and we prayed that the white men watching didn't see him either.

I whispered to Stacey. "You think he'll be all right?"

Stacey looked from the forest to the coffin, now being lowered into the ground. "He came here to see his daddy and see Morris laid to rest. He's done both. Now all he's got to do is get out of Mississippi alive."

Reverend Hubbard began to pray. I closed my eyes and bowed my head. "Amen" was said, and I opened my eyes and looked again to the forest. There was no sign of Moe. I hoped that my prayer was answered.

After the funeral, I walked the forest alone. So much had happened in the last few days and I was shaken, but there had been little time to reflect on what it all meant. Morris had put his life on the line. Medgar Evers had put his life on the line. Much had been accomplished to ease us toward first-class citizenship, to assure us equal rights, but there was still much to be done. Despite all of Morris's efforts, only a few people had been registered to vote. Most of us saw that as discouraging; Morris had seen it as an achievement. He had refused to be beaten by the system. If one Negro could be registered, hundreds more could be registered. Thousands more. Every Negro of qualifying age in the county, every Negro person of age in the state of Mississippi could one day vote, and when that happened it would mean equal rights for all of us. It would change the state. That was Morris's dream. Little Brother Morris. I thought of Grandpa Paul-Edward and how he had gotten this land.

I thought of all the sacrifices Big Ma, Papa, and Mama had made to keep it. I thought of all who had gone before.

I stayed long in the forest, thinking on all that. What Morris had begun remained unfinished. Registration drives were scheduled to resume in other counties. Without Morris, the Spokane County drive could falter. I couldn't let that happen. I had no reason not to return to Mississippi and continue the fight. My roots were here. My beginning was here. My family would always be tied to this land. I left the forest having made up my mind. I was home now, and I would remain here. I was going to stay in Mississippi.

"You sure you want to be out here, Papa?" I asked as Papa and I sat alone on the front porch swing early Saturday morning. Papa was still in his pajamas and wore the robe I had given him for Christmas. He had spent much of the last two days in bed, getting dressed only to go to Morris's funeral. He said he felt all right, just tired. Still, that was so unlike Papa; it scared me. Now, as I sat beside him, I was assured he was all right. Papa was a strong man. Nothing could happen to him.

Papa smiled. "I'm fine, Cassie. Got tired of that bed. Sun feels good."

"Not too hot yet," I observed. "Will be soon though."

"That's for sure." I looked at Papa and smiled. Papa took my hand in his, looked across the lawn, glistening emerald under the morning's dew, and to the forest. I kept my eyes on him. As handsome as ever, Papa looked so good, so well.

"Beautiful, ain't it?" Papa said, his eyes on the forest, still dark before the full sunlight made its way through the trees standing tall, guarding our land.

"Yes, sir," I agreed. "Nothing more beautiful."

Papa laughed and glanced over at me. "Oh, there are a few things I could think of more beautiful and they're all right here in this house."

I smiled wide and squeezed his hand. For the moment, I was happy. Then I told Papa I would be staying. I was going to carry on the drive. Papa squinted as he looked at me. "You sure this is what you want to do?"

"I'm sure."

"Well, then, Cassie . . . I'm proud of you. Always have been. Just give me another reason to be."

I had Papa all to myself. Big Ma was in the kitchen, already planning a special supper for the boys' last night here, and Mama was at her desk, seeing to bills. Stacey, Christopher-John, and Man had taken care of chores before breakfast, then they packed up several dishes Big Ma had prepared and took them over to the Turner farm. They wanted to see Moe's father before heading back north tomorrow. Uncle Hammer had gone with them. When they returned, the boys and I would go to Jackson to attend Medgar Evers's funeral. The wake had been on Friday and after the wake there had been a protest march from the funeral home to downtown Jackson with protesters demanding Medgar Evers's killer. Little Willie had called and told us. Dr. Martin Luther King and Dr. Ralph Bunche, Nobel Peace Prize recipient and the first Negro to be appointed United States ambassador to the United Nations, were among the marchers. Dr. King and Dr. Bunche and other notable black leaders were to be at the funeral, which would be held at the Masonic temple on Lynch Street, approximately a mile and a half from downtown and right in the heart of the Negro community. Medgar Evers's NAACP office was located in the temple.

"You know what, Cassie girl, you know what I'd like to do?" Papa said, his eyes still on the forest.

"What's that, Papa?"

"Later on, or maybe in the morning before the boys leave, like to take a walk down to the pond. You, the boys, and me." He nodded, gazing across at those old trees. "Yeah, I'd like to do that."

"We'll do that, Papa," I said, squeezing his hand again, and turned my gaze toward the forest too.

We headed for Jackson. Passing the fallow fields, which for years had been planted in cotton, and the old oak still standing tall on the hillside separating our land from the Granger plantation, Stacey's Oldsmobile sped along the dusty road. As we approached the Wallace store and the crossroads, Stacey slowed. Several vehicles were parked in front of the store, one of them a sheriff's car. As usual for this time of year, white men sat on the porch. Several others, including the sheriff and his deputy, stood in front of the store. As we eased past, the men watched us. We turned onto the road leading to Strawberry without acknowledging them. Stacey kept at the slow speed and kept glancing in the rearview mirror. We passed the Negro school. No one was on the grounds. Stacey seemed to relax and sped up, then suddenly slowed again.

"What is it?" I asked. I was sitting next to him.

Stacey's eyes were on the rearview mirror. "They're behind us."

I turned. Christopher-John and Man looked too. In the distance was the sheriff's car. Behind the sheriff's car, two trucks followed. "Could be they're just headed to Strawberry."

"Maybe." Still, Stacey was cautious.

One of the trucks came from behind the sheriff's car and sped up, coming fast up the road. Stacey swerved the Oldsmobile toward the side of the road to avoid being hit, then slammed on the brakes as the truck passed and stopped abruptly in front of us. Statler and Leon Aames stepped out. In the back of the truck were four of their boys, all grown. The sheriff's car stopped behind us. Behind the sheriff's car was Charlie Simms and his sons. The sheriff, his deputy, and Charlie Simms joined Statler and Leon at the driver's side of the Oldsmobile. The sheriff tapped on the window. Stacey rolled it down.

"Where y'all headed for in such a hurry?" the sheriff asked.

"I didn't realize we were speeding," Stacey said.

"Not speeding exactly," the sheriff said. "Just in a mighty hurry. Where y'all going all dressed up?"

Stacey was silent a moment, then answered. "Jackson."

"Y'all mighty dressed up all right," commented Charlie Simms. "Must be something important, big doings going on in Jackson."

"Y'all wouldn't happen to be going to

that Medgar Evers's funeral, wouldja?" asked the sheriff.

This time Stacey didn't answer.

The sheriff took his silence as a yes. "Well, we won't hold you long. Just got a few questions for y'all."

"Questions?" said Stacey.

Statler gave no time for the sheriff to answer. "Yeah, more questions!" He stepped past the sheriff and closer to the car. "Seems like we just seen y'all at a funeral. Funeral for that Turner boy."

"Yeah," continued Leon, "seems like a lotta folks dying round here."

"Like our brother Troy," Statler said. "Course now, that was some while back, but seems to me, that friend of yours, nigger name of Moe Turner, was the cause of it. He done killed our brother! Now look what done happened since. Our brother's dead, now his brother's dead!"

"Yeah," took up Charlie Simms, "funny thing. Seeing that the Turner boy dead, we expected that Moe Turner to turn up, show his respects."

Statler agreed with his uncle. "There's

been talk that he's been seen through here. But so far we ain't seen him. Been watching for him, but ain't seen hide nor hair of him." He leaned down and peered into the car. "By any chance, any y'all seen him?"

None of us spoke.

Statler pulled back and straightened. "Maybe you'd better ask them, Hank. Seems like they don't want to answer my questions."

"Maybe they don't like the way you're asking them, Statler," suggested Leon. "They step out the car we can put them questions somewhat more direct."

"You boys calm down," the sheriff said, then again addressed Stacey. "Now, we want to know if y'all helped that Moe Turner get back down here."

Stacey solemnly answered. "No, sheriff, we didn't help him get back down here."

"Uh-huh." The sheriff studied Stacey, then, as Statler had done, leaned down and peered into the car. He took a long look at each of us before stepping back. "Well, we believe that boy's back here. Believe he had help getting here. Talked to his family, but they ain't had much to say."

Statler again moved close to the car. "Y'all know where that nigger is, and we figure we can persuade y'all to tell us. Get on out that car, boy!"

"Hold on now, Statler," cautioned the sheriff. "You too, Leon. I think they'd best go on into town with Roger and me." He looked back to us. "Got a few more questions for y'all. Won't keep ya long." Then he turned again to Statler and Leon. "Y'all go on ahead. This boy'll follow in his fine new car here, and we'll follow him."

Statler started to object. "But, Hank —"

"Just do like I say. We'll talk about it once we get to the jail." He glanced over at Charlie Simms. "Charlie, you and your boys follow me." The two Aames brothers and Charlie Simms went back to their trucks. The sheriff and his deputy went back to their car and, once in, honked the horn, and we all drove to Strawberry. When we reached the jail located across the street from the town square, several colored men were gathered on the square. We knew some of them. They all stared as we stepped from the car. Stacey gave a nod to one of the men. The man nodded back with understanding. My brothers and I looked at each other. At least other colored folks knew we were here. The sheriff took note but said nothing as he ushered us inside.

We were not jailed. Instead, we were seated in wooden chairs in the one-room office that faced onto the street. We sat there and waited. It was hot in the office. There was no air conditioning. There was a fan, but the sheriff did not turn it on. Sweat poured down our faces and dripped along our bodies. We were scared, and the sweat pouring down was as much from our fear as from the sweltering heat. The sheriff and the deputy took their own good time about questioning us. After telling us to be seated, they stepped outside and stood on the sidewalk for some time talking to Statler and Leon and Charlie Simms. We watched them through the large plate-glass window. They were in deep discussion, which we knew was about us. Twice we heard Statler's voice rise and twice we saw the sheriff's hand pat his arm, as if to calm him. When the sheriff and Roger, the deputy, came back inside, they kept questioning us for more than an hour. Finally, the sheriff said abruptly, "Y'all can go now. Mr. Simms'll see y'all out."

We stood to leave, and Stacey said, "Thank you kindly, sheriff, but we know our way out."

"Suit yourself," said the sheriff, and opened the office door. He walked out in front of us. We stepped outside with the deputy following. Statler and Leon and their boys were gone, but Charlie Simms and his sons remained, their truck parked behind the Oldsmobile. Across the street on the square, the same colored folks who had been there when we entered the sheriff's office were still there. The sheriff looked across at them and hollered, "Y'all nigras gathered yonder, ya get goin'! Don't be loitering on that square! Get on 'bout your business!"

Reluctantly, slowly, the men dispersed. The man to whom Stacey had given a nod nodded back once more and we went to the Oldsmobile and got in.

"Y'all drive safe now," said the sheriff.

Stacey glanced over at the men leaving the square and pulled out. Charlie Simms in his truck pulled out behind us. The sheriff and his deputy stood on the sidewalk watching. We rolled slowly through the town, barely meeting the speed limit.

"What do you think?" asked Christopher-John, glancing back at the Simms truck.

"What do I think?" repeated Stacey, checking the rearview mirror. "I think we're in real trouble now."

Within minutes we were out of Strawberry and on the rural road that led to the highway. All around us were fields. Soon there would be only woods, dense, dark woods. "We could make a run for it now," suggested Christopher-John.

I looked back at him. "What, and have them shooting at us?"

"Better them shooting at us than they take us over and we end up on one of those back roads. What you think, Stacey? We going to make a run for it or not?"

Stacey did not reply. He sped up. Charlie Simms and his boys sped up too.

"We can easily outrun them," Little Man said.

"Not hardly," said Stacey. "Look who's parked up yonder."

I sighed. "Oh, Lord." Up ahead was the Aames truck.

"They're going to try to block us in," said Christopher-John. "They'll do it before we hit the highway."

As we neared Statler's truck, it swung out in front of us. This time Statler didn't stop, but his speed was slow. Stacey had to slow down too. We rolled on for more than a mile. Our fear mounted. Forest was all around.

Man leaned forward, his right arm resting on top of the front seat. "Stacey, we can still outrun them. Up ahead where there's that crossroads, then that store and the gas pumps, there's enough room you could swing right in front of those pumps, round that space, and get in front of Statler. He won't be able to keep up with this Oldsmobile."

I glanced at Man. "You know they've got to have guns."

"Course they do," Man acknowledged, "but we're going to have to take that chance before they force us off onto one of these back roads."

Christopher-John and Clayton were right and we all knew it. The knot of fear that had begun to swell since the sheriff first stopped us was about to burst. I wanted to throw up. We approached the crossroads. Stacey made his move. Suddenly ramming on the gas, he turned sharply and sped toward the store. Statler stopped his truck. Charlie Simms followed us toward the store. Stacey rounded the pumps and got in front of Statler's truck. At that, Leon leaned out the passenger window. A shotgun was in his hands. He shot right at us and hit the trunk of the car.

"What the —"

"Lord have mercy!"

"Good God A-Mighty!"

"Get down!" Stacey shouted, and jammed the gas pedal to the floor.

"But what about you?" I cried.

"I'm going to drive like a bat out of hell! Now, get down, Cassie! All of you, get down!"

We all followed his orders. There was no terror greater for black folks than being chased by white folks on a back country road. I bent down, my chest to my legs, and wrapped my arms around my knees. I could see the rusty dust rising and billowing around the car as Stacey drove at a reckless speed, and I prayed that Stacey's skills as a big-rig driver all those years ago were still intact. If we could just reach the highway maybe we would have a chance. I wanted to see how close Statler and Leon were behind us, but I kept down. I turned my head, looked at Stacey. His hands were gripping the wheel as if they were glued to it. His face was like stone, his eyes straight ahead. I said nothing to him, not even to ask him to slow down. He didn't need that from me right now. Stacey had been at the wheel when we sped through the mountains of Wyoming, and he had been at the wheel when we had fled the wrath of white men while taking Moe to Memphis. He had our lives in his hands and he knew that. As we fled toward the highway, our terror swelling like a coming thunderstorm, I thought of Morris, of what his fear must have been as he was chased into the Rosa Lee. After several long minutes, the car began to slow — not much, but enough for me to know we were merging onto the highway. I heard other cars whizzing past. Then Stacey changed lanes and sped up again. "Can we get up now?" I asked.

Stacey glanced at the mirror. "Wait until we're closer to Jackson."

"Are they behind us?"

Stacey shook his head. "Don't see them."

I sat up. So did Christopher-John and Little Man. "Jackson's too far," I said. Stacey just glanced at me, then looked back to the highway. Christopher-John, Little Man, and I looked behind us, checking for ourselves that the trucks were no longer following. We began to breathe easier. All of us were shaken by the ride and none of us spoke as Stacey, hands still tight on the wheel, drove toward the city. The time seemed endless, but there were no sirens, no trucks following us. I continued silently to pray.

Finally, we reached Jackson.

■ ■ ■ ■

We headed toward Capitol Street. It was far too late for the funeral. We were on Farish Street, which intersected with Capitol. From there we planned to turn up Capitol toward the Old Capitol building at the end of the street and head for Little Willie's. Traffic was slow as we neared downtown. Then it moved to a crawl. Then it didn't move at all. The south end of Farish going north toward Capitol was a one-way street with three lanes. All of them were jammed. We were in the curb lane.

"What's happening?" I said.

Stacey tried to peer around the car in front of us. "Don't know," he said.

It was hot in the car. The air conditioner was not working. We rolled down our windows. We could hear shouting up ahead. People in their cars, stuck just as we were, began honking their horns, as if that would get the traffic moving again, but it was of no use. None of us were going anywhere. We were all blocked in. We just had to wait it out. A few white people got out of their cars to see if they could detect what the problem was. We all kept on waiting. After some time, we heard people coming, then saw them as they filled the sidewalks on both sides of the street. All the people walking were white. We rolled up our windows. As the people passed, they talked loudly, taunting the Negro passengers in cars stuck in the traffic snarl. A small group stopped beside the Oldsmobile. "Got us some northern niggers here!" one of the group announced, as he and several others took a closer look at the Oldsmobile. "Just check out them plates! Ohio!"

Another man spoke and slammed the hood with the flat of his hand. "Damn outside agitators comin' down here! We oughta show them how we feel 'bout their meddlin'. Show them some real southern hospitality and send them back to Ohio with something they ain't 'bout to forget!" He pushed on the side of the car. A few others joined him.

Little Man exploded. "That's it!" He reached for the door handle to confront them.

"Keep that door locked!" commanded Stacey.

The car rocked back and forth. Stacey revved the engine, but there was no place for us to go. The white men pushing on the car laughed and pushed harder, trying to overturn us. A white man leaning against the hood of his truck in the next lane smoking a cigarette put a stop to it. "No need for that," he said in a calm, deep Mississippi drawl. The men rocking the car stared across at the man. He was a big man, red-haired, and towering. He looked like a logger. Inside the cab of the truck a young boy was leaning out the open window. He looked to be the man's son. "They just sittin' in their car, stuck here just like the rest of us, mindin' their own business," the big man said. "Don't need trouble here today. Y'all boys jus' keep on walkin'." His steely gaze rested on the men. He expected to be obeyed.

The men hesitated, then took their hands off the Oldsmobile. They moved slowly away, but not before one of them spat on the car. The big white man who had come to our defense watched them go, then flipped his cigarette in the street, walked to the driver's side of his truck, and, without even looking at us, got in while his boy kept staring. Some colored people came walking up the sidewalk. We rolled down our windows and asked them what was happening. They told us hundreds of protesters were marching after Medgar Evers's funeral. The police were waiting for them and stopped them at Farish Street.

The traffic began to move. We came to the intersection of Capitol and Farish. The crowds that had held up the traffic had dispersed. We kept on driving. Once out of the downtown area, we managed to make it over to Little Willie's. A lot of neighborhood people were standing on the street, talking. Most seemed to be dressed in funeral clothes. All spaces for parking on the curbless street were already taken. Little Willie was standing in front of his house along with a group of men, among them Solomon Bradley. Little Willie saw us and motioned Stacey to pull into his driveway. Little Willie left the group and came over to the car as we got out. "What happened to y'all, man?" Little Willie asked Stacey. "Y'all get caught up in that march?" He didn't give

Stacey a chance to answer. "Was looking for y'all at the funeral. Course now, there was so many folks —"

"Didn't make it to the funeral." Stacey took off his coat and slung it across one arm. His shirt was drenched.

"Didn't make it?" Little Willie looked around at all of us and knew something was wrong. Then he took a closer look at the car and saw the holes. "Lord, what happened!"

"Got shot at," Stacey told him.

"What! When?"

"Tell you inside," said Stacey.

Little Willie started across the lawn to the house. "Got news for y'all too." Solomon met us at the steps and we entered the house together. Inside, two large fans were blowing at opposite corners of the living room for a cross breeze. Another large fan was in the dining room, which opened into the living room.

Dora and her eldest daughter, Maylene, were setting the table. They gave us big smiles and Dora said, "See y'all finally made it in. Just about to set food on the table. Y'all's names in the pot. Sit on down in there and we'll call you soon as we get it on." We thanked her and sat down. My feet were killing me. By now, Christopher-John and Man had taken off their coats, and they were as sweat-drenched as Stacey. I was drenched too, but I wore nothing I could take off but my shoes. I kicked them off and set them beside the sofa.

"So, what's your news?" Stacey asked Little Willie.

Little Willie looked at us with a wide grin. "Our boy's here."

I leaned forward, looking from Little Willie to Dora. "Moe's here? Well, where is he?"

"Right here, Cassie," said Moe, entering from the kitchen.

Christopher-John jumped up. "Well, we're all sure some kind of glad to see you!"

The rest of us stood to greet Moe as he came into the room. Solomon shook Moe's hand. "It's really good to see you, Moe. Haven't seen you since Memphis."

"Long time ago," said Moe.

"You were on the run then too."

784

"Never seems to end."

Solomon nodded. "Sorry to hear about Morris. We did a lot of work together. He was a good man."

"Yes . . . yes, he was. He felt the same about you."

We all questioned Moe about what had happened with him after Morris's funeral. He had made it to Strawberry walking, then had gotten a ride with a colored man headed for Jackson. The man was going only as far as downtown Jackson and had let Moe out near Capitol Street. "There I was," Moe said, "just walking toward Capitol when I saw a lot of our folks coming down the street. Looked to be hundreds of them. I asked somebody what was going on and they told me that right after Medgar Evers's funeral, young folks started gathering and singing protest songs and talking about the killing of Medgar Evers. They were angry and they started marching, marching right toward Capitol, and other folks joined along the way.

"I was standing near when they met up with the police over on Farish. There was a bunch of white folks too standing round near the police. Some of the police roughed up the marchers, rest of them didn't make a move. They just stood there waiting. They had their dogs and they had their guns. Some of our folks had bottles and some had bricks and they began throwing them at the police."

"Calvin was in that march!" interjected Little Willie. "Told Dora and me we almost had a riot on our hands!"

"That's the truth," Moe confirmed. "Would've been one too if this white man hadn't gotten between our folks and the police. He got on a bullhorn and began begging everybody to just stop where they were. Told us his name and said he was a federal agent. Said a lot of folks in the colored community knew him and knew he stood for right. Said nobody wanted a riot in Jackson, didn't want anybody getting hurt. He begged folks to go on home. Colored man then took the bullhorn and said pretty much the same thing 'bout being peaceful. Then folks began to turn around and leave Capitol. I turned with them and came over here. Now I've got to get over to the other side of town, where I left my car. Like I said, left it with the family of a friend of mine works at the plant with me."

"Well, I'll take you over," volunteered Little Willie. "And why didn't you just bring your car over here in the first place?"

"Didn't want you mixed up in it. Don't want them coming after you —"

"You wait until early morning to leave before light," interrupted Stacey, "maybe we can get on the road at the same time, watch out for you."

Moe shook his head. "No. No way. Who knows what could happen before we get out of Mississippi? Could be some by-chance thing and the police get involved, see our northern plates, run a check, and then you'd be in trouble. No, I'm going alone. Like I said, don't want y'all mixed up in this."

"Well, too late for that," declared Little Willie. "We been mixed up in it since we took you to Memphis more'n twenty years ago. More'n that. We been mixed up in it since we been born, that's how long we all been mixed up in it. And one more thing. I'm taking you over to get your car and that's the end of it. You done enough walking."

Moe didn't say anything.

"Anyways, one thing you gotta do 'fore you get on the road is change your plates. You still got those Michigan tags on your car they can spot you. I can get you some Mississippi plates." Little Willie gave a confidential wink. "I know people."

Throughout the time we had been talking, we had been standing. Now Little Willie ordered us to sit down, and once we were seated, he wanted to know what had happened to the boys and me to keep us from getting to the funeral. We recounted the events of the morning, about the sheriff and Statler and Leon Aames and Charlie Simms, about our flight from them and finally making it to Jackson and getting stuck in traffic.

"Well, y'all sure 'nough been through it," commiserated Little Willie. "That traffic y'all got tied up in was 'cause of the march."

"Know that now," said Stacey.

"You're just lucky to have made it in," observed Solomon. "But seems like to me, you've got yourselves another prob-